The Man Who Drew Triangles

Magician, mystic, or out of his mind?

The Man Who Drew Triangles

Magician, mystic, or out of his mind?

Haraldur Erlendsson

& Keith Hagenbach

COSMIC
EGG
BOOKS

Winchester, UK
Washington, USA

First published by Cosmic Egg Books, 2016
Cosmic Egg Books is an imprint of John Hunt Publishing Ltd., Laurel House, Station Approach,
Alresford, Hants, SO24 9JH, UK
office1@jhpbooks.net
www.johnhuntpublishing.com

For distributor details and how to order please visit the 'Ordering' section on our website.

Text copyright: Haraldur Erlendsson & Keith Hagenbach 2015

ISBN: 978 1 78535 147 1
Library of Congress Control Number: 2015939701

A CIP catalogue record for this book is available from the British Library.

Design: Stuart Davies

Printed and bound by CPI Group (UK) Ltd, Croydon, CR0 4YY, UK

We operate a distinctive and ethical publishing philosophy in all
areas of our business, from our global network of authors to
production and worldwide distribution.

CONTENTS

List of maps

We dedicate this book to the Sacred Realm and the Blessed
Beings who inspired it

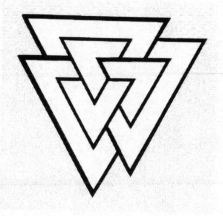

Hail to you Védís the Wise in Mount Hoffell
Hail to you Bard the Bright in Mount Snæfell
Hail to you Bran the Blessed guardian of the Grail Mountain
We offer rose petals at your feet

Heill sé þér Védís Vitra í Hoffelli
Heill sé þér Bárður Bjarti Snæfellsás
Heill sé þér Bran hinn blessaði sem bikarinn helga ber í
Skálarfelli
Við færum rósablöð fram fyrir fætur ykkar

Author's Preface

The book you are about to read was conceived four years ago when Haraldur was showing me maps like those you will find scattered through the narrative. I asked what he was doing to raise awareness about research which left me spellbound. "Nothing, really." He smiled. "I could write a learned paper about them, but only a few academics would read it, and what use would that be?" Having no idea what I was getting myself into, I told him I was a published author and suggested we weave his discoveries into a work of fiction.

Near neighbours, we met weekly to discuss and chart progress. Sharing a profound belief in the metaphysical realm and its largely ignored influence on human lives, we soon realised we were being supported and guided in our work. I found talking to Haraldur was like watching a firework display: entrancing, brilliant concepts and dazzling ideas. My job was to find ways of incorporating them into a coherent and engaging story. You will be able to judge for yourself how successful my efforts have been.

Certain themes lie close to both our hearts, and thus to the heart of our book. Our work – Haraldur's as a psychiatrist, my own as a psychotherapist – has taught us that alienation, separation and disconnection cloud the lives of many human beings. We believe that the journey to rediscovering our true selves is always within our reach and our capability, although we may need to call on the wisdom of others to achieve it.

In our experience healing journeys are rarely smooth and comfortable and summoning the courage to face and embrace pain may be a requirement. Equally, the guidance we need to find our personal healing is always available to us. The key is to be sufficiently open-minded to recognise that which is 'hidden in plain sight'.

Paradoxically, questions are more valuable to the seeker than answers, so be ready for unanswered questions. We do not claim to offer truths here, but to inspire you to embark on a quest for your own truth. We wish you an enjoyable and rewarding journey, for which you will find a wealth of further information on the links below:

www.themanwhodrewtriangles.com
olafurbardarson@themanwhodrewtriangles.com
Keith and Haraldur
Sussex and Reykjavik
April 2015

Chapter 1

Touchdown

Tuesday 7th June 2011

"This is not an exercise. I say again, not an exercise. Clear, Miller?"

"As crystal, sir..."

The bearded policeman in midnight blue uniform and chequered cap, semi-automatic rifle cradled in his arms, gave an almost imperceptible shake of the head. What did they think he was – stupid? Getting on for ten on a Tuesday night, with South Terminal half-empty and just him and Kenny Hall sent to maintain surveillance on a lone target? Hardly likely to be one of their bloody simulations, now was it?

"Doesn't look like he's spotted you..."

Inclining his head, Miller spoke softly into the shoulder mike. "I don't think he's even checking, sir..."

Not for a moment did his eyes stray from the angular figure, bent slightly beneath the weight of the pack slung across his shoulder, who continued with the same rituals he had been performing ever since Miller arrived. He circled the deserted area in front of carousel number one at a leisurely pace. Every so often he stopped and crouched before launching himself into a swallow dive that propelled him across the floor on his stomach. After lying prone for a few seconds, he clambered to his feet and the sequence began again.

"How long do we reckon he's been in here now, sir?"

"Four, maybe five minutes before you and Hall turned up. So...call it twenty..."

"Couldn't have just got the wrong one, could he...?"

"No way…"

Beyond his line of vision, ground staff in Day-Glo jackets would be performing well-oiled routines; shepherding the public to a safe distance, erecting and manning barriers. Closer at hand, Kenny would be shifting position in a dance choreographed to keep himself, Miller, and their target at the points of an imaginary equilateral triangle, as prescribed by the training manual.

"What's he's doing now…?"

"Reading the out of order sign…?"

"Assuming he understands English, French, German or Spanish…"

"Hang on, sir…"

He had shrugged off the backpack, leaned it against the carousel and with one athletic stride mounted the gleaming metal surface. Easing himself down until he was sitting straight-backed, he folded his legs beneath him, guru-style. Without haste, he placed his hands on his thighs, palms upward, and allowed his eyes to close. Tall and wiry, he was wearing jeans and a faded, red checked shirt. Miller studied the contours of chest and lower body. From thirty odd yards, no sign of tell-tale bulges. Not that he expected any; nothing as crude as a body-belt could have evaded both metal detectors and pat-downs. They'd have checked the bloke's sandals, too: which just left the backpack…

"What do you make of that…?"

Miller sighed. "Search me, sir. Praying…?"

"Possibly…"

Praying. Last rites, or whatever it was they did. Maybe they had their own manual and the bloke was following instructions. If so, he'd skipped the bit about making bloody sure you didn't attract attention.

"Couldn't be more conspicuous if he was waving a flag, sir…"

"And playing a trombone…"

"That too, sir. Could be a decoy…"

"Don't worry your pretty head about that, Miller..."

"I'll try not to, sir..."

"No sign he might be, but if he is, it's our problem. Yours is dealing with him..."

"Didn't look round before he hopped up there. And if there's anything in that pack he's not bothered about keeping it handy..."

"Could have a remote..."

"True..."

"We need his hands where we can see them..."

"Soon as I can, sir..." Miller sniffed. "What do you think – give him a couple of minutes? If he hasn't made a move by then, go in and have a word...?"

His suggestion was met by silence; he wondered how many they'd got crammed into the ops room.

"Fair enough. Hall will remain on your right flank. Take it nice and easy, okay. There's no rush..."

Miller pursed his lips. What did they think he was going to do – run at the bloke shouting and waving his gun? The target was rocking gently to and fro, chin held high. He had a long face, fair curly hair, gingery moustache and a beard trimmed tight along a fine jaw line. Miller put him somewhere between twenty-five and thirty.

"Okay, Kenny...?"

"Yeah..."

Hall sounded bored, but then he invariably did; nothing ever seemed to faze old Kenny. That was what made him exactly the wingman you'd have picked when anything might happen.

"Right..." Miller muttered, to himself. "Let's do this thing..."

He advanced a dozen or so paces, forefinger nestling alongside the trigger guard. Minimal pressure on that trigger was all it took to launch 5.56mm rounds from the Heckler & Koch's stubby barrel at a velocity in excess of 3000mph. Halting in mid-stride he turned his head and listened.

"…Gátt Gátt Gátt
Gát Gát
Geit Geit
Goat Goat Goat
Good Good
God God…"

"Hear that, Kenny…?"

"Just about…"

"Hear what…?"

"Buggered if I know, sir. Singing is he…?"

"Chanting more like…" offered Hall.

"Could be. Something about 'goat'…?"

"Goat and God…"

A hurried discussion Miller did not quite catch was taking place in the ops room.

"I want you to close in and engage, Miller…"

"Both of us…?"

"Just you. Hall stays back…"

"Right, sir…"

"Keep fanned out…"

Miller resumed his advance. The figure perched on the carousel had not altered position and his eyes remained closed.

Over the public address came a call for the three remaining passengers on Air Somalia flight 027 to Mogadishu to go immediately to gate 4B, where their flight was about to close. There would not be many people scanning the screens for that one; Miller recognised a coded message letting ground staff know a partial terminal evacuation was in progress. The singsong chanting continued.

"Ó-la-fur Ei-lí-fur Ó-la-fur Ei-lí-fur
Ó-la-fur Ei-lí-fur
Ó-la-fur Ei-lí-fur Ó-la-fur Ei-lí-fur

Ó-la-fur Ei-lí-fur...

Treading lightly, Miller veered to his left to avoid positioning himself directly in front of their quarry.

"Good to go, sir...?"

"You know the form, I'll leave it to you..."

Miller's lips twitched; for exactly how long would they be able to resist interfering? "Thank you, sir."

The big policeman eased down onto his haunches. According to the manual this offered a smaller target and less menacing appearance. Had they asked him, Miller could have told them it also made it a damn sight harder to move quickly if you needed to. He moistened his lips with the tip of his tongue.

"Hello...I'm speaking to the gentleman on the luggage carousel. Hello there..."

The man gave no sign of having heard.

"Louder, maybe..."

He had his answer: all of ten seconds.

"Good idea, sir..."

"All right, Miller. In your own time..."

He cleared his throat. "I'm sure you can hear me. It's important you speak to me, sir. Right now, if you please..."

A tremor ran through the man's body, as if he had been struck by a blast of cold air; the chanting died away and Miller found himself looking into an unusual pair of eyes; one cornflower blue, the other a translucent green. As he ran his gaze over Miller's face, uniform and weapon the eyes grew wider and a frown furrowed his brow.

"Heill og sæll minn kæri..."

"Do you speak English...?"

His enquiry was delivered with a smile calculated to reassure without appearing overly friendly. The man glanced at Hall, giving Miller a glimpse of his profile. At his school, a nose like that would have earned the owner the nickname Beaky.

"English, sir. Do you speak it...understand it...?"

The man's frown turned into a hopeful smile. "You are...guardians of the portal?"

"Not exactly, sir. I'm Sgt Miller of the Sussex Police armed response unit. My colleague over there is..."

The man dismissed the introductions with a shake of the head. The smile seemed uncertain whether to stay or go. "Yes, yes. But you have been sent to look after me. You are Gog and Magog, yes...?"

Miller sucked his teeth; he had been called a lot worse. "Well, yes, we're here to look after you, in a manner of speaking..."

"The gun..." the man hurried on. "What use are guns if the dark forces try to stop me, if they wish to resist the light? Come here, sit..." he patted the metal strip at his side. "Tell your friend to come, too. Quickly...quickly. If you are not my guardians, we must invoke those who can..."

He might babble nonsense but at least it was in pretty decent English. Looking down the business end of a semi-automatic tended to make people twitchy enough; it didn't help if they couldn't understand a blind word you were saying.

"Please raise both hands above your head, and keep them there..."

"My hands...?" He glanced down, frowning as if he had not noticed them before.

"That's correct. Above your head. Nice and high, please..."

With a bemused look, he did as Miller asked. His shirtsleeves were rolled to the elbow and he wore no watch.

"Thank you, sir. I'm not sure who you think I am, but I need you to give me some information..."

"What did they say about me...?"

"They...?"

"The ones who sent you..."

"Well, not a lot, sir. I don't think they know much. That's why they..."

The man shook his head. "Do not know – or did not tell you...? Think, Mr Miller. If they did not know I was coming, you would not be here, would you...?"

"We need an ID, Miller. Get his name..."

"Ah, well..." Miller gave a rueful grin. "I don't get told everything. They just said to have a word with you, sir..."

Even to Miller the words had an implausible ring; judging by the thoughtful nod they earned, however, the man on the carousel found reassurance in them.

"Sometimes it is the same for me. They do not always explain..."

"Let's start with your name, sir..."

"Name...?"

"That's right..."

The man closed his eyes and took a breath, before answering in solemn, reverential tones. "*Ólafur Bárðarson...*"

"O-laf-ur Bard-arson..." Miller repeated. "Did I get that right...?"

"A name of such strength and beauty, no? As you speak it, can you not feel its power, Mr Miller?" His eyes locked onto the policeman's with a disconcerting intensity.

"It...well, it does have a ring about it..."

"A ring, exactly, yes...! A sound...a sound like no other..." He peered at Miller. "You have an ear for such things..."

"Not sure I'd say that, sir..."

"Move it along, Miller. I need port of embarkation..."

"Your flight's not long in is it, sir? Well, obviously you've had to get through immigration..."

The man shrugged. "An hour...two? I do not know..."

"And where did you board...?"

"You did not recognise my language...?"

"Tell you the truth, I didn't..."

It was superfluous to volunteer the information that his command of foreign languages was limited to ordering draught beer in halting Castilian.

"Not many people would…"

"And I'm certainly not one of them…"

"Yes, yes…" The man paused. "That was why in the war your military often used us for passing secret messages. Did you know that…?"

"I didn't, sir, no…" Miller shook his head. "So, where did you fly from…?"

"Keflavík…"

"And…where's that, exactly…?"

The man frowned. "It is the international airport of Reykjavík, Mr Miller."

"Right. Got you…"

"Better brush up your bloody airports, Miller. Keep him talking, see what you can get, but don't push it…"

"Where are you heading when you leave here, sir…?"

The man considered Miller's question for a moment, then cocked his head. "How do I know it is safe to trust you…?"

"Trust me…?" Nonplussed, Miller stared at him. "Well, for a start there's the uniform, isn't there…?"

"Do you trust people who point guns at you…?"

"Fair point, but if you have a good look you'll notice it's not actually aimed at you, sir. That'd be against regulations, and my people are sticklers for regulations. My job's not shooting people, you see. It's the exact opposite, really – it's keeping them safe…"

"You are here to protect me, then…?"

"Exactly…" Miller gave him a nod of encouragement. "If you were in danger. Which you're not, obviously…"

"I hope you are right…" the man pursed his lips. "My arms are tired, Mr Miller, can I put them down…?"

"No, he bloody can't…!"

"Not yet…" It was sharper than he intended but had the desired effect. Miller conjured up a smile. "I'd like you to keep them where they are for the moment, if you would. Now, there's a couple of things I'd like to know…"

"What things, please…?"

"First off, I'm wondering what you're actually doing over here. That equipment's out of order, you see, it's not working…"

"I am aware of that, Mr Miller…"

"In that case…"

"I was looking for a quiet place. Crowds make me feel uncomfortable. So many people, all moving about, making noise…" He shrugged. "Do you work in this place all the time…?"

"Not just in reclaim, no. My unit keeps an eye on the whole place, both terminals. "

"Then you are used to it, but I am not. It made my head hurt, Mr Miller…"

"Feeling better now, are you…?"

"In a place like this it is very difficult to hear my guides. When that happens I do not know what to do or where I should go and that is a bad feeling – it makes me very nervous. I came over here so I could be still and I hoped maybe I could connect with them again…"

He suddenly broke off. Frowning, he gazed round the hall before meeting Miller's eyes.

"Something has happened…something is wrong…" lowering his voice he leaned towards the policeman. "It was full of people, wasn't it? But do you see, now…there is no one. Where are they – where have they all gone…?"

"It happens…" Miller shrugged. "You'd be amazed, you really would. I've been in here with the place absolutely heaving, then there's a gap between arrivals and…the next minute I was pretty much on my own."

"But so quickly…? No, this is not normal…"

"Listen, it's after ten and there's a lot less night flights. It is normal actually, sir – there's not a thing to worry about…"

The young man shook his head. "How can you be sure…? So many people disappearing like…like ghosts…?" The odd eyes

11

grew wider. "What if something bad has happened...something very bad? Maybe the dark powers have learned where I am and they want to make sure I disappear..."

Sweat glistened on his brow and Miller noted under the checked shirt the Icelander's chest had begun to heave.

"Nice and easy does it, calm him down. Don't let him get excited..."

"Like I said, there's nothing to worry about, sir. You're safe as houses with me here. Try a few nice deep breaths, that always helps..." He paused, but the Icelander ignored his advice. "No one can take you anywhere without my say-so."

"You don't understand forces like those. If they wanted to, they..."

"Doesn't matter what they bloody want," Miller snapped. "I wouldn't let 'em, simple as that. And it's not just me, is it? Don't forget there's my mate over there. And he's a hard bloke. No one messes with Kenny, believe me."

Glancing in Hall's direction the man nodded, drawing down the corners of his mouth. "You think so...?"

"I know it. Me and Kenny go back a long time, sir..."

"We need to check that pack over now. Purely precautionary, tell him, no big deal..."

"You were explaining why you've come and sat down here..." The man nodded. "Yes...?"

"Let me make sure I've got this straight. You don't have any more bags, right...?"

"That is correct, Mr Miller."

"Your pack and nothing else...?"

"Nothing else."

"Fine. Now, you understand we're going to have to take a look at it...?"

"I can show you..."

"I'm sure you could, but it's all got to be done by the book, I'm afraid. We need to take it away so some of our lads can give it a

12

thorough inspection..."

"Good job. Hall, when Miller gives the word, move in and get it."

"Right you are, sir..."

"The explosives boys are standing by. Okay. Miller?"

"Let me tell him what's going on..."

The Icelander stiffened abruptly, eyes wide. "Who are you talking to?"

"Well, it's actually..."

"Who are they, what are they telling you...? Did they say I can go, or to keep me here...?

"Level with him. Can't do any harm."

"I'm on a radio link to my unit commander, okay? He didn't say anything about keeping you here. He'd like you to keep your hands where they are while Kenny collects your pack. We have to make sure there's nothing nasty in there, so the bomb squad are going to take a look. That's all..."

The man stared him in silence for a few moments, then shook his head. "They really think I...would have something like that?"

"It's nothing personal, sir. It's what we have to do. If there's a query about any luggage, the experts check it out. Simple as that."

"Why would I have a bomb...?"

"You don't, then?"

"No, no..."

"So there's nothing to worry about. They'll do their thing – doesn't usually take long – and then we can move on, can't we? So..." he continued, cheerfully, "Kenny's listening in, and now I'm going to ask him to take it away. Okay?"

"If it is really necessary..."

Hall came ambling in. Dry mouthed, Miller offered a hasty prayer this would not be the moment Gatwick South terminal building was rocked by an explosion and he, Kenny, and a foreign national believed to be of Icelandic origin became headlines on the evening news bulletins. Scooping up the pack as nonchalantly as he might have taken a supermarket basket, Hall retreated to a position somewhere out of Miller's line of sight. The pack's owner watched his departure with a bemused expression.

"Good so far. Keep him occupied, but for Christ's sake don't let him start getting upset again…"

Miller moistened his lips. How the hell were you supposed to avoid upsetting someone who had made it clear their grip on reality was pretty loose at the best of times?

"Moving on, then, sir. Once they've got their bags most people head through customs then go off to…wherever they're going. But you haven't, have you? Now, if I've understood you, that was because you wanted to get in touch with these…guides of yours. Tell me about them – who are they, exactly…?"

"Beings who guide me…" The man shrugged. "I needed to talk to them, make sure all was well…"

"Okay. And what did they…?"

"And I felt I should salute the goddess – the lady of your land. I once changed aeroplanes here, but this is my first real visit to her country and I wanted to show proper respect. Give her greetings from our mountain gods. Oh, and ask for her help and protection…" He paused. "I thought maybe it was *Védís* who had sent you and your friend…"

"Did you? No, I don't think it was her…"

"The Irish know her as Danu. I am not sure what name your people would use…if you remember her at all. It is sad, but you have forgotten so much of the ancient wisdom, haven't you? Danu is a goddess of the land, but a water goddess, too. Lady of the lake as well as queen of the hidden beings of the earth…" The man nodded to himself.

"Okay. He can drop his hands…"

"Regular little multi-tasker, she is, then…" Miller moved his finger a few millimetres further from the trigger-guard. "You can put your hands down now if you like, sir."

"Thank you…"

The young man flexed his shoulders, rubbing his hands together before clasping them in his lap.

"Your legs okay, sir? I'd be getting cramp by now…"

"It is not a problem, thank you." He inclined his head. "In *Bodh Gaya* we meditated in the lotus position for many hours at a time…"

"In…where, sir?"

"Bodh Gaya."

"Is that in Iceland…?"

"India, Mr Miller…"

"Many hours…?" Miller repeated, shaking his head. "Rather you than me. Mind you, you're probably a good bit younger than me…"

"You must know how old I am…" The man smiled.

"No, just guessing. When were you born, sir?"

"At sunrise…"

"Ah. What I meant was…"

"And I am a Piscean, but you must know that, too. You say it is not so, but you know all about me, don't you? Who I am, where I come from…even why I was sent. Nothing is hidden from people like you, is it, Mr Miller? And knowledge is power, so you must possess great power. You could keep me here if you wanted to, or make me disappear like the others…"

"That might be a bit beyond my pay grade, sir. Whatever you may think, I'm just a cog in the great wheel…"

"True, Miller…"

The sound of the man's clap echoed eerily round the great, deserted space surrounding them. He peered at Miller as if trying to see what lay behind the policeman's eyes.

"You are a good actor, but there is no need – you do not have to pretend…" he went on. "The one you talk to on your radio, your commander, he must know all about me, too. He tells you what you must do, he controls you, yes, of course, but do you realise there are others, much higher powers who give him his orders? You did not? Oh, it is true – there is a great hierarchy, Mr Miller. It ascends through higher and higher levels until you reach the very top, the peak, the summit. Of course, only the chosen ones are allowed to enter those realms. Lesser beings could not survive the spiritual energy, you see. At those levels the psychic charge is so great they would burn up like moths in a flame..." He snapped his fingers. "In an instant...! That is where the supreme spirits dwell, with the celestial light beings who are their guard protectors..." He paused, rubbed his hands together and chuckled. "You are wondering how do I know all this? I will tell you. Because I have been in the presence of such beings myself, can you believe that? No? Well, it is true. I have been initiated into the great mysteries, the wisdom has been revealed to me, Mr Miller. Me, Ólafur Bárðarson! Now do you understand why I know what you are doing – I know this is just a trial, a test...?"

"Hang in there. Just go along with it, agree with whatever he says..."

"There's no fooling you, is there...?"

"They began testing me as soon as I reached the airport..."

"Did they?"

"No, no, not your airport, Mr Miller. In Keflavík..." He paused, frowning. "Just after I saw Brynja..."

"Was it...?"

"Yes, but she is not like them. They are tricksters, Mr Miller..."

"Are they? But..." Miller hesitated. "But you spotted them anyway?"

"When they asked me to take my shoes off..."

"Bit of a give-away, that..." Miller nodded. "You mean...they didn't ask the others?"

The man grimaced and shook his head. "No, no. You do not understand. Everyone had to do it. But without letting them see what I was doing I watched very, very carefully. I saw them tell the others they must take off their shoes and put them in plastic trays..."

"Ah, I see..."

Miller wished he did see. He had strayed into Alice in Wonderland territory; nothing was what it seemed, but he must pretend otherwise. He hoped they were not expecting him to play charades much longer; it was alien to him, it made him uncomfortable and he suspected he was unconvincing in the role. Something else they could add to their bloody simulations.

"But if everyone had to do it..." Miller went on, cautiously, "why did you think it was strange they'd asked you?"

The Icelander wagged a playful finger at him. "It was the way she spoke to me, you see. This woman – a young one, younger than me and quite pretty – she looked straight into my eyes, Mr Miller. For a long time, longer than you would say is normal or natural. And then she said, 'Shoes, please. But not in the same tray as your pack'. Of course, then I knew for sure they were testing me, trying to trick me. They hoped I would give myself away..." He gave a high, brittle laugh. "But I was too clever for them. Gave them no sign, just did what she told me. Casually, you understand, as if I had noticed nothing..."

"Very canny..."

"Canny...?" He frowned.

"Smart, sir...clever."

"Ah...canny, yes, I think so. They knew I knew and let me through so I can carry out my work. But you understand why I must still be very, very careful..."

"Oh, yes," Miller agreed. "I'm a great believer in careful."

The Icelander's smile vanished. He stared at Miller, eyes suddenly cold and hard as steel.

"If it had not gone well and they had tried to stop me, even if it was dangerous, I would have had no choice. You understand what I am saying...?"

"You would have had no choice...?"

"In my place, don't you think you would feel the same...?"

"I might, I guess..."

"No choice but what? Find out..."

"When you say no choice, sir, what exactly would you have done if they had tried to stop you?"

"At certain times fire must be answered with fire, the sword drawn against the sword. When it is necessary for blood to be shed, so be it..." He nodded at the semi-automatic. "You carry that, you must understand how I felt..."

Miller hesitated; whatever the man was on about, he clearly expected an affirmative.

"I think I do, yes..."

"If you are facing people who are ready to use violence, you do what you have to do, no?"

"It's all you can do..." ventured Miller.

"Even though we are not men of violence, you and me..."

"Absolutely not."

"But we are not blind and we are not stupid. We are aware violence exists, and we know some people are violent. Just as we know that to protect ourselves – and perhaps others – we may have to resort to methods that do not come naturally to us..." He gave the slightest shrug of the shoulders. "Which is what I would have done..."

"But you'd have preferred not to."

"Exactly..." He gave an approving nod. "It is good to talk with someone who can see my meaning..."

"I'm doing my best, sir..."

Regular workouts in the gym kept him in pretty good shape, but Miller had been down on his haunches for a long time in his bulky flak jacket, nursing a semi-automatic which, at four kilos plus, was no lightweight; his hips and knees were beginning to feel the strain.

"I'm going to stand up, sir. Didn't want to alarm you, just

making myself a bit more comfortable."

"You are most thoughtful, Mr Miller..."

Until recently he could have risen to his feet without needing a steadying hand on the ground but, to his annoyance, it was no longer the case. Odds-on Kenny would make some smart-arse comment about it later, it would not have gone unnoticed. Which, of course, he would have done had the situations been reversed. Looking down at the man on the carousel, he took a deep breath.

"Do you think we will be here much longer, Mr Miller?"

"I'm hoping not, sir. We're probably just hanging on for the all clear on that pack of yours, but you've said there's nothing in it, so..."

"Don't speak to me, okay. Makes him jumpy. But we need to double-check that ID he gave."

Miller shifted feet and flexed his back. Glancing round in search of inspiration he saw only Kenny away to his right, placidly chewing gum.

"Never been to Iceland myself..." He paused. "There's shops by that name over here...I've been to one of them..."

He knew trying to lighten the atmosphere would be a mistake almost as soon as he began; if he had been in any doubt the man's blank look confirmed it.

"That name of yours, common back home, is it? I mean, take Miller." He smiled, "There's loads of us. Anywhere in the UK, you'll find Millers all over the shop..."

"No. Mine is not like yours, not at all common..."

"Bard..." Miller shook his head. "Sorry, could you remind me..."

"You do not remember...?"

"Just want to make sure I've got it right..."

"Ólafur Bárðarson..."

"Thank you, yes. Olaf-ur Bar-dar-son," he repeated.

"Clumsy, but you got the job done, I suppose..."

19

"Anyone meeting you, is there...?"

"Why...?" The man gave him a sharp glance. "Why do you want to know...?"

"It's not important. I just thought maybe we could get a message to them, let them know you've arrived, but due to circumstances beyond your control you'll be a bit delayed. That's all..."

"No one is meeting me, Mr Miller. I know no one in your country."

"How about accommodation? We could give them a ring so they don't let your room go..."

"It is not necessary, thank you."

"No problem."

Miller bit his lip; he was running short of inspiration.

"You picked a pretty good time to come over. We've been having a heat wave..."

"In India I became accustomed to high temperatures..."

"I imagine you would, yes..." Miller nodded. "Holiday, that trip, was it?"

"I would call it studying..."

"And...what about now – holiday is it?"

To Miller's surprise, the Icelander chuckled.

"Your friend in immigration pretended he did not know. When I showed him my passport he asked what I had come for..." He folded his arms. "A trick, of course..."

"You think so..."

"Yes, but so obvious, Mr Miller. They must think I am very stupid..." He tipped his head to one side. "You do not think I am stupid, do you, Mr Miller?"

"I don't, sir, no...." Miller shook his head. "Mind you, those passport pushers aren't the brightest buttons in the box. Anyway, you didn't fall for it..."

"Fall for it...?"

"Let them trick you..."

"No, no. I gave him a nice, friendly smile and said, 'I am a tourist, sir'."

"Nice one..." Miller gave an approving nod. "And he was happy with that...waved you through, did he?"

"He put his stamp on my passport, handed it back and said 'enjoy your stay'..."

"Well, I never..."

The Icelander gave a wry smile and shrugged.

"By now they must know there is nothing dangerous in my pack. I would like you to ask your commander if there is a problem, Mr Miller."

"I can try..."

"Yes, please..."

"Right you are..." He cleared his throat. "Sgt. Miller to control, come in please..."

"Don't overdo it, Miller..."

"Mr Bardarson's getting a bit concerned about how long that pack check is taking, sir. According to him there's nothing suspicious in it..."

"There isn't. So far, anyway..."

"So—"

"There's a laptop. They're taking a good look at it right now..."

"And what would you like me to tell the gentleman?"

"For the moment you will carry on doing exactly what you're doing. You will be polite, you will be sympathetic, and whatever you may think of it, you will go along with any lunatic nonsense he comes up with. Do you read me, Miller...?"

The policeman tapped his earpiece and frowned. "Didn't quite catch the last bit, sir. What you want me to tell him..."

"You're not going to mention it to him, but I'd say he's in for a long night..."

"Why would that be, sir...?"

"Well, his pack may be clean, but we've got a couple of

problems with your new best friend, Miller. Number one, he sounds as mad as a fucking hatter. Number two, there was no passenger by the name of Olafur Bardarson on any flight in from Reykjavik tonight..."

Chapter 2

The Listener

Wednesday 8th June 2011

To even the casual observer it was obvious Charlie Simmonds was focused on the task in hand. Leaning back, head cradled in cupped hands, his eyes were tightly closed, his brow furrowed. His headphones were plugged into a battered iPod, placed neatly alongside his computer keyboard. With the exception of a phone and the computer – its screen currently blank – the only occupants of the desk were Charlie's size ten dock shoes. Nibbling his lower lip, he revealed a set of uneven lower teeth.

"A que hora es la proxima tren para Madrid...?"

He took a deep breath and grimaced. "Jesus...all right then..." he murmured, *"a que hora es el proxima tren para Madrid...?"*

Touching his fingertips to his brow, he shook his head; how the hell were you supposed to know if a train was masculine or feminine? And how was it, while he still wrestled with the basics, a handful of evening classes had sufficed for Sally to be able to jabber away like a native? He opened his eyes, silenced the iPod and transferred his attention to a map of Europe pinned to the wall beside his chair.

His eyes were drawn, inevitably, to the section of the Iberian peninsular where the brown smudge marking the eastern end of the Pyrenees faded into green. There, in the foothills, a few kilometres south of the border, lay *Sant Cosme*. And in a rock-strewn field on the western edge of that hamlet stood the crumbling, derelict farmhouse Charlie had set his heart on trans-forming into a retirement home. Canny old Antoni stubbornly insisted the ruin wasn't for sale, but Charlie had done his homework; in the wake of successive droughts no half-decent cash offer was going to be turned down for long.

And with only three months of his contract to see out, Charlie had time to play with. Sally had been nagging him to get into security consultancy, and he had put out a few feelers. Not as young as he once was, but he had bags of experience and a CV which was solidly impressive if not spectacular. Twenty-five years with the Met before joining Her Majesty's Customs and Immigration, recently reincarnated as the UK Border Agency; currently with Gatwick's ground security unit. That kind of expertise was in demand, even if blokes his age could expect no more than short-term contracts.

All that could change radically, of course, if Sally just realized the boys were perfectly capable of running their own lives without Mum fussing over them. Then you wouldn't see her and Charlie for dust. Stack the venerable Range Rover to the gunwales and head for the Tunnel. Foot hard down along the *autoroutes*, follow *direction Narbonne*, before swinging south on the A9. Engage low gear for the last few kilometres up the dusty, bumpy dirt track into *Sant Cosme*.

It wasn't like he'd be dragging Sally down there kicking and screaming, either. She'd probably moan, but she was nearly as taken with the place as he was; wouldn't even mind living rough for a bit while he knocked the *finca* into shape. They had run into an ex-pat couple in the fly-blown little village bar who'd done the same thing with a ruin they picked up for half nothing. Michael, a jovial, bearded farmer-cum-builder from Wexford, had offered advice on finding cheap materials, the loan of his cement-mixer and even a hand with the heavy work. It turned out Sally and Joan shared an interest in the old Cathar stories. When they got fed up with hauling breeze blocks and whitewashing walls, they agreed they'd hop in the Range Rover and bugger off to Perpignan, leaving Charlie and Michael to get on with it.

With a sigh of resignation he reactivated the iPod, closed his eyes again and resumed his studies, failing to hear the knock on the door heralding the brisk entry of a short, overweight woman in her early forties, a green plastic file hugged to her generous bosom.

"Charlie...?"

Taking in the situation at a glance, Yvonne Nightingale frowned.

"Un billete de ida y vuelta para Barcelona, por favor..."

His visitor leaned across the desk jabbing a finger at the iPod. Its owner came upright fast, eyes wide and scowling.

"What the f...?" The scowl morphed into a weary smile. "Oh...evening, boss."

"Morning..." she pointed out. "It's twenty-five to one, Charlie..."

Without undue haste he lowered his feet to the floor, shed the earphones and glanced at a clock on the wall. He was a stocky, broad shouldered man with a crumpled face, shrewd eyes, and a bald patch he tried to camouflage by keeping his greying hair unfashionably long.

"So it is. What brings you here at this hour...?"

"The incident..." brushing a speck of dirt from the spot vacated by Charlie's shoes, she parked a well-upholstered hip on his desk. "Don't tell me you hadn't heard..."

"Actually, I was across the other side, boss. By the time I got back it was pretty much done and dusted." Charlie shrugged. "All I heard was a couple of shooters had collared some nutter..."

"Nothing else...?"

"Young bloke, foreign – Scandinavian, was it? Got to reclaim, then came on kind of weird, gave a false name..." Charlie scratched his head. "Yeah, that was about it..."

She stared at him in silence, eyes narrowed. "When I landed this job, I got a briefing on each of my team. Well...hardly a briefing, call it a thumbnail sketch. Interested, Charlie...?"

"I think you're going to tell me anyway..."

"You are – or were – considered sharp, efficient, tenacious and a first class interrogator..." she sucked her teeth. "Not to mention lazy, stubborn and devious. Big problem is, you're retiring in September, and I'm told you've switched off – coasting to your pension..."

"I wouldn't say that..."

"I'll bet you bloody wouldn't. Oh, and there's a whisper you've been running high-stakes card schools on nights when you're technically on duty..." She raised her eyebrows. "Which, if true, might explain where you were earlier..."

"Hey, hang on..."

She cut his protestations short with a wave of her hand.

"Charlie, right this minute I don't give a toss if you were in flagrante with an air hostess..."

"Flight attendant, boss..."

"I just thought you might be interested in the gossip. I'm not, but it did make me wonder if you might be exactly the person I needed..."

"It did...?"

"The cops didn't know what to make of that nutter, so somehow we've wound up with him. Twenty-seven, Icelandic national, nothing suspicious in his pockets, bags or on his laptop. If he's on any watch-lists, the counter-terrorist boys haven't shared it with us – yet. If and when we manage to wake Reykjavik up we may find out if he's got a record back home. And, yes, he was acting like a lunatic, but that could be cover – doesn't prove a thing..."

The crimson nail varnish made her look as if she had just slashed someone's face, and the absence of makeup hinted at a hasty exit from her bed. She cocked her head to one side, like an inquisitive owl.

"Tell me about the poker, Charlie. Are you just good, or

seriously good…?"

Scanning her face for any sign she might be joking he concluded, correctly, she was not. Nor was it likely she was angling for an invitation to a late night sit-down in north terminal. "You'd have to ask other people…"

"Don't be coy, Charlie…"

He sighed. "Well, I guess I…usually come out ahead."

"Thought you might. Which is about more than knowing the odds, isn't it? Winners have to be able to suss people out, read their body language, tell if they're bluffing by watching their eyes…" A smile hovered at the corners of her mouth but did not take flight. "You do that, don't you, Charlie…?"

"I'm flattered…"

Yvonne Nightingale's lips tightened. "Don't be. I don't care whether you like me. I didn't get where I am by trying to be everybody's flavour of the month. But don't ever patronise me, Charlie. Do we understand each another…?"

"Yes, boss…"

"My gut feeling is we might have a tricky sod on our hands, and it takes one to know one…"

Ignoring the challenge in her smile, he nodded. "Makes sense…"

"I've got to decide what to do with him, and he's bloody high profile, what with armed coppers swooping and the terminal evacuated. God knows how many punters filmed him on their mobiles before the shooters turned up, but of course it's all over the bloody net, too…"

"That figures…"

"Anyway, we'll come back to him. A bit of background first, though. Bear with me, you'll see why. About an hour ago, a junior Home Office minister called Oakley rang me at home. He's why I'm here, when I should be getting my beauty sleep…"

"Yes, boss…"

"And reading between the lines I'd say there's currently a

vicious little turf-war raging between a couple of the departments in that particular ministry…" She shrugged. "Nothing new in that, as I'm sure you know…"

"Yes boss…"

Charlie might not, but it was no surprise that she did. It was less than a month since the most recent in a series of unusually rapid promotions saw Yvonne Nightingale appointed the first woman to head the Gatwick Airport Ground Security Unit. Known as the odd squad, its remit was dealing with any individual, whether a member of the travelling public, air crew or airport employee, exhibiting within the confines of England's second largest airport 'behaviour which could reasonably be considered irrational, unusual, out of the ordinary or bizarre, and might represent a potential risk to self or others'.

"In the red corner, the section with responsibility for all matters pertaining to, amongst other things, immigration and border control. In the blue corner, their presumed colleagues whose portfolio includes counter-terrorism. Still with me…?"

"Yes, boss…"

She heaved a sigh and shifted position. "Charlie, I'm tired. And when I get tired I get irritable. If you say 'yes boss' again in that tone, I shall assume you're taking the piss and I may slap you…"

"I would prefer to avoid that…"

"Very wise."

It was of no great concern to him, since their paths were not fated to cross for long, but Charlie had not warmed to the unit's first female director. On their first encounter he found her brusque and sharp-edged, attributes he did not find attractive in a woman. In addition, she was reputed to have an unhealthy respect for rules and regulations while Charlie, in common with a perhaps surprising number of ex-policemen, enjoyed a greater affinity with those of an outlaw mentality. A little grudgingly, he now found himself beginning to appreciate her style.

"But if I read junior minister Oakley correctly, the warring factions have at least one objective in common. To whit, ensuring they're not perceived as having made any error or misjudgement regarding the twenty-seven year old Icelandic national, whose odd behaviour and strange pronouncements triggered a partial evacuation of this terminal..." She paused, eyebrows raised. "Now, the aforementioned Mr Oakley occupies the red corner, so his brief is...?"

"Border control..."

She aimed a crimson tipped finger at him. "Precisely. Hold that thought. Oakley left me in no doubt we are expected to handle this whole thing in a manner which does nothing to harm his department's interests, and ideally may even further them..."

Charlie spread his hands. "Sorry, you're going to have to spell it out. Whitehall wrangling goes right over my head..."

Yvonne Nightingale heaved a sigh. "You disappoint me. Oakley sees this as a chance to rack up some points and my guess is he fixed it so the cops passed the bloke to us. What he's hoping, is we can come up with reasons why CT should have spotted him as a security risk before he ever got here. Oakley then presents it as an example of border security doing CT's job better than they are. Result, a feather in his cap, and we earn his eternal gratitude and support. Well, for as long as it suits him, anyway, but it could work for us. Why? Because he and his buddies are the ones who sign off on our budgets..."

Charlie nodded. Yvonne Nightingale sounded as if she had as much of a taste for political game playing as the man who had roused her from her slumbers.

"And that's what you want done...?"

"I didn't say that. I'm telling you what Oakley would like..." she shrugged. "Which may inform our decision while not necessarily influencing it. Let me tell you what I do want..."

She counted the points off on the plump fingers of a left hand that was, Charlie noted, unencumbered by rings.

"The name he gave the shooters didn't match the one in his passport..." Pulling the offending item from the file she handed it to him. "I want to know what's going on there..."

He flicked through to the photograph; symmetrical features, high cheekbones, aquiline nose, deep-set eyes, moustache and trimmed beard, a head of tight curls.

"Do we know if this is kosher...?"

"We do. It is..."

"Okay..."

"He talked to the shooters about being on a mission, giving no clue what it was. If he is, we need to know about it. Also claimed someone – singular or plural – might want to stop him. Who, and why...?"

Charlie nodded.

"Made references to using violence. What kind, has he ever done so before? Why this time, and against whom...?"

"Got it."

"Good, because..." She glanced at an outsized, pink plastic watch which would not have looked out of place on a twelve-year-old's wrist. "I want a verbal report by one forty-five."

Reaching into the file again she produced a memory stick and tossed it onto the desk. "CCTV. Make sure you've seen the last bit, when the lead copper talks to him. We may only have a walk-on part in this show, but what we do we are going to get right. Meaning no mistakes, Charlie."

He turned the memory stick over in fingers that were, for a man of substantial build, surprisingly slender. A musician's fingers, Sally called them, although Charlie could not recall having held a musical instrument since a tambourine in primary school, sixty odd years ago.

"You want me to go talk to him, then...?"

Tossing her head back, the director of the GAGSU closed her eyes. "For Christ's sake, Charlie, what do you think I'm doing here...?"

He shrugged. "You never said..."

"I know what I said. Oh, by the way, the shooters thought he might be high; tests ruled that out. We could have anything on our hands: terrorist, homicidal maniac, paranoid schizophrenic...or just some loveable eccentric. I want to know which and I want to know fast. And yes," she added, "you got the job. Assuming you're not so demob-happy you can't get your finger out and do it bloody well..."

"In an hour? That's kind of tight..."

"Tighter still if you don't get on with it..."

"One question..."

"Jesus..." She rolled her eyes. "Which is...?"

"Why isn't he already in Maidenbloom...?"

"Quick answer, your ears only?"

"Okay..."

"Private clinics cost big bucks. Last budget review, the word – unofficially, of course – was we're expected to make serious – underline serious – economies in psychiatric services. Got your answer?"

"Yup..."

"I am not tossing this one to the shrinks, only to find myself explaining to some committee of stuffed shirts why it cost a stack of public money to decide he's only a bit of an odd-ball, after all..."

She stood up, grimaced, and flexed her back.

"Anything else...?" he asked.

"If you needed anything else, you'd have it." She wagged a finger at him. "The bloke himself. What's he's about? Is he for real or playing games? If so, what games and why. Yes?"

"Yes..."

"If you can get more than that I won't complain, but it'd be a bonus..."

"No pressure, then..."

"When you're done you can go back to dreaming of sunning

yourself in the land of castanets and toreadors. Oh, and buying return tickets to...Barcelona, was it?"

He cocked his head. "Speak it yourself, boss...?"

Yvonne Nightingale, exhibiting that lightness of foot commonly found in women of large build, was half way into the corridor. She stopped and leaned round the door to favour him with a grin. "You may find it hard to believe, Charlie, but I used to have a lover from Madrid..."

And she was gone. Listening to her retreating footsteps, Charlie grinned to himself. Tossing iPod and earphones into a drawer, he plugged the memory stick into a USB slot and turned the volume up on his computer.

Ψ

Charlie spent a few moments at the one-way mirror; appraising people before they saw him gave him a sense of starting on the front foot. Given more time he would have preferred using his own office; to his mind the interview rooms were bleak and cheerless, the lighting harsh and too bright, putting people on the defensive from the word go. Not that this one showed signs of being unduly bothered; lounging on one of the plastic chairs scattered round a plain wooden table, he was staring into space. Charlie exchanged nods with the duty officer who punched a code into the keypad on the wall and waved him in.

"Hi there, I'm Charlie Simmonds. I work for airport security..."

The man was on his feet before the door closed, darting forward to press his visitor's hand in both his own. "I am *Ólafur Bárðarson*..." He smiled. "You have good, strong hands, Mr Simmonds..."

"Have I really?" Charlie nodded. "Now, anything you need before we get going? Food, something to drink...?"

"No, thank you. They gave me water, and..." He patted a

pocket, "I always carry some seeds in case I get hungry…"

Charlie laid the blue passport on the table.

"You are strong, I think. Not just your body – as a person." He paused, studying Charlie's face. "And from your eyes…I would say you feel more than you let people see…"

"Would you, now…"

The man sat down, watching as Charlie took out a notebook and fountain pen, placing them beside the passport. Shrugging off his jacket he draped it across the back of a chair and positioned it on the opposite side of the table.

"Once we've had a chat and you've answered some questions, I'm going to recommend what action we take next…"

"You are a policeman…?"

"Nothing to do with them, no. Completely separate unit, handling airport security…"

"Are you an important man in this unit, Mr Simmonds…?"

Charlie hesitated. Not very, if he were honest. Never quite made it to senior management. Probably could have done, if he hadn't kept his head down and just done the best he could. If he'd been a bit more savvy he'd have known whose ass to kiss to get up the ladder. Not his style, though, unfortunately. Tell the truth, if he hadn't happened to be on the graveyard shift tonight, he probably wouldn't even be here talking to the bloke.

"Important…?" Charlie donned a suitably enigmatic smile. "You could say that…but I've come to talk about you, sir. How about we start with…"

"But you decide what happens to me…"

"Not so. Only recommend. Someone else decides…"

As Charlie opened the passport, the Icelander sighed and stared at the floor.

"I do not understand what is happening, Mr Simmonds. It is like a dream, but a bad one, you know? Looking down as my plane landed I was so happy – I have been looking forward to this for a long time. Then everything goes—" he broke off, glancing at Charlie. "But maybe now they will be better. I asked my guides to send help and...here you are."

"Indeed I am..." Charlie agreed, although seeing Yvonne Nightingale in the role of guide did not come easily. "Answer my questions, sir, and I'll do what I can for you. Does that sound okay...?"

If he heard, the tall man did not respond. Folding his arms, he gazed at a point somewhere in the distance.

"I was just sitting, you see...making no trouble...hurting no one. Then Mr Miller and his friend came along, with their guns. I do not know why, but they thought maybe I had a bomb. I said no, that was crazy, but I had to go with them to this big room full of men in blue uniforms. I tried to tell them, to explain, but they were so busy taking fingerprints, photographing me, and...there was this lady in a white coat – a nurse or a doctor, I don't know – who wanted blood from my arm...and my pee in a bottle. I said why, why are you doing this, but no one..." He took a long, deep breath. "I can tell you, my head was going round and round, it was all...crazy..."

"How's the head now?"

"Now...? Better, thank you..."

"Good. Listen, I hate to rush you, but I've only got an hour for this. I need your help..."

"Yes, yes..." The man leaned forward, nodding. "Let us help each other. I will help you and you will help me, yes...?"

"Like I said, I'll do what I can. What's going to help is short, clear answers..."

"I will try, but it is not always..."

"Do your best, okay? You want this mess sorted out as quickly as possible, right...?"

The Icelander spread his hands. "But what have I done, Mr Simmonds...? No one has told me. What do we have to sort out...?"

Charlie hesitated. He wanted to be asking questions, not

answering them. But he wasn't going to get far without the man's cooperation.

"How often do you fly, sir?"

"This is the first time in maybe…a year."

"You know all about nine-eleven, don't you…?"

"Of course." He frowned. "It was terrible, terrible…"

"For people like me, it was a game-changer. Since then, every security man in every airport in the world has been on red alert. These days, if we spot anyone acting even a bit odd, a bit…suspicious, we pull them in, fast…" He raised his eyebrows. "And in my book, spending an unnecessarily extended period in reclaim, throwing yourself across the floor and then planting yourself down on a carousel and…doing whatever you were doing, that's more than just a bit odd, you see. And it's definitely reasonable grounds for—"

"It was broken…" he protested. "I saw a notice. Go and look for yourself. All I wanted was somewhere quiet to talk to my guides. What is so bad about that? I tried to tell Mr Miller, but he—"

"You also gave him a name that wasn't on any passenger list. So not only were you acting in a suspicious manner, but you've given a false ID as well. And you're surprised we wanted to talk to you…?"

The Icelander gave a weary shake of the head. "I kept trying to explain but…"

"Now's your chance, sir. Explain it all to me, clear things up and with a bit of luck that could be the end of your problems…"

"Problems…?"

"Well, you've been detained by the police and now here you are in the middle of the night, still under questioning. Not ideal, is it? Annoying and inconvenient, I'd have thought if it was me. But you don't see it as a problem…"

"Well… it is inconvenient, but…"

With a shake of the head he got to his feet, thrust his hands into his pockets and paced across the room. Leaning back against the mirror, he folded his arms. Looking at the moustache and beard set in hawk-like features, Charlie wondered if pirate might perhaps feature in the Icelander's genes.

"It is as it is...I must accept it. And trust everything is unfolding as it should, and in the end all will be well. You see," he went on, "I believe when you are doing the universe's work, Mr Simmonds, it provides whatever you need. You talk about problems, but I say no, they are not really problems at all..."

"What would you say they are, then?"

"Tests, challenges. And finding the answers is all part of my journey, you see. Each answer is like..." He waved a hand, "like a burning torch..."

"You've lost me..." Charlie shook his head.

"They light the way, help me see the path to my goal..."

"Right. Which is an interesting way of looking at it, but..." Charlie tapped his watch. "Why don't you come and sit down...?"

The Icelander shook his head.

"As you wish. Right, your name, then..." Charlie licked his finger and leafed through to the photograph page. "Let's get that sorted out..."

"I am Ólafur Bárðarson..."

"That's not what it says here. According to this you are Mr Haraldsson...how do I say the first name?"

"Þormóður."

"Thank you. So, the name in your identity document is different from the one you gave Sgt Miller and now me. I need to know why..."

"It is no great mystery, Mr Simmonds..."

"I'm pleased to hear it. Go on..."

"In my country a child takes the name of its father. My father was *Haraldur* so I am *Haraldsson*, son of Harald. If I had a sister – but I do not – she would be *Haraldsdóttir* which means..."

"Okay, I get the picture..."

"You have a son?"

Questions were always a judgement call. Brush them aside and you risked antagonizing people; answer too many and you were inviting them to run the show.

"Two, actually. Why do you ask?"

"In Iceland, Charlie is Karl, so your sons would both be called *Karlsson*..."

"Right..." Charlie nodded. "Except that wasn't really what I was getting at..."

Returning to the table, the Icelander picked up the paper cup and stood looking down at Charlie, cradling it in his hands. "No. You wanted to know why, when someone asks who I am, I do not say, 'I am *Haraldsson*'. Yes...?"

"Yes..."

"Because it is not who I am – it is a name, yes, but not my identity, Mr Simmonds. And they are not the same thing, are they? Whatever we put on the collar of a dog it is not a name. I would call it only..." He shrugged, "a label. When people ask me who I am, I wish to give them the truth. Did you teach your sons to always speak the truth...?"

The quality of Charlie's parenting, it turned out, was of insufficient interest for the Icelander to wait to learn more about it.

"*Haraldsson* is the label round my neck," he went on. "It may tell you who my father was, but does that matter? No, because I am not my father, am I? But *Ólafur Bárðarson* is different. Quite different. Try closing your eyes and letting it ring through your consciousness, like the sound of a Tibetan bowl. Do more than hear it, Mr Simmonds, feel its vibration. That will tell you everything about me. My history, my nature...even my spirit..." He paused, eyes shining. "*Ólafur Bárðarson* has an energy like no other name, you see. It is unique, as each snowflake is unique. Billions and billions of them, never two alike...did you know that?"

"I've heard something of the sort, sir. Let me get this straight, then. You don't dispute what's printed here is...I'll call it your official name. But it so happens you prefer...Bardarson...?"

He planted his hands on slim hips and a pained look flickered across his face, the cheeks now glazed with a faint coppery stubble.

"Prefer? No. It is because my name must tell my story, Mr Simmonds. *Ólafur* was the first settler in my village, a little place called *Ólafsvík* – the *bay of Ólaf*. It is a name that goes back hundreds of years in our history, and is rich in meanings. *The white one*, and also *the power of the ancestors*..." He pursed his lips. "And it rhymes with *Eilífur*. That is harder to translate, but you could say it means...*the eternal one*..."

Charlie opened his mouth, but the Icelander's eager expression told him trying to interrupt would be futile.

"...Now you understand *Bárðarson* is 'son of *Bárður*' yes? *Bard* means bright, and *Bárður* is a great god of the snowy mountain – people have written sagas about him. And at special moments I can feel my whole being soar just as the peaks of *Bard's* mountain ascend into the heavens. And every part of me, Mr Simmonds – my heart, my mind, my spirit and my body – is like a living tuning fork, resonating with *Ólaf's* village, *Bárðar's* mountain, with my ancestors, the people of my country...my motherland itself..." The green and blue eyes held Charlie's prisoner. "Now do you see? It is not a matter of *prefer*, I have *chosen* the one name – the only name – that holds my truth..."

His voice faded away; the men exchanged nods.

"I hear you..." Charlie told him.

"If that is true, I am happy..."

"Now I need you to hear me..."

"I will become the listener..."

"I do understand about the names. Which is a start, but time's short, and we've got to move on..."

"Yes, yes, of course, but..." The man returned to drop back

into his chair. "I have been here many hours now; the dark ones must know where I am – you realise that, don't you? Nothing can be hidden from them for very long, Mr Simmonds – they have eyes and ears everywhere…"

"Not in my unit," Charlie told him.

"Thinking that way is dangerous. It is not possible to recognise them – they are too clever. They want you to think you are safe, but you are not. No one is safe from them. Believe me, Mr Simmonds, if they wanted to make me disappear this moment, you could do nothing…"

The man had a haunted look in his eyes; his breathing was quick and shallow. Things were slipping away from Charlie; he sensed he had about ten seconds before they were irrevocably beyond his grasp.

"Who could, then…?"

The Icelander frowned.

"Could what…?"

"You said I couldn't stop these dark…people. Who could, then?"

"The light workers…?" The Icelander's eyes narrowed, then he nodded. "Yes, I think so. They are trying to raise consciousness on the planet, you see. Find ways to bring in more light…" He paused. "So the dark ones are very fearful of them. Think about it, Mr Simmonds, think what will happen as the light grows stronger and brighter. There will be no place for the darkness, no shadows where it can hide. In the end, no more darkness – it will cease to exist…"

Charlie moistened his lips.

"These guides you talk about, are they, like…light workers?"

"Of course…"

"Okay, then. As soon as you'd asked them for help, I turned up, that's what you said, remember?" He paused, eyebrows raised. "So they must have sent me to protect you. Stands to reason, doesn't it?"

The man's eyes searched Charlie's face; whatever he saw triggered a faint smile.

"It is possible. Why not...?"

"If they sent me, you can trust me, can't you...?"

"Well..."

"And I can definitely keep you safe..." insisted Charlie, "but only if tell me everything."

"You think so...?"

Charlie spread his hands. "We're on the same side, aren't we?"

"If I tell you, you may be in danger, too..."

"Listen, we're handling high-risk situations twenty-four seven. That's what they train, equip and pay us for. You and me, we'll be fine, absolutely fine. All you have to do is trust me, it's as easy as that..."

"You are sure...?"

"I don't make promises I can't keep...so," Charlie went on, "this mission of yours. Start at the beginning, please. The people who sent you, tell me about them..."

The young man hesitated, took a sip of water and brushed his lips with the back of his hand. "Well...they came one night saying there was work to be done here..."

"Meaning England...?"

"By the time they returned, I had started preparing myself. The second time, they told me where to go, what to do."

"How could you prepare, if you didn't know where you were going or why?"

"By spending many hours studying maps, getting to know your country and its history. And making my own maps..." He grimaced. "If I had my computer, I could show you..."

"You can do that later..." Charlie folded his arms and leaned back. "And why did they pick you? I mean, did you approach them, or did they...come looking for you?"

"Approach...?" He gave a puzzled shake of the head. "You think it is possible to summon them, Mr Simmonds, order them to come...?"

"Well, maybe not...I'm just trying to get things clear in my mind, that's all. Anyway...first meeting, no details..." He paused. "Why would that have been – didn't they trust you...?"

"Of course, always. But that night maybe the time was not right..."

"When was that exactly, do you remember?"

"The winter solstice..."

"Remind me, please...I'm not good on the astrological stuff..."

"No...? December the twenty-first...so," he added, "it will be half a year exactly..."

"When you say 'it'..." enquired Charlie, "what are we talking about...?"

"The moment my work will be finished...completed."

"Ah, yes..." breathed Charlie. "Go on..."

"My journey will be over, the divine purpose fulfilled..." He sighed. "It will be a special moment, I will feel proud to have been a part of it. It is a great honour to be chosen...whatever happens..."

"It sounds as if you don't know..."

"How could I? Mighty energies will be unleashed, set free after such a long, long time, Mr Simmonds. It will be like..." Puffing out his cheeks, the young man shook his head, "...like water bursting from behind a great dam. Maybe those who sent me know, but not a mere human like me...All I can do is exactly what they asked me, and trust..." He placed his palms together. "As always, what will be, will be..."

Charlie picked up his pen, slowly turning it end over end in his fingers.

"These...energies. Sounds a bit...risky, dangerous. Must take courage to do something like that..."

"*Cour-rage*..." the Icelander seized on the word. "Rage of the heart. But if the heart tells you your action is right action, what is there to fear? Yes, maybe there is danger, but what does it matter...?"

"Well, it all depends, doesn't it?" Charlie scratched his head with the end of his pen. "I mean, if there's a chance you might wind up dead, for example, it might matter quite a lot..."

"You think so...?" the Icelander enquired, smiling. "But why? Don't we live many lives?"

"Looked at that way, I suppose..." conceded Charlie.

It had happened to him occasionally; finding someone evasive and elusive to begin with, leading you round in circles, making you wonder if they were playing games. Then you said or did something and it turned out to be the key; from then on it was all plain sailing, effortless. Sure, you might still have to nudge them along, toss in the occasional cue, but the hard graft was over. From that point the trick was to avoid being too eager; keep them on track without them being aware. Trust, that wily old Met trainer had told him all those years ago; it's all about winning their trust. That and making them feel you're their best friend, so they can't wait to tell you whatever it is you want.

"Mind if I call you Olaf...?"

"Please..."

"I interrupted you, didn't I? You were saying it'll be exactly six months from beginning to end. Which takes us to...?"

"The night of mid-summer. Do you see the beautiful shape of my journey, Mr Simmonds? If you could see it now it would be a perfect arc..." With a sweep of the hand, he drew it in the air, "Starting at moment of deepest winter..."

"The shortest day, right...?"

"People think of it as that, but look deeper, you will see more. Consider what happens at midwinter. Light begins its return to the planet and with light, warmth – two energies which support and nurture life. So, it is a time of new beginnings, of rebirth, yes, but light of a different kind also returns – the light of consciousness and awareness. That is the essence of my mission, you see. I am sure it is why they chose to visit me on that night of all nights..."

He paused, head cocked, waiting for Charlie to go on.

"Looked at like that, it makes sense, doesn't it?"

"Perfect sense, if you accept that what happens on earth reflects the patterns of the heavenly bodies. As above, so below. All part of the cosmic dance..."

"Nicely put..." Charlie assented.

So far, so good; a firm date, clues as to timing. More than enough, he guessed, to put a smile on the face of the shadowy Oakley and maybe Yvonne Nightingale, too. Play his cards right now, he could scoop the pot. For sure they would find enough on the laptop to establish the target beyond doubt, but why deny himself the satisfaction of strolling in and telling her himself?

"A couple of weeks, then. Not long, is it...?" Charlie sucked his teeth. "And is everything set up, or do you have to, you know...put in the final touches?"

Olaf looked puzzled. "What kind of thing...?"

"No idea..." Charlie waved a hand. "Just wondering..."

"You must understand I am..." Olaf paused, resting his brow lightly on his fingertips. "What is the word for...something you must add for a chemical reaction to take place? In Icelandic we say *hvati*..."

"Can't think...Anyway, you were saying...?"

"There is a word..." he insisted, frowning.

"Do you mean you've absolutely got to be there, or the event doesn't happen...?"

Snapping his fingers, the young man came upright so fast Charlie recoiled.

"Catalyst!"

"Got it..." Charlie nodded. "So, come midsummer night, that's your role – you're the catalyst...?"

"You must understand, Mr Simmonds, I am not doing, I am being. Being fully present in that place, at that moment. And so honouring its dark history and the blocking energies, so they can be set free again..."

He rose to his feet, arms wide, his voice taking on a reverential tone. "...Attuning to and honouring the heights and the depths, the heavenly bodies above and the earth below..." He paused. "And then, my work is done..."

With a self-conscious smile he let his arms drop slowly to his sides.

"That is going to be quite something..." Charlie assented, softly.

"I know it. Something so beautiful, natural and simple..."

When you came down to it, it was all about timing, Charlie thought; picking just the right moment. And his gut told him this was it.

"So, walk me through it if you would, Olaf. On that night, when the moment comes...the climax, let's call it..."

"Yes, that is the word...climax..."

"Where is that place – where exactly are you going to be...?"

The Icelander gave a rueful smile and slumped back into his chair. "Can't you get me my computer, Mr Simmonds? Everything is there..."

"Later..." Charlie shrugged the idea away. "Listen, if you don't remember the exact location, give me a rough idea..."

"I have been there once, well...in meditation. I attuned to it, felt its energy. It has been blocked for centuries, but once it is cleansed and healed again its full power will return, I am certain. Just by tuning in I could feel it...and it is so powerful. My whole body was shaking, I could not control it..." He took a deep breath, exhaling slowly. "You can imagine what it will be like on midsummer night, Mr Simmonds, at the moment sun and moon move into alignment..."

Charlie pushed pen and notebook across the table.

"Show me that place, Olaf. Draw me one of your maps..."

"You need to see it, everything, or you will not understand

properly. The patterns, the calculations, all my research..." He glanced at the door. "Maybe they have finished with it..."

Watching Charlie unscrew the cap, a slow smile spread across Olaf's face. "Ah, you have a Montblanc – they are so beautiful..."

"Anniversary present from the wife. Tell you the truth, I'm a bit old-fashioned – fountain pen addict, you might say. Can't be doing with biros and felt-tips and roller balls and that modern rubbish..." He offered it to Olaf. "Don't mind using these, do you...?"

Olaf ran his finger the length of the fat lacquered barrel, black as a raven's wing.

"Of course not but...it has such a fine nib..."

"Don't worry, I dropped it once, and believe it or not it just bounced. They're tougher than they look..." Charlie opened the notebook, smoothing the page with the flat of his hand. "Take your time..."

Head cupped in his hands, he resisted the urge to watch as Olaf began sketching with firm, precise strokes. A smile tugged at Charlie's lips as he recalled his concern about having insufficient time. Not only would he be way ahead of schedule but delivering far, far more than she could have expected. Savouring the prospect, he realised Olaf had spoken. "Sorry, I was miles away. Are you done...?"

"I said I think it is better if I make two..."

"Sure, why not...?" Charlie shrugged.

Turning the page, Olaf resumed his labours.

"It will be easier to understand..."

"Great..."

Olaf, satisfied with his efforts, finally spun the notebook round. Charlie found himself looking at a single vertical line beside which Olaf had printed three names.

"An imaginary line connecting Glastonbury in the south with Ben Macdui in the north..." Olaf indicated each one in turn with the gleaming gold nib. "You know Ben Macdui...?"

"No, I don't..."

"It is the second highest mountain in Scotland. And here..." the nib hovered above the third name. "Scafell..."

Charlie glanced up to find Olaf beaming at him. "Okay..." Charlie nodded. "But that doesn't really..."

"Sacred sites, Mr Simmonds, all of them. And I discovered they are in perfect alignment. Perfect..." He repeated. "Later, I will show you the measurements..."

Charlie Simmonds needed more than imaginary lines; a lot more. Hardly breathing, he stared at the page, willing what he saw to make some kind of sense. Finally, he forced a smile and kept his tone casual. "Yeah, interesting...and the other one?"

"Yes, of course..."

With a flourish worthy of a conjuror pulling a fluttering dove from his top hat, the Icelander turned the page and jabbed a finger. "Here are three islands." He announced. "Holy islands. You see the names?"

"Anglesey, Lindisfarne...Arran..." Charlie intoned, moistening his lips. "Olaf, I still don't..."

"What do they make, Mr Simmonds? Don't you see...?"

"All I see is a triangle..."

"Look again, please – observe the angles. I have marked them for you...forty, fifty and ninety degrees..."

"Olaf, I thought you were going to..."

"The golden triangle of Pythagoras, Mr Simmonds. And look..." He pointed again. "Here...on what is mathematically the exact centre point of the base...do you see...?"

Charlie stared blankly at the neat, clear capital letters. "Yeah, I see..." He was unable to keep the frustration from his voice. "But what the hell has any of this got to do with...?"

Olaf held up both hands. "Scafell...that is what you wanted, isn't it?

"What are you talking about...?"

"That is where I will be on mid-summer night, Mr

Simmonds..." Olaf smiled. "Isn't that amazing...?"

"Yes..." agreed Charlie Simmonds, faintly. "Bloody amazing..."

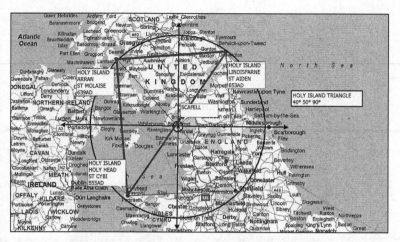

Image 01 Mount Scafell and the Holy Islands

Chapter 3

Maidenbloom Hospital

Wednesday 8th June 2011

Dr. P. L. Wingfield MBChB PhD FRCPsych, Maidenbloom Hospital's medical director, did not relish the prospect of his first two appointments of the day. Evidence to support his misgivings about them was as yet no more than circumstantial, but he suspected that both involved the risk of becoming embroiled in situations he would have preferred to avoid.

Some two hours earlier, scanning the front page of the *Daily Telegraph* over coffee and muesli, he guessed it was probable the 'mystery Icelander who brought chaos to Gatwick' would have found himself sectioned and dispatched to Wingfield's psychiatric unit. That in itself caused him no great concern; the airport authority's contract had been designed to cover eventualities of precisely that nature. The source of his unease was a message relayed to his smart phone by Doris, his secretary, requesting that immediately the patient's initial assessment had been completed, his findings should be communicated to a junior Home Office minister of whom he had never heard.

In the second case, that of Ms Chloe Spenser-Nelson, alarm bells began to sound when he noticed that Doris had attached to the cover of the patient's file a pink post-it inscribed with the letters, 'O.C.C.' and, unwilling to place her trust in its inherent adhesive qualities, had reinforced them with not one but two staples. While a contract of any nature between the two organisations was beyond the realms of possibility, their geographical proximity had resulted in several former members of *The Order of Cosmic Consciousness* arriving on Maidenbloom's doorstep

In the course of providing it, any illusions Wingfield might have harboured regarding the nature of this secretive cult were dispelled. Suggestive of brotherly love and universal wisdom though its title might be, its true colours were revealed to be of a more sinister hue. Eager for any opportunity to bask in the reflected glory of a well-publicised stable of celebrity devotees, the *Order* adopted a highly defensive stance should any disenchanted member of its congregation seek to air their grievances in public. Thus far Wingfield had successfully side stepped direct confrontation with them, but he did not doubt they possessed both the resources and the will to deploy formidable legal forces any time they might deem it necessary. His sense of unease was in no way alleviated by unsubstantiated but persistent rumours that *Order* converts included the wife of the CEO of USCARE, a Los Angeles based conglomerate numbering Maidenbloom Hospital among its European assets.

Sir Giles Spenser-Nelson had delivered Chloe to the hospital claiming she was in urgent need of mental health care. Reading her notes, Wingfield hoped to find some indication of how he had managed to wrest her from the notoriously determined clutches of *The Order,* but the report by the staff member on duty that night offered no insights. While previous experience with such patients suggested that her father's insistence on mental health treatment was justified, it did not prevent him regarding Chloe's case as a potential minefield, to be negotiated with circumspection.

The slight, bare-footed figure enveloped in a pale blue towelling bathrobe two sizes too large entered his consulting room without knocking. Leaving the door gaping, she padded silently across the deep pile carpet to his desk. Without sparing a glance for Wingfield, who was occupying his favoured position beside the window, she folded her legs neatly beneath her and dropped onto a leather chair, eyes averted and slim shoulders hunched, exuding defiance.

"Good morning, Chloe..."

Unhurriedly, he closed the door before returning to where he could enjoy the feeling of sunshine on his face. A small, dapper, bespectacled man in his late fifties, Wingfield had a shock of prematurely grey hair, fleshy, boyish features and a sensual fullness to his lips.

"Do you know who I am?" He enquired.

"It's Morgana, actually..." She drew the robe tighter round her neck. "Your name's on the door, so obviously I do. You're some kind of shrink, presumably..."

Wingfield eased his hands into his jacket pockets. His suits, tailored by a small family establishment just behind Bond Street, were one of his extravagances and he treated them with care. Sunlight glinting on his glasses, he nodded. "I'm medical director and yes, I'm a psychiatrist."

Lips pursed, she looked across at him, displaying her pallor and dark rings surrounding wide-set, translucent blue eyes. Fair skinned, with high cheekbones and a cascade of shoulder length auburn ringlets, she reminded Wingfield of that breed of wraith-like creatures immortalised by William Morris and his followers.

"God knows why I'm here. Maybe you can tell me..." She shrugged. "There's absolutely nothing wrong with me..."

"That's a good start..." Wingfield's smile was not returned. "So, how are you this morning, Morgana...?"

"My father told you all about it, didn't he...?" She gave a toss of her head. "He and my mother really got their knickers in a twist..."

Late the previous evening a chauffeur-driven Bentley bearing Sir Giles and his daughter had swept up to the hospital entrance. Following what he referred to only as her 'exit' from *Cosmic Centre*, two days earlier, he claimed Chloe's subsequent behaviour had been erratic and had included violent episodes. Notes by the duty psychiatrist, a young man from the Indian sub-continent whom Wingfield suspected might have been slightly daunted to find himself dealing with a knight of the realm, indicated Chloe challenged none of her father's assertions, showing more interest in hastening his departure. Shortly before leaving he issued a warning the young woman might be 'a danger to herself', but declined to elaborate. Medical records requested from the family GP, if and when they arrived, would hopefully throw further light on the subject.

"Well, he expressed pretty serious concerns about your well-being..." Wingfield assented, crossing to his desk. "Quite frankly, though, I'm more interested in whatever you've got to tell me."

She sighed and propped her chin on her hand. "What do you want to know, then...?"

"You may be absolutely right, there may indeed be nothing wrong with you, but that wasn't the picture your father painted and I'd like to hear yours..."

"I was a bit out of it last night. What did he actually say...?"

"That he received a text message from you on Sunday afternoon, which left him in no doubt you were distressed..."

"Sent to my mother, actually. She knew where I was..."

"He didn't...?"

"God, no..."

"I see. Anyway, he brought you home but then they both became worried about you. According to him, your behaviour was not normal..."

"Oh, come on..." She gave a contemptuous shrug. "My family wouldn't know normal if they saw it..."

"In that case, let's move on..." Wingfield clasped his hands on the desktop. "Tell me how you're feeling..."

"The man's a control freak. I can tell you now he'll want you to tell him everything I say. Are you going to...?"

"Would it bother you if I did...?"

"Surely there's some kind of...I don't know, confidentiality thing...?"

"At twenty-four you are no longer a minor. Your father can

demand all he likes, but nothing you disclose to me can be communicated to him – or anyone else for that matter – without your permission. Does that make you feel any better...?"

"He'll still try..." She sighed. "He's used to getting his own way, and he's bloody manipulative..."

"Is he indeed...?'

Her voice had the ring of an expensive private education. Wingfield wondered if Sir Giles had also picked up the bills for the therapists whose jargon came so readily to her lips.

"It sounds as if you have a challenging relationship with him..."

"I'm not going to get into all that stuff..."

"There's no need..." He smiled. "So, let's get back to you and how you're feeling..."

"Feeling...?" She made no effort to hide her irritation. "I don't think you're listening. I said I'm fine – there is nothing wrong with me..."

"I did hear that, but it doesn't answer my question, you see. For example..." He shrugged, "You appear to be frustrated. Would that be so...?"

"Of course I am. Who wouldn't be? You think I want to be in this bloody place...?"

"You have made that clear..." He smiled.

"Look, I don't know what you want me to say..."

A degree of petulance and reluctance to cooperate neither surprised nor concerned him. Having just escaped the clutches of one set of oppressors it was predictable she should cast him in similar mould. She would almost certainly have been subjected to techniques triggering feelings of powerlessness and vulnerability, and their effects would need time to dissipate. At this stage his role was to offer measured, sympathetic responses and find out as much as possible about her mental state, while fostering the belief that although the betrayal she had suffered might be painfully raw, she was now in safe hands.

"I really have no interest in your doing anything particular, Morgana..."

"So, what do you want...?"

"Well, it would be of real help if you simply answer my questions as openly and honestly as you can..."

She reached up, took a lock of hair and twisted it round her finger. "What do you think I'm doing now...?"

"I appreciate you don't want to be here – that's natural. What I'm trying to understand is how you're feeling. What the experience is like for you..."

"How do you mean...?"

"Well, you described it as frustrating. What other words come to mind...?"

"Oh, my God..." She shifted uncomfortably, clutching at the robe.

"Is something wrong...?"

"I don't know..." She bit her lip. "I just thought...what if they're out there...?"

"Out where, Morgana...?"

"There..." She pointed at the window. "Waiting for me. They could be, couldn't they...?"

"What makes you think they might be...?"

"Because it's exactly the kind of thing they'd do. I mean, they went absolutely crazy when my father turned up and said he was taking me away. God, they were so pissed off...so they could be, really they could...right outside that window. And if I come out they'll..."

"Would you feel better if we checked...?"

"You do it – you look..." She hunched her shoulders. "I don't want them to see me..."

"All right, that's exactly what we'll do..."

Wingfield pushed his chair back and stood up. Hands clasped behind him, he paced to the window and spent a few moments scanning the car park. Glancing over his shoulder he shook his head.

"No sign of them…" He told her. "Nothing. Do you feel better now…?

"A bit…" She watched him return and resume his seat. "You think I'm paranoid, don't you?"

"I would say you are understandably nervous after a most unpleasant experience," He told her. "So I want you to be aware of a couple of things. First, we have CCTV cameras covering the grounds, and…" He gave a wry smile, "more security guards than you'd believe. In addition to which we have an arrangement with Crawley police. In an emergency they absolutely guarantee to have men here in eight minutes. You have my word that no one, and I mean no one, Morgana, except myself and my staff, can get within a hundred yards of you…"

"Okay…" She sank back into her chair with a sigh. "I mean, you probably think I'm exaggerating but…you don't know them like I do…"

"I don't, that's true…now," he went on, "a few deep breaths should help calm your system a bit. Would you like water?"

"How about a rum and coke…?"

"Sadly, we lack the necessary license," he told her, earning a wan smile. "Would it be fair to say, given the concerns you mentioned, you're feeling nervous or…anxious?"

"Nervous…?" She puffed out her cheeks. "A bit I suppose. I mean…I don't really know…"

"And if you did know?"

"That's one of those tricksy questions shrinks ask, isn't it…?" Her lip curled.

"Is it…?"

"Yeah, and it's the kind of stuff they do…"

"They…?"

"*Them*…They're always trying to confuse you, get you mixed up – you know? They are serious mind-fuckers…"

"And you think I'm like them? Trying to…fuck your mind?"

Her laugh was sudden, brief and humourless. She tipped her head to one side. "I bet you don't say fuck much, do you, Doctor?"

"We were talking about you..."

She frowned. "I don't know anything about you, do I? I mean...you could even be working for them..."

"From what I understand..." Wingfield placed his elbows on the desk, fingertips touching, "I think it is no exaggeration to say *The Order of Cosmic Consciousness* regards my profession with fear and loathing. Among the darkest of the dark arts..."

Chloe Spenser-Nelson wrinkled her nose. "Yeah...I think that's right, actually..."

"On which basis, I'd suggest it's extremely unlikely they'd have me on their payroll..."

"I suppose..." Pursing her lips, she gazed down at chewed fingernails. "I bet you do think I'm paranoid..."

"I hoped I'd answered that..."

"You didn't really..."

"I try to avoid forming opinions until I'm confident I am in possession of all relevant facts. In this case, I'm still trying to establish them..."

"The only thing you seem to be interested in is how I feel..."

"Maybe not the only thing, but your emotional state is significant, certainly..."

She ran a weary hand across her face; defiance softened into resignation. Taking a deep breath she put her head back and closed her eyes.

"All right then, if you must know...I'm tired. That's what you wanted, isn't it? Not just tired, actually...like, shattered. Totally and utterly shattered..." The dark eyes sprang open. "They force you to stay awake for hours and hours, even when you're dropping. Did you know that...?"

"It sounds most unpleasant..."

"Unpleasant...?" she snapped. "It's not unpleasant, it's bloody horrendous. Literally any time they think you might go to sleep, they start playing really loud music or one of them runs up and starts shouting at you or tells you you've got to start dancing, or…"

"How did you feel when they did that…?"

"How do you think…?"

"I'm hoping you'll tell me…"

"Pissed off, for Christ's sake. Wouldn't anyone be? I mean treating people like that, it's…so unfair."

"In what way…?"

"In every way…To start off with they're always drumming into you how wonderful their workshops and course things are, how they've helped millions of people all over the world so if you do exactly what they say, of course it'll work for you, too. They make it sound like a bloody miracle. By the time you've finished you'll be a better person, everybody's going to adore you and you'll feel fantastic…" She stopped to squint at him. "My father said you'd treated loads of people they've got at. You must know all this stuff…"

"I wouldn't say loads, but a significant number, yes…" Wingfield nodded. "But the experience is different for each person, you see…"

"I got into it by accident really. I remember doing some on-line questionnaire and I must have given my contact details because suddenly they're bombarding me with texts, emails, calls…everything. To get them off my back in the end I said okay, I'd go along for some open day – which turned out to be just for me and one other poor girl. Anyway, they were really persuasive, desperate for me to sign up for a workshop. And in the end, like an idiot, I went along with it."

"You needn't blame yourself. They're very clever…"

"You're not kidding. What they do is convince you you've got all this emotional baggage you absolutely must get rid of or it'll fuck up your whole life. But once you've dumped it, everything will be fantastic and marvellous and wonderful and you'll live happily ever after. And, surprise, surprise, they know exactly how to help you do it – in fact they're the only ones who can. So you pay up and it's serious money, I kid you not. That's clever, too, because then you sort of try to get your money's worth by doing exactly what they tell you. You try really hard, do your best, but instead of helping they bloody well...torture you."

"Torture...?" He echoed. "Strong word..."

"So? It's what they do. Not just stuff like stopping you sleeping, either – they really get in your head. Like Saturday night, I think it was, they kept on and on wanting to make me tell them everything I'd ever done that was bad or nasty or...evil, you know? I mean ever, in my whole life – even when I was a kid. Especially stuff I was ashamed of – they zeroed right in on that. And if I couldn't think of anything they'd scream at me...tell the others I was lying, I was hiding something..." She clenched her jaw, fighting the tears. "Had I ever stolen anything, or cheated on a boyfriend, or lied to my parents? And really sick stuff, like had I ever had group sex, or let people abuse me as a kid. Can you imagine? *Let* them..."

She met Wingfield's eyes, folded her arms and glared at him.

"Oh, for Christ's sake...it's so obvious what you're thinking. No, I was *never* abused, okay...?"

"Do you have any idea why they asked...?"

"They probably ask everyone, I don't know. Because they're sick bastards with twisted minds, that's why..."

Burying her face in her hands she wept, muffling the sounds with the robe. Wingfield slid a box of tissues towards her and waited.

"And I mean sick..." she went on, without raising her head. "We all told them things...you know, everyone's done stuff they wish they hadn't...they're not proud of, haven't they? And do you know what they said...?"

"You don't have to go on if it's too painful..."

Her head came up quickly, eyes bright with tears.

"They said if I tried to hide anything, if I wasn't completely honest about every horrible thing I'd ever done, they'd know, and they'd tell everyone about me. Family, friends...everyone." She bit her lip, "and when they found out what a disgusting little shit I was, all those people were going to hate me. Just...hate me, and refuse to have anything to do with me ever again..."

"Is that how you see yourself?"

"That's what *they* said. You're a shrink, for Christ's sake – how shitty is that...?"

"I would describe it as insensitive, disrespectful and abusive..."

"And what did you have to do to stop all of it ruining your life...?" She snatched a handful of tissues. "Easy peasy. Sign up for more of their fucking courses..."

"Morgana, it's obviously upsetting to revisit it, so I'm going to ask you to stop right there. For your own well-being. Are you okay with that?"

"God, I must look a wreck..." She dabbed at her eyes, took a fresh wad of tissues and blew her nose. "Yes, I'm okay with it. You're probably right..."

"There are one or two other things I'd like to know..."

"Such as...?"

"How have you been sleeping...?"

"I haven't. Last night some nurse gave me a pill she said would knock me out. Well, it didn't..." Her face puckered. "Every time I closed my eyes I saw these faces..."

"Of people you knew...?"

"Theirs – the ones who...there was some guy called Donny, he was kind of group leader. Really nice to start off with, you know, all smiley and friendly and helpful...but he was actually the worst of the lot...God, he was such a sod..." She crushed the ball of tissues in her fist. "Do you know what I'd really enjoy? Kicking him in the balls. Wiping the smile off his smug bloody face..."

"You saw Donny. Any others...?"

"I can't remember the names. There was Roger, and...Heidi, I think..."

"Don't worry, it's not important..."

"Okay..." She shivered, drawing the robe round her. "It was pretty scary at times, actually. You felt like you couldn't get out, like you were a prisoner, you know? You'd get tired and confused and they'd twist what you said, or make you say things you didn't want to. I mean, after a bit your head's spinning, it's like a really bad acid trip..." She shot him a defiant glance. "Well, anyway, they call it downloading. Confessing all your shit..."

Wingfield, wearing a sympathetic half smile, nodded. It told him nothing new and the details were of little importance, but letting her tell her story was part of the process. Sleep deprivation, bullying, confessions extracted under threat of exposure and the rest were, he knew, the currency in which *The Order of Cosmic Consciousness* habitually dealt. Borrowed from the interrogators' handbook, they were effective in breaking the subject's will; steadily undermining their confidence and self esteem until, exhausted, disorientated and disheartened, they would accede to practically any demand. The medical director's first priority, however, was his patient.

"If it's all right with you, I'd like to move on..."

"Go ahead..."

"Your father told us that after you were rescued you seemed to believe Donny and the others could read your thoughts. Do you still think so...?"

"Did I really say that...?"

"So he said..."

"Listen, I was out of it. Who knows what crazy stuff I came up with..." She shrugged. "But now, do you mean? No, how could they...?"

"But earlier you were concerned they might be outside, were

you not…?"

"That…?" She waved a hand. "That's different. I just suddenly got…a bit frightened, that's all. I'm perfectly okay now…"

"I see." He paused. "Apparently there were also occasions on which you struck out at your mother, accusing her of being in league with the *Order*…"

Morgana heaved a sigh. "She was probably fussing over me and I just wanted her to leave me alone. That other stuff? Quite honestly, I don't remember…"

"You don't remember wanting to harm her?"

"I wouldn't have meant to…"

Wingfield paused. "What about self harm, Morgana? Do you have any history of that?"

She recoiled as if he had struck her.

"Self-harm…?"

"I need to be very clear where we stand on safety issues…"

"You mean am I going to top myself…?"

"I was asking about any self harm. Have you had thoughts of—"

"No I bloody haven't…" She glared at him.

"And you have never intentionally harmed yourself…"

"No…" she insisted, tight lipped.

"I see…"

"Look, I'm sure you're a brilliant shrink. With all those letters after your name, you ought to be…" Her smile lingered longer than necessary. "But I'm afraid you're not getting it. The whole thing was ghastly, but it's over, thank God. I'm okay, and…that's it, really." A look of alarm flickered across her face. "You can't keep me here if I don't want to stay, can you…?"

Wingfield shook his head.

"Unlike our friends down the road, we do not hold people against their will. In due course," he continued, smoothly, "you and I will discuss the wisest course of action. It's very important you don't fall into the trap of underestimating the psychological impact of what you've been through..."

"Meaning...?" She twisted another lock of hair.

"It takes time to make a complete recovery from something like that. You must have read about people who were assaulted, or even just witnessed a road accident, and were traumatised..."

"Are you saying I'm traumatised...?"

"I am saying it's a possibility we should not dismiss lightly..."

She glanced toward the window, frowning. "How could you tell if I was?"

"Seeing the faces is a form of flashback..."

"Is that really serious...?"

"It's a symptom. As is worrying that people are planning to abduct you..."

"Abduct...? You make it sound like it's aliens..."

"That wasn't my intention. All I'm trying to do is alert you to the fact that some of your recent behaviour has been neither normal nor rational. On the contrary, it indicates the thought processes of someone who may be, temporarily at least, mentally disturbed..."

"God, you make me sound like I'm a complete nut-case..."

"The purpose of meeting you is for me to determine whether you need support to deal with the effects of your recent experiences, and if so, of what nature..."

"Me, need help? You must be joking. Christ, they're the ones who need a shrink..." She gave a mirthless laugh. "It wouldn't do my parents any harm, either..."

"Not a view I assume you would share with your father..."

"It was a joke..."

"Was it indeed...?" He smiled.

"Did I say my father's a control freak...?"

"You did mention it, yes..."

"And my mother lets him walk all over her..." She sighed. "Always has. Mind you, most people do. He's used to getting his own way..."

"It doesn't sound as if he would have approved of you doing that workshop..."

"God, no..." She grimaced. "That's why I didn't tell him. My mother must have. I shouldn't have told her, but she's always been interested in that kind of thing..."

"What kind is that...?"

She hesitated, running fingers through her unruly mass of hair. "Oh I don't know...you'd probably call it quote, 'the metaphysical', unquote..."

"That's a broad term..."

"She's always seen auras and...stuff. I have, too, ever since I was a little kid. Anyway." She waved a hand. "I got the idea *they* were into that, too...but it turned out I'd got that bit wrong. All they're into is selling their courses and making money. End of story."

"As a matter of interest, if you did decide to discharge yourself, would it be to the parental home?"

"Christ, no. I've got my own place..."

"And do you live alone?"

"I don't, actually..." She sniffed. "I live with a Persian cat called Gandalf..."

Wingfield nodded. Flashbacks hinted at possible PTSD, for which outpatient treatment would probably suffice. She was mildly delusional, which carried a risk of susceptibility to external influences, real or imagined. Much of the time her behaviour was rational, but it was often the case that those initially presenting as normal subsequently became unpredictable and could even suffer psychotic episodes. He must also consider the possibility he might find himself dealing with Sir Giles.

"As I've said, the decision as to whether you stay or go rests with you. So what I propose to do is give you exactly the advice I would give to my own daughter under identical circumstances.

Yes…?"

"Go for it…" She folded her arms.

"It's conceivable, albeit unlikely, that if you left here now you would suffer no further ill effects. But given what you have been subjected to you are, in my clinical judgement in a more vulnerable state than you appreciate. You also told me you would be returning to your own home, where you would be alone…"

"Except for Gandalf…"

"Indeed. I was thinking more in terms of…"

"I know what you were thinking…"

"So, my advice is that you remain with us, on a strictly temporary basis. I'll prescribe medication now to help you relax and sleep. Within twenty-four hours, you'll have a further consultation, either with myself or a senior staff member, so we can keep the situation under review. How does that sound?"

She took a deep breath, peering at him through narrowed eyes. "You really meant that bit about walking out if I want to…?"

"Certainly…"

To Wingfield's satisfaction, she nodded.

"Okay…let's go with that, then…"

"Excellent…"

"For the moment…"

"That's understood…"

Wingfield got to his feet, leaned across the desk and shook her hand. "A thoroughly mature decision if I may say so…"

"Thank you, kind sir." A grin lit her pale features. "Catch you later, then…"

Unfolding her legs she got lightly to her feet and glided to the door, which, as before, she did not trouble to close. Wingfield would not have suggested as much to his daughter but Sir Giles, whatever his shortcomings as a father, was probably a better judge of her condition than she.

Ψ

The medical director shrugged off his jacket and draped it across the back of his chair, careful not to disturb the white carnation Roma had pinned in the buttonhole. He always associated that particular flower with funerals, but trusted it did not constitute his wife's subconscious motivation for so doing. The warmth tempted him to also dispense with his bow tie, but he dismissed the thought; that would be taking informality a trifle too far. Quitting the outsized, smoked glass desk occupying centre-stage in his generously proportioned consulting room, Wingfield had once more stationed himself at the window. The Icelander was ushered in by a pair of male nurses in white jackets who, at a nod from Wingfield, positioned themselves on each side of the door.

"Hello. My name's Peter Wingfield. Would you like to sit down?"

The man planted his hands on his hips. "Last night they put an injection in my bum..."

"Is it painful?"

"You are the medical director, yes...?"

"I am. You like to be called Olaf, I understand..."

"You are in charge...?"

Wingfield surveyed the tall, long-limbed figure with his mass of tight curls, trim moustache and beard, and unusual eye colouring. His jeans were worn but looked clean enough; the sleeves of his checked shirt a shade short for long, sinewed arms.

"That is also correct..."

"How can you let them do that...?"

"According to my information, on arrival you were assessed by three staff members, one of whom is an approved mental health care professional. In his expert opinion, Olaf, you were in a highly agitated state, hence he felt it necessary to administer olanzapine, which is the recognised medication for—"

The young man clapped his hands to his temples. One of the

white coated men edged forward but Wingfield caught his eye and gave an almost imperceptible shake of the head.

"Do you know what this olaz...this stuff does to you...?"

"Certainly. And I appreciate it was done against your wishes, but he felt—"

"You have never taken it, have you, mister medical director? It is like they filled your head full of sawdust – you can't think. And you start dribbling, like a zombie. You know zombies...?" He took a few stiff-legged robotic steps, tongue lolling. "And when people talked to me, I could not understand what they said..."

"I regret the staff thought it necessary to act without your consent, but you must understand everything was done in the interests of safety..."

"That is crazy. Why would I hurt myself...?"

"Not just your own, Olaf. I am told you resisted. Quite forcefully, in fact..."

The Icelander threw his arms wide. "What do you expect me to do? Some man is going to inject me and I don't know what with or why. At the airport I was patient, I answered all the questions. I let them take blood, gave fingerprints, I made no problems, not once. Ask them if you do not believe me. But I did not want drugs put into me, okay? He did not say what it was for – only I must have it. And when I said no, he brought in some big guys..." He glanced over his shoulder, "maybe these, I don't remember..."

"Which made you angry, and it sounds as if you still are..."

"Yes. I told you, it made my head feel like...I don't know..." He spread his hands. "You are in charge. Why do you allow this...?"

"Because when a person is detained under section 136 of the Mental Health Act of 1983, which you were, Olaf, the holding authority is empowered to administer such medication as they deem necessary, with or without the consent of—"

"You can do anything you like and it is legal..." The Icelander waved a dismissive hand. "Anything is okay, yes...?"

"Why don't you sit down, so we can have a proper chat..."

The Icelander shrugged the invitation aside. Sinking his hands into his pockets, he glanced round the room and moved to stand in front of an imposing array of awards, diplomas and certificates occupying one wall.

"These tell me you are an important man, Dr Peter Wingfield..." His visitor observed moving along the rows, nodding to himself. "Oh yes...very important."

The ease with which people could be impressed never ceased to surprise and, if he were honest, gratify Wingfield. It was a source of amusement to him that not a single visitor had yet noticed that, alongside evidence of an enviable range of professional qualifications and academic achievements, he had chosen to display something of a very different nature. Encased in a slim silver frame, inscribed in copperplate and adorned with an ostentatious gold seal, hung a faded certificate attesting to the fact that Peter Lewis Wingfield, aged nine, had without artificial buoyancy aids completed three lengths of Battersea public swimming baths.

"May we begin...?"

The Icelander nodded and lowered himself into a chair, rubbing his face with the heels of his palms. "My head still does not feel right..."

"There are sometimes unfortunate side effects, but—"

"There is no such thing as a side effect," Olaf insisted. "They are all effects..."

"If you wish. But we've found it is effective for patients who show signs of—"

The man's hands dropped to his lap and he frowned at Wingfield. "You will not give it to me again, will you?"

"That particular medication is used once only. After that, if it were necessary, we might give you some tablets..."

"They could make me feel the same way..."

Wingfield glanced at the men by the door. Dismissing them might reduce the tension in the room and lessen the man's agitation; equally it could leave Wingfield uncomfortably exposed.

"I need the answers to a few questions. They should give me a much clearer idea of what's going to be best for you. Now, if that includes medication of any kind, I'll explain it, and—"

"No injections..." The young man held up his hands.

"Olaf, last night you were anxious and distressed..."

"What if you went to another country and the same thing happened to you? They said all you had to do was tell them who you were and why you had come. So you did, you told them everything they asked for, but they did not believe you, and..."

"I would probably find that just as difficult as you have, but let's take it one step at a time. That was the situation last night, wasn't it? Do you feel the same now...?"

"Now...?"

"Now. Sitting here with me in this room..."

"Well..." The young man shrugged. "My head does not feel right..."

"You did mention that. But you can hear me and you understand what I'm saying, is that correct...?"

"Yes, yes..." Olaf gave an impatient flick of the hand. "But I still can not hear...the others."

"What others would they be, Olaf...?"

"If I tell you, maybe you will..." He jerked a thumb over his shoulder, "...you will tell them to give me an injection..."

Wingfield peered at him over the top of his glasses.

"Tell me, would you feel better or worse if I asked the nurses to go...?"

"Go...?"

"Leave us by ourselves."

"Better. You will do that?"

"They were sent because there was a risk you might get angry and become violent." Wingfield paused. "Tell me, do you think that might happen?"

"Violent? No, there is no risk, Dr Wingfield."

At a nod from Wingfield, the nurses exchanged glances and made their exit, closing the door softly behind them.

"Now perhaps you can relax a little..." Wingfield smiled, "and tell me about whoever you would like to be able to hear, but can't..."

"Okay..." Olaf nodded. "My guardians. Who are always with me – always. They take care of me, guide and protect me. When I lose contact with them..." he lowered his voice, "how could they warn me of danger, tell me when the dark powers might strike...?"

"I can see that would be difficult for you..." Wingfield nodded. "So how do they get messages to you...?"

"After that drug, it was like I was behind a thick, heavy curtain. I could not hear them any more..."

"Don't worry – the effects wear off, given a little time..." He smiled. "So, do you actually hear their voices?"

"I talk to them, they talk to me..."

"Yes, but I'm interested how you do that. I mean, are their voices inside your head would you say, or do they come from somewhere...outside you?"

The young man gave no sign of hearing the question. "It will wear off, you are sure...?"

"You have my word..."

"I hope it is soon..." The Icelander slumped back in his chair.

"Does knowing that make you feel better...?"

"Yes...but those men were rough. I do not like people treating me like that..."

"Of course. That's perfectly natural..."

The Icelander's eyes narrowed. Staring hard at Wingfield, he clenched his fists. "If they try again, I will fight them..."

"I completely understand how you felt. Do you feel that way

right now...?"

"No, no, not any more..."

"But you get angry, sometimes..."

"If people treat me badly, if they hurt me..."

"Right..." Wingfield nodded. "And do you have any history of violence. Olaf? What I'm asking is, have you ever intentionally harmed another person...or yourself?"

His words hung in the air, evoking no response from the Icelander. Studying the figure opposite him, tight jawed, motionless, eyes without warmth or expression, Wingfield saw a hunting animal, poised to attack.

"Do you find that question...upsetting?"

"Is that what they told you I did...?"

"No one has told me anything, apart from what happened here, last night. I'm simply asking about your history."

Another silence.

"I never hurt anyone..."

"Okay..."

"Never."

"I hear you," Wingfield told him. "But you still seem upset..."

"They said I did, but it was not true. They were lying..."

"Who said you did...?"

"All of them..."

Wingfield waited.

"The police, the newspapers, the television people...even people who knew me..." His eyes dropped. "Strangers wrote letters accusing me..."

"Accusing you of...?

"They wanted someone to blame. I do not know why. You are a psychiatrist, maybe you know. They would not leave me alone, they kept asking questions, the same questions again and again. I could not believe it – they took what I did say and made it sound like I said something different. Anything they did not know, they guessed, they just...made up. They were so cruel..."

He shook his head. "Then they tried to blame *Brynja*. How could anyone do that to her...?"

"You were blamed for harming someone, but you didn't do it, you were innocent. Is that what you're telling me...?"

Chest heaving, Olaf's gaze flickered round the room before returning to Wingfield's face.

"I saw her yesterday, at Keflavík...she must work there. I did not know, you see. I got there late, I missed the bus, and...she was at one of those ticket desks. Her uniform was the same colour as her eyes. The first time I have seen her in...I don't remember, three, four months, maybe more..." He shook his head. "She saw me, too, but there was no time. I was late because of the buses. No time to talk, I wanted to...it made me sad...so sad..."

"It sounds...distressing."

"It was not my fault. I wanted to, but they said I must run or they would close the gate, and I...the flight would leave..."

His voice faded; he stared blankly at Wingfield.

"But now you know where she works, Olaf..." Wingfield reminded him, gently. "You could probably find her again if you wanted, couldn't you...?"

"Maybe..."

"Okay..." Wingfield paused. "I'd just like to go back to that time you felt you were wrongly accused. Tell me more about that..."

The Icelander folded his arms. "It was a long time ago..."

"But it obviously still troubles you. I wondered if those old memories could have been stirred up by the meeting at the airport..."

"It is possible."

"Just...possible?"

Olaf stared past Wingfield, shaking his head. "They did not tell me about this – they did not warn me..."

"Your guides, you mean...?"

"You say it will wear off, but how can you be sure...? If I can never talk to them again, you know what will happen? The dark powers will triumph – they will make sure I can not complete my work..."

"Olaf, trust me. It will wear off..."

The Icelander was on his feet, making a slow circuit of the room, arms outstretched, palms turned upwards. Staring at the ceiling, he muttered the same words over and over again, too low for Wingfield to make them out. Returning to the desk he let his arms sink to his sides, and shook his head.

"It is the same. I am trapped, a prisoner..."

"Olaf, I really have no interest in keeping you here a moment longer than necessary..."

"I will never see her again..."

"The lady you saw...?"

"Brynja..."

"And she's...important to you?"

Olaf shook his head. "She was the mother of my son..."

"You have a son...?"

The man stared at Wingfield, his mouth twisting into a grotesque, clown's grin. "Do you still go swimming...Peter Lewis Wingfield?"

"You didn't tell me..." Wingfield reminded him, softly. "You have a son...?"

The grin faded. "No, Doctor, I do not *have* a son..." his voice was barely more than a whisper. "I *had* one..."

Chapter 4

New Patients

Wednesday 8th June 2011

The early morning traffic was lighter than she had anticipated; they were making good time beneath a cloudless sky promising more good weather. None of which prevented Dr Patricia Carragh feeling ill at ease, painfully aware of the distance between her son and herself. Not physical distance, for it would take only a moment to move the hand she was resting lightly on the gear lever to touch his; her concern lay with distance of a different nature. Colm was negotiating that mysterious and sometimes treacherous territory separating adolescence from young adulthood; territory into which he seemed reluctant to invite his mother.

Tall and spare of frame, he was plugged into a white iPod and held a mobile phone across which his long fingers skipped quick and light as a dancer's feet. Playing a game, Patricia wondered, or sending another in a seemingly endless stream of text messages? Whichever it might be, it was part of a private world.

"Colm...?"

His fingers danced on.

"Pet...?"

Her touch on his arm brought a hurried glance from eyes like a startled deer's. As dictated by current fashion, his fair hair was shaved almost to the skull; his face, like his body, was lean and fine-boned. He tugged at the earphones and frowned.

"Yeah...?"

She smiled. "Er...nothing."

"What...?"

Should she risk the truth? Sorry I made you jump. It's just that I need to make contact, somehow. For the last few months it's felt as if you and I inhabit different worlds. Sure, you visit mine now and then, when you need something: a lift, maybe, or help with exam revision, or clean clothes. Or to hoover up the prodigious quantity of calories required to keep that restless fast-growing body functioning. You're my son and I love you very much, but I can tell all is not well on that remote planet where you spend most of your time. My heart hurts because I'm not sure exactly what's wrong, so I can't be sure what I can do to help, and not knowing makes me feel sad, helpless and guilty.

"Just wondered how you're doing, that's all..."

She tried to make her words light and casual and hoped she had succeeded. His blue eyes were deep-set and brooding, disconcertingly like his father's.

"Fine..."

"Really?"

"Yeah." His brow furrowed.

"Well, we haven't talked much about..." She waved a hand, vaguely, "how you are with this stuff. You know...seeing Tony."

"It's all right." He shrugged, eyes drawn back to the mobile.

She bit her lip; her opening gambit should have been something he might actually want to converse about. Like basketball or revision or what he'd like to do in the summer holidays; anything, in fact, but therapy. She had promised herself she would not intrude; she would give him space, and trust he would raise the subject in his own good time. He had not done so, her resolve had failed, and now it was too late to backtrack.

"Just wondered...do you think it might help?"

"I've only been once..."

"Yes, I know, darling."

Perhaps she was going too slowly; a lorry loomed uncomfortably large in the rear view mirror. She accelerated and the Volvo reluctantly picked up speed.

"I mean sometimes it's easier, isn't it?" she went on. "Talking to someone who's not, you know, family?"

"Yeah." He glanced up. "Tony's like, a shrink, same as you, right...?"

From the moment she first broached the subject, she had taken great pains to explain the process as clearly as possible, presenting it as ordinary, unexceptional. Since he had shown little curiosity and asked practically no questions, she assumed he understood. Perhaps she had been mistaken.

"No, pet. I told you, don't you remember? I only see people who've got something really wrong with them. When they're what we call mentally ill."

"I'm not, then?"

Fine golden fuzz shone above his top lip, running along the line of his jaw. Liam had made a song and dance about giving him a fancy electric razor last Christmas, which was probably premature. Her hand strayed back to his arm. To reassure him, she wondered, or herself?

"Absolutely you're not. That's what I'm saying. Tony's a psychotherapist, which is completely different. All kinds of people go to them because...well, they're just finding life a bit difficult, that's all..."

"Oh. Okay."

"You're no more mad than the rest of us, pet."

He looked at her blankly. "Right..."

He set about plugging in the earphones, signalling an end to the exchange, but Patricia persisted.

"I know it hasn't been easy, what with Dad leaving and every-thing. I thought you might like to talk it all over with someone..."

"I'm okay with it, Mum..."

With Liam leaving or seeing Tony she would have liked to ask, but the earphones were back in place. Tony would not have disclosed what passed between Colm and himself even if she had asked – not that she would dream of doing so; sixteen-year-olds had as much right to client confidentiality as anyone else. But did Colm really talk to him, did he pour out all the things he could or would not share with her? Not just how he felt about the separation, although, God knows, that had been traumatic enough for the poor kid. Had he touched on the darkness that sometimes engulfed him; the night terrors that could bring him to her bed in the small hours, incoherent and ashen faced? Did Tony know about the drinking, for on a couple of occasions she was pretty sure she had smelled alcohol on Colm's breath? If so, did the therapist see it as harmless experimentation, a rite of passage for kids of that age? As she might have done, had she not witnessed the painful years before her own father finally succumbed to cirrhosis of the liver.

She glanced at him, wondering why it sometimes seemed so difficult to provide the love and support he needed to cope with his angst. Maybe it was because her own teenage years had been such a contrast with those of her son and daughter. At sixteen, Patricia O'Leary was a good Catholic girl, living an all-too-quiet existence in a Mayo backwater. Each school day she was up early to don her dull grey uniform and catch the wheezing rattletrap of a bus for the long haul to Westport, where she attended St Mary's Ladies College. With her sights already firmly set on a career in medicine, the eldest of the three O'Leary sisters had little time for anything other than her studies. After school she returned directly to do her homework, then help Mum out with Sinead and Muirin. Her mother was a worrier, a timid nervous woman, whose health was never the best, even though at that time Dad could still hold down a regular job. While Patricia's life would have seemed excruciatingly dull and boring to Colm or Caitlin, it had been, to the best of her recollection, happy enough.

Among Patricia's most vivid memories were the alternate Saturdays when she journeyed by bus and then on foot to Grandma Frances' tiny hillside cottage, practically within sight of

St Patrick's very own mountain. She never failed to cross herself assiduously before ducking through the low door. However much she might look forward to those visits, to step inside was to leave the world with which she was familiar and enter one which, however beguiling and bewitching it might be, felt illicit and perhaps even sinful. It was certainly a world of which Father Coyle would have fervently disapproved. Not that there was anything remotely dark about Frances herself. Bright-eyed and bird-like, quick of word and movement, the old lady always had biscuits or freshly baked soda bread awaiting her favourite granddaughter. It was the tales with which she was regaled that sent a frisson of fear and excitement down Patricia's young spine; tales of leprechauns and fairies, mountain spirits and even visitations from the departed, God rest their souls. And this from a woman who, although no one in the family ever spoke of it, had herself once entered a convent.

Patricia took a deep breath. Whatever dark currents might run in my family, she prayed silently, please do not let them surface in my son.

She drew to a halt outside a row of identical modern bungalows, each with picture windows and a stiflingly neat garden. Pocketing mobile and iPod, Colm clambered awkwardly from the car. On the sports field he was capable of moving with effortless grace and elegance: away from it, he could be as clumsy and ungainly as a newborn giraffe. She held out an envelope. "For Tony. Don't forget, okay?"

"Yeah."

"You've got money for the bus back?"

With a brief nod, he closed the door, changed his mind and tugged it open again. Planting a knee on the passenger's seat he craned over to kiss her.

"Bye, Mum. Catch you later..."

She watched him push through the gate and lope up the path to the front door, earphones dangling from jeans threatening to slip from his slim hips at any moment. He could be distant, unavailable and monosyllabic, then lift her heart with one small, spontaneous gesture; just as his father had – at the beginning, anyway. With Liam, of course, the periods of withdrawal and disconnection had grown increasingly protracted and the heart-lifting moments increasingly rare. In her naïveté she had assumed this must be her fault, her responsibility. Even when she discovered the painful truth, guilt haunted her like a stubborn ghost.

Easing back into the traffic she became aware of what sounded ominously like a new rattle beneath the Volvo's bonnet and grimaced; noises of that nature had a habit of proving costly. During the separation, when he was maddeningly tight-fisted over money, she could never understand why Liam had been so willing to cede ownership of this tank of a car. Subsequent visits to the local garage provided the explanation.

Twenty minutes later, negotiating the sleeping policemen guarding the car park with such extreme caution her passage would barely have disturbed their slumbers, she pulled into a vacant space alongside the medical director's gleaming new Mercedes convertible. Among her colleagues there were those who found the spectacle of a man Peter Wingfield's age behind the wheel of a sports car faintly ridiculous. "Talk about taking your virility substitutes on four wheels," said the mocking voices. "Christ, he's a shrink – can't he *see* it?" The medical director's choice of transport, however, did not feature in Patricia's thoughts when, later that day, she made her way to his office.

Ψ

Peter Wingfield toyed with a letter opener in the shape of a miniature sabre, his attention divided between Patricia and a tennis match on the wide-screen, wall-mounted television. He had lowered the sound as a gesture to his visitor but their conversation was punctuated by the muted thud of felt on gut and periodic eruptions of applause or groans.

"This morning I assessed a young lady who had recently been delivered from the clutches of our local purveyors of spiritual truth and light…" His eyes flickered to Patricia's face. "You know who I mean…"

"I can guess."

"She's suffering the after-effects of their rather unpleasant brand of tender loving care…"

"I've heard about that…"

But his attention was now with the tennis.

"…To whit, sleep deprivation, isolation, forced confession of sins…et cetera."

"That lot are unbelievable…" she murmured.

"And persist with state of the ark techniques. You or I could make a fortune bringing them up to speed. Not that they'd ever give us the chance, of course…"

He shot her a sideways glance to make sure she appreciated the humour and seemed satisfied by a wan smile.

"She was distressed, but angry, too, and I always think that's a good, healthy response. The ones who worry me more are those who go into withdrawal, or just collapse. She'd certainly had quite a hard time – the way she described the confession routine, the Spanish Inquisition would have been more fun…"

"You handle those cases yourself, don't you…?"

The miniature sword flashed in the air like a conductor's baton.

"So far, yes. After confession," he continued, "they hit her with guilt. She was bad wicked and evil and her only hope of salvation lay in enrolment in their on-going programme. Several thousand pounds' worth, payment in advance…"

"They've been doing the same things for ages.".

"Indeed they have…"

"They are such bastards…"

She was hoping he would get to the point. He had surely not summoned her to interrupt his enjoyment of the tennis and be instructed about the modus operandi of the *Order of Cosmic Consciousness*. She shifted restlessly in her chair. Wide set green eyes and open features, framed by simply cut, shoulder length auburn hair gave her a deceptively youthful appearance.

"*Le mot juste*. Didn't someone once remark of George Bush the younger that he acted in a manner calculated to bring discredit on bastards as a class...?" Wingfield frowned. "Or perhaps it was Nixon...?"

"What I don't understand is how they go on getting away with it. I mean, after all this time, you'd think there would be some kind of investigation..."

"Not going to happen, Pat." He shook his head. "Bastards they may be, but they're rich, devious and powerful ones. With friends in extremely high places..."

Patricia's jaw tightened. From childhood she had stoutly resisted all attempts to abbreviate her name. At a tender age she had sensed that, in some way she could not have explained, the diminutive belittled her. So determined was she that her mother learned to introduce her as 'my daughter Patricia. *Not* Pat, if you please.' Soon after starting work at Maidenbloom she had made her preference clear to the medical director, but if he heard he chose to ignore her. She suspected he was reminding her of the balance of power in their professional relationship; Peter Wingfield was known to have a taste for keeping people in his comfort zone rather than their own.

"What state is she in...?"

Prolonged applause signalled a break in play. Wingfield met her gaze and drew down the corners of his mouth. "I'd describe it as...shaky. Her father's an extremely determined character and when he got wind of what was going on he pulled her out. God knows how – I'd have thought it would take Mossad or a squad of Ghurkas at least. Anyway, he brought her to us last night. She's agitated and anxious and there are signs of paranoia – at one stage she insisted I look and make sure they weren't waiting for her outside. Hasn't been sleeping and she's having flashbacks. Sir Giles reported mood swings and aggression. Took a swing at her mother, apparently. Not," he added, dryly, "that the picture she paints of the family environment suggests everything there is sweetness and light..."

With a sinking feeling, Patricia realised she was being told more than she needed to know about a patient who, after all, was not her responsibility.

"Presumably her father knew your record...?"

"I expect so." He shrugged. "Not that there's anything special about that kind of case. It's generally just a matter of medicating and keeping them under observation for a few days..."

"Right..."

"And therapy – that usually helps, of course. It probably will with her..." He took off his glasses and set about cleaning them with a tissue. "But I'm happy to rely on your judgement..."

"Why mine? She's not my—"

"I've decided to place her in your very capable hands..."

He put his glasses on again and slid a file across the dark, glass desktop. She estimated his smile at three parts self-satisfaction and a dash of sympathy. He nodded at the screen. "Ever been to Wimbledon...?"

Patricia folded her arms. "Peter, it's out of the question. I've got more on my plate than I can handle now. You know that..."

Events on the manicured grass of SW19 appeared more compelling than his colleague's protestations until, abruptly, he swung his chair to face her and planted his elbows on the desk. "I do realise you're pretty hard pressed."

"I used to have a team of five. Do you know how many I have now?"

"Well, of course I..."

"One support worker." She held up a finger. "One..."

"Which, I agree is not ideal..."

"In the same period, my case load has gone up from twenty-one to thirty. Thirty, Peter, and all I've got is a ward manager, an OT assistant and a part-time psychologist..."

"And I'm also aware it hasn't been easy for you the last few months, one way and another..."

"Forget the domestic stuff – that's my problem and I'm handling it. This is about my work..."

"I understand..."

"If the regulations didn't stipulate I had to have one, I'd probably have lost my social worker, too."

"But they do, and you haven't..."

"You know what I'm saying..."

"Yes, I do..."

"And the whisper on the wards, you might call it, is the last round of cuts are not going to be the last..."

"A possibility I'd love to rule out, but I can't, I'm afraid. Our lords and masters did not like last year's profit and loss account, and they're sniffing round for more economies. By the way," he went on, "what news of your mother?"

"You know what chemo does to you..."

He took a deep breath. "I do indeed..."

"I'm slipping over this weekend, actually. Taking Colm along for a break from revision..."

"Should do you both good..."

"I'm counting on it..."

Unwilling to let him steer her further from the subject, she nodded at the file. "Peter, seriously, there's a limit and I'm at it...no," she corrected herself, "I'm beyond it. And this isn't just me moaning about being overworked. We've got a duty of care to our patients, you know, and I'm getting to the stage where I'm not sure..."

Wingfield was nodding like a toy dog in the window of an old saloon. "A lot of people in this place are feeling exactly the same way, I'm sure you appreciate that..."

"Of course I do, and like them I'm coping – but only just. What I cannot do is take on any more responsibilities."

Finally abandoning all interest in the All England Lawn Tennis Club, the medical director reached for the remote control, aimed it at the television and the screen went blank.

"What you need is a break. Not just a weekend..." He waved a hand. "A proper break. Recharge the batteries..."

"Which will be just grand – if and when I get a chance. For the time being, I'm actually better keeping busy. Less time to think about things, you know what I mean...?"

"So, I'm helping, aren't I?" He gave her a wry smile. "Keeping you busy."

"They're looking to make more cuts – you just said so. And if they're looking, they'll find. Do you realise what you're asking me to do is take on another patient when the chances are my team's going to get even—"

"I do know how you feel..."

"If that's true, how can you ask me to take on this...Chloe?"

Over the past few months, she had grown accustomed to reaching home, exhausted, to resume the role of single parent to the troubled Colm. Her relationship with Caitlin had suffered too, their communications becoming ever more brief, frosty and mutually uncomfortable; painful reminders that, in her daughter's eyes, responsibility for the marriage breakdown rested firmly on Patricia's shoulders.

"I don't enjoy this, I don't like pushing people to the limit. But I'm between a rock and a hard place, Pat. I'm getting non-stop pressure from the board in L.A. wanting cuts. And when I tell them exactly what you've told me; we have a duty of care towards our patients, they don't actually come out and say so directly, but they make noises that mean, well if you won't do what we want, we'll find someone who will..." He paused. "Which may not be the same kind of pressure you're feeling, but it's pressure, believe me…"

"Yes, I'm sure it is…"

"And I look round at a lot of hard working, conscientious, dedicated people – like you – knowing that wherever we make cuts some of them are going to suffer. Believe me, it's not always easy to sleep at night…"

"I can imagine…"

"Of course I could give the girl to someone else, but because of well…let's call it the sensitive nature of her case, I need a very, very safe pair of hands. You understand what I'm saying here…"

"Is it really that sensitive…?"

"It is really that sensitive. What we're dealing with is an organisation which, if it was an individual, would probably be diagnosed delusional and definitely paranoid, and locked up in the top-security wing. They're terrified, literally terrified of even a whiff of bad publicity. So they see this young woman…" He leaned forward to tap the file, "as a threat. Now, she's free, white and twenty-one, and whatever she chooses to say or do about them is up to her…once we've discharged her. But if she does anything they don't like while she's still our patient, as far as *they're* concerned it's guilt by association, and they will do anything to discredit us…"

"You really think so…?"

"Which absolutely must not happen…"

"Okay…"

She picked up the file, glanced blankly at the patient's name and shook her head. Determined to defend her position, she had capitulated in the face of his first appeal to her better nature.

He spread his hands and spoke softly. "You may not realise it, but you make a rod for your own back by being very, very good at what you do…"

"That sounds like a compliment I could do without…" She began getting to her feet, but he waved her down.

"There's just one other…"

"One other what...?"

"Patient..."

She stared at him, slack-jawed. "You're not serious..."

"Wait a moment..." He held both palms towards her. "There's a very specific reason why you should handle him. You, and no one else."

"Peter, I..."

"I know what you're going to say, and I understand why. But before you say anything, I'd really like you to hear me out. Would you do that, please...?"

She wanted to speak, but no words came. The anger surged up from somewhere just beneath the waistband of her plain grey skirt, leaving her throat hot and dry. Peter Wingfield opened a second file.

"This one's a twenty-seven-year-old from Iceland. His name's completely unpronounceable, but don't worry because you won't need to – he wants to be called Olaf..." He slipped off his glasses and looked up, narrowing his eyes. "Another one who rejects his given name...interesting. Anyway," he continued, "ground staff at Gatwick decided he was acting strangely, so they picked him up and questioned him and he was eventually shipped over here. There was some counter terrorism involvement, apparently, but they seemed to lose interest..."

"Lose interest? You mean they cleared him..."

"My guess is they may be keeping an eye on him, from a distance. Anyway, we're getting to the nitty-gritty now."

"That's good..." she said, dryly.

"Now, during the assessment he mentioned, *en passant*, he came here on the direct instructions of spirit guides. Which was not an isolated incident, in fact, far from it. Ever since childhood he's been in communication with them and they seem to play a central role in his life. For reasons which he never made entirely clear, the aforesaid spirits despatched him to spend midsummer night on top of some mountain in deepest Cumbria..." He paused. "Or possibly inside it. He claims that among other powers he is able to enter mountains at will..."

"You said something about the nitty-gritty..."

"Nearly there," Wingfield smiled. "He makes these spirits of his sound a pretty benevolent bunch, but you never know with disembodied beings, do you? Tricky, unpredictable lot if you ask me. One minute they're preaching universal love and under-standing, the next they're telling you to go and butcher complete strangers with a machete. Now..." he added, closing the file, "do you see why I immediately thought of you for Olaf. Or," he corrected himself, "Olaf for you...?"

"Frankly, no..."

"I distinctly remember you telling me you belong to a special interest group at the college. Yes?"

"Yes, but..."

"And that you're supposed to be putting a paper together for a presentation to them, but you haven't got started – or you hadn't when you told me about it. That is so, isn't it?"

"Yes, but..." She ran a hand wearily through her hair, "what's that got to—"

"And I'm sure you said what you really wanted to do was present something on hallucinations, delusions, hearing voices..."

She gathered herself to resume her protests, but he held up a hand.

"All of which are common in psychosis, understood to represent unprocessed primal urges, blah, blah, blah. But I gathered you're more interested in a rather different angle. You want to come at them from some kind of..." He made an airy gesture, "call it a spiritual perspective. Communing with angels or demons or...God knows who else."

Patricia could only nod. She vaguely recollected mentioning it when they were chatting after a staff meeting a few weeks earlier. What surprised her was that he remembered it in such detail; at the time his attitude had seemed mocking, dismissive.

"Well, yes, I was…something along those lines…"

"Was? As in, no longer…?'

"Still am, then." She shrugged.

"This man hears voices and always has. He actually came here because they told him to. In that particular case it was in what he called a dream, but maybe it was some kind of vision. Anyway, he hears them when he meditates, in self-induced trance states – you name it…" Wingfield smiled. "You have to admit, he's tailor-made for your research, isn't he…?" Subtlety might not be Wingfield's strong suit but he knew what he wanted and how to get it. A surfeit of calls on her time meant the paper had been relegated to the back burner, where it remained in spite of the presentation date getting uncomfortably close. Assuming the medical director had not overplayed his hand, the case material Olaf could supply might indeed be the answer to a maiden's prayer.

"Possible…"

"Better than possible. Probable, I'd say. And as far as Chloe's concerned, I don't see anything very different from the others. Why don't I get their files to you so you can have a look. Procedures are pretty routine…"

"I'd appreciate that…"

"Oh, there's one other thing you should be aware of…"

Patricia gave him a wary glance. "Which is…?"

"He didn't want to talk much about it, and I didn't pressure him, but there is something else that could have quite a bearing on how he responds to stress…" Wingfield peered at her. "About a year ago, his son – his only child, I gathered – disappeared. Just…vanished."

"My God. How old…?"

"Young – only four or five. All very mysterious, and it sounded as if for a time people – the media, anyway – pointed the finger at him. Which he found deeply distressing…"

"I can imagine…"

"And also at the mother, from whom he's since split…"

Patricia shook her head. "The child…disappeared?"

"We didn't go into the details. But no body was ever found, apparently…"

"How do you begin to come to terms with that…?"

"You might like to find that out."

"Assuming he has, of course. Anything else?"

"Nothing you won't find in his notes."

"Okay…" She gave him a weary smile. "You know, sometimes you remind me of a T-shirt of Colm's…"

"It must be particularly elegant and stylish, then…"

He placed the Icelander's file on top of the young woman's.

"Dream on, Peter. We're talking teenagers…"

He raised an eyebrow. "Enlighten me…"

"It's got a crocodile across the front. A big, smiling, green crocodile…"

"An Irish one, then…?"

She shook her head. "Underneath which it says: *Trust Me, I'm a Doctor.*"

The medical director raised an eyebrow.

"You don't trust me?"

"These two and that is *it*." She got to her feet. "Absolutely no more, not at the moment. Can I trust you?"

"Why wouldn't you…?"

"I'm serious."

"I know. And I appreciate your understanding." As she turned for the door, he added, "I really do hope that fellow turns out to be useful."

"Not as much as I do…"

"I'd be interested to see a copy of that paper when you've finished it…"

"I'll email it to you…"

Closing the door of her consulting room, she deposited the

files on her desk and stared down at them. Part of her wanted to take the damned things and ram them into her shredder. Better still, march back and slap them across Peter Wingfield's smug, self-satisfied face. Arguing with him was like playing chess against a grand master; checkmate was only a matter of time. She slumped into her chair, trying to decide whether she felt more angry with him or herself. Not for the first time, when she needed to put in strong, clear boundaries with him, she found herself looking on helplessly while he trampled them. In one breath she pointed out her workload was grossly excessive, in the next tamely agreed to let him add to it. It was like a drowning swimmer screaming for a lifebuoy and accepting a lead weight instead.

The pattern was as familiar as it was unwelcome; giving the needs of others higher priority than her own. Even in primary school, little Patricia O'Leary would not be found in the rush for the door when class was dismissed; she departed only when all the chairs were stacked, the last book tidied away. Not seeking gold stars but because she took it for granted it was her job, her task, her role in life; if there was work to be done, she was there to do it. A pattern she had repeated so often with family, husband, children, and now Peter Wingfield. Yet when she felt vulnerable, when she was floundering and in need of help or support, stating her needs seemed impossibly hard. And on those rare occasions when she did so it was in such tentative, apologetic terms her voice often went unheard.

It was among the lessons learned at her mother's knee; her gentle, kind-hearted, thoughtful and long-suffering martyr of a mother. When she first detected the telltale lumps, Fiona O'Leary told no one, for who was she to trouble them? She took the long bus-ride into Galway alone, tramping through fine rain to the University Hospital where kind, sympathetic folk in white coats inspected her, asked questions, took blood samples, ran tests, and instructed her to return a week later. Which she did, on her own once again, pale and drawn, guarding her fears as closely as if they had been shameful, guilty secrets. So when she received the news she had prayed so long and hard she would not receive there was no one to hug her, comfort her, or assure her they loved her and would help her face the purgatory of the treatment. When she finally broke the news to Patricia, in a tentative phone call, it was in an apologetic tone, for most of all her mother dreaded being a burden to others.

Peter Wingfield bustled in, clutching a handful of files.

"Cult victims, as promised…"

"That was quick…"

He peered at her. "Are you all right, Pat?"

"Yes, fine…" Forcing a smile, she took the files. "Thanks for those, I'm sure they'll be useful."

"Excellent." He smiled. "And let me know what you make of our space cadet."

She looked at him blankly, then nodded. "Oh, him. Yes, okay."

"And I know it's not the way we'd normally handle things, but with these two, I'd appreciate being kept in the loop, please." He eased his hands into his pockets. "Seeing that they're special cases."

"Olaf as well…?"

"They're being rather cagey about why, but the Home Office are taking an interest in him…"

"Might that be to do with the terrorist angle…?"

"Possible. They were very keen to know what I made of him…"

"What did you say?"

"Blinded them with science." He smiled. "I told them he was subject to persistent and recurring delusions and heard voices which he called his guides. I gave an initial diagnosis of manic state with psychotic symptoms and possible schizoaffective disorder."

"Were they happy with that?"

"I don't know how much it meant to the chap I was talking to. He seemed more interested in whether I thought all that was consistent with Olaf being a terrorist..."

"If there was evidence of anything like that he wouldn't be here, would he?"

"I very much doubt it. I said I couldn't rule it out, but if I was recruiting someone for that sort of thing, someone as unstable as he seems would not be my choice."

"Me neither..."

"With Chloe, as you appreciate, I want to avoid alarm bells ringing in Los Angeles. I have absolute confidence in you, Pat, it's not about that – it's just that I'd like to be kept in the picture."

"No problem." She nodded, wearily.

"Good. Let's have another word when you've seen them." Glancing at his watch, he gave her a tight-lipped smile.

"I think that's it then. We shall meet again soon, no doubt..."

She waited until the door closed and took a deep breath; she badly needed a silver lining to this particular cloud. On impulse she opened the Icelander's file, checked which ward he was on, and rang the duty nurse.

"Mariette, it's Patricia Carragh. You've got a Mr Haraldsson with you, is that right?"

"We have..."

"I'd like to talk to him. Could you get someone to bring him along to my room, please?"

She heard a sharp intake of breath at the other end of the line. Mariette was one of several staff members recently arrived from Martinique. Leaving no stone unturned in their hunt for the least expensive labour, USCARE took advantage of the fact that, for employment purposes, that remote Caribbean island was a region of France and hence the EU.

"I'm really sorry, Dr Carragh, but I'm not sure I can do that..."

"Oh. Why would that be, I wonder...?"

"Well, Mr Haraldsson got quite angry after he went to see Dr

Wingfield this morning, you see. After he got back he stuck this notice on his door. It says he's not talking, not to anyone..."

"Is that so?"

"There's some more things it says, too. Do you want to know what they are...?"

"Yes, please..."

"Will you hang on a little minute, now..."

The phone clattered down. Patricia waited, wondering what Peter Wingfield had said or done to trigger that reaction.

"I wrote it down for you," Mariette told her. "It says, '*If you will not listen, I will not speak. Leave me in peace*'."

"Well, that's pretty clear," agreed Patricia. "Listen, don't worry about sending him along. I don't have a lot of time right now, but I'll come down first thing tomorrow morning."

Chapter 5

The Silent One

Thursday 9th June 2011

Clipboard hugged to her chest, Dr Patricia Carragh cut a neat, businesslike figure in plain white blouse and loose, knee length, grey jersey skirt. At some point during adolescence she had become convinced her thighs were too broad, her wardrobe thereafter being selected with an eye to disguising this unsatis-factory feature. When an unfortunate boyfriend was bold enough to comment favourably on her legs, she rounded on him angrily; how could his words be anything other than empty flattery, when they conflicted so sharply with her self-image? He was sent packing with no idea why genuine admiration earned such an unexpected and unwelcome reaction, nor the oppor-tunity to make the same mistake a second time. Without ever thinking about it too deeply, Patricia had always assumed she was quite plain, in spite of attracting sufficient male attention to persuade any woman with more vanity than she that the truth might be otherwise.

Making her way briskly along wide, brightly lit corridors, past a succession of glass-panelled doors and tasteful impres-sionist prints, she reflected that, whatever moral reservations she might still entertain regarding private health care, in terms of working environment it had much to be said for it. Her training seemed to have been conducted principally in cramped, overcrowded, antiquated buildings, where too few staff waged a brave campaign to meet the needs of too many patients. Many of whom were not only unwell but anxious and confused.

Entering some of those grim old hospitals had been enough to make her queasy, for which neither her own nervousness nor the faint odour of industrial cleaners and disinfectants could be held entirely responsible. As a medical student she was dimly aware she might be the victim of subtle, less tangible influences, among them an acute sensitivity to her environment. She even pondered whether the patients' psychological state, their apprehension and unease, might in some mysterious way influence her own physiology.

Such things were rarely discussed, but from time to time patients – and occasionally colleagues – spoke of sensing an atmosphere in this or that hospital, or even individual ward. When it was described in negative terms, Patricia had heard the word 'energy', sometimes branded 'heavy' or even 'dark'. The terms held no meaning for Patricia's scientific mind and she initially granted such notions no more credence than she might have accorded flying saucers, voodoo or those surprisingly common tales of hospital mortuaries frequented by ghosts. As time went by, however, she found herself allowing the possibility that they might perhaps indicate the existence of invisible forces capable of impacting on mind and body alike.

In recent years she had to some extent overcome it, but Patricia was aware that her reluctance to explore such essentially metaphysical territory might lie in its association with her grandmother. Frances, God bless and preserve her, claimed to have access to realms inhabited by shades, beings and spirits; realms against which Father Coyle regularly warned his flock, branding them satanic. The priest's views on that particular topic, however, could be extreme; only last Christmas Eve, had he not solemnly reminded a group of excited children that Santa was an anagram of Satan? In any case, to Patricia's mind her grandmother suffered scant damage to her immortal soul from her beliefs; on the contrary, she gave every sign of relishing and enjoying life. As the years went by her back had become a little bent, but she continued to display a zest and vitality belying her age and was rarely without a smile. Her isolated cottage, with its smoke-stained walls and aroma of peat, might be no palace but it was, she cheerfully maintained, plenty big enough for herself and her beloved books. For all the strange and disturbing tales of encounters with leprechauns, elves or the giants whom she insisted made their homes in nearby hills, she radiated a child-like delight in life. Observing those assembled at Mass, Patricia sometimes wondered, privately, whether the same could be said of many of Father Coyle's most devout parishioners.

Ψ

Patricia found Mariette, a small, neat figure in the Maidenbloom livery of pale aquamarine, on the phone at the nurse's station. A frown furrowed her brow as she peered at the computer, a forefinger hovering over the screen.

"No, I am really so sorry, madam. I can tell you a patient of that name has been admitted, but I am not allowed to give you any information about them." She gave Patricia a wry smile. "Yes, yes, of course I understand...you are family, madam...Yes, I do believe you, really, I'm sure you are who you say...But, you see, you are not here, so it is not possible for me to know this for certain...No, and the rules do not allow us to—"

Rolling her eyes, she pointed at a door with a piece of paper stuck to the glass panel using surgical tape. Patricia gave her a sympathetic touch on the shoulder and moved on.

The message had been scrawled in capital letters with a thick, red felt-tip. Patricia carefully removed it, knocked twice and waited. Hearing nothing, she knocked more firmly with the same result. Opening the door she slipped inside to find the blinds open, the room bright with sunlight. The lean figure stretched out on a pale blue cotton blanket appeared to occupy its entire length. The man's pose reminded Patricia of a carved figure she recalled seeing atop a crusader burial vault in a gloomy cathedral side-chapel in southern France. Sculpted in gleaming marble, resplendent in crested helmet and full suit of armour he lay, eyes closed, arms crossed on his chest, gauntleted hands gripping a broadsword with a jewel-encrusted hilt. The man on the bed possessed a similar warrior-like quality; she noted the high cheekbones, prominent nose, a determined jut to the jaw and military precision of moustache and beard.

"Hello there, Mr Haraldsson. I'm Patricia Carragh..."

Something told her he would not respond, and so it proved.

"I'm sorry to disturb you. I did knock a couple of times but perhaps you didn't hear me..."

The figure on the bed remained motionless. Patricia caught her breath; could he have self-harmed, somehow laid hands on pills or a syringe...? On the point of reaching to check his pulse, she detected movement of the chest; slight, but regular. His shirt collar was frayed and it looked as if an amateurish attempt had been made to dye his jeans, leaving them the mottled blue and green of an old bruise. Her maternal eye registered a hole in the toe of one thick blue woollen sock and scuffed walking boots placed neatly under his bed beside a bulging backpack.

Placing his sign on the bedside table, she cleared her throat.

"And in case you were wondering, I did read what you wrote. It sounds as though you feel people aren't listening to you, so that's what I've come to do..." She paused. "You can talk, I'll listen..."

Perhaps taking time out to come and see him had not been such a good idea; her schedule for the day was already full.

"I'm a colleague of Dr Wingfield's. He tells me you and he have had a chat..."

Good idea or not, she was here and not inclined to give up on him just yet.

"He told me a little about you, but I decided I'd really like to talk to you myself and hear what you have to say..."

A pair of pine-framed chairs with burgundy leatherette seats and backs flanked the bed. Patricia sat down, crossed her legs and smoothed her skirt over her knees. It was not unusual for a patient to be reluctant to communicate, although, according to Peter Wingfield, this one was more than happy to talk given the right encouragement; her first task was persuading him to re-engage. Taking his file from her clipboard she placed it on her lap and leafed through it.

"According to your notes…" she went on in conversational tones, "you were taken into custody at Gatwick on Tuesday evening. Would that be right?" She paused to glance at him. "And if you're wondering why I mention that, perhaps I'd better explain. The airport security people detained you under section 136 of the Mental Health Act, 1983, you see. Technically that gives them powers to take you from a public place to a desig-nated place of safety – like this – if in their opinion you might be mentally ill or in need of care or control, to protect you or others from harm…"

She paused again, keeping him in her line of sight so she would be aware of any movement he might make.

"Now…the next thing I think I should tell you is that, under this particular section of the Act, you can be held for seventy-two hours. That's three days, isn't it? Let's see, today's Thursday, so that means we've got until tomorrow evening to make up our minds about you. No rush, then…"

She turned the page and her ring caught the sunlight and sparkled. A silver band with an old-fashioned clutch of three small, square-cut emeralds set in the form of a shamrock, Liam used to call it her engagement ring, although he had never bought her such a thing. When Frances learned her eldest grand-daughter was to wed, the ring had been her gift, for it was, she explained, an heirloom handed down from her own grand-mother. Patricia's gold wedding ring had been consigned to a velvet-lined box at the back of a dressing table drawer, but her attachment to this one was greater. When Caitlin married,

Patricia had decided, it would be passed on to her.

"So there's no mad rush, but I imagine you wouldn't want to be staying here longer than absolutely necessary, would you now?"

She skimmed through the next couple of pages.

"If we haven't sorted things out by Friday, we might have to hold you under a different section of the Act. That would be section 2…"

She sighed and shook her head. "Hopefully not, because if it came to that it would be an altogether different matter. I mean your situation would become more…serious. You might be kept here – or somewhere like this – for anything up to twenty-eight days. Now, that's quite a stretch, isn't it…?"

Soon after they moved to Putney, Patricia went to yoga classes for a few weeks in a friendly, shabby, little community centre on the fringe of Clapham Common. With two small children and work to contend with, finding the time had not been easy, but off she cycled, through the unnerving traffic, to join a group run by an improbably supple young Jamaican woman named Pleasure. The last ten or fifteen minutes were spent lying in the position Haraldsson had adopted, eyes closed, breathing slowly and deeply to a background of Pleasure's relaxation tapes; sleep-inducing music which she recalled washed over her like a soothing Caribbean breeze.

Perhaps the young Icelander had entered just such a state, or an even deeper one; serene as a sleeping cat, he might be oblivious both to her presence and her voice. Looking at his face, Patricia felt a pang of envy; achieving that degree of relaxation in an environment most people would find stressful was no mean feat. She should see if she could track down local yoga classes; a little more peace and calm in her own life would not come amiss.

"According to someone who interviewed you at the airport, you're planning to climb Scafell. Is that right…?"

Unexpected direct questions could sometimes do the trick.

Like in those old World War II films, when the escaped British prisoner of war remembered to speak German until the moment some wily Gestapo officer addressed him in English.

"Yes, here it is. On midsummer night, the twenty-first? Today is the ninth. If that's right, being held for twenty-eight days would be a bit of a problem, wouldn't it...?"

Closing the file, she leaned back and folded her arms.

"I really did come to listen, but..." Patricia paused. "The trouble is, if you're not going to say anything, me sitting here listening isn't much use to either of us, is it now?"

She considered the possibility – albeit a remote one – he might be catatonic. Rigid physical state was among the principal indicators, but she detected no sign of tension or rigidity; in fact, the reverse was true. She could try gently moving his hand or foot, checking for resistance or compliance, but felt no inclination to do anything other than sit and continue her monologue. Even if he could enter trance states at will, the research suggested those in trance or even coma were usually able to understand anything said to them. Getting to her feet, she crossed to the door.

"I'm just stepping out. I'll be back in a couple of minutes..."

There was no sign of Mariette; two nurses she did not recognise were in conversation behind the desk. They looked up as she approached.

"Hi, I'm Dr Carragh. I'm with Mr Haraldsson in room 27 and I just wanted to check if he's had any medication."

One of the nurses spent a few moments typing; after studying the computer screen, she glanced up. "Olanzapine on arrival, that was 2.20 a.m. Nothing since then."

"Has he asked for anything? For a headache, maybe, or to help him sleep...?"

"Nothing, Doctor."

"Any visitors?"

"The bursar popped in to see him just before he went to Dr

Wingfield. Just routine, checking if he wanted to call home or let anyone know where he was…"

"Do you know if he did?"

"Apparently not. But now you ask, I gather the patient did talk to someone…or—" She hesitated, then corrected herself, "…something, maybe."

"Some thing…?"

"Well, when he got back from seeing Dr Wingfield, he asked if he could go into the garden. The instruction was he shouldn't go anywhere by himself so a male nurse went along. When they came back I asked if he'd enjoyed the walk and he gave me a big smile and said, yes, and he'd talked to an angel…"

"In our garden…?" offered the other nurse, laughing. "That would be a first…"

"An angel…" repeated Patricia. "Did he now…?"

"He went straight back to his room and not long afterwards he stuck that note on the door."

"He hasn't mentioned it again? Or any other visitations?"

"He hasn't said a word to anyone, Doctor."

On her return Patricia found everything as she had left it; apart from the rhythmic rise and fall of his chest, Olaf gave no more sign of life than a fallen tree. As she sat down his sign caught her eye. She turned it over and glanced at the back to find a map of the British Isles and the Irish republic on which three lines had been superimposed, joining Bristol, Middlesbrough and Dublin. At each point of the triangle were notes and what looked like calculations.

"Would all this be your own work?"

The enquiry, as she had expected, elicited no reply.

"Now, I don't know if you'd recognise my accent, Mr Haraldsson, but I'm from Ireland myself and it's got me scratching my head about what the connection might be between Dublin and these other places. Might these notes help, I wonder…?"

In contrast to the sign, they were written in small, neat script, but she felt sure both were in her patient's hand.

"Next to Dublin, it says '*Skerries Islands, goat*'…the Bristol one says '*Goatacre*', and I see '*Goatland*' beside Middlesbrough. Not that I'm any the wiser for that…" She shook her head. "No, I've no idea what it means. I'd need your help to make sense of it. Always assuming it makes sense to you, of course. Does it…?"

Her question hung in the air like a leaf caught in a spider's web. Leaning back, Patricia stared up at the ceiling.

"The Skerries," she murmured, frowning. "You might be interested to know I've been to them. My family lived right across the other side of the country, out west in County Mayo, but we used to visit relatives in Balbriggan, on the coast a wee bit north of Dublin. And one time we took a boat trip out round the Skerries…"

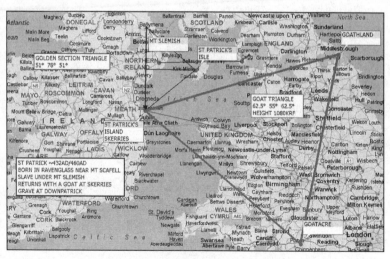

Image 02 St Patrick and the Goat

She recalled a rare windless summer's day, bright and warm, the sea flat as glass and the lazy chugging of an old diesel as their vessel slowly circled the islands. Seals, gleaming like polished riding boots, sunned themselves at the water's edge while quarrelsome herring gulls and guillemots circled overhead. Here and there, cormorants stood motionless on the rocky shore, hanging their great dark wings out to dry.

"Hang on a minute..." she added, "It was a heck of a time ago, but I don't remember a goat island. One was called St Patrick's – because he was supposed to have lived there – and there was Rockabill, which is actually two separate islands. But..." She shook her head, "I'm sure there wasn't a goat island. Maybe you've made a mistake about that, otherwise it's a mystery..."

"Like me...?"

Staring at the map, absorbed in childhood memories, the question caught Patricia by surprise. She blinked at him. "Like you...? I suppose you could say that."

"It may be a mystery to you, but there is no mistake."

"Okay..."

"Would you like to know why?"

"Definitely. I'm curious, Mr Haraldsson." She paused. "It is your work, then? The triangle...these notes?"

"All mine." He nodded. "Please call me Olaf."

"And I'm Patricia."

Raising himself on one elbow, he reached to clasp her hand in his, then lay back. "You are really interested, or is it just that you want to know if I am mad?"

Patricia shrugged. "Both, I guess..."

According to the notes he was twenty-seven; she would have guessed he was older. For a man his age there was a lot of grey in his beard and hair, but it was more the depth and intensity of the extraordinary eyes, hinting at experience longer and more profound than his years suggested.

"You were sent here for us to assess your mental state so that's part of it, obviously," she agreed, nodding at the map. "But I would like to know what this is about..."

He took a deep breath and rolled onto his side, supporting his head with a hand under his chin.

"Dr Peter Lewis Wingfield thinks I am crazy."

"Does he, now? Did he say so?"

"He would not say that to a patient, would he?"

"I'd be surprised if he did, but you seem to think…"

"I could tell…"

"I see…"

"I did not like him. He thinks he knows more than the rest of us. He does not listen to what you say, and I told him I did not like that…" He shrugged. "Maybe that is why he sent you…"

"Anyway, here I am. How do you feel about talking to me…?"

He swung his feet to the floor and leaned back resting on his elbows. For a few moments he searched Patricia's eyes in silence, then nodded slowly. "Your energy is not like his…"

"I'm not sure what that means. Could you explain, please?"

"Dr. Wingfield likes to control people. You prefer…cooperating with them…"

"There's probably something in that. The bit about me, I mean…" she added quickly.

"You are more open to receive, I think. To listen…"

"It's a big part of my job – just listening…"

"Your job, yes. But also who you are. So," he went on, "let us begin with the goats."

"Goats…?" she looked at him blankly, then smiled. "Oh, yes, them. Why not?"

"You really do not understand?"

"I do not."

"There are places named Goatacre in Bristol, and Goatland in Middlesbrough…"

"But no Goat island in the Skerries, as far as I'm aware."

He wagged a playful finger at her. "You need someone from Iceland to remind you about Irish history?"

"Is that what we're talking about?"

He pursed his lips. "Well, if not history, legend. You were right, one of the Skerries is named after St Patrick because he lived there after he escaped from slavery and came back to Ireland. And there is a story that one day while he was visiting the mainland, people stole his goat. They took it home, killed it and ate it." Olaf smiled. "You did not know this story?"

"I must admit it doesn't ring any bells..."

"There is more. You wish to hear it?"

"Absolutely..."

"Even saints can lose their temper. He found the robbers but when he asked if they had taken his beast, they said no. So he stopped them from speaking. They could only make noises like a goat! Good punishment, no...?"

"It fits the crime, sure enough. And that's what you've done, is it – link two towns where there are goat place names with Dublin, which has a goat folk-tale...?"

He inclined his head. "The explanation for your mystery..."

"I see..." However tenuous the connection might be, there was one – in his mind, at least. Some people devoted inordinate amounts of time and energy to constructing model cathedrals using matchsticks, knitting teapot covers, or recording the numbers on passing trains; scouring maps for goat associations might be higher on the eccentricity scale, but it was hardly the stuff of insanity.

"Why is this strange man so interested in goats...?" The Icelander raised his eyebrows. "You were asking yourself, no?"

"I won't deny it." She laughed.

"In your work, Dr Carragh, you must find that what is obvious, what is on the surface may be easy to see, but is not usually very useful. To find what is of value you must...dig a little deeper. Is that not true?"

"It is not uncommon..."

"Then let us take our friend the goat, and dig deeper," he said. "Did you know, for example, he is an ancient symbol...?"

"I know it's one of the signs of the zodiac," she offered, "but apart from that..."

"It is related to midwinter and so to the house of Saturn and Janus. And you are right, there is an astrological connection. The sun enters Capricorn – for which the sign is the goat, of course – at the precise moment of the winter solstice." He paused. "Shall we keep digging?"

"By all means." It seemed the Irish history lesson was now to be followed by an introduction to symbolism. As yet, no hint of spiritual beliefs or experiences; for the moment she must be patient and trust she would learn more of his inner world.

"Goat can represent a beginning, or maybe the path leading up a mountain – the kind of path goat walks with ease. The mountain itself, of course, can be a symbol of entry into a higher level of consciousness. In the traditions of my own country, the goat was linked with milk being given in the holy tree – a drink for the warriors of Wodan. We also have the legend of Thor and Loki, and two goats who pull Thor's wagon..."

"You've obviously done some serious study..."

He leaned forward, gazing into her eyes. "I am curious, Doctor. Never content to take anything at face value. I want to discover the hidden meanings, which are almost always the true ones. And you see what happens when we look closely at mister goat? What seems at first a humble, ordinary creature becomes a mighty messenger. And he opens up the possibility of whole new worlds of meaning, does he not?"

"It seems so," she assented.

Reaching under the bed, he hoisted his backpack onto his knee and rummaged inside, producing a sheaf of papers which, with a theatrical gesture, he tossed onto the floor.

"There..." He waved at them. "Just a few – I have made many of them..."

"Maps...?"

"Call them patterns I find on the surface of the earth..."

"So it's a kind of...hobby?"

"No..." The Icelander shook his head. "A passion. Look..."

He bent to pick one from the floor, but Patricia held up a hand. "Hang on a minute, I'm sure they're all interesting, but I want to understand about our goats..."

"Go even deeper...?" He smiled.

"I want to know why you chose these particular cities, for a start. My geography isn't much better than my Irish history, but I bet if you looked hard enough you'd find dozens...no, hundreds of places with goat in the name, or where they pop up in local stories..."

"You are right." He nodded approvingly, as if she had just solved a complicated problem. "I am sure there are many..."

"So, that's my question. How come you chose Bristol, Middlesbrough and Dublin, and not others...?"

The bed creaked as he crossed his legs, clasping his hands round one knee.

"Chose...?" he repeated. "It is not a question of choosing..."

"But you agreed there must be..."

"Choice is usually a logical process. That is not how I find my patterns. I do not even look for them, you see. I tune in to the land, then wait and see what it tells me. You could say I...listen and let it guide me." He met her eyes and smiled. "Do you understand?"

"Not really..."

"Perhaps my connection to the land, to the planet also, is different from yours..."

"It sounds that way. Tell me more, please."

"I try to enter the stream of the guiding consciousness of the earth. That means I do not rely only on my logical, rational mind. I pay attention to what you psychiatrists would probably call...delusions or hallucinations."

"Really? So for you, what I might describe as a delusion..."

"Could be an important message contained in the field of transformation, leading me to a deeper level of understanding..."

"I see..."

"Do you, Doctor...?" He cocked his head.

"In broad terms, I think so..."

"You are trained to see delusions or visions or schizophrenia as something wrong with people, something to be cured, is it not so...?"

"It depends on the way the individual's behaviour is affected..." she told him. "But, I take your point. That kind of thing is often pathologised..."

"Even though they might be states of consciousness people need to enter before they can receive the wisdom of the planet...?"

Patricia took a deep breath and folded her arms. "I'm not taking issue with you, but I'd really need to understand some of those terms better before I could give you an opinion..."

"Yes, of course..."

"Could we go back to your map...?"

"Of course. It was not choosing those cities but allowing the planet to guide me to them. When I drew the patterns – like our goat triangle – I found they were mathematically precise. To me that was validation of my intuitive choices." He paused. "Which is in the shamanic tradition, is it not...?"

"You've hit on something else I don't know much about, Olaf..." She smiled.

"Really...?"

"Really. What is the connection between your patterns and the shamanic tradition?"

"They enter altered states to do their work. Not just shamans – all kinds of spiritual guides, medicine men and healers do similar things. It is an accepted part of the culture and tradition in their countries. In yours..." He shrugged, "they are sent to places like this, someone like you decides they are mad, and they are locked up..."

"Are you worried that might happen to you...?"

Olaf peered at her through half-closed eyes. "Do you think I should be locked up, Doctor...?"

"Nothing you've told me so far suggests you're a danger to yourself or anyone else..." she told him. On that basis, the answer is no..."

"Good..."

He took the map from her hand and traced the lines with a finger. "Did you notice this is not just any triangle...?"

"Is it not?"

"Two sides are the same length, which means it is an isosceles triangle. The chances of a triangle with such properties occurring by chance is practically zero." He delved into the pack once more. "I can show you the calculation..."

"Not right now, thanks all the same..." Patricia shook her head. "I'll take your word for it."

"Pick any of them..." He waved a hand at the papers scattered across the carpet like autumn leaves, "and I will show you perfect geometric shapes. You will find them all over the planet..."

Gathering up a handful he began passing them to her. "I studied the English ones because I was coming here, but, look, they are everywhere..."

They appeared before her faster than she could read them, but she glimpsed Ireland, different parts of England and Scotland as well as France, India and the Holy Land, Switzerland and the United States, each bearing shapes and patterns. Triangles seemed to be the Icelander's favourites, alone or in combinations of two, three or even more, but there were rectangles, an occasional pentagram, and once what looked very like a Maltese cross.

"Fascinating..." She glanced up at him. "Yes, I see what you mean..."

"These are not created by my imagination. All I have done is link together places on the planet which possess special associations," he explained, studying her face. "And please remember, none of them could occur by chance – that is impossible..."

"And do other people accept your work as...valid?"

"I have not shown them to many people." He shrugged. "A few, I expect, would understand, would accept. Most, probably, would not..."

"How would you feel if your ideas were...rejected?"

"The work of pioneers in any field of human knowledge is often rejected." He smiled. "But think how important patterns are. You use them, don't you?"

"Triangles...? I don't think so..."

"No, no. But right now you are comparing me with patterns of crazy people..." He pulled a face and squinted at her. "Mmm. I wonder. What pattern does this Olaf fit? A pattern of sane men or mad ones...?"

"Fair enough." She smiled. "I accept the analogy. The difference is, the kind I use to draw conclusions about patients are based on research. They reflect the findings of expert medical professionals, repeated in many tests over long periods. With respect, Olaf, yours aren't quite like that, are they? Yours are something you have discovered, working alone, and you've said yourself most people probably wouldn't understand, let alone accept them. Would you not agree they're two different animals...?"

"How long is the history of psychiatry? How old is this profession of yours, Doctor...?"

"Pass." Patricia shrugged, brushing the hair from her face. "Everyone you ask would give you a different answer."

"And your own?"

"Modern psychiatry...?" Drawing down the corners of her mouth, she shrugged. "Okay, my best estimate would be...late nineteenth century?"

"Is that all – only two hundred years?" Olaf brandished his maps in the air. "What I am holding is based on human experience going back..." his voice dropped, *"thousands of years..."*

"How so?"

"Remember that goat. I did not invent the symbolic meanings – they are centuries old."

"True enough."

"Researching my patterns, I looked at all kinds of holy places and sacred sites. Places where people believed gods or spirits lived, so they have been going there to honour and worship them since ancient times…" He paused, eyes shining. "You see what I mean?"

"A fair bit longer than people have been lying on the therapist's couch." She laughed. "I have to admit that…"

"I am glad you agree…"

"Okay, let me see if I've got the picture…" Leaning back, Patricia counted the points off on her fingers. "Your maps and patterns and so forth mean a lot to you and you must have put in enormous time and effort to come up with such a lot of them. And what you're doing, essentially, is join up places which…" She waved a hand, "which you believe have historic or cultural or religious significance. And the way you decide whether they are or are not significant or meaningful is based on a kind of…mathematical analysis." She took a deep breath. "Now, does it sound to you as if I've been listening – have I followed you?"

He considered her words in silence for a few moments, smiling faintly. "Yes, thank you. I think you have listened and started to understand." After a moment's pause, he added, "But that is not why you came to talk to me. You have been patient and polite and you have asked many questions about my work. But that is not what interests you. You really want to know about me, is that not true…?"

"I told you, my job is deciding your mental state. Anything and everything you say helps me to do that."

"What do these tell you?" he enquired, nodding at the maps.

"That you have an interesting and original way of seeing the world. But you're quite right," she added. "I shall need more. My concern is that, if I ask you more searching questions, you'll respond as you did to Dr. Wingfield, and refuse to talk at all..."

"What kind of questions?"

"For example, I understand you told him you came here on the instructions of some family members – people who are no longer alive. I'd like you to tell me all about that."

Olaf's eyes lit up at her words and he clapped his hands.

"Wonderful..." he exclaimed. "It is true, and when they sent me, they said they would make sure there were people to guide me. You are one of them, Doctor, aren't you..."?

Chapter 6

The Abbey and the Angel

Thursday 9th June 2011

If Patricia had found it difficult to command the medical director's full attention at their morning meeting, when she returned to his office later she found him less distracted than irascible. He insisted she tell him first about her meeting with Chloe yet became increasingly impatient as she did so. He interrupted her more than once, and when she referred to her new patient as Morgana did so again.

"What's that name stuff all about...?"

"Didn't she tell you she's a psychic...?"

"What do you mean, a psychic...?"

He glared at her as if the term offended him.

"She...gives readings."

"Those people and their damned readings," he snorted. "Ironic, isn't it? She finishes up here because of the mumbo-jumbo she's been fed, and it turns out she does exactly the same thing..."

"It's hardly the same, Peter. What she does is..."

"There's not much difference in my book..." He waved an impatient hand. "Anyway, what's that got to do with changing her name...?"

"Well, she decided Chloe didn't fit very well with what I gathered is a pseudo-Arthurian, mystico-romantic persona. So she looked round for something else and Morgana had the right kind of ring. Having adopted it for professional purposes she found she liked it enough to start using it all the time. Probably," she added, "also two fingers to Daddy..."

"It really isn't so very different from the *Order*, you know…" he insisted. "All she's doing is play on people's minds – usually the impressionable ones with an irrational belief in supernatural causality…"

He paused to peer accusingly at Patricia. "You don't go along with me on that, though, do you…?"

They had crossed swords on the subject before but with the medical director in his present mood she was not tempted to do so again. He had as yet given no hint of the reason for his ill-temper, leaving her to speculate if it might be work related or possibly triggered by something closer to home. Perhaps the pale, ethereal Mrs Wingfield, compliant Roma, had finally put her foot down. Or might the blonde ex-stewardess mistress, Peter Wingfield's open secret, have provoked him? She had once been pointed out to Patricia, causing the green-eyed monster to stir, albeit only momentarily. The post of inamorata to the choleric medical director might not be one to which Patricia aspired but it was difficult not to envy the sexual magnetism of present incumbent.

"I'm not saying I'm convinced there's anything to it, but I don't dismiss the possibility there might be, that's all." She shrugged. "It's like anything else, isn't it – you've got charlatans and you've also got people who seem to have genuine gifts…"

"If you'd call anything about them genuine…"

Lifting a fist-sized, bronze, Gordian knot from its wooden stand on his desk, he peered at it as he turned it in his fingertips. She hoped he was not going to pursue the subject further and was relieved when it became evident he was not.

"So, what do you have in mind – meds, presumably," he went on, "and keep her under observation for a few days…?"

"And if she keeps having flashbacks, I shall do some work on them with her…"

"Fine. Is that it…?"

"Not quite, no…"

"Oh...?" He did not seem pleased to hear it.

"Well, I was surprised but she did hint that some time, maybe – just maybe – she might actually go back..."

Wingfield grimaced. "Oh, dear God. To them, you mean...?"

"It sounded like just a thought, she doesn't have plans..."

"What, then?" He held the gleaming bronze at eye level and squinted at her.

"She's obviously spent a lot of time going over it in her mind. And the impression I got was she's started wondering if it was really as bad as she first thought, or could it possibly have had something to do with her..."

"They really know how to get into people's heads, don't they...?"

"Have you ever had anything like that with other people you've treated?"

"Not that I remember. Go on."

"She seems to be toying with the idea the way to deal with it might be to go back and confront them. As if she might be able to show them she's stronger than they are..."

Wingfield shook his head.

"Recipe for disaster. Which you made clear, I hope..."

"Peter, I've said, at this point she has no plans. It's just..."

He dismissed her protestations with a wave of the hand. "So, what did you say?"

"Much the same things you would have done, I expect. Asked didn't she remember how awful she was feeling when she texted for help, and didn't she think there was a real risk exactly the same thing would happen again..."

"And...?"

"It wasn't what she wanted to hear. I mean, she's pretty headstrong, isn't she? And does not respond at all well to anyone she sees as an authority figure..."

"That is certainly true..."

"So she changed the subject with some haste..."

He lowered the bronze slowly onto its stand and sighed.

"It could create real problems…"

"Absolutely…"

"Not for her – for us. You see what I mean, don't you…? Devoted father rescues daughter from the clutches of the loonies, and we let her walk straight back in…"

"It's hardly our remit to…"

"The hell with our remit," he snapped. "That cuts no ice whatsoever with the tabloids…"

"You really think it would get to that?"

"God forbid, but it could – easily."

"But we know the character structure of the kind of people most likely to be attracted to an organisation like that, don't we? Emotionally immature and highly impressionable, hence vulnerable and open to manipulation. So how could anyone seriously hold us responsible…"

"We're not talking about what's fair and reasonable, for God's sake, Pat. We're talking about the media. They work on the assumption we can fix people like that and if we don't we're incompetent, negligent, or both. It comes down to whatever the editor of the bloody Sun thinks would make a good headline…"

"If that's the case," she said, "and you've got more experience than I have, what's your advice…?"

He slipped off his glasses and stared at the window for a few moments. "She's definitely toning her story down then…?"

"You know the line they're always peddling. There's something wrong with you and the only way to fix it is our way. So maybe, in spite of everything, they did get through to her and she's seriously wondering if they've got a point…"

"When I saw her she was extremely angry with the group leader chap…" He clicked his fingers. "What was his name…?"

"Donny…?"

"That's right…"

"That's changed, too. Now it's more like well, maybe he was

just doing his job. It's a kind of variation on the Stockholm syndrome, isn't it? With her forming a strong attachment in response to psychological and emotional abuse..."

"And an over controlled environment..."

"Exactly. Reminds me of all those battered women who get drawn back into violent relationships over and over again..."

"Possible..." he agreed, putting on his glasses and nodding. "If she did go back, of course, they aren't going to let her slip through their fingers a second time."

"Peter, she's self-referred. Short of locking her up what can we actually do?"

"Make sure she sees sense. Treading carefully," he added. "Extremely carefully. I've known cases when the *Order* tried hard to make contact and smooth things over. If that happened and she told them you'd pressured her to steer clear of them, they'd be right on your case..." He shook his head. "You just have to make sure it doesn't happen, Pat."

"I can do my best..."

"Did her GP records turn up, by the way...?"

Patricia nodded. "Bulimic from early puberty onwards, and an OD at thirteen. Which she always insisted was accidental but reading between the lines I'd say that was responding to parental pressure. Daddy's on the boards of a couple of blue chip companies; a teenage daughter with acute mental health problems wouldn't look too good."

"Hence his description of her as highly strung, with risk issues..."

"It fits, doesn't it...?"

"Increasing the likelihood that if she did go back they'd really get their claws into her..." He leaned forward. "For the girl's sake as well as ours, it's vital you find a way to make sure it just does not happen."

"At least she's flagged it up sufficiently early for me to work on it. And we know it's not a problem in the short term..."

"Do we?"

"She's agreed to stay here until the weekend. That gives me a couple of days. For a period after that I know she's going to be busy because she's going off to do some readings – down in the west country, I gathered…"

"Unless they persuade her not to…"

"She doesn't have much choice – she's seriously strapped for cash. That course cost her a packet and Daddy may not be short of money but now is hardly a good time to approach him…"

"True," Wingfield assented.

"I'll tell her as soon as she gets back she should come in to talk to me again, so we can get an idea of how she's doing. And then take it from there…"

"I'm not sure that's…"

"Peter, if I come on too strong, the chances are she'll think I'm being controlling and just walk out. But if I recommend she comes back as an out-patient, I'm pretty confident she'll go along with it."

"What if she did talk to them…?"

"I'll make it clear that would be extremely unwise in view of her condition, and I'd like her to agree to have absolutely no contact until she and I have met again and discussed it fully."

Wingfield pursed his lips and scribbled a note on his pad.

"I hope you're right," he told her. "And you'll keep me posted, of course…?"

"Certainly…" She nodded. "Now, there's Olaf…"

"Oh yes…bloody Olaf…"

His vehemence took her by surprise. Pushing back his chair he got to his feet, thrust his hands deep into his pockets and strode to the window where he stood with his back to her, gazing out. "I had a bad feeling about that one from the start…"

"Really…?" She pursed her lips; interesting he had omitted to mention that before. "Bad in what way…?"

"Nothing I could put my finger on. But I was right…" He

turned to face her. "Turns out he's the centre of two storms. A political one and a diplomatic one."

"Olaf…?"

"I've been fielding calls all day. Apparently, first thing this morning, the prime minister of Iceland sent their ambassador to deliver the strongest possible complaint about our treatment of one of their citizens…"

"What on earth are we supposed to have done…?"

"Not us…" He waved a hand, "the British authorities. The media reports mentioned possible terrorist connections and his people are up in arms about that. They insist the charges are without foundation, he's totally innocent and should be released immediately…"

"But that's not why he landed up here…"

"They're claiming it is. And I am working hand in glove with the security services…"

"I still don't get it. Is Olaf someone special…?"

"Not as far as I know, but I rather gather there's history between Her Majesty's government and Iceland…"

"Are you serious…?"

"Around the time of the economic crash some minister or other in Whitehall – could have been number ten – dropped dark hints the Icelandic banks were major money launderers for the Russian mafia and some unsavoury Arab regimes. That, of course, triggered a flight on…whatever their currency is, and according to them nearly wrecked their economy. At the time they accused us of financial terrorism, and they're still smarting about it. That's one reason why they're choosing to make our man a *cause celebre*. Or so I've been told…"

"What are these people on…?" She shook her head. "Anyway, presumably they want us to discharge him, like now…?"

"Well…"

"That happens to be exactly what I was going to suggest. I mean, yes, some of his ideas and behaviour are pretty eccentric, but I see absolutely no evidence of risk. So..." She shrugged, "problem solved, yes...?"

"If only it was that simple. That may calm the diplomatic storm, but there's the other one..."

"Peter, I don't believe this..."

"We are not at liberty to simply release him. That is not an option..."

Returning wearily to his desk, Wingfield resumed his seat and leaned back, cupping his head in his hands.

"The Home Office left me in no doubt on that score. They absolutely refused to say what evidence they base their decision on, but someone – presumably MI5, or..." He waved a hand, "whoever has responsibility for such things, is far from satisfied Olaf hasn't come for nefarious purposes..."

"My God, they think he's working for Al Qaeda...?"

"No idea what they think. When I tried to find out they clammed up. Talked about national security..."

"Speaking of which, are you supposed to be telling me all this...?"

"They know he's your patient, so you have to know what's going on..."

"So what do they want, exactly?"

"To put him under close observation..."

"So we're to keep him...?"

"It's not as simple as that. While he's locked up in here, he's obviously very restricted in terms of making contact with other people who might be involved. On the other hand, keeping an eye on him gets more tricky if he's discharged – more tricky and requires far more resources. They want me to organise some kind of half-way house, so he's in one place and has to stay in touch with us, but he's also got a degree of freedom..."

"What did you have in mind...?"

"That's the whole point, I don't..." he snapped. "I told them, I can't just wave a damned wand and produce something like that

out of thin air – the idea's ridiculous. They don't seem to understand I run a private psychiatric hospital, not a rehab – we don't
have half-way houses..."

"So, what now?"

"If I get a direct instruction to keep him as an in-patient, we
will. Otherwise, if you think we should discharge him, I'll tell
them that's what we're going to do, and they'll have to run their
surveillance operation the way they would for anyone else..." He
heaved a sigh. "Any flashes of inspiration...?"

"How about the abbey...?"

Wingfield stared at her for a few moments, frowning.

"The Standingstone place...?"

"They have a retreat centre," she told him. "I've stayed there
myself..."

"Have you really...?"

"A couple of times, actually, when I needed a bit of peace and
quiet for a couple of days. It's perfect for that. I got to know
Abbot Thomas, too. He's a good man and I'm sure he'd find space
for Olaf if I asked..."

"Manna from heaven..." Wingfield's tone brightened. "It's not
far away, either, is it?"

"Fifteen minutes drive..."

"They'd presumably put the place under some kind of
surveillance. You're not going to tell him that, are you...?"

"I don't think he needs to know, does he? I'd just say I wanted
a sort of..."

"Half-way house...?"

"No. I think I'd call it a...refuge. He'll understand that..."

Peter Wingfield took a deep breath, placed his fingertips
together and nodded. "Excellent, Pat. Good thinking. I shall
communicate the glad tidings..."

"Best to wait until I've talked to Thomas..."

Wingfield nodded. "But you'd have been quite happy to
discharge him – delusions and the voices notwithstanding?"

"You said it yourself, Peter – does it matter he believes he's getting these messages, if they're always completely benign. I think what happened was running into the mother of his child at the airport temporarily destabilised him..."

"Which could happen again..."

"Possibly, but without a trigger of that magnitude, the chances are remote," she pointed out. "I take your point, though, I'd say he's never really dealt with the child's disappearance. When he flew into Gatwick he was in a manic state but he's functioning perfectly well now. Absolutely no reason I can see not to discharge him..."

"So how are you going to explain the abbey idea...?"

Patricia folded her arms.

"I'm sure I can come up with something. After all, we're only talking a few days aren't we...?"

"They told me they wanted about a week..."

"Well, I can tell him I recommended a discharge, you insisted he's kept under observation and we compromised on the abbey. How does that sound...?"

"Fine. If the other stuff hadn't blown up, I'd have preferred to hold onto him a bit longer anyway. He was sectioned, so technically we've got until tomorrow night..."

"I'll recommend we do some work together on the child's disappearance..."

"And you get a chance for some research..."

"I might well..."

"A win-win, then..." he offered.

"Let's hope so. If that's it, I'd better get on," she said, getting to her feet. "I've still got a couple of patients to see..."

He glanced at his watch. "At this time?"

"Yes." She nodded, grimly. "At this time..."

"Let me know as soon as you've worked your charms on your friendly monk..."

"Yes," she said. "I will..."

Ψ

Following Liam's final, sullen departure, Patricia had been tormented by grief, guilt, and an abiding sense of failure. However deftly she deflected enquiries regarding her well being, she could not hide the fact she was working obsessively long hours, shedding too much weight too quickly and had rings round her eyes the shade of storm clouds. When a ward sister took her aside to tell her about Standingstone Abbey she listened politely, expressed appropriate gratitude and dismissed it from her mind. A few days later, passing the gates, she turned in with the intention of doing no more than seeing what the place looked like. Within an hour she had received a guided tour and learned it was run by a Catholic order whose community work included providing retreats for those of any faith in need of temporary sanctuary. On Colm's next visit to his father she booked herself a simple room for the weekend. Father Thomas proved a patient and compassionate listener and that first visit marked the beginning of a friendship. Hearing his voice when she rang was enough to lift her spirits.

"Of course, that would be no problem," he told her when she explained what she was looking for. "How soon would you like him to come?"

"Is tomorrow morning possible?"

"Friday? Yes, I can organise that. I hope you'll be bringing him over in person, Patricia. It's far too long since we had a chat. Tell me how you are…"

"I'm fine, thank you, Father…"

"Fine," he repeated, as though the word was unfamiliar. "Are you, indeed? I met a counsellor the other day who told me in her profession 'fine' is considered a mnemonic…"

"Is that so…?"

"You didn't know?"

She could not bring herself to spoil the pleasure enlightening her would give him.

"I have a feeling you're going to tell me."

"There are, I understand, several versions, of which she told me only two were fit for my ears. The first was: flustered, insecure, nervous and exhausted. The other was: frustrated, inadequate, neurotic and emotional..." The abbot chuckled. "Which one are you, may I ask...?"

"Okay, I think I'd better come for that chat."

"Excellent. Is there anything I need to know about our guest?"

"He's an odd character, Father. I haven't come across anyone quite like him. But he's extremely engaging, has some interesting perspectives on the world, and I have to admit I rather like him." She paused. "I do get the feeling he's maybe...let's say a wee bit of a lost soul."

"I believe the popular term for that is a deal-clincher," the abbot told her. "You knew I wouldn't be able to resist the opportunity to minister to one of those. I'm intrigued, though – what makes you say that?"

"I can't really put my finger on it, but I'd say he's looking for something, without knowing quite what. All a bit vague, I know, but it's the best I can do. Oh, and I should warn you, some of his spiritual beliefs are, well...unusual to put it mildly."

"There are those who would say the same of my own," he reminded her.

"Our man believes he's in direct contact with spirit beings who send messages to guide him..."

"And if I admitted receiving spiritual guidance, might I too find myself on your couch?"

"That rather depends. Does yours come from giants who live inside mountains, or dead relatives?"

"Ah, well, there might be a difference, I admit. But he sounds interesting..."

"He is, Father. If you get a chance, have a talk to him. And if you do, I'd be really interested to know what you make of him..."

Ψ

She found Olaf sitting cross-legged on his bed, laptop balanced on pillows piled in front of him, a sheaf of papers spread out on the blanket. He looked up as she entered.

"I did not expect you back so soon…"

"I need to talk to you. It looks as if you're busy…"

"I have been playing with King Arthur…"

"Have you really…?"

He smiled. "Well, maybe not in person. But look what I found…"

He turned the laptop towards her and she found herself looking at a triangle superimposed on a map of southern Wales and an area of the west country south of the Bristol channel.

"You know the legend…"

Patricia shook her head. "You keep forgetting – I'm not English. I do know he had a lot of knights and a round table big enough for them all…"

"It is very simple, look. Tintagel was the place of his birth…" His forefinger traced the lines on the screen. "Glastonbury is

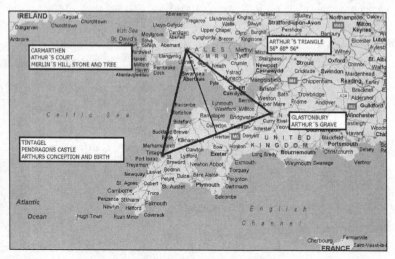

Image 03 King Arthur from birth to grave

where he is buried and here…Camarthen, which means Arthur's Court. Forming another special triangle…"

"I've told you about me and geometry…"

"An isosceles one…" He grinned. "Which I will add to my manuscript, with the rest of my research…"

He closed the laptop and folded his arms. "I hope you have come to tell me I am free now…"

Patricia turned a chair to face the bed and sat down. "Not exactly, but I have come to tell you that if you're happy with what I'm going to propose, you won't have to stay here…"

"Wonderful!" He clapped his hands.

"But I'm afraid that doesn't mean you're free to go anywhere you like. Not yet, anyway…"

Olaf's smile faded, to be replaced by a puzzled frown. "I do not understand…"

"I've just had a meeting with the medical director to discuss what we think would be best for you. I said in my opinion we could discharge you, but for various reasons Dr Wingfield felt differently. You may not realise, but what happened at Gatwick attracted an awful lot of media attention. That's put him under pressure, and he felt an immediate discharge would be premature…"

"And he is the head man…"

"He is, but I have clinical responsibility for your case. So, yes, we had…different perspectives but in the end we agreed a way forward…"

"Oh…?"

"I told him I thought you would feel much happier once you were out of the hospital…"

"They are meant to be places of healing, but I feel little healing energy in your hospital, Doctor. From a few people, yes, but mostly it is hard…harsh."

"Is it, really? Well in that case," she continued, "you'll be happy to know tomorrow morning we can transfer you to a very different kind of place, called Standingstone Abbey."

"An abbey sounds old…"

"It is quite old and surrounded by parkland so you'll find it nice and peaceful. It's run by monks and I've arranged a room in their retreat centre…"

"I like the sound of it…" He closed his eyes for a few moments, then nodded. "And I will be there for how long?"

"You and I will arrange to meet so we can talk, probably two or three times. If things go well, I'd expect about…a week at the most, maybe less."

"I am happy with your plan…" he told her, placing his palms together and inclining his head.

"That's good…"

"I am also interested, Doctor. If you were ready to discharge me, what will we talk about in our meetings? Or…" He nodded at the laptop, "would you like me to show you more of my patterns, perhaps?"

"I'm sure that would be fascinating, Olaf, but I have one or two other things in mind…"

"Tell me, please…"

"Well, so far we've really only talked about how you are right now, because the first priority is always what's happening for people in the present moment. We need to find out how they're coping, how well they're dealing with life, if you like. So initially, at least, we're not so interested in their history. But that's what I'd like to explore with you next…"

"My history?"

"Particularly your experiences relating to your son, and what happened to him…"

"Björn…?" He folded his arms. "That was a long time ago…"

"For a tragedy like that a year doesn't seem long to me. And it sounds as if the memories are still painful. Would that be true…?"

He moistened his lips with the tip of his tongue, looking at her for a few moments in silence. When he finally spoke it was not to answer her question.

"You said there were other things…"

"One, actually. You could say it's more personal. It would be a favour to me…"

"What kind of favour?"

"Well, I'm writing a paper on people's experiences of communicating with what they understand are beings from…the spirit realm."

He peered at her through half-closed eyes. "Have you ever done that, Doctor…?"

"Me, no…" she said, more hastily than she had intended. "But I've certainly met people – you being the most recent one – who have done. Or believe they have. And it's a subject that interests me; I'd like to know more about the whole process. Would you mind talking about something like that…?"

"No…" He shrugged. "I would not mind at all…"

"Although it would be of great help to me, obviously, there would be no therapeutic value for you…"

"That is not a problem…"

"But on the other hand, I believe talking about your loss could have. Perhaps more than you think…"

He lifted the laptop to the bedside table, straightened his papers and swung his feet to the ground before replying.

"Even though it's been a year…"

"The wounding from bereavement can take a long time to heal. Sometimes," she added, "it never does…"

"Are you saying that is the case for me?"

"I'm going to answer your question with one of my own." She smiled. "And that is, whether you think the way you were acting at Gatwick might have anything to do with unexpectedly running into Brynja just before you flew out…"

Olaf took a deep breath. "You think it did?"

"I'm interested in what you think, Olaf."

"It is possible..." He shrugged. "It was...difficult, I would say."

"Which suggests it is possible the mourning process is not yet complete as far as your son's death is—"

"Disappearance..." he said, sharply. "His body was never found..."

"As far as his disappearance is concerned," she corrected herself. "Did you have any kind of counselling afterwards...?"

"No. I talked to friends, of course...one was a priest. That helped, I would say. Then I went away, to India."

"Even if your reaction to meeting her was only one factor, Olaf, it still suggests something similar could happen again..."

"No, I do not think so..." he insisted.

"And you may be right, but both Dr Wingfield and I think talking it through could be a help..."

"I do not think it is really necessary but I will think about it, Doctor..."

"I'd really encourage you to do that..."

"Tell me the kind of thing you need for your paper..."

"Well, for a start I'd like to know more about your life experience. All the people in the group I'll be presenting to are psychiatrists, and they'll expect me to provide background in the form of what we call patient history. That doesn't necessarily mean going into detail about everything, but I would like to hear about what you feel are the main events in your life – the formative ones," she told him. "Since I'm here, we could begin now..."

"I am meeting someone in the garden later..."

"How much later?"

"I do not have a watch..."

Patricia glanced at her own. "It's nearly ten past five..."

"We agreed half past..."

"Okay." She nodded. "Well, that's enough time to make a start. Tell me about your early life – what was that like...?"

Olaf pursed his lips and gazed towards the window for a few moments before replying.

"Well...for the first five years, everything was normal, I would say. When you are little, you do not remember much, do you...?"

"Some do, some don't. Were you happy...?"

"Happy...?" He stroked his chin. "Yes, I think so. Happy enough, you know. My mother looked after us most of the time. My father farmed and he was also a fisherman..."

"Really – he did both...?"

"We did not have much money – he had to work hard to feed us. In Iceland our winters are often long and very cold so farming is not easy. Many men have to do more than one job just to make a living..." He paused and smiled. "One thing I remember very well. A friend of my father came to see us and I told him fish grow on trees. Everyone laughed and I was unhappy because I thought they were laughing at me. But my father did not laugh, he put me on his lap and asked was I sure about that. I said, yes, of course, because I had seen them in the trees near our house. He explained they did not really grow there – in good weather he hung up some of the fish he caught to dry. He was a kind man..." His smile faded, "but then he died..."

"What happened...?"

"He went out fishing and there was a bad storm – a really bad one that went on for days and days. My mother told us not to worry, he would be safe, he would come back, but we could see she was frightened. Maybe because one of her brothers was a fisherman and he drowned in a storm the year before..." He shrugged. "None of the men with him came back. They found the boat floating upside down, and two bodies were washed up later...but not his..."

"That can make the mourning even more difficult..."

"I was young." He shrugged. "Children do not think about things, they accept what happens, don't they?"

"As small children we may not think much, but we are

sensitive and we feel a great deal," she said. "Did you?"

"I must have been sad. That would be normal, wouldn't it?"

"It would, yes..."

He took a glass of water from the bedside table and sipped at it.

"After that my mother went a little crazy and life was...it all changed. They took her away I never knew where she went..." He waved a hand round the room, "probably a place like this. People told us it was so they could make her better..."

"Who do you mean when you say 'us'?"

"I had a brother, Magnús. He was two years older. We were both sent to live with our family, but not together. I was with my mother's parents for...I don't remember how long."

"Months..." she enquired, gently. "Years...?"

"More than one year..." His brow furrowed. "Yes, it must have been, because I had two birthdays at their house. In the end my mother did come back, but they did not make her better. She was different from before, it was...strange. She was there but sometimes it was like...she was somewhere else. You could talk to her but she did not always answer. And she cried a lot..."

"That must have been difficult for you. You'd just lost your father, and you were only little..."

"Maybe...I do not remember..." He peered at her. "Is this the kind of thing you want to know?"

"Yes, it's fine."

"Too much, too little...?"

"Whatever seems important to you..." She nodded.

"Okay. Well, after about a year, maybe two, she found a new husband. His wife had died having a baby and he had two children a bit older than Magnús and me. I think maybe he wanted someone to look after them. He was not a nice man. Well..." he corrected himself, "he was okay with his own kids, but not us. He drank a lot and when he got drunk he shouted at us and hit us. All of us – Magnús, me, my mother..."

"She didn't stand up to him...?"

He shot her an impatient glance.

"She was frightened of him – we all were. Also..." He shrugged, "a woman with two children, it is not so easy to find a husband. You understand?"

"I understand." She nodded.

"So I tried to keep away from the house, from him. I often went up into the hills or the mountains, sometimes to the sea. I loved being near the sea in bad weather, when the wind was strong and there were great big waves...but I was happiest in the mountains..." With a wistful note in his voice he added, "They were my friends..."

"And family...?"

He shrugged. "And family, maybe..."

"You just went wandering around the countryside by yourself, at that age...?"

"I did not feel like I was by myself..." He shook his head. "Not after I started meeting spirits."

"How old were you when you started doing that...?"

"Seven, eight, maybe...I do not remember exactly."

"Okay. And then...?"

"I did the things children do – like going to school, making friends, you know. My friends were important because I could not be with my spirits all the time, so you could say I kind of...adopted myself into my friends' families. I spent more time with them than my own. I did okay at school, worked hard. I liked mathematics and languages and I did well enough to get a place at the University of Iceland in Reykjavik."

"And when you weren't working hard?" she enquired, smiling. "How about sport or girlfriends?"

"Sport?" He shook his head. "I was no good at ball games. But I really liked mountain running..."

"Seriously – you ran up mountains...?"

"Yes, yes, most weekends..." He chuckled at her incredulity.

"In Iceland it is very popular. Not just up and down once –
sometimes we go eight or ten times. I think I loved it because I
was at home in the mountains. Sometimes, getting near the top,
I felt a great surge of energy, ran past all the others and it felt like
I flew to the top..."

"Must have been a good feeling."

"People could never understand how I did it, when they were
getting tired..."

"And what did you read at university...?"

"Philosophy. But for me it was..." He grimaced, "...too dry
and dull. After one year I was so bored I gave it up. I looked at
other courses, but there was nothing I liked. I knew I wanted to
do something practical, something creative, not waste my time
writing essays analysing other people's theories and ideas. In the
end, I dropped out and found myself a job with some
builders..." He shrugged. "And that is what I do now..."

Patricia nodded, expecting him to continue but he showed no
inclination to do so without being prompted.

"I noticed you speak of your brother in the past tense..." she
told him. "Does that mean...?

"Magnús? He is dead..."

"I'm sorry."

"He married when he was twenty. But it lasted less than two
years – the girl left him for someone else and I think it broke his
heart..." He clasped his hands and sighed. "One day he drove
out to a big waterfall, left his clothes in the car and jumped into
the river. The currents are very strong, you cannot get out, they
just sweep you over..."

"Were you close to him?"

"Close...?" He paused. "Not really. We were very different
from each other but...he was my brother."

"That must have been about the time you went up to
university..."

"In Iceland we go up at nineteen..."

"Eight years ago," she said. "So by the time you were twenty you already had experience of terrible losses, hadn't you…?"

"I had friends whose fathers had been fishermen and died in accidents," he told her. "It is not so unusual…"

"But still painful, surely, even if it's not…"

"Yes, I suppose…"

"And there was Magnus…"

Olaf shifted uncomfortably. "After we were separated as kids, we never really…connected again."

"That's understandable," she told him. "So, tell me about Brynja. When did you meet her?"

"Soon after going to university, at some party. We were introduced, and I really liked her name; in our language it means love. We talked and found we were interested in a lot of the same things. I liked her, she liked me, you know, and after a few months we started living together. It was quite a surprise when she told me she was pregnant…"

"A good surprise…?"

He paused to run the back of a hand across his lips. "We did not plan a baby but, yes, we were pretty happy, we both wanted him. He was born on the sixth of January 2004. It was not an easy birth. He was a big baby and *Brynja* is small, slim, with narrow hips…you understand?"

"Yes…" Patricia nodded. "I understand."

"He was normal, healthy, and a really easy baby. He slept well, fed well. We did not have so much money, but our parents helped us. Well…*Brynja's* did…"

His voice faded away. He reached for the glass, took a few sips of water and sat cradling it in both hands. A mini tractor dragging a mower rumbled slowly up and down the lawns outside the window; a trolley went rattling past the door. The sounds served only to magnify the silence which filled the room.

"Between then and now…you know about that…"

"Some of it…"

He got to his feet. "Look, I am sorry, but I promised I would be there…"

"It's okay – not a problem. And thank you for what you've told me. It will give me a context for the rest. So…" she went on, "I'll collect you at eight-thirty tomorrow morning and we'll go to the abbey…"

"Thank you…"

"I'll see you then…"

The door closed behind him and she took a slow, deep breath. She crossed to the window and pushed it as far as the security catch allowed. The mower had completed its work, leaving textured rows across the lawn; the fresh, summery smell of cut grass lingered on the air. She was on the point of turning away when she caught sight of the tall, slim figure striding towards a wooden bench between a pair of cherry trees. It seemed to be unoccupied until the young woman who had been lying on it raised herself on one elbow, then sprang to her feet. She ran lightly to meet the Icelander and hug him

"So the angel has a name…" murmured Patricia under her breath. "Or maybe two…"

Chapter 7

With the Abbot

Friday 10th June 2011

The main routes were always heavy with rush hour traffic at this time in the morning and Patricia threaded her way towards the abbey using smaller, less congested roads. As they left the soulless sprawl of suburban Crawley behind them and entered a succession of leafy Sussex lanes, she glanced across at her passenger. The Icelander had said barely a word since she had picked him up.

"How does it feel to be out of there…?"

Olaf drew down the corners of his mouth. "I would like it better to be free…"

"I'm sure, but it's a step in that direction, isn't it…?"

"I hope so…"

"I think you'll like the abbey – it's a completely different environment…"

"For just one week, yes…?"

"I very much doubt it'll be longer than that, but let's see how things go…"

"Our meetings, you mean?"

"Have you thought about what I suggested…?"

"Talking about *Björn*…?"

"That's right…"

"You spoke of a mourning process. I do not understand what that means…"

"Well, different people deal with grief and loss in different ways…"

"But you were talking about me…"

"It may help if you understand a bit about the theory. One of the early ones was what's called Freud's hydraulic model. According to that, if we don't express a feeling it stays inside us. Over time, unexpressed feelings build up like water behind a dam. Then we reach capacity, the dam breaks, and all the accumulated feelings burst out and overwhelm us..."

"Are you saying I did not express what I felt when *Björn*..."

"That's an old model, Olaf. Freud's been dead a long time; we've developed newer, better theories. Most of them are still based on the extent to which each person is able to fully experience the emotions associated with whatever has happened to them. For some people, of course, that's just too painful, too difficult. And don't forget," she added, "we're talking about more than losing Bjorn. At about the age he was when he disappeared, your father died. Effectively, you then lost your mother for a long time too, didn't you. That sounds to me like an awful lot for a little boy to deal with..."

He stared straight ahead as if searching for something in the distance. "That was more than twenty years ago..."

"Agreed, but what if, for a child – which you were – it was all too much...?"

"I do not really remember..."

"I believe that within every experience, however terrible or traumatic it may be, there's the potential for emotional healing. But to achieve it may mean exploring some deep, painful places which, understandably, we may be reluctant to revisit..."

"And that is what you want me to do?"

"It's not about what I want or don't want," she told him. "But I do feel talking about those experiences and what they were like could be of real benefit..."

"You think it would help me? Going back, stirring up old memories...?"

"It's not something I would suggest if I didn't. I am a mother, remember, and I can't even begin to imagine what losing a child would be like…"

"I am not sure…"

"I may be wrong, but we won't know without talking about it, and that was all I had in mind. In the end, of course," she added, slowing for a turning, "it's your choice whether you do or not…"

She swung in between twin whitewashed stone gateposts marking the entrance. He ordered the gates to be removed, Father Thomas once explained, to signify there were no visitors whom the monks would not welcome. A simple notice read: *Standingstone Abbey. A Place of Peace.* Which was true; she sensed an air of tranquillity about the place each time she visited it. She eased the Volvo gingerly along the cracked and rutted concrete drive, which wound through an expanse of rolling parkland dotted with stands of oak and ash.

"This abbey of yours…" observed Olaf, "looks more like a prison…"

His reaction matched her own on the first occasion she had glimpsed it through the trees. Ahead of them loomed a gaunt, forbidding, two-storey Victorian edifice of dove-grey stone. Occupying three sides of a central quadrangle, it boasted an imposing arched entrance; two rows of narrow, barred windows lined the walls. Flanking it they could see half a dozen low modern buildings with clean, uncluttered lines.

"It was originally built as a workhouse…"

"Workhouse…" Olaf echoed with a shake of the head. "What is that…?"

"Where poor people who couldn't feed themselves used to be sent. They weren't usually treated very well but it was better than starving, I guess. This one dates back to the mid 1800s. It had been empty for ages when the Benedictines took it over…"

"There are many monks…?"

"Around twenty, I think. The order does a lot of educational and community work…"

She identified the buildings as they drove by.

"That long, low one is the sanctuary – which is where you'll be staying. The main building's been turned into a school for special needs kids. The place with the curved roof and bell-tower is the chapel, and the hall next to it is a venue for concerts and lectures. I came for an evening of Gregorian chants there once…"

Olaf glanced across at her, eyebrows raised.

"You enjoy chanting…?"

"I can't say I've done much since," she confessed.

"In India, they are much more advanced in their under-standing of the power of sound vibrations than we westerners."

"I did enjoy the evening…"

"They use sound in all kinds of ways. To help you relax, to give you energy – even to heal. Every organ in our body has its own vibration; you can sing or chant them into balance, into a natural, healthy state…"

"Really? Can you do that…?"

"I was there only a short time. It takes long study and proper initiation. But I did learn certain mantras and sacred words I use when I want to awaken Shakti – or enter deeper states of consciousness." He paused and smiled. "Perhaps you should study such things, Doctor. Think what it could do for your patients…"

"It's an interesting idea…"

"But a mad one, you mean…"

To begin with she had felt self-conscious and was reticent about chanting; only slowly, gradually, had she found the courage to join in. She recalled being surprised and gratified not only by the unexpected richness and power of her own voice but the sense of liberation she experienced as she allowed it full rein.

"I'm pretty sure I'd have a fight on my hands to persuade Dr Wingfield," she told him. "Unless you've got a magic method of convincing him, too…"

The chapel had been designed in the form of a pentagon. The walls were clad with vertical planks of natural pine, and a shallow tiled roof sloped up to the central wooden tower which housed a single, gleaming brass bell. Patricia parked across the road from it and glanced at her watch. A young monk in black tunic shirt and grey trousers came briskly down the chapel steps and made his way to the car.

"I'm brother Anthony." He smiled. "You must be Dr Carragh...?"

"I am indeed..."

"The abbot asked me to show our guest to his quarters. He's tied up for the moment, but he promised he will be along as soon as he can. If you have time he hopes you can wait..."

Olaf hoisted his pack from the back seat and took Patricia's hand.

"Thank you for bringing me. When do we talk again...?"

"I'd like a word with the abbot but that won't take too long because I have appointments," she told him. "Let's meet back here in say twenty minutes, and we'll sort something out. Or I can call you – you have a mobile...?"

"I do not like them," he told her. "They make my head hurt..."

"And no watch, either..."

"I will find you. I will send you a message."

"But if you don't have...?"

"There are other ways..." He smiled, placing his palms together. "Namaste..."

"Namaste...?"

"I salute you or...I honour the God in you..."

He shook hands with brother Anthony and Patricia watched the contrasting figures move away; a neat, compact young monk alongside the taller, rangy Icelander. She did not have long to wait before Father Thomas bustled up to open her door, usher her out of the Volvo and hug her. In his late fifties or early sixties, the abbot had a broad, open face, firm jaw, thinning grey hair and the build of a man who, once active, was now engaged in a losing battle with middle age spread. Like brother Anthony, he wore a black shirt open at the neck and neatly-pressed grey trousers.

"It's very good to see you, my dear. I'm sorry to keep you waiting…"

"It's okay, honestly. I only arrived a few—" she began, but her host was in full flow.

"…I had a meditation to lead which mercifully ended on time but I got ambushed, you see. A section of the main building is being refurbished and the architect just wanted five minutes…" He dabbed at his brow with a blue handkerchief. "Which, as it invariably does, became ten…"

Patricia assured him she had relished the luxury of a few minutes to herself, taking the opportunity to close her eyes and enjoy the soothing sound of hymns being sung in the chapel.

"I hope you've time for a walk?"

"Do you mind if we make it a quick one?"

"Busy…?"

"Extremely…"

"I shall not insist on the full guided tour, then." He smiled. "But you absolutely must see our hydrangeas. They are simply stunning this year…"

Linking an arm through hers, he led Patricia away, regaling her with insights into the trials and tribulations of overseeing building works of which, he assured her, he possessed neither technical knowledge nor understanding. She allowed his words to wash over her, more aware of birdsong and the warmth of the sun until he paused and peered at her.

"You look weary, my dear. Am I boring you…?"

"You are not…" she assured him, brushing her hair from her brow. "It's just that I've got a lot on my plate right now. And I didn't get much sleep last night…"

"Stress can do terrible things to sleep…"

"It's not that – I rarely have problems sleeping. I don't get many, but I had a nightmare, woke up freezing cold and never seemed to get off to sleep again..." She gave him a wry smile. "To tell you the truth, Father, I'm not much use for anything this morning."

He frowned. "It was that bad...?"

"It was, actually..."

They walked on for a few moments in silence.

"I find talking them through can help. It seems to sort of..." He waved a hand, "dispel them, you know...?"

"Sometimes, yes. But I think I'll just sit with it for the moment..." She sighed. "Just thinking about it gives me goose-bumps..."

"Then I suggest we find something more enjoyable to do..."

"I second that."

"I shall take you to the Peace Garden and show you those hydrangeas..."

"That would be nice, but I thought there was a rule of silence. Isn't it reserved for prayer and meditation...?"

"True, but there's not much point being abbot if you can't break the rules, is there now...?"

"Are you sure you're not Irish, Father...?"

"Now there's a thought..." He chuckled. "Anyway, between you and me, I don't think we'll find many people to disturb at this hour."

He led the way to an arched, wooden door on heavy, wrought iron hinges, set in a head high wall which had all but vanished beneath a blanket of ivy. Pushing it open, they entered an enclosed area overlooked by the main building. Criss-crossed by gravel paths, it had stands of birch and oak and carefully tended flowerbeds provided a dazzling display of hydrangea and rose bushes, marigolds, chrysanthemums and ranks of sunflowers, faces turned to the sky. A shallow stream, meandering among the freshly cut lawns was traversed by a series of small bridges built of buttery stone.

"I must admit, I always thought of workhouses as grim, soulless places," she told him. "This one always comes as a surprise..."

Despite a quick glance to confirm they would not be overheard, Patricia found herself speaking in hushed tones.

"I'd say Standingstone's the exception rather than the rule," the abbot agreed, "but one of the early governors was quite an enlightened man. He had a passion for gardens – we know from the records he paid people out of his own pocket to come and instruct his inmates in growing flowers and vegetables. Just look at those now, are they not food for the soul...?"

He drew her to a halt beside bushes heavy with pink and white roses.

"My guess is he was a religious man, too. He planted quite a number of these and they feature prominently in Christian symbolism. And did you notice," he added, pointing them out, "some flower beds are arranged in cruciform...?"

"If you're interested in symbolism you'd better have a chat with Olaf," she told him. "The first time we met I was doing my best to assess him and he was busy giving me a lecture on that very subject."

A few moments later as they were crossing one of the bridges, Patricia paused, folded her arms and leaned over the balustrade. She gazed down at king cups, like miniature golden galleons swaying on the current which tugged lazily at ribbons of waterweed just beneath the surface.

"Patricia...?"

"Yes...?"

She glanced up to find the abbot studying her with an expression of mild concern.

"Are you quite sure you're all right? You look pale..."

"I keep getting images..."

"Really...?"

"Which makes me wonder..." she went on, slowly, "if maybe

you're right. If I told you about last night, whether it might help..."

"You never know..."

She felt curiously protective towards the nightmare haunting her. However benign the abbot's intentions might be, she was reluctant to subject it to the harsh light of an analytical mind.

"But...I don't think I'm ready to try to work out what it all means..."

"No, no. I understand..."

"I remember when Colm and Caitlin were little and got upset by scary dreams, all they needed was to tell me about them and for me to say everything was okay. That was enough – they'd usually go straight back to sleep. Mind you..." she added, "it may make more sense as I'm telling you about it..."

"Which is also possible..." assented the abbot. "Doubtless you'll find out..."

"A lot of it was pretty bizarre..."

The abbot scratched his head. "Dreams seem to me to have a logic of their own, the problem being it's quite different from the every-day logic we're used to..."

"Okay, let's see what happens..." she took a long, slow breath. "Well...I was stumbling round on a steep mountainside. It was night time, but now and then I could see things because there was a moon – could have been full, now I come to think of it – but it kept disappearing behind clouds so I couldn't really see a thing..." She paused, frowning. "I could have been on Croagh Patrick...do you know it?"

"Of it, but I've never been there..."

"I used to go up there with my gran as a kid. I'm not sure it was, though..." her voice tailed off.

"Then it's probably not important..." offered the abbot.

"True. Anyway, I knew there was somewhere important I had to go, but for the life of me I couldn't remember where. On top of which I was completely lost. And I remember feeling a whole rake of things: stupid, frightened and…so frustrated I could have cried. Not to mention, half the time I couldn't see where I was putting my feet and I knew one false step and I might go crashing down…" She clasped a hand to her heart. "So I stopped and shouted for help. That was really spooky, because there was an echo…but it said different words back to me. You understand…?"

"I do," he assured her. "Very disconcerting. Do you remember what you shouted, or what came back…?"

Patricia thought for a moment and then shook her head.

"Afraid not. I think I just shouted 'help', or 'help me', but I can't remember what the echo said…"

"Don't worry, I just wondered…"

"Not the actual words, but I felt it was saying I was stupid for getting myself into that mess. Which, obviously, I didn't want to hear so I shut up and went on. It was still scary, but I had a sense I wasn't alone. As if there was someone above me, sort of…keeping an eye on me…"

She put her hand to her face again. "Actually, there were two of them. Yes, that's right…a man and a woman. And I really wanted them to come and, I don't know, hold my hand, so I'd feel safer, but they just sort of…hovered around. They were there, but not there, you know…?"

"Did you see their faces?"

"No, I was just aware of them sort of…hovering behind me. Actually, I had the strangest feeling one of them…" She pursed her lips, "…could have been the man I've just handed over to the charming brother Anthony…"

"Olaf, isn't it…?"

"It is, and even for a dream that is pretty surreal…"

"Or not…" he murmured.

"At that point I heard a voice shouting for help. A child's voice, so I set off, scrambling down towards where I thought it was coming from, shouting I was coming. And that was strange, too, because although I had no idea who it was, I remember shouting 'Rose, I'm coming, Rose, I'm coming'..."

Patricia shook her head, glanced at the abbot and gave a wry smile. "I probably never mentioned it, Father, but I do *not* like heights. To be more accurate, I'm practically phobic. Liam and I took the kids to Paris one time to see the Eiffel tower. And..." She touched a hand to her throat. "I just about made it to the first level. Then they left me clinging to a railing for dear life while they waltzed up to the top. When I woke up this morning I felt the same sensations I did that day..."

"Which were...?"

"A sort of cramp-like ache along here, " she told him, bending to run her hands along the back of her thighs. "It always gets me in the same spot – even imagining being in a high place sets it off. I get nauseous and a bit dizzy..."

"It certainly was a nightmare, wasn't it...?"

"You're not kidding." She nodded with a wry smile. "And it didn't get better..."

"I feel guilty now for getting you started..."

"My choice..." she reminded him, waving his apologies aside.

"Sure you feel like going on...?"

"I've started so I might as well finish..." she told him. "Okay, so I follow the sound, stumbling and slipping and sliding, terrified I'm going to fall, then, suddenly, out comes the moon, and I see him..."

"Not Rose, then...?"

Lips pursed, she shook her head. "A little boy. I don't know...five or six? I thought it must be Colm, but I was in a kind of panic...Anyway, I could see he was standing on this kind of...ledge. Beyond which there's just nothing...an abyss...sheer drop, way, way down to the sea..."

"The sea...?"

"I thought it was a mountain, but this bit's more like a cliff..."

The abbot smiled. "I see. And then...?"

"Well, then he sees me. He's as frightened as I am, crying and shouting over and over again he's lost..."

She raised a finger. "Actually, I'm not sure if he was saying he was lost, or he had lost someone – or something. All I know is, I have to get him off the ledge, fast, but as I reach out for him, I see this snake at his feet. A huge thing, like a...boa constrictor, or something. Now, I'm about as fond of snakes as I am of heights, so I just, well...freeze. And I'm standing there like a statue, can't move a muscle, and everything goes into slow-motion. All I can do is watch as the snake winds itself round the kid's leg...launches itself off the ledge, and they both disappear into the abyss...which is when, thank God, I woke up..."

"Just when you were on the point of rescuing him..."

Patricia stared down at the stream and shook her head. "Unless the snake got us both, of course..."

"My goodness. Powerful, indeed..."

Linking his arm through hers once more, he led her across the lawns to a varnished wooden bench set in the shade of a group of spreading oaks. High overhead an aircraft whispered through cotton-wool clouds. Shading her eyes, Patricia stared up at the glistening dot, trailing vapour trails like twin feathers etched on the sky.

"How are you feeling now...?" he asked.

"Better than when I woke up, that's for sure. I lay there going over and over it and I could not get the idea out of my head the little boy was Colm. It probably sounds crazy, but in the end I had to go up to his room and check to make sure he was okay. Which, of course, he was..." She shivered.

"I'm sorry. Maybe this wasn't such a good idea..."

"It's not your fault, really. It'll fade in a day or two – they always do. Oh," she added, "and sorry about the blasphemy, Father..."

"I hardly noticed." He smiled. "I rather doubt He would have done, either..."

"There's a theory that when we dream we're sorting through whatever's happened recently..." she told him. "Filing things away, making sense of them..."

"Do you think that's how it works...?"

"If it does, my filing system went haywire last night..." she broke off, laughing. "And now it's like trying not to scratch an itch – it's hard to resist trying to work out what it all means..."

"You don't have to..." The abbot smiled.

"You could get lost in the imagery and symbols, but what stays with me is the intensity of the feelings. I was terrified from start to finish and even after I woke up..."

"And helpless and frustrated, wasn't it...?"

"You needn't be Freud or Jung to figure out that bit. I've been worried about Colm for months. Right now he's in the middle of exams, which is bound to be pretty stressful, but to be honest he's been struggling ever since Liam and I separated. He can get withdrawn and monosyllabic and spend hours locked away in his room on the computer..." She paused. "And oddly enough he's been having nightmares of his own, but he clams up – won't say a word about them, not to me, anyway. I'm hoping he talks to his therapist – not that I'm supposed to say he's seeing one..."

"So he's on your mind. Anything else that might make you feel you're slipping and sliding...?"

"Where do I start? There's Mum, of course. She's coping pretty well with the chemo – or so she says, which isn't necessarily the same thing. That's nagging away at the back of my mind, for sure. And things aren't great with Caitlin. We're barely talking, actually. She still thinks I was to blame for what happened with Liam..." She leaned forward, cupping her chin in her palms. "Work's a nightmare, too. There've been cutbacks, and my caseload is..." She shook her head, "...insane, but the medical director chooses to ignore that. Yesterday he dropped a couple of new patients in my lap. Olaf and a refugee from the *Cosmic Consciousness* people. You've heard of them...?"

"Nothing good..." He nodded, with a wry smile.

"Get the wrong side of them and all hell can break loose..."

"Sounds as if you don't like to admit it, even to yourself, but you're feeling exposed, worried about losing your footing and maybe falling..."

Patricia gave a mirthless laugh. "All of the above..."

"You could have come and talked to me before now, you know," he chided her gently. "Or do you prefer keeping everything bottled up...?"

"Guilty on both counts..."

"I'm not giving you a hard time. I'm just saying..."

She put a hand on his arm. "You're right, but you know what it's like, Father. I know what I could, should and need to do, but finding the time, energy and will-power is something else." She glanced at her watch and grimaced. "Sorry, but I must get back..."

A group of children passed by, chattering and laughing, deaf to the stage-whispered exhortations of an earnest young monk that they observe the rule of silence. A dark-haired girl in tie dyed T-shirt and cut-off jeans gestured towards the bench.

"What about them?" she protested, indignantly. "They're talking..."

"They are, Ginny," the monk conceded, "but very, very quietly..."

"I have a nasty feeling," the abbot observed with a sigh, "that brother Steven is going to find a way to draw that incident to my attention next time we speak..."

He got to his feet, and they began retracing their steps.

"Interesting 'rose' should crop up in that dream. I must check in my dictionary of symbols..."

"Along with mountains, high places, echoes, moons..."

"Full moons..."

"That's right..."

"And snakes..." He waved a finger at her. "Mustn't forget

them…"

"I'd prefer to. But that's the problem, isn't it? You're sure to find they all have a dozen possible meanings, and you wind up more confused than ever…"

"The obvious thing is you've got an awful lot on your mind, it's probably a bit overwhelming, and you need to look after yourself much better…"

"Physician heal thyself…"

"Exactly…"

"I don't seem to be very good at that. What's the magic formula, Father?"

"Heaven alone knows. All I can do is give you a little common sense advice. Talk to people you trust, tell them how things are, ask for advice and guidance, then do what feels right. Above all, seek the help and support of God." He paused. "Are you doing any of that, Patricia…?"

"Well…sometimes."

She still considered herself a Catholic but since her marriage had increasingly rarely practised the faith in which she was raised. The most tangible legacy of his Plymouth Brethren upbringing was Liam's fierce rejection of any form of religious belief. That particular brand of faith had forbidden him practically every pleasure or indulgence enjoyed by young men, notably alcohol, dancing, and sex. From the outset of their relationship, even slipping away secretly to attend Mass felt like an act of disloyalty to him. Against their father's wishes she had insisted on baptism for both children, but the battle she had to wage was so long and bitter she chose not to fight it again when the time came for confirmation.

"Would that be…not very often?"

"No…" she protested, then met his eyes and laughed. "Or to put it another way, yes."

"Whatever the true significance of your nightmare, let's assume you were guided here today for a reason. And let's also assume that reason was for you to enlist the aid of a higher power..."

"All sounds reasonable to me." She nodded.

"I know you're pressed for time, but why don't the two of us slip into the chapel right now and spend a few minutes in prayer...?"

Patricia nodded. "You think He would overlook the fact I've been absent rather a long time...?"

The abbot put his hands behind his back, closed his eyes and turned his face toward the skies for a few moments.

"I would say..." he announced solemnly, "the chances are good..."

Ψ

Patricia glanced in the wing mirror, opened her window and returned her host's farewell wave. When she told him she always left his abbey feeling lighter than when she arrived, the words were no empty platitudes. The sense of a burden lifted from her shoulders was tangible; if she were to discover she had shed a pound or two when she next stepped on the scales it would come as no surprise. Ostensibly nothing in her life had changed, yet she felt calmer and more trusting, aware that finding a different perspective on a disconcerting dream had played its part. Viewing it through the prism of the abbot's dispassionate consciousness helped sap its power to disturb and unnerve her. The tranquillity of the Peace Garden had probably helped, too; time in nature had always held a healing, nurturing quality for her. Or had it really been those few final minutes, kneeling in the cool, serene beauty of the chapel, inhaling the heady scent of roses cut from the abbey's own gardens? If Father Thomas and Olaf did meet, she reflected with a smile, they would have a field day on the symbolic significance of roses...

The thought made her suck in her breath and apply the brakes so hard the Volvo's tyres squealed in protest. The arrangement with Olaf had slipped her mind and he was probably searching for her. She executed a hasty U-turn and drove back until, on a grassy bank, opposite a section of the main building festooned with scaffolding, she spotted him lying on his back, an arm protecting his face from the sun.

"Olaf, I'm so sorry," she called as she hurried towards him. "I completely forgot. I was practically out of the gates..."

"It is not a problem..." Looking up at her, he smiled. "I knew you would come..."

"Some time, you mean...?"

"No..." He shook his head. "I meant now."

"Oh really...?" Patricia frowned. "You sound very sure..."

"I told you I would call you..." he reminded her.

"I know, but..."

"And I did..."

"Did you?" She assumed it was a jokey reference to mobile phones, but saw nothing in his expression to confirm it. "Well...I'll put it down as a missed call..."

"Missed? No..."Olaf shook his head. "If it had been, you would not be here..." Climbing to his feet he bent to brush the grass from his jeans. "I got here just as you were driving away..."

"Yes, I really am sorry..."

Joining his palms, he smiled. "Please, do not be. I lay down, made myself comfortable and...tuned in."

"I see..."

"And it worked." He shrugged. "You came back quite quickly, didn't you...?"

"I...suppose so."

If he enjoyed playing the game that he possessed telepathic powers, she had no problem with that. In fact, she found it intriguing and made a mental note to explore it with him further when there was more time.

"Are we going to talk now?" he enquired.

"Olaf, when I said we could arrange a meeting I didn't mean today..."

"No...?"

"I'm afraid not. I've had to cram in extra appointments because I'm flying to Ireland tomorrow with Colm. I'll be back on Monday evening though, so why don't we get together first thing Tuesday morning...?"

"You are taking your son with you?"

"That's right..."

Olaf folded his arms, turned his face towards the sky, and closed his eyes. After a few moments, he nodded.

"On a healing journey..."

"Possibly, but...I'm not sure what you mean..."

"They are telling me it is for healing..."

Patricia stared at him, momentarily nonplussed.

"Are they really? That sounds positive..." she said, awkwardly. "For Colm, you mean...?"

"For both of you..."

"What do you think they mean by that...?"

Opening his eyes, he squinted at her.

"Think of your dream..."

"Dream...?"

She repeated the word as if it were unfamiliar. It was not completely beyond the bounds of possibility the man really could communicate telepathically. Inferring he had knowledge of her dreams, however, was on a different scale; one which was not only unsettling and disturbing but also made her feel indignant.

"Olaf, what are you talking about...?" she demanded.

"The snake. You have forgotten...?"

It was the stress, of course. She should have recognised the signs earlier. It affected people like that; good God, didn't she see it every day in her consulting room? Patients whose minds played tricks, distorting and bending reality into unfamiliar, frightening shapes, like some demonic balloon sculptor. It could happen without warning any time emotional or mental demands overloaded the nervous system and sent it spinning out of control. People imagined events, hallucinated, heard voices. With an enormous effort, she willed herself to reply in casual tones.

"Did the abbot tell you...?"

"We have not talked yet..."

She could see nothing but concern in his extraordinary eyes; no hint of wildness or madness.

"You look pale," he told her. "Are you all right...?"

"How could you know that...?" she demanded, her voice little more than a whisper. "How...?"

"You know how, Doctor..." He spread his hands. "You saw me..."

She stared at him, biting her lip. The only thing that mattered now was to get away, to find a quiet place where she could make sense of what was happening.

"Sorry, I have to go now..." she told him, turning for the car.

"And we meet on Tuesday...?" he called.

"Sure, yes. First thing..."

Chapter 8

The Stone & the Rose

Saturday 11th June 2011

Father Thomas emerged blinking into the sunlight and set about wiping brick dust from his hands. Removing the garish, yellow plastic safety helmet which the contractors insisted he don for site visits, he ran the back of a hand across his brow and glanced around. As he filled his lungs with blessedly fresh air he caught sight of a tall, spare figure leaning against a battered, rust stained cement mixer, stranded like a beached ship in the middle of an untidy pile of builders' rubbish. Hands deep in his pockets, the man was peering up at a ragged gap in the brickwork where a pair of workmen in blue overalls were painstakingly manoeuvring a steel girder into position.

"Hello there..." called the abbot. "Lovely morning..."

The man glanced at him. "Komdu blessaður og góðan daginn, ábóti..."

Flicking his handkerchief in the air, he stuffed it back into a pocket. "Would that be Icelandic, by any chance...?"

"Yes..."

"Then you must be Olaf..."

"Yes..." came the reply, but he offered nothing more.

"My name is..."

"I know who you are. I was at Mass..."

"You were up early, then..."

"Six...?" The man drew down the corners of his mouth. "You think that is early...?"

"Not for a monk," the abbot agreed. "But for a lot of people..."

"I suppose…"

The tall man gave a perfunctory wave and turned away, stepping carefully through rubble and discarded timber like a long legged water bird.

"Are you going…?"

He looked back over his shoulder.

"Yes. Why…?"

"I know Patricia Carragh…"

"Oh, do you…?"

"Yes, we met a couple of years ago. She's an interesting woman…"

"Yes…" said the Icelander without meeting his eyes.

"When she asked if we could give you a home for a few days, she suggested I have a chat with you…"

Olaf swung round. There was something defiant about the way he planted his hands on his hips as he frowned at the older man.

"About what…?"

"Nothing in particular." The abbot waved a casual hand. "She just said you had some…views on the world she thought I'd find intriguing…"

"Oh."

"My inspection didn't take as long as I expected," he went on, nodding at the building, "so I've got half an hour or so to spare. I wondered if you'd care to join me for a stroll round the grounds. Of course, if you've something else you want to do…"

His half question hung in the morning air. Olaf nodded but did not move from where he stood, as if he preferred to maintain a safe distance.

"You work for them, do you…?"

"I'm sorry…?"

"Peter Wingfield."

"I'm not sure who…" The abbot scratched his head. "Do you mean Patricia's boss…?"

Olaf came striding across the clutter of timbers, boxes and debris to confront him.

"She said she had somewhere quiet for me. A place I would like better than her hospital, because I did not really need to be there. Do you know that place...?"

"Maidenbloom? No I..."

"I tell you, being locked up in there would drive anyone crazy. But now you want to ask me questions, yes...?"

"Not necessarily. All I said was—" the abbot began, but found himself cut short.

"So you can tell her what I say..."

"Good Lord, no..."

"I know what they are trying to do. Maybe they think I am stupid, but I am not. They want an excuse to take me back and keep me there, don't they...?" Olaf's eyes glittered. "Why? I do not understand why. Have I hurt anyone? No, I would never do that. So why are you helping them...?"

"You were at Mass, yes...?"

"I told you..."

"That is my work, Olaf. I am a monk. I am not a part-time spy for Dr Wingfield or anyone else. Do you understand...?"

"Why else would you want to talk to me...?"

"I told you. Patricia Carragh..."

"Your friend..." Olaf sneered. "Who told you all about me?"

"That is not so..."

The finger stabbed at him again. "She did not warn you I see people who are not there and hear voices in my head? And that I was sent here for a reason, but they do not really understand what it is, so they are frightened of letting me go. So what do they do...?" He gave a humourless laugh. "Hope I will think I am safe and do what you do with priests – make my confession..."

"You keep talking about 'they'. Who are 'they'...?"

"People like you..."

"Okay…" The abbot spread his hands. "And what am I like…?"

"Anything you do not understand or agree with is a threat. So is anyone who does not believe what you believe," Olaf snarled. "You know Wych Cross…?"

Confused, the abbot shook his head. "I do, but I don't see what that's got to do with…"

"They burned witches and heretics there, no? Your church, Father. Why? Because they did not accept your beliefs. That made them dangerous, so they had to be silenced…"

"I don't think you've got your facts quite right…"

"And they think I am dangerous…"

"Olaf, come on, now. Stop…" The abbot took a step forward and held up both hands. "Before we go any further, I want you to answer one simple question. Will you do that, please?"

The Icelander pursed his lips.

"I'll take that as a yes." The abbot smiled. "My question is – are you crazy…?"

"What are you saying…?"

"It is a serious question and I'd really like to hear your answer," the abbot told him. "Are you crazy, Olaf?"

"I am no more crazy than you. Why do you ask that…?"

"Then please stop talking as if you were…"

The banshee scream of a metal grinder shattered the tranquility of the morning. Both men flinched as a shower of glittering sparks cascaded, like a giant Catherine wheel, from the ragged gap in the brickwork. The abbot took Olaf's arm and shepherded him to a safe distance.

"You're right, I don't understand you, but how could I? I know nothing about you. Except," he added with a wry smile, "you're pretty angry about something and I'm getting blamed for it. Right?"

Olaf stifled a sheepish smile. "Maybe…"

"So, what do you want to do? Go off somewhere by yourself

and cool down, or take a walk with me? The offer's still open..."

The younger man glanced round as if looking for a reason to decline, but he did not find one.

"I do not want a lot of questions..."

"You have already answered the only important one," the abbot told him. "If you want to walk in silence then that's what we'll do. If not you can choose any subject you like. How's that?"

"Okay, I suppose..." Olaf nodded.

"Excellent..."

The abbot led the way back to the drive and past the chapel. The pair walked side by side, casting long shadows across grassy banks dotted with cowslips, buttercups and crimson poppies delicate as tissue paper. It was Olaf who finally broke the silence.

"She really told you nothing about me...?"

"Practically nothing. Oh..." the abbot corrected himself, "she did say you're something of an expert on symbolism..."

"Expert? No..." he dismissed the idea with a shake of the head. "But interested, yes..."

"She and I had been talking about roses, and what they signify..."

Olaf glanced across at him. "The wounds of Christ crucified, you mean..."

"The red varieties, yes. I associate the white more with our blessed Lady..."

The abbot waited, but Olaf showed no interest in pursuing the subject. Mercifully the metal grinder was no longer in use, and the still of the morning was broken by nothing more intrusive than intermittent birdsong and their own footsteps. Damp patches remained on the rutted tarmac drive in the shade of the copper beeches lining it.

"I must say, your English is remarkably good," the abbot said, glancing at his companion. "Practically perfect, in fact. Have you lived here?"

"No, but we have your television channels in Iceland. I read philosophy at university, too, and many of the books were in English..."

"Ah, yes..."

"And spent nearly a year in India, where English is the second language..."

"In India, were you? I was there myself once, but only briefly. I was sent on a week's course at a beautiful little Benedictine abbey in Kappadu, down in Kerala. I would have loved to stay longer and travel round but it wasn't possible..."

Olaf nodded. "Go back if you have the chance..."

"It sounds as if you enjoyed it..."

"It was a rich experience..."

The abbot glanced at him and smiled. "Am I permitted to ask you about India, or would that be prying...?"

"What do you want to know...?" Olaf did not return his smile.

"I just wondered what you did for that length of time..."

"Studied..." He caught the abbot's eye and went on, "Mainly ancient texts on spiritual wisdom, but also yoga and meditation. And I learned how to use breathing to enter altered states of consciousness..."

"Fascinating..."

Olaf shot him a sharp glance. "But works of the devil..."

"Are you telling me, or asking me...?"

"Not the sort of thing you did in Kerala..."

"No, but that doesn't mean they're works of the devil. Not to me, anyway," the abbot told him. "I believe the important thing is the intention with which they're used. Surely that can be prompted by the devil...or by God."

He drew Olaf to the side of the drive as a red post office van picked its way past. The driver slowed to look at them, acknowledging the abbot's wave with a quick nod before moving on. The abbot glanced at his watch and frowned.

"Odd. Usually as regular as clockwork, but he's a good hour early today..." he observed. "Not our usual man, either..."

As the van disappeared round a corner, Olaf cleared his throat. "You said you thought I was angry..."

"That was the impression I got..."

"I am sorry. I should not have..." Olaf waved a hand. "You know, said those things..."

"It's not a problem." The abbot told him with a smile. "I'm sure there's a reason."

"I was so excited to be coming to England...really looking forward to it. But from the start things happened I did not expect..." He glanced at the abbot. "It is hard to believe Dr Carragh told you nothing."

"I would not expect her to divulge information about a patient."

"A patient..." Olaf repeated. "Exactly. I did not expect to become a patient..."

"I can imagine that could be...disconcerting."

"Being put in a psychiatric hospital when you have done nothing is worse than that," Olaf told him, with feeling. "Not just put there, either. They held me down and injected me with drugs...for no reason."

"Did they...?"

Olaf stopped and clapped his hands to his temples. "It made my head go numb...I could not think straight. It was so bad I could not understand what people said to me. I heard the words, but they did not mean anything..." He grimaced. "It was frightening..."

"Did it last long?"

"They said it would not, but it was days..." he went on, the angry edge creeping back into his voice. "Even now it is sometimes hard to hear my guides. They poisoned me..."

"And you really believed I might be part of...all that?"

"It seemed possible..."

"And all that when you had been looking forward to coming..." offered the abbot. "Has it been completely ruined? I mean, are you planning to go straight home?"

"Of course not!" Olaf shook his head. "I spent many months preparing."

"Preparing...?"

"Studying your history. Reading your legends and folk stories, researching sacred sites..."

"Churches, cathedrals...?"

"A few of the very old ones like Canterbury. I was more interested in places like Stonehenge and Avebury. Some islands, too, like Holyhead, Iona and Holy Island..."

"Well now..." the abbot told him as they resumed their walk, "I really am curious. What kind of work could you possibly have to prepare for by researching Iron Age sites and English folklore...?"

Aware his curiosity might meet a hostile response, the abbot was relieved to see a smile spreading across the face of the younger man.

"I have tried to explain it to a lot of people. I am not sure any of them understood..."

"Sounds frustrating. I warn you, I may not either..."

Olaf stared at him for a moment. "I think you will. My work," he went on, "is about healing the land..."

"You'll have to say more..."

"I am to go to a place which in ancient times was a place of worship. Being such a place it actually became holy, invested with spiritual power, if you like. In those days, that power flowed like...like a mighty river. But over the centuries things changed, people worshipped in different ways and in other places, and it lost its power. The mighty river shrank to a tiny stream..." He paused. "I have been sent to help that energy to flow the way it used to..."

"Well..." The abbot puffed out his cheeks. "I'm not sure what to ask first. Whether it's when, where or how. I'm not even completely clear on why..."

It was the first time he had heard Olaf's bubbling laugh.

"Ask whatever you like…"

"Let's start with where. Where are you going to perform this…healing? I assume," he added, "we're not talking about a church…"

"No. I am going to the top of a mountain called Scafell. If you ask when, the answer is midsummer night. Because at the moment of midsummer there is a special alignment of Sun and Moon. It creates a wonderful opportunity for making connection with spiritual forces."

"At that specific moment…?" echoed the abbot.

"Yes, yes…" nodded Olaf, eyes sparkling. "Think of the journey of Sun and Moon like the rise and fall of a cosmic tide. Midwinter is low tide, but then light and consciousness begin their return to the planet, and the tide is full at the moment of midsummer. Which is why that is when I must be standing on the very top of Scafell…"

"And what will—?" began the abbot, but Olaf threw his arms open and went on.

"The eternal gates will be thrown wide and heaven and earth closest to one another. That means the veils that separate them can be drawn aside for us to enter the realm of spirit. Do you not think that is wonderful…?"

"I can see it's inspirational for you…" The abbot smiled. "Now, tell me how you'll achieve your healing goal."

"I shall not be alone…"

"You're going with other people?"

"Beings…"

The abbot glanced at him, eyebrows raised. "Ah…"

"Many of them. Those who possess the powers to restore energy to ancient spiritual paths and so heal the land. They will come flooding in along the midsummer line which runs away to the east, through Iona…" He tugged at his beard. "I could tell you so much about Iona…"

"Maybe later...?" suggested the abbot. "You were telling me about..."

"They come from the east, but there are others. The protectors of Scafell, and all the holy places right across the planet. Anywhere people have gathered to worship: mountains, hills, temples, groves of sacred trees, stone altars..." He paused. "In Icelandic we call such beings *verndari*. You would say guardians..."

"Would you include churches in your list...?"

"Of course. Every church has its guardian..."

"I had no idea..."

"Think how many bear the names of saints. The saints who are their guardians. In fact," he went on, "I was sent by one of our most famous mountain lords, named *Bárður*. I act as his messenger, a channel for the consciousness of beings like him..."

The abbot, who momentarily considered offering an alternative perspective on the subject, noticed the toes of his black shoes had been dulled by a coating of dust. Not the ideal footwear for a stroll round the grounds, but strolling had not featured on his original schedule. Glancing at his companion, he wondered if he was typical of his fellow countrymen. Could it really be that the most popular topics of conversation in the coffee bars and sitting rooms of Reykjavik were spirit guides, mountain lords and the dance of the planets?

"Healing is needed for all the dark, troubled energies Scafell has absorbed over thousands of years. Just imagine it. The accumulated pain and sadness and suffering carried up there by every person who went to pray to their gods..."

The abbot stretched out a hand to take Olaf's arm, drawing him to a halt. "I've just had an idea. Did Brother Anthony show you our famous stone?"

"He promised he would when—"

"Excellent. Then I shall do so myself. It's not exactly Stonehenge, I'm afraid, but we can be there in five minutes or so…"

"Your holy stone?"

"I'm not sure I'd call it that. You can decide for yourself."

He led his visitor away from the drive, following a path which took them across a stretch of rough, grassy ground towards a group of spreading oak and more slender ash trees.

"You have a few days in hand," he pointed out, "which is lucky, isn't it? If you'd flown in a few days later and all this had happened you might not have made it for the big night…"

"If you believe in luck…"

The abbot chuckled. "You, I gather, do not…"

"When people call something lucky – or unlucky – they feel they have explained it. No need to think any more about it. I find it more interesting to ask another question – if there was a reason, what might it be…?"

"So you think there's a reason for everything…"

"Exactly…" Olaf nodded. "I do not believe any event happens by chance or is random. I believe each one carries a message, even though it may not be obvious…"

"Good heavens…" The abbot smiled. "If I thought that I'd never get anything done. I'd spend all my time trying to work out what every tiny thing meant…"

"If you look at them all separately, I agree. But I do not do that."

"Oh. So what do you do?"

"Try to recognise patterns…"

"Explain, please…"

"Patterns, groups, connections. One piece of a jigsaw may mean little; put all together you have the picture. I got to England," he went on, "and strange things started happening. Things I never expected, did not understand, and some I did not like at all. Does it help to think I am unlucky and get upset and angry? Or step back, look at what is going on and ask – if there is a message, what might it be…?"

"Admirably philosophical. So right now, when instead of being wherever you thought you'd be, events have conspired to have you here, chatting to me..." The older man paused. "What do you read into that...?"

"There are many possibilities..."

"Indeed. What is the first one that comes to mind...?"

Olaf fell silent for a few moments. "Maybe I did not really understand the reason for my journey. Maybe I am being asked to stop and think more deeply about it and...discover the truth."

"That would certainly make sense..."

"Maybe I was also meant to walk and talk with you..."

The abbot inclined his head. "I would like to think so, but I rather doubt anything I say will be that important..."

"And what I may say to you...?"

"Good point..." He chuckled. "Puts me in my place, doesn't it...?"

Olaf suddenly wheeled away from the path, took a few high-kneed steps through the tall grasses and dropped to his haunches. Reaching out he took the stem of a tiny, deep blue wildflower between finger and thumb. "What is the name of this, please?"

"If I'm not mistaken," said the abbot, squinting, "what you've got there is columbine..."

"St Columba of Iona..." Olaf exclaimed with a grin. "And we were just talking of saints and holy islands, weren't we...?"

"We were, yes. What a..."

"Coincidence...?" Olaf raised his eyebrows.

"You're about to instruct me in the truth of the matter..."

"Truth – who ever really knows that?" Olaf enquired. "We spoke of Iona and Columba – so they were in our consciousness. Then what happens...? I am walking along, my eye is drawn to this little flower, and I find it shares its name with St Columba. Interesting, no...?"

The abbot moved to Olaf's side, took a pair of spectacles from his shirt pocket and slipped them on. He leaned forward, hands on knees, studying the bloom nestling between the Icelander's fingers.

"You believe there's some connection...?"

"Believe...?" Olaf shook his head from side to side. "It fits with my picture of the universe and how it works..."

"And if I still think it's coincidence...?"

Olaf spread his hands and smiled. "Then for you, that is what it is. For me it is a reminder that everything is connected. And whether it is or not, surely looking at it like that makes life more interesting..."

The abbot slipped off his glasses and pocketed them. Hands clasped behind his back, he walked on with slow, deliberate strides. "I must admit, I don't feel the need to search for hidden meanings or...cryptic messages," he offered. "I simply accept God moves in mysterious ways..."

"Or the gods...?"

"Not for me..." the abbot replied, firmly. "Tell me about your messages though. Where would you say they come from...?"

"Do you expect a simple answer...?"

"I don't really mind as long as I can understand it..."

"I will do my best. First, I believe everything that exists has a level of consciousness..."

"Absolutely everything...?"

"Without exception, so I include Mother Earth. Now, since she is our home and always around us, it is easy to take her for granted. If we do we may not realise she is constantly communicating with us – or trying to, if only we would listen. And her messages come in very simple, very clear terms – so simple even a child can understand. In fact, children often understand them better than adults. But," he went on, "most people have forgotten how to listen. We do not trust our instinct or intuition – we are taught to believe only those things our rational minds can grasp and for which there is scientific proof. Everything else, we ignore..."

"Are you saying that is what brought you here – a message from Mother Earth...?"

"In a way, yes, but not the Earth as a separate entity. All things are connected by virtue of the fact that all exist in the clear space of the field of consciousness of the universe..."

"This takes me back to my theology lectures at Cambridge, heaven knows how long ago..." the abbot told him with a faint smile. "I used to get out of my depth then, too..."

"Would it be easier if I said God instead of universe?"

"Possibly..."

"Perhaps there is no difference. So..." he went on, "I believe the universal consciousness inspired my mission. But it is only a tiny part of a far greater process. One embracing many different aspects: clearing, cleansing and healing but also transformation and the expansion of consciousness. So whatever I do will benefit not just Scafell or England, or even the planet but..." He threw his arms wide, "the entire cosmos..."

"Hang on, Olaf..." the abbot told him. "Let's bring this whole thing back to earth – literally. You obviously subscribe to the Gaia theory. The planet as a living organism..."

"Alive and conscious. And not just the planet – everything in it and on it..." He broke off to gesture at the oak trees ahead of them, silhouetted against a cloudless sky. "When I say I believe they live, I do not just mean they grow taller and their leaves come and go. I mean, each one is a spiritual being with its own unique wisdom, its own consciousness. It is literally aware of our presence as we pass..."

"Just as I would say God inhabits it and inspires its growth. And its magnificence is proof of God's existence..."

"Because you are a man of great faith..."

"Aren't we both in our own way...? I mean," the abbot went on, "you don't know for certain what you'll achieve on midsummer night. Even so, you're obviously prepared to put up with a lot of inconvenience and hassle because you're deter-mined to go through with it. Isn't that a sign of faith...?"

"Possibly." Olaf assented. "But surely, many people set out on sacred journeys without knowing why."

"You see my point, though? You must be extraordinarily trusting of who or whatever sent you..."

"I do not need to understand the reasons in my head..." Olaf told him. "My heart tells me something wonderful is going to happen..."

"How will you know if it does? I mean, if the mountain or you – or it could be both, presumably – is blessed with this myste-rious healing...?"

Olaf spread his hands. "I will not know until it happens, so maybe you will ask me when I come back..."

"Then I hope you will..." the abbot told him. "But I'm right, aren't I? You simply don't know..."

"Only the mountain will know what happens for the mountain. For me it could be anything..." Olaf smiled. "Some new understanding maybe, or insight...or vision, like St Paul...?"

The abbot glanced at him. "Are you expecting something like that...?"

"I expect nothing and allow all possibilities. And do not forget," he added, "I believe all things are connected. So if I do have some wonderful revelation it will be a gift for the whole planet, not just me..."

"You're in good company..."

"How is that...?"

"Wasn't it Confucius who said, a man who cultivates his spirit within the walls of his own home, even with doors locked, benefits the whole kingdom...?"

Olaf glanced at him and nodded. "I agree."

"A case of great minds thinking alike...?"

"Maybe..."

"Not fools seldom differing, I hope…" The abbot chuckled.

"Fools…?"

The Icelander's tone brought a hurried glance from the abbot. The young man's smile had melted away and there was a dangerous glitter in his eyes.

"That is what you really think…?"

"Absolutely not…" The abbot waved a hand. "It's just a saying…"

"That I am foolish, stupid…?"

"Olaf, believe me, it was just a joke. A rather lame one, I'm afraid…"

"You are like the others. The men at the airport, Peter Wingfield, your friend Patricia. You all pretend, don't you? You listen, say nice things, tell me you are interested, you understand. But all the time you are thinking, this guy is mad, there is something wrong with him…"

"I don't think anything of the kind…"

The Icelander stopped to face him, arms folded, feet planted apart, jaw set at a defiant angle. There was a disdainful curl to his lips as he went on.

"Maybe I was a fool." He gave a humourless laugh, "to trust you…"

"Stop Olaf, for heaven's sake…" The abbot held up his hands. "First, I have absolutely nothing to do with the authorities, or Maidenbloom…"

"You are her friend…"

"Patricia Carragh is an honest, decent woman…"

"She could have let me go…"

"Maybe so but at least you're not locked up, are you?" the abbot pointed out. "You're here in pleasant surroundings, able to—"

"She is clever. Asking questions, trying to make me say something to give them an excuse to keep me locked up. That is what they really want, isn't it? A way to stop me doing my work…"

"I don't know about the others, but you're wrong about Patricia…"

"You think I do not know the dark forces are trying to block my path? That is why they gave me that drug – to confuse me, so I would not know what was going on. But I do, I see it all. Even without my guides I see it…" Eyes flashing he pointed an accusing finger at the abbot. "It is all a trick, a game, but you will not deceive me…"

The abbot took a deep breath. It was like sailing and finding himself caught unawares by a sudden squall. And it called for a similar response: remain calm, avoid getting swept up in the man's anger and wait for the storm to blow itself out. He was at pains to keep his voice soft but even. "You seriously think that's what I'm doing – playing some kind of—"

"Why would you want to talk to someone like me…?

"Because I am fascinated by—"

"No…" Olaf shouted. "No, no, no. She told you, this Olaf is a crazy, a lunatic. We have to lock him up, but he is careful what he says to me because I am a head doctor. Be nice to him, pretend to be his friend and he will trust you. Away from the hospital he will feel safe, he will tell you everything – his craziest ideas. Then we can—"

"Olaf, even if she'd asked me, which she would not, I would never have agreed. Think about it. I asked if you wanted a walk," the abbot reminded him, "and you said yes. No one forced you to…"

"It was a bad idea…" Olaf glanced round like a wild animal sensing hunters. "I should go back now…"

"If you must, but before you do, hear me, please…"

The abbot's tone commanded respect. Olaf opened his mouth to speak, met the older man's eyes and hesitated.

"You may be right about everyone else, maybe even about Patricia – I can only tell you what I know of her. There could even be another agenda here – something I don't know about. I'm not denying it's possible, but I am saying if there is it's nothing to do with me. I want to make that crystal clear."

Olaf passed a hand slowly across his jaw. "Okay…"

"And you misunderstood my words. I may not go along with all your views, but I respect your right to hold them…"

"Okay…"

"Most important of all, I do not believe there is anything wrong with you. Other people may come to different conclusions and they have as much right to their opinion as I do to mine." He smiled. "Now, if you've had enough of my company I understand, but I want you to know I shall be sorry if you decide to go back…"

To the abbot's relief he saw a faint smile flicker across the young man's lips.

"I hear, and…I believe you."

"Olaf, have you considered that we might both be seekers of truth, but we happen to be following different paths?"

"I do not know why…I felt like you were attacking me…" He joined his palms. "I am sorry…"

"I didn't take it personally," the abbot assured him. "So, are you going back, or…?"

The Icelander took a slow, deep breath, the tension ebbing from his frame. "No…" He shook his head. "I will come with you…"

"Excellent. So for the time being at least," the abbot said, stepping forward and hugging the younger man, "our paths converge…"

They walked on without speaking for a time, following the footpath as it wound through clusters of oak and ash, sunlight dappling feathery ferns and holly bushes beneath them. Swift as a shot from a catapult, a squirrel sped across the clearing a few yards ahead of them. Pausing on a rotting branch it studied the intruders suspiciously before scaling the nearest tree with effortless grace. The silence was disturbed only by pigeons cooing soft, private love songs.

"Are you a typical Icelander?" the abbot enquired. "I mean, do they all see the world from your...metaphysical perspective?"

"Not really..." Olaf gave a firm shake of the head. "But we do have great respect for nature and what you probably call the supernatural..."

"So spirit guides like the ones you mentioned wouldn't be considered unusual...?"

"I am thinking of everyday life. For example, friends of mine have a small plot of land opposite their house, with maybe a dozen rocks on it. Big ones – maybe eight or ten feet high. And a few years ago a developer bought the plot. But when his men tried to clear it their machinery kept breaking down. Cranes, bulldozers, diggers...they all just stopped. The local people told the man the problem was fairies – the nature spirits who lived in the rocks. They were angry and just would not give up their homes..."

"So what did he do...?"

"Grumbled, argued and...in the end, went away. Left the fairies in peace..."

"It's a nice story..."

"Nice or not, it is true. Those rock are still there – and so are the fairies. My friend's wife can see them..." Olaf spread his hands. "The point is that things like that do not seem odd or strange to us. We accept there is more to life than things we can see or touch..."

"I've heard stories like that about Ireland. They're careful not to upset the little folk, the leprechauns, but it wouldn't happen here..."

"No...?"

"If machinery didn't get the job done, they'd try a few sticks of dynamite..."

"I would not like to live in a house they built after they did that…"

"Are you superstitious, then…?"

"In India I soon learned that in their culture the supernatural is woven into every aspect of life, and it felt right to me…"

"You must have been at home there…"

"At first it felt like I was on another planet. But quite soon I was seeing everything in a new light."

"It's a long way to go. Were you on another mission…?"

"No…" Olaf pursed his lips. "No, not that time…"

"What, then…?" The abbot glanced across at his companion. The smile that sprang so readily to his lips, lighting the Icelander's clean-cut features, had vanished and he wore a haunted look.

"Sorry. I'm prying again. You don't have to explain…"

"You could say I was running away. From a tragedy in my life, something which was…truly terrible. But however terrible things may be, you have to find a way to go on. For a long time, I could not see how I could possibly do that. In fact…" He moistened his lips, "…at one point, I thought it would be better to die."

"What St John called *la noche oscura del alma*…" murmured the abbot.

"But such things are happening to people everywhere, all the time, aren't they? Innocent people are caught up in civil wars, religious conflicts…tribal massacres…they or those they love are blown up by bombs…"

"In my experience, the fact others are going through their private hell doesn't really make our own easier to bear…"

"But you have to find strength…"

"Maybe just the strength to endure the pain."

Olaf stared at him for a moment. "You believe we must pass through darkness to reach the light…?"

"Some people interpret the story of Christ in those terms…" offered the abbot. "Those three days in the darkness of the tomb…"

"Maybe I was blessed..." Olaf told him. "When I was desperate for help, it was sent. An old friend told me about his experiences in India. I can still remember, as I listened I could feel a kind of...a knot deep inside..." He pressed a clenched fist into his solar plexus. "You know...?"

"A gut feeling..."

"Gut...exactly. And I had no idea why or how, but I felt certain that was where I must go..."

"And you trusted the feeling, obviously..."

"Feeling or...a knowing. My friend told me how to contact teachers he had met. I went to the Indian embassy for a visa and a few weeks later I found myself half asleep, in the middle of the night, on an old bus rattling into Delhi from the airport. From that moment my whole life began to change..."

"For the better..."

"Much, much better. And the strange thing was, I had no idea I would make that journey, but once I had it felt completely natural. As if I planned it long, long before but then forgot the plan..."

"Might be a difficult one to answer but, of all the things you learned while you were out there, what made the greatest difference...?"

"You are right, that is not easy..." Olaf told him. "Just one...?"

"Just one..."

They walked on, raising puffs of dust from the dry earth with each step. Olaf stared ahead, eyes narrowed.

"Perhaps it was that our ideas and beliefs about ourselves and the world actually create our life experience," he said, slowly. "There is no such thing as 'out there' and life is a reflection of whatever we hold within..." He paused and smiled. "Is that more than one...?"

"I will allow it..."

"Then I need two..."

"Then I will allow another..." the abbot told him.

"The two go together, you see. The other is that we have the power to change any belief that does not work for us, or does not serve us. It may take time and energy but...it can be changed. And when we change what is within us, of course, something magical happens – our outer world is transformed. And that," he added, "is life-changing. Literally..."

"The principle being we become master of our own destiny. That's an attractive concept, isn't it...?" The abbot nodded to himself. "So tell me this. When you got home after all your learning and discovery, armed with new self-knowledge and insights and understandings...did you experience life any differently?"

"You called me philosophical..."

"That is the impression you give..." the abbot nodded.

"As a student I wanted to change the world. I joined protest groups and went on marches. Now I try to flow with life instead of resisting or struggling against what is..." He stroked an invisible cat. "Accept life...surrender to it."

"Mmm. A little too passive for my taste," the abbot told him. "There's a saying, that he who swims against the tide reaches the source. I resist the idea of giving in to everything, even if—"

"No, no. I do not mean giving in like that. I mean not wasting energy being sad or angry because things happen to be the way they are. Use that energy to respond in the best way possible. And when you choose to act, do it with power and purpose..."

"That's better!" The abbot nodded. "Yes, much more to my taste..."

"And I have explained how I feel about chance or coincidence..." With a grin, Olaf raised a forefinger. "Instead allow the possibility there is divine logic behind everything, but because we are humans we find it hard to understand..."

"So let me ask you what's probably the only question which really matters..."

"Which is...?"

"You described going to India as running away..."

"I did..."

"I'm not asking you any details because it's nothing to do with me, but if it drove you to thoughts of suicide, it must have been traumatic..."

"It was, yes..."

"So you run away. But a year or so later you come back again, with wonderful new discoveries about yourself and life. New understandings, new perspectives..." He waited for Olaf's nod of confirmation. "And that makes me wonder – did they help you cope with the trauma any better – did they take away the pain...?"

"Was it a magic wand...? No." Olaf shrugged. "Did it help...? Yes, there is no question about that..."

He stopped and glanced eagerly about him. "Are we getting close...?"

"You'll see it in a moment..."

Leaving the trees behind them, they were traversing an expanse of undulating scrubland, following a path little more than a wellworn, rutted deer track. Winding between gold tipped gorse bushes, tangles of brambles and knee-high grasses it had begun to ascend a gentle incline.

"Do you know the stone's history...?"

"I don't, I'm afraid. According to local people it's been here a long time...maybe several hundred years."

"Do they visit it...?"

"The druids do. When the chief druid got in touch to ask if they could, we realised we must have been up at Cambridge around the same time, but we'd never met. I read theology and he did anthropology. Charming chap. Told me druid means oak tree and said they'd like to plant a dozen of them in a circle round the stone. I told him to go ahead – I have no problem with it..."

The prospect of reaching their goal had put a new spring into the Icelander's stride. The abbot, breathing heavily, quickened his pace in a vain effort to keep up as the stone came into view. Occupying the top of a small hillock, it stood etched against the skyline like a giant flint arrowhead. Pausing to shade his eyes, Olaf gazed at it.

"We are in the presence of an ancient rock lord," he said in a reverential tone. "Will your druid friend come to celebrate the summer solstice?"

"They've got their own name for that..." He tugged at his chin, brow furrowed, then snapped his fingers. "*Alban Hefin* – that's it. I understand it means 'light of the shore'..."

Olaf's attention was now focused on the giant stone and the abbot allowed his companion to reach it first. Irregularly shaped and nearly twice the young man's height, its colours ranged from rich, chocolate browns to pale shades of translucent grey, flecked with specks and veins of quartz which sparkled in the sunlight. Tapering to a rough point at the top, the base was six or eight feet broad and had been sunk deep into bare earth trodden flat by two and four-legged visitors. Completing a leisurely clockwise circuit, halting now and then to study it from different angles, Olaf retreated a few steps, turned his back and stood without speaking, eyes closed.

"I sense real power here. Our friend carries many memories...he sings the history of the land..." Opening his eyes he turned to the abbot. "We talked about places of worship. I would say people have come to this place for...who knows how long? So it resonates with their vibrations. Their hopes and dreams, fears and prayers. Do you feel it...?"

"Not the way you seem to. But," the abbot went on, "I admit I have a soft spot for the thing, and I always enjoy coming up here. Showing it to visitors is an excellent excuse, of course. And I can't explain it," he added, "but every time I do, I get the feeling that I am in the right place here at the abbey – I'm exactly where I should be..."

"Ah..." Olaf smiled. "So the rock lord speaks to you, then...?"

"I wouldn't go that far, but if you're getting these vibrations, presumably you think there's some mystical quality about it..."

"About both. The stone and the place in which it stands." Olaf slipped off his sandals. "Which might explain why you like visiting it. Maybe you are attracted by the spiritual energy..."

The abbot chuckled and shook his head. "You ascribe a great deal of influence to these mysterious planetary forces of yours, don't you?"

"They are not very mysterious. If you like, I can explain more about them..."

The abbot folded his arms. "You are determined to convince me they exist, aren't you?"

"All I would do is share a few discoveries I made while I was researching sacred sites..."

"Okay. Fire away."

"First, I need something..."

Sandals in hand, he retraced his path down the slope, peering to left and right, finally swooping like a bird of prey to snatch up a gnarled stick. He bounded back to where the abbot waited in the shadow of the stone, smoothed an area of cracked, dry earth with the sole of his bare foot and dropped to his haunches.

"Have you heard of a place called Rose Dale?" he enquired, squinting up at his companion.

"Better than that – I've been there. It's a beautiful spot, pretty remote, way up on the Yorkshire moors. An old Cistercian nunnery, dating back to the late twelfth, early thirteenth century if memory serves..."

"So, imagine here we have Rose Dale..." Olaf scratched a rough cross into the earth. "And Grey Abbey...?"

"Ah, now..." the abbot echoed, tugging at his chin, "that's in Ireland, isn't it? Cistercian, again – a monastery..."

"And right next to the Rose Mount..." Olaf busied himself with his stick once more. "So, the second cross is Grey Abbey and this line – which is supposed to be straight – joins what I will call two rose sites. Now, this is where it gets interesting. Do you have any idea what lies on the centre point of that line...?"

"No idea, I'm afraid." The abbot peered at the marks, shaking his head.

"The mountain I am to climb on midsummer night..."

"Scafell, does it...?"

"Whose name tells you it is no ordinary mountain. Scal or skull means the place of the lost grail or the mountain of God. So," Olaf went on, "here we have a monastery, which I will call a symbol of the masculine. Across the Irish Sea a nunnery – symbolising the feminine. The pair located east and west of, perfectly aligned with, and equidistant from... a sacred mountain."

"Well, well..." The abbot murmured.

"With the nunnery towards the rising sun and the abbey towards the setting sun of the equinox. And what is the equinox...?" Olaf spread his hands. "A moment of perfect balance. Day and night, male and female...perhaps even heaven and earth."

"You actually see the planetary movements in those terms, do you?"

"So does your church..."

"Not as far as I'm aware..." The abbot looked puzzled.

"Even though Easter, the day you celebrate the transformation of Jesus, is determined by the dates of the equinox and the full moon...?"

"Well, yes, in that sense..." The abbot folded his arms and nodded at Olaf's patterns. "But I can't get as excited about this as you do. I mean, are you really claiming the locations of these places, relative to one another, possess some kind of mystical significance...?"

"Maybe, maybe not. It depends on your point of view..."

"Which you could say of almost anything..."

"Exactly..." Olaf smiled. "So you prefer to believe the pattern was created by chance or coincidence...?"

"I'm aware of your views on that one, but you've put your finger right on it..." The abbot gave an apologetic shrug. "Pure coincidence..."

"Even though Scafell occupies the exact centre point of the line..."

"Which is intriguing but it doesn't change my mind..."

"And the distance from Scafell to nunnery and abbey is the same – five hundred and twelve thousand Roman feet. A sacred number, by the way..."

"And you will not persuade me by citing numerology..." protested the abbot only to find his words brushed aside.

"You could say Jesus is the gateway from both sites to Scafell, the mountain of God. In this case a feminine mountain..."

"Wait..." The abbot held up a hand. "What makes you say that?"

"The true name of Scafell is the mountain of the goddess, Rose – or Sophia..."

"Is it really...?"

"So..." The Icelander flung his arms wide, "Jesus opens the gate, bringing the spiritual seeker closer to God. The Son of God is the intermediary between the seeker and the divine. Prayers are made to Him because He will intercede. He will help the person praying to approach God..."

Olaf paused, eyebrows raised; the abbot tugged at his lower lip.

"That introduces some interesting theological questions, but let's do our best to remain grounded. Let us consider what you have drawn here. Leaving aside the question of coincidence, I'm not at all sure people had the means to measure distances with that accuracy nearly a thousand years ago..."

"That is not in doubt..."

"You sound very sure..."

"Because we know the Romans could. To build their famous roads they had to be capable of calculating extremely fine alignments," Olaf reminded him. "Which is why Roman surveyors were extremely highly rewarded for their work. Speaking of the Romans, did you know their first capital in England was Colchester...?"

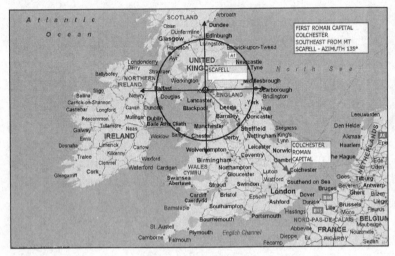

Image 04 Colchester

"I did..."

"And that Colchester lies exactly south east from Scafell?"

"I don't need to answer to that one, do I?" he said with a wry smile.

"Let me add to your list of coincidences. Our two rose sites are a certain distance from one another, in Roman feet. Now, although the unit of measurement is different, that distance is exactly the same as the one separating Rome from its holy mountain of Jupiter and also Jerusalem from Mount Ararat..."

"A clear sign that mysterious consciousness of yours is at work again, I suppose..."

"I allow that possibility..." Olaf smiled.

"I'm sure you do..."

"While you remain a doubting Thomas..." Olaf teased him.

The abbot returned his smile, but did not reply.

"I shall show you what happens when we add yet another rose to our pattern..." Painstakingly inscribing a third cross, he scratched lines linking it to the first two.

"This is a little place called Roseberry which is not far south of Edinburgh..." he explained. "Would you like to guess how far it is from Scafell...?"

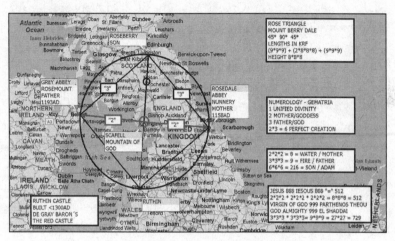

Image 05 Rosemount and Rosedale

"I suspect," replied the abbot gravely, "it will turn out to be the same number of those wretched Roman feet..."

Olaf flourished his stick with the triumphant smile of a man who had just solved a complicated problem. "And you are right. Which might also be chance. But there is a particular reason I think not..."

"Enlighten me..."

"It is a significant number."

"In what way...?"

"Five hundred and twelve is eight times eight times eight. And 888 is the sum of the Greek letters forming the word Jesus..." He leaned forward to trace the outline of the triangle with a finger. "So what you see here is Jesus lines connecting three roses. Jesus who opens the door for us to the divine..."

The abbot puffed out his cheeks. "I don't deny those places – their names, anyway – possess some degree of religious significance..."

"And the rose, we already agreed, is a Christian symbol..."

"One of many, but yes..."

"With a history, however, going back much, much further..." Olaf pointed out. "The Greeks thought of it as Aphrodite's, for the Romans it was the flower of Venus. Both goddesses of love..." Olaf paused, lips pursed. "Which makes me wonder if Mary is a more modern symbol of the divine feminine..."

The abbot was bending forward, hands on his knees, peering intently at the pattern before him as though concerned he might have missed something. "I see where you're coming from. It's food for thought, but..."

"But the ideas of a man who is quite clearly mad." Olaf chuckled.

"I didn't say that..." the abbot protested. "I am not making the same mistake twice. What I would say, is the connections which are blindingly obvious to you, seem to me...well, tenuous at best. It would take a great deal more evidence to convince me..."

"I do understand..." Olaf told him, inclining his head.

"Time and time again, I have noticed that if someone believes passionately enough in any idea and they're sufficiently determined to find proof to support it, they will keep on digging away until they think they've found it..."

"So, you are not persuaded...yet?"

"Not yet..."

"But do you allow the possibility – however small – that all this..." He pointed with his stick, "might be evidence of something magical? The spiritual wisdom of our planet manifesting in patterns on its surface...?"

"I seem to recall..." The abbot frowned, "hearing something

very similar from people desperate to explain crop circles..."

"But you do not believe it..."

"Surely you're choosing to ignore a simple fact about your rose-related sites. Men built a monastery or a convent here, an abbey or a church there..." He paused. "Men, Olaf..."

"Men resonating with and in the field of planetary wisdom...?"

"Or guided by the Almighty..." insisted the abbot. "But I'm not really clear how you come up with patterns like these..."

"In most cases, the clue is in the name. Shared meanings and shared sounds can also be significant. Sometimes the link lies in their locations or their orientation relative to one another. On occasions, I have found the link through studying folk stories and legends. The Earth." Olaf smiled as he went on, "is wonderfully creative in finding new ways to manifest its consciousness."

"So it seems..."

"Have you ever noticed how many references there are in the Old Testament to mountains as the dwelling places of God...?"

"That is an interesting point..."

"So I would say the holy mountain between them might be a channel directing divine energy to Rose Mount and Rose Dale, and I can show you hundreds more patterns just like these, from all over the planet. They link cities, tiny villages, churches, mountains, hills, streams and rivers – holy places of every kind. And once you accept the patterns exist then..." Olaf spread his hands, "the only question is: who or what created them...?"

"And they have become a passion..."

"Psychiatrists are not so kind; they say I am obsessed..."

The abbot rubbed thoughtfully at the earth with the toe of a dusty shoe.

"I am a priest, doing my best to serve God. To my mind, your question has been answered. God is the ultimate power in the universe, so if your patterns are real and meaningful – about which I remain sceptical – then they were created by and are the handiwork of the Lord and reminders of His sovereignty over all things..."

"Maybe we are in agreement and it is just that our understanding of God is different. But please be aware, Father..." Olaf joined his palms, "I do have the greatest respect for your beliefs..."

The chimes of the chapel bell echoed through the stillness. The abbot glanced at his watch and grimaced. "Good heavens, I'd no idea we'd been so long. I'm afraid I have to get back, Olaf. Do you want to stay here or...?"

"I will come with you, but first I must say farewell to your rock..."

Turning to face it, Olaf touched his palms together, bowed his head and murmured a few words under his breath. Waiting until he had finished, the abbot stepped forward and patted it.

"A loving touch..." Olaf smiled.

"Something I am in the habit of doing before I leave," admitted the abbot with a bashful shrug. "I'm not sure why. A little ritual, if you like..."

"Would you do something else this time?" Olaf asked. "An experiment..."

"I don't have a lot of time..."

"A minute or two will be enough..."

"All right..." The abbot cocked his head. "An experiment of what kind...?"

"You feel affection for it..."

"I suppose I do, in a way..."

"Let us see how it responds to you. I will go round to the other side and place both my hands on it," Olaf told him. "I invite you to do the same."

"I see..." The abbot frowned. "And that's...it?"

"Then close your eyes, allow your awareness to be with your friend, and...see what happens."

Before the abbot could reply, Olaf had circled the stone, placed his sandals on the ground and taken up his position opposite the abbot.

"One minute. I will tell you when time is up…"

The abbot took a deep breath, glanced round and was relieved to see they were alone. Not that it mattered, of course, because he was free to use that minute in any way he pleased. Taking awareness to the stone sounded much like blessing it, which was what he decided to do. Feeling more comfortable, he laid his hands against the cool, weathered surface, leaned forward for it take his weight and closed his eyes. The next thing he knew, Olaf was touching him lightly on the arm.

"You did not hear me…?"

The abbot stepped back, ran a hand across his brow and shook his head. "No, I didn't, actually…"

Olaf spent a few moments studying the abbot's face. "Are you all right…?"

"I'm fine, yes. It's just…I'm not sure what happened just then…"

"After you closed your eyes…"

"Yes…" The abbot thrust his hands into his pockets. "I'd decided to bless it, actually, but the moment I closed my eyes, I had this strange feeling I could see into the rock…almost as if it was made of some kind of dark glass…" He paused, brow furrowed. "And it was as though I could see a person in there. That sounds crazy, doesn't it?"

"A little girl…?" Olaf nodded. "Yes, I saw her, too. Interesting…"

"Are you serious…?"

"Wearing very old fashioned clothes…"

"Olaf, I am beyond surprised. That's absolutely extraordinary…"

"Is it…?"

"Yes. There's a piece of local folk-lore about this rock. I was going to tell you on the way back…"

"Please, tell me now…" Olaf nodded encouragement. "I like stories…"

"Well, they say that ages ago, there was a tremendous storm and the next day the stone was found on the ground. You can imagine how heavy it is, and how difficult it would have been to lift, so it didn't get put back – it just lay there for years. The story goes that the governor of the workhouse and his good lady desperately wanted a child but the poor woman kept on having miscarriages. Until one night her husband dreamed a little girl came and begged him to put the stone back in place. Which he did. He rounded up all the men he could find, brought them up here, and somehow managed to do what she'd asked…" The abbot paused, smiling. "You can guess the rest, can't you…?"

"Nine months later one healthy baby arrives…"

"One healthy girl baby…"

"Exactly so…" The abbot nodded. "So you can see why I was a bit…taken aback…"

"Of course. But that story has the ring of truth…" Olaf told him. "The mighty rock lord is brought low…falls from his appointed place…the earth invites the governor into a space of consciousness and asks for his help…he hears, responds, acts…bringing healing to the rock lord and his own family…" He paused. "What do you think of that…?"

The abbot turned and ran his gaze slowly over the stone. Meeting Olaf's eyes once more, he nodded. "Maybe you are right." He smiled. "Maybe anything is possible…"

Chapter 9

Under Croagh Patrick

Saturday 11th June 2011

Patricia leaned towards the oval window, gazing down at clouds spread out like God's own freshly laundered duvets beneath a gleaming silver wing. She might complain about the noise and traffic, but living in close proximity to an airport could be a blessing, too. Not that it made getting Colm up and running any easier; with a body clock set on teenager time, the chances of persuading him to go to bed before two in the morning were roughly the same as those of getting him perpendicular before midday. How much longer, she mused, could whoever designed school timetables steadfastly ignore elementary human biology?

While early morning flights held little pleasure for either of them, today Colm's resistance was lower than expected, which she ascribed to artfully planted reminders they would be visiting Gran Fran, the name he gave her as a small child. The bond between them was evident from his earliest years, when Patricia's resources were stretched almost to breaking point by the demands of two small children, plus senior house officer duties at a Dublin hospital. These included extended periods on call, endless overnight stays at the hospital and ridiculously little sleep; visits from her mother and grandmother were life savers. She harboured reservations about the stories with which Frances regaled the child at bedtime, but the delight each evoked in the other was compensation enough. The guilt she felt about leaving him was largely assuaged by the fact he was so content to be left. To Patricia's regret this was rarely the case when Fiona assumed child care duties, although, Caitlin, thank heaven, was as happy with one family member as the other.

Hunched over his laptop, Colm's fingers flickered across the keyboard. She had once asked to be initiated into the mysteries of computer games and he selected one he assured her was simplicity itself. Her total ineptitude had taken two minutes to expose, at which point class had been terminated. The neurological wiring of his generation, quite different from that of her own, seemed to incorporate an almost magical ability to intuit their way through technological intricacies as impenetrable to her as mandarin. She closed her eyes and laid her head on his shoulder, making him shift uneasily.

"Yeah...?"

"Nothing. I'm using you as a travel pillow. You don't have to stop..."

Stretching long arms towards the seat in front of him, he flexed his shoulders and yawned. "How much longer...?"

When the children were small she discovered the best way to deal with this recurring enquiry was to choose a figure at random. Accurate or not, provided it was delivered with confidence it invariably did the trick. She made a show of consulting her watch.

"We shall be landing at Ireland West in...thirty-one minutes and sixteen seconds..."

Colm groaned. "Mum, I'm not six. How long really...?"

"Really? I'm not sure..."

"Anyway, I thought we were going to Knock..."

"It's just a fancy name for Knock, pet. And I know how old you are, but I thought I'd see if the old methods still worked."

"Are we renting one of those terrible old bangers of mad Mick's...?"

Lifting her head from his shoulder she adopted a pained tone.

"They are not old bangers. They may not be in the first flush of youth but they do everything we need, don't they? And Mick's not mad, he's a grand fellow. He gives me a special price, too, because I'm a Doctor..."

"It's probably because he fancies you," Colm offered, returning to his game.

Mick O'Hare would have looked more at home among horses than cars. In his sixties, a Sweet Afton drooping from his lips, he had the bow-legged build of a jump jockey and wore corduroy trousers, hounds-tooth jackets and trilby hats.

"You're a bold boy. I do not fancy Mick and I'm sure it's mutual..."

She delivered the rebuke with mock indignation, but his playful tone pleased her; it had been all but absent in recent months. She made to ruffle his hair but he recoiled at such an affront to teenage cool.

"You want me to get a sports car, I suppose?"

"Doesn't have to be." He shrugged. "But something, like, halfway decent, at least. Do you remember that time Dad got an Alfa...?"

A note of reproach in his voice, real or imagined, sent the needle on her self-esteem meter sinking into the red zone. Colm read her expression at a glance.

"Mum, that's not what I meant..."

"I know. It's okay, pet..."

He peered at her and shook his head.

"You looked really wiped out last night," he told her. "Are you really okay...?"

She thought she had done a better job of camouflaging the weariness at the end of a day which had started well, until that brief, disturbing exchange with the Icelander. She summoned a smile. "Me? I'm fine..."

His eyes told her he was not convinced. "You're worried about Grandma, aren't you?"

She reached for his hand and squeezed it. "A bit, yes. I'm sure she's getting good treatment, but it's a tough time for her. Seeing us cheers her up, though. We'll call and let her know we landed all right – she still doesn't trust planes. Listen," she went on, "you might have a point about hire cars. Why don't we treat ourselves...?"

"Seriously...?"

"Maybe we should give old Mick a miss – just this once, mind – and see if we can't find something with a bit of...oomph."

"Won't that cost more...?"

"Aren't we worth it?" she demanded. "So, resident motoring expert, pray enlighten me. What would be even better than an Alfa...?"

"Are you serious...?" he asked.

"You'd better believe it, kid."

Her attempted transatlantic drawl earned a pitying look and a faint grin. She was unsure whether it was an expression of amusement or resignation. Within the hour, however, she found herself sliding behind the wheel of a gleaming Audi smelling like a saddlery. To Colm's disappointment, she vetoed an even racier sports saloon on the grounds it was an automatic. Her enjoyment of a fast car, she explained, would be seriously compromised if she had to spend the weekend mastering two pedals rather than the customary three. Pulling away for the first time, she experienced almost guilty pleasure at the car's sheer power. Any lingering reservations about the disparity between the charges levied by Mr Hertz and mad Mick O'Hare faded into the distance as swiftly as the bleak, functional architecture of Ireland West Airport.

Ψ

Before Patricia had parked outside the garden gate, Frances materialised at her front door, beaming. The cottage resembled a child's drawing with its uneven walls, irregular windows and curiously undulating roof. She might have turned eighty, but to Patricia's eye her grandmother had changed extraordinarily little over the years. True enough, her step had lost some of its spring but the smile was as warm and eyes as bright as ever. Patricia offered up a prayer that her own array of oils, creams and lotions would be half as effective in preserving her complexion as the Mayo air had been for Frances.

Colm bent to receive a welcoming kiss, folded the diminutive figure in a hug and nodded towards the gate. "Look what we've got. Isn't that cool...?"

"Well, well!" Frances clapped her hands. "Isn't that a fine, shiny machine?"

"It's an Audi..."

"'Tis a grand yoke, whatever it is. We do not see many such up a boreen like this..."

"I talked her into it, but she really likes it. She wants to get us one..."

Patricia planted her hands on her hips. "Dream on, young man..."

"You know you do."

Frances waved a forefinger at the youth towering over her like a dockside crane. "Keep working away at her," she advised. "Your mother was never one to buy nice things for herself. Were you, pet?"

Shading her eyes, she peered at Patricia over the rim of her spectacles.

"Nonsense, of course I was..." Patricia protested. "Now, are you going to invite a pair of weary travellers in, or do we stand out here all day talking about motor cars...?"

"Weary travellers who have come all of five miles in their fine carriage...?" Frances shook her head. "And on a wonderful, sunny Sunday morning, too. How is it you've not walked over, taking in fine fresh air and acquainting this child with the beauty of Mayo?"

"You do well to get young ones on their feet at all," Patricia told her. "Things have changed from your day."

"I'll have this young fellow on his later, you see if I don't," the old lady told her. "Now, I want to hear how you found that daughter of mine..."

"Not too bad. Better than I expected actually..."

"She always tells me she's grand, but would she say if it was otherwise?" Frances shook her head. "Come on in, now. You'll be wanting a cup of tea..."

"Lovely..." Colm nodded.

Patricia frowned. "You never touch tea at home..."

"We're not at home..." he reminded her.

Patricia shook her head. "Go on, the pair of you. I'll be in directly..."

Frances led her great-grandson past the confection of old bamboo poles and patched wire netting that passed as a chicken run. If the local foxes didn't take the old lady's hens, thought Patricia, it could only be as an act of kindness. Returning to the car, she opened the boot to retrieve a cellophane-wrapped spray of freesias she had found at a garage shop, and a cardboard box of provisions from Thornhill's tiny village store. She pointed the fob at the car then paused and shook her head. What in heaven's name was she doing, in the depths of the countryside, with Flaherty's ramshackle farm the only building in sight? Slipping the keys into her jeans, she pushed open the gate, the inviting smell of freshly baked bread wafting down the path to greet her.

Ducking through the door she found Frances, match in hand, bending over an ancient hob to light the gas under a blackened, battered kettle. Colm was reclining in one of the sagging leather armchairs, bursting with horsehair which she recalled prickling her own young legs and making them itch.

"Your mother never told you about your name...?" she was asking, in the tone she would have adopted had Patricia failed to tell Colm the identity of his father.

"Not that I remember..." Colm shrugged.

"Shame on you, Patricia O'Leary..."

Frances had never taken to Liam, declining to use her grand-daughter's married name. In doing so, Patricia privately admitted, she had demonstrated admirable prescience. Wiping her hands on the faded, sunflower patterned apron she wore over a plain blue cotton dress, Frances shot Patricia a reproachful glance.

"He should be told…"

Patricia had begun unpacking her box, but it was not easy to find space for the contents amongst the little kitchen's crowded shelves and cupboards.

"I'm sure he was…" she murmured, knowing her protestations were unlikely to deter Frances from pursuing the subject. "He probably wasn't listening. Will I get cups out…?"

"'Look yonder, 'tis all done…" Frances nodded at a low wooden table on which she had set crockery, cutlery, and a plate of sandwiches.

"Eggs laid this very morning and you have home-grown tomatoes and bread fresh from the oven. Now, will you sit yourself down and stop fussing, woman…"

"I remember something about a saint…" offered Colm in his mother's defence. "Is that what you meant?"

"That's not the half of it." The old lady gave a shake of the head. "You mean they don't teach you about names at that fancy English school…"

He exchanged glances with Patricia. "I guess…well, not really."

"There's schools for you," Frances lamented, "and wasn't it always so? Filling the young ones' heads with facts and dates and all manner of nonsense, not the slightest use nor value when it comes to living life…"

"When they should be teaching them about names…" Having decanted a bag of sugar into an ornate cut glass bowl with a chipped rim, Patricia began searching for a vase.

"You would not be mocking me I hope, young lady…?" Her

spectacles had slipped down her nose, and Frances stabbed them back into place.

"Me? I would not be so bold..." Patricia assured her.

She found a slender, blue glass vase, filled it from the kitchen tap and smiled; hearing herself addressed in those terms took her back thirty years. She planted a quick kiss on Frances's cheek.

"Can I have a sandwich?" asked Colm.

"I did not make them for show, pet. Eat up, now, you'll have your tea in a minute."

"What's the stuff about my name, then...?" he enquired, taking a moment to select the largest sandwich.

"Ah, yes...Columba," intoned Frances. "Did you know the first time I clapped eyes on you, I told your mother it would be a fine, strong name for the fine strong baby you were...?"

"Did you, honestly...?" He glanced at Patricia for confirmation. To the best of her recollection, practically every member of the family had at some point taken her aside to suggest names for him. Unwilling to spoil whatever her grandmother's account might be, she nodded. "Now you mention it, Frances, it could have been yourself..."

The old lady gave a satisfied smile. "T'is from the old Irish, *Collum Cille...*"

"Okay..."

"Which has several meanings, one being 'dove of the church'..."

"What else...?" he enquired through a mouthful of egg and tomato.

"Well, church can mean circle, and dove can be something high and bright. So...bright bird in the sky...?"

"Cool..." Colm's tone suggested he had been hoping for something more dramatic.

Patricia took a moment to savour the fragrance of the freesias before clearing space for the vase among a display of framed family photographs on the heavy, dark oak sideboard. Leaving the other one for Frances, Patricia perched on the broad arm of Colm's chair while Frances filled the teapot with boiling water and warmed to her theme.

"Dove of the church indeed, for didn't he bring Christianity to Scotland? Not only that, he was missionary and warrior, founded monasteries and performed miracles and still found time to convert the heathen..."

"Wow..." Colm was more impressed.

"I've half a dozen books about him, so I have. Would you like one to take home with you...?"

Patricia avoided Colm's eye, knowing he would be less than enthralled at the prospect of wading through a dusty tome on his namesake. "It's not the best time, Frances. He's in the middle of exams right now..."

"Yeah, that would be great..." he told her, licking his fingers.

"Then so you shall. People are fearful ignorant about names these days, and it should not be so..."

"I'll Google it," he told her.

Patricia shook her head. How was it possible, when she was driven to despair by the hours he frittered away on Facebook, computer games and YouTube, that one word from his great-grandmother was enough to have him researching ancient Irish saints?

"You'll do what to it...?" Frances demanded.

"Look it up on the internet," Patricia told her. "That's where the kids go to find everything these days."

"Hey, you don't have a computer?"

"I do not..."

"You should..." His eyes gleamed. "A laptop. I could show you how to work it..."

"At my age...?"

"They're so simple, aren't they, Mum?"

"Well, I..."

"You see...?" He grinned. "Honestly, it would change your

life. You and me could skype."

"I shall have to think about it." Slipping a knitted cover over the teapot, she carried it across to the table in both hands, stepping carefully across the uneven floor. "Although so far, I have done very well with just my books..."

Colm surveyed the dark wood shelves stretching from floor to low ceiling, which housed her library. "Have you really, like, read all of them?"

"Indeed I have and haven't they been my companions and teachers all my life?" She ran her fingertips tenderly along the spines, eased one out and blew the dust from its pages. "You'll find no shortage of saints here. This one's about St Teresa of Avila and this..." She drew out a second volume, "is a biography of St Francis..."

"The animal guy?" asked Colm.

"After a manner of speaking..." She peered along the row. "There's plenty more beside the holy men. This one's about devas and nature spirits..."

"Devas – what are they...?"

Frances did not appear to hear his question. "You should be taking in the wisdom..." she went on briskly. "Why, it would do you more good than all your googles..."

Colm, about to respond, caught his mother's eye and thought better of it. He reached for another sandwich.

"And what about Padre Pio...?" Frances leafed gently through the pages. "A modern saint, this grand fellow. Did you hear of him...?"

"Afraid not..." Colm shook his head.

"If I had favourites he'd be one of them. For he had the stigmata, he could heal all manner of sickness with a touch of his hand and..." her voice sank to no more than a whisper, "he could appear in two places at the same time..."

"How could he do that...?" Colm asked.

"People said he could do things only our good Lord himself

could do. And didn't that ruffle a few feathers in the Vatican..."

"Two places at once, though..." Colm insisted. "That's impossible..."

"Some would agree with you," Frances admonished him. "Others would not. Be that as it may, when you've finished your tea we'll be away for a walk. Not too far mind, for the old legs are not what they once were, but it is too beautiful a day to sit inside, is it not?"

Before setting off, Frances took her visitors to inspect an array of vegetables. Gazing at rows of plump broad beans and lettuces, peas and potato plants, Patricia could only admire the old lady's energy and industry.

"They'd win prizes at any show, Frances."

"And so they should. All planted in harmony with phases of the moon..." she purred.

"Why do that...?" Colm wanted to know.

"It ensures healthy growth and the very finest flavour. What did you think of those tomatoes...?"

"They were really good, actually..."

"Ah well," she went on, lowering her voice, "I have also made friends with the garden spirits who tend them..."

"Do you reckon there are any of them in our garden, Mum?"

"Nature spirits...?' Patricia repeated.

"Of course there are..." Frances chuckled.

"I'm not so sure..."

"Some things are so," insisted Frances. "Whether you believe them or not..."

Her grandmother's chosen route came as no surprise to Patricia. From the cottage it ran eastward, towards the smooth, symmetrical profile of Croagh Patrick. Some three or four miles distant, the mountain rose above undulating countryside dotted with gorse bushes. Following the narrow, uneven track, Patricia was content to hang back a little and enjoy the sight of Frances and Colm deep in conversation. Linking his arm through hers,

Colm shortened his stride, leaning down to catch his great-grandmother's every word. Patricia revelled in the fresh, sharp edge to the air, the serenity and stillness, and the landscape's rich palette of assorted greens and browns. Colm had been only five years old when they moved to England, yet she could still feel like a stranger there. Each time she set foot on home soil was like donning a reassuring, familiar, comfortable old coat. Her rational voice, however, insisted it had less to do with the mystical qualities of Mayo than putting a few hundred miles between herself and Maidenbloom Hospital.

"Mum!" Colm called over his shoulder. "Mum..."

"What, pet?"

"Gran Fran didn't know why Croagh Patrick is that shape..."

"Nonsense. She knows everything there is to know about it..."

He drew Frances to a halt to let her catch them up.

"She doesn't. We did mountains in geography. The really old ones get worn to a forty-five degree angle. Did you know that?"

"At your age, I knew everything. As you get older you start forgetting it again. Wait a few years and you'll see what I mean. Anyway," she added, "doesn't it depend whether they're weathered by weather or glaciers...?"

"What this handsome young fellow did not know," Frances informed her, with satisfaction, "is that its ancient name was Mount Aigli..."

"Aigli...?"

"Eagle. Not that you'll see many of those fine creatures round here nowadays, more's the pity."

Colm gazed at the mountain's summit. "Are we going to the top?"

"If you are it will be without me," Frances told him, "and I'd better make a bed up for you, because, let me tell you, 'tis three times further away and twice as high as it looks from where you're standing..."

"One day we will," Patricia promised, "but definitely not now.

You'd need time, plenty of water and the right shoes, none of which we have. When I was a little girl it used to be a really slippery climb, but they've made a proper path now. Even so, it's quite a hike."

They had reached a point where the path traversed a broad valley with rough ground sloping up gently on both sides. A stream wound between clumps of reeds, no more than a shallow rivulet stained translucent gold by peat-rich earth. Frances nodded at a narrow bridge fashioned from rough-cut logs, on the far side of which their track began a steady ascent.

"This is as far as I take myself, nowadays," she told them. "You young folk can go on, but it's my habit to stop here, take the weight off my feet and sit by the stream awhile."

"Sounds good to me." Patricia glanced at Colm. "Do you want to go on a bit further, work off some energy?"

"No..." Colm shook his head. "I'll hang out with you guys."

"Michael Flaherty has been known to turn his cows loose up here, so you'd better mind where you're sitting yourself down," Frances warned. "You would not want that fancy motor of yours smelling like a farmyard, would you now?"

"Indeed we would not," Patricia assented, with feeling.

Picking her way gingerly across the scrubby, uneven ground, Frances clasped Colm's arm as she lowered herself onto a patch of grass near the bridge.

"So your man here has been educating you about your own mountain, has he?" Patricia said, sitting down nearby.

"He may know all about slopes and angles and such like," said Frances, smoothing her dress across her knees, "but does he know the magic of mountains, I'm wondering..."

"What kind of magic...?" He bent to pick up a stone and sent it looping high into the air, landing in the water with a faint splash.

"Not the Harry Potter kind," Patricia told him, "that's for sure..."

"Mountains can sometimes whisper to you, you see. So do streams, or a forest when winds rustle the leaves..." She paused to take a deep breath.

"I don't get it," Colm glanced at his mother. "How could a mountain talk to you...?"

"I don't think Frances means it quite like that..."

"How then...?"

'T'is a matter of learning to still the mind and...listen. Be open to whatever you might hear..."

"It's not talking the way we are now," Patricia offered. "It's more..."

"I will give you an example," Frances told him. "A few years back, things were difficult and I needed a little help. Some guidance..."

"Okay..."

"At full moon it was – a honey moon, or rose moon as some call it. And I climbed all the way to the very top, and stayed the entire night there..."

Colm dropped to his haunches, eyes fixed on her face. "Seriously? All night...?"

"It was in my younger days, pet..."

"And heard, like, voices?"

Watching his rapt expression, Patricia felt again that mixture of awe and trepidation with which she had once listened to tales of little folk, banshees and fairies. When she spoke of mystical matters, the old lady's voice took on a lilting, hypnotic quality.

"Voices, no. But I had a dream. That is how messages sometimes come..."

"Oh..." He frowned, disappointed. "So it wasn't really the mountain...?"

"Indeed it was..."

"But you can dream anywhere..."

"You can. But you might have different dreams in different places..."

"Yeah, but…"

"And I believe I had that dream on that particular night, not by chance," she went on, "but because I was surrounded by the wisdom of Croagh Patrick itself. I've been back since, and the same kind of thing has happened…"

"Oh, okay…"

Frances peered at him. "Are you disappointed there were no voices?"

"No. I was just wondering…"

"Wondering what, pet?"

"Did you always have, like…good dreams?"

"Dreams are dreams, are they not…?" she asked. "Neither good nor bad."

"Yeah, but…"

"But…?"

"Well, I mean, you couldn't say nightmares are good, could you?"

"If someone gave you an unwelcome message, would you call that person bad?"

Patricia sat very still, hardly daring to breathe. Perhaps it was naïve, but she had assumed he would speak of his night terrors in the privacy of the therapist's chair. But for some reason she could not even guess at, it might be here, in the middle of the Irish countryside, witnessed only by his great-grandmother, his mother and the looming presence of the holy mountain. He stood up and thrust his hands into the pockets of his jeans.

"No…" He shrugged. "Why…?"

"I think of my dreams as messengers, you see…"

"Always…?"

"If not always," she conceded, "then often…"

"Okay…" He gazed into the distance, alone with his thoughts.

"Would you have a reason for asking…?" Frances enquired, in a voice so soft Patricia hardly caught her words.

"Well…" He shrugged, without meeting her eyes. "Kind of…"

"Come to me…" Frances said, extending her hand.

He turned to look at her, took a step closer, and sank back onto his haunches. Leaning forward, Frances laid her hand on his knee, very gently, as if calming a frightened animal.

"Why…" She smiled. "You're trembling, pet…"

"Yeah, well…" He bit his lip.

Patricia wanted to make it easier for him, explain to Frances what had been going on, offer him a lead. Colm glanced at her, and something in his eyes told her to hold her peace.

"It's like…" he told Frances, "I have these…nightmares."

"Do you, now…?'

"And they really scare me…"

"They can do that…"

"But it's pathetic. I mean, it's not like I'm a baby but they really do…" the words came in a sudden torrent. "And I know it's just a dream, but it's still…I don't know what to do, and…"

"Darling, it is not pathetic…" Patricia began, only to catch a small movement of the old lady's hand, no more than flexing the fingers, but she knew what Frances was asking, and stopped herself.

"If it's frightening, then that's the way of it…" Frances pointed out.

"Yes, but…"

"Whether you are nine or ninety…"

"I suppose…" He poked at the ground with his fingers. "But letting it do that to me just feels…stupid."

"Nightmares…" said Frances, her tone suddenly businesslike. "Now would that be the same one over and over, or different ones?"

"The same one…"

"And how long has it been going on…?"

"How long…?" His gaze flickered from Frances to Patricia. "Dunno…do you, Mum?"

"They seemed to start around Christmas…"

"Yeah, I reckon…"

"And they upset him really badly…"

"It, Mum…" he corrected her.

"Sorry. It…"

"Yeah…" He ran the back of a hand across his brow. "It does. I mean…sometimes I lie there for hours. Trying not to go to sleep…"

"You never told me that…"

"Did you tell anyone about it…?" Frances wanted to know.

"Not even Mum," he admitted. "It's just…pathetic."

"Not to me," Frances told him, firmly. "So if you feel like telling your Gran Fran, then you may. And if you'd prefer not to, we shall speak of other things." She looked across at Patricia. "Like why I have not heard from Caitlin. Isn't it months since that bold girl made even a telephone call…"

"I don't mind…" Colm said.

"It is up to you, my pet…"

"But I don't see the point. I mean, telling you won't make any difference, will it…?"

"The truth is, I don't know. It is also a fact that you will not find out if you don't. So my advice is to close your eyes, take a few lungfuls of fine Mayo air, and do whatever feels right. And if that is to tell me I'm a nosey, interfering old woman and should mind my own business, you go ahead. But…" She narrowed her eyes, "be warned, if you do, you will like as not get a bang on the ear for your disrespect…"

"Right…" With a wan smile, Colm folded his arms and did as she had suggested.

Patricia heard the sound of running water and, somewhere in the distance, the cry of a sparrow hawk. She watched the rise and fall of Colm's chest and waited for his eyes to open. When they did he gathered himself and nodded.

"Okay…"

"Would you like me to go?" Patricia enquired. "And give you two some space..."

"No," he said, quickly. "I'd prefer you stay..."

"That's fine..."

"Grand..." Frances patted the ground at her side. "Now, you don't look comfortable, perched there like a bird that just might fly off into the sky. Sit yourself down..."

He hesitated for a moment before lowering himself to sit cross-legged. "Er...I'm not sure where to start..."

"The beginning is often a good place, don't you think...?"

Colm nodded, but his smile faded as he began. "It's always the same. I'm in this, like...hole. Well, more of a cave, really. It's kind of dark, but not totally...I can see a few random people hanging around. No one I know, so, I'm not sure who they are or what they're doing, except it feels like they might be waiting for something..."

"How about you?" enquired Frances. "Are you waiting for something, too?"

"Maybe. I don't know. No idea..." He shrugged. "All I know is...I can't move. It's not like I'm...tied up, or anything. More like my body isn't working. Or it's working, because I can breathe, but...I can't actually move. Like I'm paralyzed...you know?"

"Paralyzed...?" echoed Frances. "That's an awful bad feeling so it is..."

"Really scary..."

"Sure, wouldn't it frighten the life out of anyone...?" She nodded. "And then...?"

"Then I realise the other people are all...looking in the same direction, and...I can't move my head, only my eyes, so I look, too, and..." He moistened his lips, "and...this really old lady sort of...appears out of the dark. And she's staring straight at me with these weird eyes and she's got a harsh look on her face, like I've done something that's made her really angry. But the worst bit is she's kind of...covered in snakes. You know, twisting about, all over her..."

He drew sinuous circles in the air round his head and shoulders. A tremor ran through his slim body, as if he was caught in a draught of chill air.

Resisting the urge to comfort him, Patricia hugged her arms tightly to her chest.

"...Loads of them, everywhere. And I can't stand them, can I, Mum...?"

"It's not just they frighten him..." Patricia told Frances. "It's a full-blown phobia."

"Ah, you poor fellow." Frances reached out once again to touch his knee.

"Anyway, she just walks towards me, with that look on her face, you know. And there's all those snakes...the way they move around, kind of...in and out of her hair, and I can see their eyes, and their fang things flicking in and out...the way they do."

The colour had drained from his face. Stiff and still, a hand clasped to his throat, it took an effort for him to continue.

"I can't, absolutely can't move. But she's getting closer and closer and...I'm looking at them slithering over her, and their fangs...and I know they're going to get me. I just know it, but I can't do a thing. I want to scream at people to stop her, to help me, but I can't. Can't even speak. God, it is so horrible." He shuddered. "Then, just as a big snake kind of rears up, ready to strike, I always wake up..."

"Breathe, pet..." Patricia told him.

He waved her words aside. "Don't fuss, Mum. I'm...okay."

"Are you now?" enquired Frances. "Because I would not be, if it were me..."

"But it's so stupid..." he insisted. "I mean, it's always the same. I wake up before anything terrible actually happens. I kind of...know I will, but I forget. Does that make sense...?"

Perfect sense, pet..." murmured Frances.

"And I just want it to stop..." He shook his head.

"Your woman is a kind of Medusa, isn't she now…?"

"A what…?"

"And there's one to keep away from," Frances gave a grim smile. "Not only has she the serpents, but one look would turn you to solid stone in the instant…"

"Feels like she already has…"

"Now the only way to deal with her was to cut off her head…"

"Was it…?"

"Which Perseus did…"

Patricia shot her a sharp glance. Frances might not think so, but this was not the moment for a class in Greek mythology. He needed to be comforted, reassured that fear was a natural response to imminent physical danger real or imagined, and affirmed for his courage in admitting to it. All of which she herself was ready to do, but he might find it easier to hear coming from Frances.

"You talked about dreams sometimes being, like…messengers," he said. "Do you think mine might mean something?"

Frances' attention seemed far away. Gazing into the distance she sat, eyes half-closed, rocking back and forth.

"Mean something…" she echoed, absently. "Indeed it might…"

"Like…?"

"Frances, quite honestly I don't think it really matters what —"

"Quite right…it does not. Not when there is work to be done."

"What do you mean…?"

Frances shook her head, and reached out her hand.

"Help me up, pet…" she instructed.

He helped her clamber stiffly to her feet.

"Now then…" she announced, "we must go back directly…"

"What's the rush, Frances? I'd really like you to…"

"Yes, yes, all in good time. Now…" she told Colm, "take my

arm, young Colm…"

"But I still don't see…"

"I'm sure you don't…yet," she told him. "But never fear, you will. All you need to know for now, is the reason you've been plagued by her these past few months is because some healing work needs to be done."

"And you're going to…"

"You will find out in good time." Glancing skywards she frowned. "The weather's turning. Come along now…"

Patricia, on the point of objecting, caught Colm's eye. He gave a shake of the head; however crazy it might seem, he wanted her to go along with whatever Frances had in mind. As they retraced their steps, Patricia, bringing up the rear once again, found it hard to decide if she was more angry with Frances, or herself. She could have cut short discussion of his nightmares and avoided the whole situation. She could have trusted that, when the time was right, he would broach the subject in the safety and security of Tony's study. Instead, she had naïvely imagined that an octogenarian pseudo mystic would be of more help to Colm than a trained therapist.

She halted, took a deep breath, and looked about her; it was too late to fret about it now. Wiser, surely, to put it out of her mind, focus on the peace and beauty of what she saw and heard and ground herself in the reality of the moment. She was immediately aware of a chill in the air and hugged her arms across her chest. Without her noticing, the clouds had grown darker and heavier, and away to the west the sky was turning an ominous, steely grey. When she reached the cottage she found Colm leaning against the sink watching as Frances, on her knees, opened each drawer of the sideboard in turn and rummaged through the contents. She slipped an arm round his waist, and kissed his cheek.

"Okay?"

"I'm fine…"

"Did she explain...?"

"About Medusa, yes..."

"Terrific..." Patricia rolled her eyes. "We'll go soon..."

"Not yet..." he insisted. "Please..."

Frances gave a sudden cry of delight. Climbing to her feet she beamed and waved a hand in the air.

"There, I knew I had it, and I was right..."

"What is it...?" asked Colm.

"Why..." she announced, holding out a reel of crimson cord, "it is exactly what we need..."

"And for what purpose," enquired Patricia, coolly, "would we need a piece of coloured string...?"

"Cord," Frances corrected her. "Cord, my lovely. Now then, where are my scissors?"

Bustling into the kitchen, she unwound a length of the cord and snipped it off. Pushing her glasses into place with a forefinger, she turned to Colm.

"Now, I want you to pay heed to what I tell you." She glanced at Patricia. "The both of you..."

Colm nodded. His mother, arms folded, did not.

"Whether you understand the why of it matters not, but I ask you to do exactly as I say. Now, you know the St Patrick story...?"

"Everyone does..." Colm told her.

"Everyone *thinks* they do. They think he banished the serpents on the mount that bears his name," the old lady continued. "But it is not so, you see. The deed was done in another place, nearby, called St Patrick's Head." She glanced at Patricia. "You'll know it...?"

"Frances, of course I do..."

"But you may not know it lies at the end of a magical earth line. One that runs east, passing through the very heart of Ben Bulben..."

Patricia tightened her arm round Colm's waist; their visit was taking on a surreal quality. The time had come to put a gentle halt to the old lady's rambling, take Colm away to a saner world and talk to him calmly and rationally about what he had shared. She opened her mouth to speak, but Frances was in full flow.

"…On through the blessed saint's chair – and his well – crosses the Irish Sea, and ends at the highest mountain in England—"

"Frances, I'm sorry, but we really have to head back soon," Patricia broke in. "I promised Mum we'd…"

"Hang on a sec." Colm shook his head. "I want to know about this line…"

"Ben Bulben was once *Ben Culben*," she said, addressing him alone, "which is but another form of Columba. So you are to go to the mountain whose name you bear – and there is no time to lose…"

"Ben Bulben?" exclaimed Patricia. "Do you have any idea what you're saying? It's miles away. I mean, *miles*. And why would we, anyway?"

"You would do well not to delay…" Frances tied a bow in the cord before handing it to Colm. "There, I have woven a little magic into it. Protection, should you need any. Now, when you reach Ben Bulben, approach it from the southwest and you are to find a yew tree…"

"What do they look like…?" He frowned.

"Your mother will tell you…"

"Hang on. This whole thing is completely crazy. You can't be serious, Frances…"

The old lady smiled. Her gaze was unwavering, her voice firm.

"Indeed I am, and well you know it." Looking at Colm, she went on. "Now, once you have found it, tie your cord over a branch. And be sure to tie it good and tight, so it cannot slip off. Is that clear, now?"

"I think so, yes." He nodded, frowning. "Go towards this Ben Bulben from the south west, find a yew tree…and tie the cord to it..."

"Perfect!" Frances patted his arm. "You have the entire picture..."

"Just wait a minute..." Patricia held up both hands. "You're not listening to me, either of you. A few minutes ago we were hearing about Colm's nightmares. The point of that, as far as I was concerned, was seeing how he could be helped over them. Now, suddenly, that's all gone out of the window and it's magic lines, bits of string, and..."

"Cord..."

"Whatever." She grimaced. "Not to mention suddenly going all the way to Sligo. Now it may make perfect sense to you, Frances, but to me it sounds like complete and utter madness..."

"I don't understand it either, Mum. But Gran Fran obviously believes it would help...somehow." He looked into old lady's eyes. "That's right, isn't it...?"

"I do..." she assented.

"Help how?" Patricia spread her hands. "I do not get how any of that stuff can benefit Colm one bit. Apart from which, we came over to spend time with Mum. It's a while since she's seen your man here, and you know how much it means to her..."

"I am well aware of that." Frances nodded. "As I am of how much her grandson's health and happiness mean to her. For that is what we are talking about, is it not?"

"I was hoping so, but..."

"She told me Sinead and the little ones are with her today. So she has company the next few hours, which is all it will take you..."

"A few hours is right..." she agreed with a wan smile. "I mean, at least tell me why we have to go all that way. It's a hell of a drive, and I can find you plenty of grand yews this side of Sligo..."

"I do not doubt it. Any more than I doubt that if you truly wish the dark energy to be lifted from the young one's shoulders, the work must be done beside Ben Bulben…"

"And that's it – the only reason you can give me? You have a feeling about it…"

The old woman stepped forward and placed her hands on Patricia's shoulders. "If you will hear me out, you shall have others…"

"Go on, then…"

"Out yonder by the stream, the guardians of the threshold spoke to me. They have something planned for him – call it a test of the heart. If he overcomes his fear and does as they bid him, there is a healing in it…" She glanced at Colm and nodded encouragement. "For him, and for all of you…"

Patricia opened her mouth, but Frances reached up to place a finger gently against her lips. "He has been called, do you see? He could remain trapped, caught in the snare of darkness, or he could free himself, pass through, wake to his inner truth and…follow his path…"

Patricia ran her fingers through her hair and sighed.

"I'm none the wiser…"

"Sure there's one way and one only to find out if I'm right, is there not?"

"How far is it, Mum?"

Patricia shook her head. "I don't know exactly, but it must be…I'd say a good couple of hours each way."

"That's not so far," he protested.

"Oh, really? You're not doing the bloody driving…"

"No. Sorry…"

He looked crestfallen. Angry with Frances, she had vented her frustration on him. She put her arm round his shoulders and hugged him. "That was unfair. It's not your fault pet…"

"I get it. Four hours is a hell of a lot…"

Taking a deep breath Patricia gathered herself. "I still don't understand what good it can do, and I still think it's madness. But your Gran Fran's certain, isn't she?" She paused. "And if we don't go, I'm always going to wonder what would have happened if we had. Does any of that make sense...?"

"No..." Colm's face was lit by a broad grin "But it means we're going, right?"

"Right..."Finding herself enveloped in a bear hug, she peered at Frances over Colm's shoulder. "Are you at least going to explain why Ben Bulben?"

"Now there's a question, and if we had the time I would give it the answer it deserves." Frances shook her head. "For now, just remember it's a place where magical and mysterious things can happen."

"What kind of things...?"

"Things that defy all your fine logic and reason...!"

"Cool..." Colm shrugged. "I was just wondering. The line through it you said ends up at a mountain in England. Which mountain...?"

"Why, the highest in the land..." Frances told him, smiling. "But if they ignore something as important as names, I do not suppose they teach you about mountains, either..."

Over the harsh, insistent ring tone of her mobile, Patricia heard Colm reply.

"They do, actually." He laughed. "It's Scafell, isn't it...?"

Chapter 10

Ben Bulben

Sunday 12th June 2011

Thinking about it later, Patricia could not remember whether Colm had answered Frances's question before her mobile rang or after. Clear in her memory, however, was her surprise the call reached her at all in that remote location.

"Good heavens, Frances..." she exclaimed, fumbling in the pocket of her jeans, "you get a signal right out here in the sticks...?"

"I wouldn't know." Frances shook her head. "For I have only the old kind with wires."

Patricia found her phone and clamped it to her ear.

"Is that you, Pat...?"

She recognised the voice; her heart sank.

"Peter...?"

"It is I..." he told her. "Are you there...?"

"Yes, I'm just surprised..."

"Understandably. Are you alone...?"

"No...why?"

"Might be better if you were. Can you find somewhere...?"

Frances and Colm regarded her with quizzical expressions. Colm silently mouthed 'work?'; she nodded and turned for the door.

"I'm outside now. Alone..." she added as she ducked out into the sunshine. "Has something happened...?"

"I'm aware you're away..." he said as if she had no right to be. "But it's that Olaf chap..."

"What is...?"

"Your friend from the abbey…what's his name?"

"Thomas. Father Thomas…"

"He called the hospital…"

"Why, what's going on?"

"It's all right. Nothing's happened…"

"Something has or you wouldn't be…"

"Nothing to get agitated about."

"Really…?"

"Yes, really."

"Thank God for that…"

Taking a deep breath she set off along the path, pausing beside the chicken run to slip her fingers through the wire netting.

"Your friend rang because Olaf's asked if he can go away for a couple of nights. He didn't want to bother you but he wanted to check with someone to see if it was okay…"

"A couple of nights?" she repeated, frowning. "I'm not sure…"

"You don't have to be. They gave me a hot line number to the Home Office, in case anything came up…"

"I didn't know that…"

"I rang and got a call back pretty quick from some security fellow, presumably. Anyway, he knew all about Olaf' and his plans…"

"How could he possibly know…?"

"I did not enquire."

"God, do you think they've bugged Father Thomas's phone?" she asked. "Or yours…"

"Quite possibly…"

Did that mean the phone in her hand was too? Had strangers in a secret listening post been intercepting all her calls for days? She felt angry and violated.

"Pat…?

"Olaf is my patient, Peter," she reminded him. "I have clinical responsibility…"

"Which is why I'm calling you."

"So what else did they say?"

"We're to let him go."

"Are we…?"

"Apparently they suspected he'd do something like this. So he can contact…whoever he's supposed to contact. When he leaves the abbey they'll keep him under surveillance and see what he does."

"And if it's all perfectly innocent?"

"Then presumably he gets a clean bill of health. To be honest, I have no idea. They didn't tell me, and after all, he's their problem. Anyway, I want you in the picture, just in case Thomas decides to talk to you after all…"

"Do we know where Olaf's proposing to go?"

"Glastonbury, apparently."

"Really…?"

"I thought you only went there if you wanted to stagger round knee-deep in mud getting deafened by pop music, or you're some marijuana smoking hippie in search of King Arthur's tomb…"

"Do you realise someone might be listening in to us, right now?" she asked.

There was a moment's silence. When Peter Wingfield spoke again the tone was no longer casual or playful.

"Yes, well…that's it, I think," he said. "I'm sorry to disturb you like this, but…"

"No problem," she told him. "You had to, obviously…"

"Good. And…you're back Monday evening, right?"

"Right…"

"Well, if nothing crops up beforehand, we'll speak on Tuesday…"

He had ended the call before she could reply. She switched off her phone, pocketed it and glanced skyward. Clouds were gathering and she felt a sharpness to the air. The mountain, away on the horizon, was as massive and reassuring a presence as ever, while beside her Frances's precious hens continued to scratch, peck and cluck, without a care in the world. She stared at them for a few moments, envying their carefree existence. Ducking through the door into the cottage, she looked enquiringly at Colm.

"Sorry about that," she told him. "It was work, yes. Now, where were we...?"

"Do you not recall?" Frances shook her head. "Your son was giving you a geography lesson."

"About...?"

"Scafell," Colm told her.

"Ah, right..." Patricia nodded. "Which is a bit weird..."

"What's weird about a mountain?" He frowned.

"I didn't mean that, pet." Patricia shook her head, "but just as you mentioned it, my mobile rang. With a message about one of my patients who just happens to be off to that very place in a few days' time."

"Hey!" Colm grinned. "Spooky, or what?"

Frances smiled. "Then he'd be going for the solstice, would he not?"

"Yes, but we're getting off the subject again. Now, Frances, you're saying we'd have to go to Ben Bulben to do this..." She waved a hand, "this tree thing..."

"Exactly..."

"And you're absolutely sure nowhere else would do. Is that right?"

"All I am doing." The old lady spread her hands, "is passing on to you what I myself was told."

"Told...?" echoed Patricia cocking her head.

"You medical folk are awful hard of understanding sometimes, isn't that the truth, now...?" Frances appealed to Colm with a shake of her head. "That was the word I used – told. Now you would probably have some fancy psychiatrist's name for it pet, but simple folk like me would call it instinct or intuition, or maybe just a good old-fashioned feeling in my bones…"

"You did say told," Colm reminded her, gently.

"I did and I was." Frances eased herself down into an armchair. "Not in the selfsame manner you might tell me something, for goodness sake. But back there by the stream, you see, something spoke to me. And I heard it clear as a bell." She peered over her glasses at each of them in turn. "But now it's up to you. The pair of you must do as you see fit."

"That something didn't explain why it's so important we slog all the way to Sligo, I suppose…?" enquired Patricia.

"You suppose right. It did not." Frances smiled.

"Or what will happen if we do?" Patricia paused. "Or don't, for that matter?"

"Aren't you after wanting everything neat and tidy, cut and dried, the i's dotted and the t's crossed?" Frances shook her head. "You would think we were talking about some dry old lawyer's contract. But we are not…"

"Which is the problem." Patricia sighed, perching on the arm of the other chair. "I'm not at all sure what we are talking about."

"Then, let me tell you what I think," offered Frances. "If you ask my opinion, 'tis not by chance that the Medusa dream keeps returning to your man. It has something to tell him."

"You think it's got like, a message, then?" asked Colm.

"I do indeed. And once you have heard and heeded it, why, the dream will go away, for its work is done."

Colm and Patricia exchanged glances.

"Go away, really?" he asked. "Just like that?"

"Now, I don't pretend I can explain it because I'm not that clever. But the simple things I do understand. The first of them being, you chose to speak of it within sight of the blessed mountain. I do not believe it was by accident or happenstance you should do so."

"Okay." Patricia folded her arms. "Let's say you're right so far..."

Frances nodded but her eyes were fixed on Colm.

"You have a terror of snakes, yet in your dream, who should appear but the Gorgon herself, with heaven knows how many of the things wriggling and writhing about her..."

Colm nodded reluctant assent.

"It's no mystery what you're wanting, pet. That is, to stop your woman from waltzing in, scaring the bejazus out of you and ruining your beauty sleep. Am I not right?"

Colm edged to Patricia's side and nodded again. "You couldn't be righter..."

"Then would it not be the most natural thing in the world that the person whose help you should seek would be the very one who mastered those same creatures and sent them packing from these shores for ever?"

"Which is a nice story, Frances," Patricia pointed out, "but when it comes down to it, that's all it is. One of those old folk-tales we like telling our children..."

"Maybe so, and maybe not."

If her grand-daughter's scepticism troubled her, the old lady gave no sign.

"So what we'd be doing is, like, asking Saint Patrick to help get rid of my snakes," Colm offered with a glance at his mother. "How cool is that?"

Her son's eyes might be shining at the prospect, but Patricia had yet to resign herself to hours behind the wheel of the hire car.

"Getting a major saint on your team sounds like a good move. But..." She gestured at the door, "when we've got his personal mountain practically on Fran's doorstep, I'd still like to know why on earth we can't do whatever needs doing right here."

"But Gran Fran said, Mum," Colm insisted, "that isn't the actual place he did the...whatever he did. Is it?" he appealed to Frances.

"You're right, pet, but now you're like your ma, getting

altogether too literal and logical," Frances told him. "If you do as I tell you, it will be because you trust in the mystical and magical – in things you do not understand." She spread her hands. "I cannot tell you why you'd be guided to the mountain that bears your own name and not his. Neither can I explain why you should ask for help from the spirits of that place, or honour a yew tree and not some other. I have a notion why the deed is best done this day of all days, but it is not important. All I can tell you…" Placing both hands on her chest, she met Colm's eyes and held them, "is that I firmly believe in this old heart of mine, the act holds a healing for you…"

"Is that what you'd call it?" Patricia frowned.

"And why wouldn't I? Sure your snake is a scary creature but it's more than that, is it not? It is an ancient symbol of healing, which you should not need me to remind you, Patricia O'Leary, you being a medical person yourself." Frances shook her head, reproachfully. "What about that staff with its serpents?"

"Well, yes…" Patricia shrugged grudging assent. "I suppose."

"I didn't really understand that bit about helping spirits…" Colm told her.

"No, no. 'Tis you seeking their help, pet. But don't fret about that, for won't I be instructing you how to ask them for what you need?"

"Cool…"

Patricia sighed. Frances was right; the only way to make a decision was probably to ignore reason and logic, and trust her instincts. She glanced at Colm's eager expression, then the patient smile on Frances's wrinkled face.

"Okay." She sighed. "Let's do it."

"Seriously, Mum?"

"You'd better be quick," she told him. "Don't give me time to think about it…"

"Brill…"

Patricia found herself folded tightly in Colm's arms. "Come

on, then!"

"A little patience, if you please." Frances rose to her feet and bustled into the kitchen. "You asked how you should call on the powers at Ben Bulben to aid you. I shall jot a few words down for you. Speak them out loud just before you tie your cord on the tree." She turned to Colm. "You have it safe, I hope?"

He tugged it from the pocket of his jeans, earning a nod of approval.

"On that sideboard you will find an old jar and in it some pencils, pet. Bring me one sharp enough for serious writing. While I am doing that," she told Patricia, "you'll find a fresh loaf in the crock and tomatoes on the side. You'll need sustenance for your travels."

"Your pencils are blunt, Gran Fran," Colm groaned.

"I've a good knife here. Put a point on one for me," she told him, stretching up for a pad of paper dangling from a nail driven into a beam above the sink. "These are for my shopping lists," she said, "but they'll be grand for a message to the spirits..."

"How do you know about all this stuff, Gran Fran?"

"And what stuff would that be?"

"You know." He shrugged. "What you've been talking about. Mountains and holy places, and writing to spirits..."

"Sure am I not an Irish woman?" she asked, eyes twinkling. "Wouldn't it be in my blood, now?"

Colm handed her the pencil and glanced across at Patricia, busy slicing tomatoes and buttering squares of sweet-smelling, brown soda bread.

"So's Mum," he pointed out, "but it doesn't seem like it's in hers."

"There are those who are offered the gift and accept it," the old lady told him solemnly, "and those who are offered the gift, and do not."

Watching them exchange glances he frowned.

"What do you mean...?"

"One day your mother may tell you..." She pulled up a wooden chair, sat down at the small square of pine that served as a kitchen table and pursed her lips. "...Or, of course, she may not. Now, Ben Bulben...let me see..."

Patricia licked butter from her fingers and looked up from a growing pile of sandwiches. "You'll find an empty water bottle in the car, pet. Would you fill it up? And while you're out there give the windscreen a wipe."

"It's not locked, is it?"

"Heavens, no." She brushed the hair from her eyes. "Why on earth would I do that...?"

Patricia waited until she heard the clatter of the gate, followed by the sound of Colm opening the car door.

"He's really excited about this, Fran. I hope he's not going to be disappointed."

Frances looked up. "He will be rewarded for his courage. No need to go fussing over him now. That young fellow will be grand, mark my words."

"He trusts you."

"He is learning to face his fears. He is learning to trust others, and most important of all, himself." She resumed writing in large, spidery script. "How can anything but good come of it, will you tell me that...?"

Patricia piled the sandwiches onto a plate and covered them with a tea-towel. "What was that about my refusing a gift?"

"As a child, you were drawn to the wisdom," replied Frances, her hand moving purposefully across the paper.

Patricia frowned. She was uncertain what Frances meant, recalling only that at some point, sensing conflict between the teachings of Father Coyle and her grandmother's fanciful tales, she had made a choice. "I'm not sure about that..."

"Twas plain to see and no surprise, for you always had a fine mind." She glanced up to meet Patricia's eyes. "But the wisdom never goes away. 'Tis always waiting to reveal itself when we are

225

ready for it."

"Do you have foil or cling film for these...?"

"I do not countenance such things in my kitchen," Frances told her. "In the drawer in front of you, you'll find good old-fashioned grease-proof paper."

"The wisdom is all very well," Patricia pointed out, "but I enjoy my work and I'm proud of what I do..."

"I have no doubt that is true." Frances put down the pencil, "but who knows what wonderful things might happen, if you were to weave a little magic into that fine medical work?"

"You'd be surprised at some of the things I'm doing already."

"Would I, now?" Taking off her glasses she polished them on the hem of her dress. "Go ahead, surprise your gran, pet."

"Well, I belong to a group discussing how to introduce greater spiritual awareness into psychiatry."

"Greater spiritual awareness, indeed!" Frances, wide-eyed, nodded approval. "Well, now, that would be a grand thing, and no mistake."

"Most psychiatrists think talking like that means you're certifiable."

Colm burst into the room like a whirlwind, flourishing an empty plastic bottle. "Done. Windscreen and windows. Can we go now?"

"When you've filled that with water and thanked Frances for the tea, the sandwiches, the walk, and..." She sighed, "sending us to Sligo."

Folding the note, Frances proffered it to Colm. "Put this somewhere safe, now. Once you find your yew, before you attach the cord, read it. Out loud, mind. Do you hear what I'm saying, pet?"

"Defo..." Colm, busy at the tap, glanced over his shoulder and nodded.

"You are asking the universe to aid you in your work, which must be done with proper respect. And," she added, "there is one thing more."

"Which is?"

"Keep an eye out for eagles," she instructed, waving a finger at him.

"You can if you like," Patricia told him with a shake of her head, "but you won't see many of them, I promise you."

"Okay," he told Frances, throwing his arms round her. "I'll let you know how it goes."

"I should hope so…"

"I bet anything it works. That'll be awesome…"

"Indeed it will," Frances assented as Patricia embraced her, "and before you're away, I will tell you one last thing. Do you know what day this is?"

Colm, puzzled, shook his head. "Sunday?"

"But not just any Sunday!" She grasped his arm and smiled up at him. "'Tis the seventh Sunday after Easter. Whit Sunday, the festival of Pentecost, when the Holy Spirit himself descended upon the disciples of Jesus. And how did he do so? Why, in the form of a dove. A white dove. Do you understand what I'm telling you?"

"Wow!" He hugged her again. "Yeah. I do…"

Ψ

Dark clouds were gathering like mourners at a funeral; driven from the west by a relentless, blustery wind. Sweeping across the Atlantic wastes, they carried imminent threat of a storm. In her early years, Patricia came to know sea and sky intimately; their moods and habits, colours, sounds and even smells. A sixth sense told her it would not be long before squalls came rolling in to deliver heavy downpours. She heaved a sigh; setting off on a wild goose chase was bad enough without the prospect of tramping the Sligo heights drenched by driving rain. The shower proof jackets she had packed would offer scant protection against conditions like that.

"We'd better find a garage and get a map," she announced as the engine purred smoothly into life. "I only know the first bit of the way..."

"It's okay, the hire people gave us one," he said, reaching into the glove locker. Finding what he sought he unfolded and spread it across the steering wheel.

"Right. If I show you where we're going, are you up for navigating?"

"No prob."

She traced their route with a fingertip. "We take the N17 through Ballyvary and Swinford, as far as Westport, then the N4 for Sligo. After that we should be able to see it – it's big enough."

"Doesn't look that far to me," Colm told her.

"Maybe it's not as bad as I thought," she conceded, "but Irish roads aren't exactly the M25, pet."

"You're not kidding..." Colm grinned, pointing.

Rounding a bend, they found their progress halted by a dozen or so sheep meandering aimlessly along the middle of the narrow road. A sharp blast on the Audi's horn sent them skittering into a field of gorse and thistles.

Reaching Thornhill ten minutes later they swung onto Cockle Strand, where a scattering of whitewashed bungalows with dove-grey slate roofs huddled beneath the meagre shelter of wind-sculpted trees. Patricia bit her lip; even if Frances was right and this would banish the night-terrors, she still felt guilty spending time away from her mother. It was some relief to see her sister's people-carrier parked outside the gate. She put a hand on Colm's knee.

"Go in and tell your gran I'm taking you on a little trip. Don't try explaining – it'd take too long. Just say it's important. Oh and tell Aunt Sinead we'll be back by teatime. Okay?"

He unclipped his seat belt. "That it?"

"No. Looks like it could bucket down. Grab those jackets I

brought and ask gran if we can borrow an umbrella, otherwise we're going to wind up looking like a couple of drowned rats."

She had barely brought the car to a halt before he was out and away, effortlessly vaulting her mother's low stone wall and loping to the front door. Patricia waited, fingers drumming on the wheel, pondering how she was going to explain their mission to the family when they got back. She was still undecided when Colm reappeared with an armful of clothes and an elderly umbrella.

"I told her it was Gran Fran's idea and she was totally cool with it. Just said try not to be late for tea," he announced, closing the door. "Okay, pedal to the metal..."

"Where did that come from...?"

"Dunno." He grinned. "Some old sixties movie..."

Patricia had traversed the coast road to Westport countless times, in a variety of cars, aboard school and country buses, pedalling ancient bicycles and even on foot. Sunday traffic was mercifully sparse and she was now sufficiently accustomed to the car to maintain a brisk pace.

The first few miles took them through flat countryside, offering occasional glimpses of the broad expanse of cold, grey ocean, away to the north. As so often in the prelude to a storm, it had taken on the appearance of a sheet of gleaming steel.

Carrowkeeran, Killadangan and Streamstown passed in a blur. A wide avenue, lined with neat houses painted assorted pastel shades, led them through the heart of Westport where the town clock, set in its odd, bulbous little tower, told them it was twenty to one.

"Fifteen minutes..." Colm nodded his approval. "You're doing great. Follow the signs for the N5."

Patricia looked across at him. "How are you feeling, mister? It's been a bit of a strange day one way and another, hasn't it?"

"I'm good..." He shrugged.

"Even talking about the bad stuff...? It didn't look like that was too comfortable."

"Well, no, I guess not. Glad I did, though."

"What, so she could send us flying off like this? On a completely daft trip to a magic mountain where we're supposed to find one particular tree and lasso it...?" She laughed. "On top of which it looks like we'll be doing it in a force nine gale..."

"You think Gran Fran's dotty, don't you?"

She found it hard to suppress a smile at the delight behind his accusation.

"I mean, it's pretty obvious," he went on, "the way you, like, look at her sometimes..."

"And what times would those be?" she demanded feigning indignation.

"You know. When she starts on about white doves and magic...and that guy she says can be in two places at once..."

There had been times over the last few months when she had almost given up hope of seeing him bright-eyed and vibrant again. She reached out to touch his arm and he took her hand and squeezed it. It was all worthwhile, whatever the outcome; driving any distance and being soaked into the bargain was a small price to pay for this moment.

"If they marched your great-grandmother into my consulting room and she told me she believed in all those things," Patricia told him, "she'd probably wind up in the top security wing..."

His brow furrowed. "You're kidding..."

"As a matter of fact, I am..." she admitted, tightening her grip on his hand. "It so happens I've got a patient right now who reminds me a bit of Fran. And if I had my way, I'd probably discharge him..."

"So you don't really think she's a nut case?"

"I know psychiatrists – including my boss – who seem to think they have a hotline to the truth," she told him, "but I don't. When you think about it, everyone's on a line somewhere between sane and insane. The important question is, when does it start to matter?"

"But you must have some idea about her..."

Patricia paused and took a deep breath. "When you were tiny and we were living in London, I still remember one time, pushing you along in your pram and seeing a lady in a bus shelter. A nice, well dressed, pretty ordinary looking, middle-aged lady. The only thing was, she happened to be chatting away to someone I couldn't see." Patricia paused. "And I remember wondering, is one of us mad? And if so is it her because she's talking to someone I can't see, or me because I can't see them?"

Colm nodded slowly. "I don't really understand everything she talks about," he admitted, "but I can't see anything bad about it. I mean, that lady wasn't hurting anyone and neither does Gran Fran."

"The same goes for my client. I think you're right," she agreed, "and Fran's genuinely trying to help. She wouldn't have come up with something like this unless she truly, honestly believed it'll work..."

"I think it will. Maybe it already has," he corrected himself. "I mean, I actually feel pretty good now..."

"In that case can we just go home...?" She turned a pleading gaze his way. "Pretty please?"

"No way..." he told her, wide-eyed. "She'd never forgive me..."

"Either of us..."

They were approaching the glittering façade of the Glasshouse Hotel, perched incongruously in the centre of old Sligo town like some marooned alien spaceship. The first drops of rain began pattering across the Audi's roof like a herd of frightened cats. The sky had become so dark she had switched on sidelights fifteen minutes earlier; now, with a grimace, Patricia did the same with the wipers.

"Are we nearly there...?"

"We should see Ben Bulben once we're through town," she

told him. "After that it's probably no more than ten, maybe fifteen minutes."

"Brilliant!" He looked at his watch. "One hour fifty. Hey, that's not bad, you know…?"

She gave a regal wave of acknowledgement. "Move over, Lewis Hamilton…"

As they reached the outskirts of Sligo the silhouette of Ben Bulben appeared against the horizon, massive and angular, towering over the landscape like an immense, sheer-walled fortress. Propelled by gusting winds, silver backed, grey storm clouds already shrouded the summit, and the rain showed no sign of abating.

"There you are," Patricia nodded at the mountain. "That's what we've come all this way for…"

"Awesome…"

They were startled by a flash of lightning followed by a rumble of thunder like a train crossing a distant iron bridge. Abruptly they found themselves in a long procession of vehicles, crawling through the downpour at little more than walking pace, tail lights painting blood-red slashes across tarmac slick with rain.

"Maybe there's an accident…"

"Funeral, more likely." Patricia sighed. "When we were doing so well…"

"Couldn't you just, like, overtake…?"

"A funeral?" Patricia shook her head. "Not in Ireland. It'll clear…"

She broke off, catching sight of a pair of diminutive, bedraggled figures at the roadside waving their thumbs. Huddled together against the deluge, their only protection was a tattered length of material held over their heads. She braked and pulled over onto the muddy grass verge beside them.

"Let them in…"

Colm already had the back door open and two bare-footed

girls wrapped in soaking, mud-spattered white dresses tumbled onto the back seat. No more than seven or eight, tousled fair hair plastered to their heads, they had identical sets of clear, flax blue eyes.

"Thanks, missus," said the taller one as her companion seized her hand. "Would yous ever take us home...?"

"Where do you live, pet?"

The car behind flashed its lights and Patricia resumed her place in the queue of crawling traffic.

"It's only Collinsford. Please, missus...please?" she pleaded, eyes wide. "The littl'un's terrible frighted with the lightnin', so she is..."

"I's not!" came an indignant retort.

"Are so, Roisin," she insisted with a warning glance. "And we'd get awful wet walking that far..." The smaller girl whispered behind her hand and she added. "Us'd catch terrible colds..."

"I don't know where Collinsford is," Patricia told her, "but we're heading for Ben Bulben. Is it anywhere near there...?"

"The oul' mountain? Tis right near us's place..." Her enthusiastic nod sent a fine spray of water over Colm, who had craned round to smile at them.

"Yous can get there real easy. We can tell yous the way, can't we, Roisin...?"

"Are you sisters...?" enquired Colm.

"I'm Niamh she's Roisin. She's only six. Everyone calls her Rosie..."

Roisin set about picking her nose but a hiss from her sibling sent her hand to her lap. Glancing in the mirror, Patricia saw Niamh was wearing a single, crumpled wing fashioned from gold painted cardboard.

"There, missus. Up there..."

She pointed urgently to a small turning on their right.

"Any idea how far it is...?"

"Through Drum East and Cloonderry," Niamh told her.

"Have a look on the map, see if you can find them," Patricia instructed Colm. "So, looks like you girls have been to a party, then..."

"We's been to a grand party, we has..." giggled Roisin.

The side road proved to be uneven and narrow, barely more than a single lane in places, tall trees on both sides making poor visibility worse. Driving as fast as she dared, Patricia prayed they encountered nothing bigger than a bicycle coming in the opposite direction. The detour was the last thing she would have chosen but leaving the sisters stranded in the rain was never an option. In the distance, forked lightning flashed earthwards like a silver rapier, followed by another rumble of thunder.

Colm switched on the interior light and peered at the map. "What were those places...?"

"Drum East and..."

"Cloonderry," Niamh told her. "And they's real places, I'm not making them up..."

"I'm sure you're not..."

"Don't see them. Maybe too small..." opined Colm.

"Us knows the way," Niamh insisted. "Yer getting there, missus..."

"Was it a fancy dress party...?" Patricia enquired.

"Rosie don't have wings but we's both angels," Niamh replied. "Proper angels, like the Jesus ones."

"Angels...?" said Colm. "Cool..."

His words brought a burst of giggles from the sisters.

Emerging from the gloom beneath overhanging trees, they found themselves at a T-junction. Coming to a halt, Patricia lowered her window and peered through the rain at a signpost on the far side of the crossing, but Niamh was already fumbling with the door handle.

"Here, missus, here..." she piped. "This'll do us grand..."

The next moment they were out of the car and half way across the road, leaving the door gaping. Hand in hand, pale feet barely seeming to touch the ground, they fluttered through wind and rain like a pair of butterflies. As her remaining wing threatened to fly off by itself Niamh grabbed at it with her free hand.

"'Bye, angels…" Patricia called after them.

Dancing across the puddles, they released each other's hands long enough to scale a sagging wooden gate beside the road sign. Patricia caught a last glimpse of them skipping along a path through waist high bracken. Colm got out, closed the door and flopped back into his seat shaking the rain from his hair like a wet puppy.

"Well, they somehow got us here," she told him, pointing. "That's our mountain…"

On the far side of the gate the ground rose until it merged into the lower slopes of Ben Bulben.

"This should take us back towards the main road," Patricia said, nodding to the left. "If we've detoured past that funeral, which I guess is possible, our angels might just have done us a good turn…"

"If we're so close, why don't we look for a tree now…?"

"Why not indeed…" Patricia nodded. "We're not going to find many up there, that's for sure."

Low and dense, the storm clouds were scudding ever eastwards. Away to the west, over the distant ocean, the sky had taken on a pale, luminous quality. It might be passing through but the storm, Patricia knew, had not done with them yet. Gusts shook the car, driving the rain against roof and windscreen in an intermittent tattoo. To her relief the rumbles of thunder were less frequent so the storm must be moving away; regardless of Fran's instructions she was not letting Colm out among trees while there was risk of lightning.

The weather might be showing signs of improvement, but they had yet to locate a suitable yew. They were commonplace in graveyards, she knew, but they had not laid eyes on a church since leaving Sligo. In truth, they had come across few enough buildings of any description, with the exception of an occasional isolated cottage or farmhouse.

"We'd better stop and ask at the next place we see," she told Colm, "or we could wind up driving around all day…"

"We won't, don't worry," he told her with a grin. "It'll be okay, I know it will…"

Envying his confidence, she was having pangs of guilt. Even in perfect conditions their search would have been far from straightforward and here they were battling poor visibility, high winds and driving rain. Had she been too hasty, reckless even; should she have thought the whole thing through? If they were thwarted at the last gasp, what might be the effect on Colm?

"Wow, Mum, why don't we ask in that place? Looks like a movie set…" He had spotted a building set well back from the road and separated from it by a wide expanse of garden behind a waist-high dry-stone wall. Patricia brought the Audi to a halt beside a pair of ornate wrought iron gates.

"Quite a place, isn't it?" She nodded. Running her gaze over towers, turrets, narrow, arched windows and crenellated walls, Patricia was reminded of fairy tale castles in the story books she adored as a child. Indeed, she thought, if a knight in shining chain mail and plumed helmet had trotted into view on the back of a white stallion at that moment, he would have looked less incongruous than the Range Rover by the entrance. A bricked drive led from the gates to a massive, arched entrance, winding through manicured lawns and passing beneath stands of tall trees swaying in the storm like drunken dancers.

Colm glanced at her. "Are we going to ask…?"

"No need…" Patricia shook her head.

"How come?"

"See those first trees on the left?"

"Yeah…"

"Yews."

"Are they...?"

"Either one will do..."

"Are you sure?" He shot her an anxious glance. "They're kind of hard to see..."

She gave a wry shake of the head. "Trust your mother, child."

"We did it..." Colm pumped his fist, then his look of triumph faded. "But it's someone's garden, Mum. I can't just barge in and..."

"You'll be in and out before they know you've been," she pointed out. "And who's coming out to argue about it in this weather, may I ask? They are perfect – practically in the shadow of the mountain." As she spoke, a faint roll of thunder echoed. "Sounds like Ben Bulben agrees..."

"Wait 'til I tell Gran Fran..."

"You haven't done anything to tell her about yet..." She laughed.

"Hang on. Got to read that thing of hers first." He searched through his pockets. "Out loud, before I tie the cord, remember?"

"I do indeed."

He unfolded the crumpled paper and smoothed it across his thigh.

"Hail O Holy Earth

Hail Ben Bulben, Binn Ghulbain, Sacred Mountain

Hail O fire in the earth and fire in the clouds

Hail to the spirits in the sky

Hail to the Mountain spirits

Hail to the Yew spirits

Hail to all creatures on land, sea and air

Hail to the guardians of the land

Hear me, Bless me, Guide me, Heal me."

"Great," she told him. "That should do the trick. Put something on or you'll get absolutely..."

Her words were too late; he was out of the car, shoulders hunched against the rain. He pushed through the gates and ran off along the drive, water splashing knee high with each long stride. Patricia stiffened, hand rising to her mouth. She could not escape the sense this might be a special moment, one they would both remember.

Colm reached the trees, looked from one to the other, and made his choice. He tried again and again to throw the cord over a low branch, only for the wind to blow it back into his face, thwarting his efforts. He looked back at the car and spread his arms in a gesture of frustration, then looped the cord round the trunk, drew it tight and knotted it several times. Pausing for a moment to rest a hand against its rough bark, he patted the tree before heading back. She pushed the door wide and he dropped into his seat beaming, face glistening with raindrops.

"Did you see…?"

"I did. Good work…"

"Do you think it'll be okay…?"

"I'm sure it will, darling."

As she slipped the car into gear, he tugged at her arm.

"Mum, stop. Hang on a sec…"

She thought he had seen someone emerging from the house but a glance showed it was not so.

"What is it…?"

"Didn't you see…?"

"See what…?"

"The name, look…" He pressed a button and sent his window sliding down. "There, can you see it now…?"

It took a moment for her to realise what had excited him. The name of the house had been carefully scripted into the wrought ironwork of the gates. In graceful lettering, set into an oval panel on each gate, it read: *AIGLI MANOR.*

"See?" He laughed. "She was right…"

"So she was…"

"There it is…" he exclaimed triumphantly. "Our eagle…"

A brilliant, jagged bolt of lightning momentarily etched the majestic silhouette of Ben Bulben against the bank of dark clouds on the mountain's far north easterly side.

Chapter 11

Return to the Wild

Tuesday 14th June 2011

Cradling a mug of freshly brewed coffee in both hands, Patricia strolled barefooted across the uneven flagstones of the small kitchen patio and onto the lawn. The sensation of dew-damp grass beneath her soles was one of her early morning indulgences at this time of year. She sauntered along the flowerbeds, breathing in the fragrance of roses and gazing in awe at the exquisite delicacy of spiders' webs strung between the stalks of tiny, blue forget-me-nots.

"Hiya..."

Startled, she glanced up to see Colm in frayed, cut-off, jean shorts, rubbing his scalp and yawning. He had inherited Liam's physique; broad shoulders, narrow hips, long limbs.

"Don't expect to see you up at this hour. Are you sleeping okay?"

"Great, why...?"

"Just wondered..."

"Can I ask you something?"

"You may ask me anything you like..."

He moved to her side and she slipped an arm round his shoulders.

"But just so I can prepare myself," she added, "I'd like to know in advance. Will it cost me sleepless nights or a lot of money?"

"Believe it or not, Mother dear..." he told her, "neither."

"Seriously?" she affected surprise. "Grand, ask away then."

"Can I go to a party...?"

"When?"

"Er...tonight."

Patricia pursed her lips. "Midweek? I thought we had an agreement, mister. Revision weekdays, weekends off."

"I did loads of revision last night. And I have all day today don't I?" He flashed her a winning smile. "I'm on top of it, honestly. And everyone's going. Like, everyone."

"You're telling me all the other mums and dads have said yes, in the middle of exams...?"

"Mum, it's a full moon party," he told her as if it must clinch his case. "It's going to be so cool."

"Chances are pretty good there'll be another full moon in roughly four weeks," she reminded him, "by which time exams will be over."

"Yeah, but..." He took a deep breath, "Sophie van Moppes asked me if I wanted to go. There'll be a whole bunch of her friends."

"The pretty Dutch girl?"

"It's in the big field just down the lane from their house. She's got to be back by one so it's not going to be, like, all night..."

He studied her face carefully before playing his trump card. "Her mum said I can sleep over, so you wouldn't even have to come and get me, would you?"

Patricia took a leisurely sip of coffee. She had always thought him self-conscious round girls but maybe that had changed without her noticing. Sophie seemed sparky and vivacious; little wonder he was keen to go. That sleep over would be a real bonus; she could stay the night in Canterbury rather than make the long drive back after her meeting.

Putting her face inches from his she stared into his eyes and addressed him in a tone of mock severity. "At one sharp your carriage turns into a pumpkin..."

Brow furrowed, he shook his head. "What...?"

"Let me put it another way. One o'clock latest. Promise?"

"Promise."

"Deal."

"Yay…" He enveloped her in a bear hug before loping off towards the kitchen, leaving a trail of glistening footprints in his wake. "I'm going to call Soph…"

"Don't forget to thank her mum…!" she called, well aware that even if he had heard her he would probably forget.

Ψ

Despite her pleasure at the exchange with her son, Patricia found the short drive to the hospital irksome. During the brief period spent at the wheel of the hire car she had developed an unexpected taste for comfort and speed; returning to the venerable Volvo was like trading a thoroughbred for a cart-horse. She felt uneasy at the prospect of a meeting with the medical director, and his first words did nothing to make her feel better.

"Looks like the bloody Chloe girl's gone back to the loonies…"

He glowered as if he held her personally responsible.

"When was that…?"

"Her father rang me first thing this morning. Hopping mad. Wants to know why we discharged her…"

"She was self-referred, Peter…"

"You said you were going to make sure she…"

"I thought I had. I mean, I talked to her, made all the points you and I discussed and as far as I could tell she was fine with it. We'd already agreed she'd go off and do whatever she had arranged over the weekend, then she was going to come back…"

"Well now she isn't…"

"She's said so…?"

"She hasn't said anything. Not to us, anyway. According to her father, when she left here she went off to Wales. Spun him some half-baked nonsense about hunting dragons, which, of course, made him wonder what was going on. Anyway, he's pretty sure she was going on to the West Country..."

"Did he say where...?"

"Not as far as I know. He called her a couple of hours ago but she said she couldn't talk to him. When he pushed her she admitted she was at loony HQ. What do they call it...?"

"Cosmic Central, or something...?"

"Something grandiose. Promised she'd call him back, but never did. Now he can't get a reply from her mobile or home phone." Wingfield shrugged. "He's put two and two together...and I have a nasty feeling he might be right."

"Yes..." She nodded. "It's a possibility, I suppose. And he's blaming us, is he?"

"I got him to see sense in the end but he obviously holds us at least partly responsible."

"What did he expect us to do, for heaven's sake?"

Peter Wingfield looked at her mutely for a few moments and shrugged. "Section her, I guess. That's what he'd like now..."

"On what grounds...?" She drew down the corners of her mouth. "People run round with the idea we can section anybody we like at the drop of a hat..."

"Despite no indication of psychosis, no hallucinations and no risk..."

"She does have a history..." Patricia pointed out. "Attempted suicide?"

"Originally he was coy about that. Less so now, I gathered."

"Selective memory hasn't he...?"

"So it would seem..."

"How did you leave it with Sir Giles, then?" she enquired.

"I said even if he manages to persuade her to come back – the chances of which are practically nil – we could only act based on how she presents." He pursed his lips. "And unless she's a hell of a lot worse than she was, sectioning was out of the question."

"Did he accept that?"

"He didn't like it. He dropped a couple of none-too-subtle hints, if we don't cooperate he can make life uncomfortable. No wonder that young woman has problems with dearest Daddy..."

"That's all we need..." Patricia shook her head. "Treat her and we've got the *Order* gunning for us. Don't treat her and he's on our case..."

"On our case and a man with no little influence..." Wingfield picked up his letter opener and peered at it, avoiding her eyes. "Damned if you do, damned if you don't. I'm afraid they've got you between a rock and a hard place."

She glanced at him; his observation told her all she needed to know about how much support she could expect from her medical director and the USCARE Corporation of Los Angeles, California, if things turned sour.

"Me, did you say...?"

"You accepted clinical responsibility for her, Pat. Now," he went on, briskly, "I'd better bring you up to speed on Bardarson..."

"I'm seeing him when we've finished..."

"Okay..." He picked up a note pad and peered at it. "According to the information I've just been given, he did exactly what he said he was going to do. Went down to Glastonbury, got there late, slept rough on Sunday night. But had a busy day yesterday..."

"How so...?"

"Having wandered round town seeing the sights he had his palm read, would you believe? Must have got on well with the gypsy lady – he spent the rest of the day with her. She must live round here because she dropped him off at the abbey late last night..."

"Well, well..." Patricia smiled.

"He made no contact with anyone else. The security people checked her out as you would expect..."

"And..."

"Nothing of interest to them. As a result they've classified him zero risk..."

"Can we return him to the wild...?"

"Indeed, which is presumably what you had in mind..."

She nodded. "He'll be a very happy bunny...There is one thing, though..."

"That being...?"

"They didn't tell you the name of the gypsy, so-called?"

"No." He frowned. "Why would they...?"

"Would you believe Chloe Spenser-Nelson?"

"You're not serious...?"

"Perfectly."

"Good Lord..." The medical director leaned back, shaking his head.

"I had a feeling there might something going on with those two. He had a rendezvous with her here he was extremely keen to keep but I'd forgotten she was heading down Glastonbury way until much later..."

Wingfield cupped his head in his hands. "Interesting..." he murmured. "What do you think – about Bardarson and the girl?"

"He went to a lot of trouble to see her – assuming that was his sole reason for going. And if they spent the day together and she brought him back..." Patricia shrugged. "Think about it. Attractive young woman with history of instability suffers emotionally traumatic episode, becomes mildly paranoid. Meets charming, good-looking young man with attachment issues, manic tendencies..." She spread her hands and smiled "A match made in psychiatric heaven."

Wingfield nodded. "Or hell..." he observed with the pained expression of a man whose martini is far too dry.

Getting to his feet, he clasped his hands behind him, paced slowly to the window and gazed out for a few moments without speaking. When he turned back he had donned a faint smile. "It would offer interesting possibilities, would it not?"

"Like...?"

"Let us assume for a moment they have indeed embarked on a liaison."

"Even if that would be slightly jumping the gun?"

"Even so..." The medical director was not to be deflected. "Bardarson might be in a position to exert...let's call it a degree of influence over her. In other words, she might be more ready to listen to him regarding the risks of surrendering herself to the tender mercies of the *Order* again than she would be to me or you..."

"But even if that were true..."

"Bear with me. And assume also they were trying to get her to support some kind of charge against us...or more specifically you." He spread his hands. "He might be in a position to persuade her to..."

"Peter, the whole scenario is completely hypothetical. We have no idea..."

"There could be a lot at stake..."

"Believe me, I am well aware of that..."

"And I am pointing out it might be prudent to bear it in mind when you talk to him."

"My first concern has to be his mental and emotional well-being, doesn't it? If I establish there is some kind of ongoing relationship with the girl that might become a factor..."

"Exactly. And I'm reminding you it is important you remain aware of..." He waved a hand, "let us call it the bigger picture."

"No. What you're saying is I should put pressure on him..."

Peter Wingfield's mouth was a thin, hard line. "You misunderstand me. I'm not suggesting anything of the kind. I am encouraging you..."

Anger welled up from her stomach in a sudden hot surge, taking her breath away; she wondered if her cheeks looked as hot as they felt. She bit back the words which sprang to her lips;

there was nothing to be gained from clashing with the man.

"And you think that would be ethical? Speaking hypothetically, of course," she added.

Wingfield returned to his desk but did not sit down. Resting his forearms on the back of his chair he looked down at her.

"An elevated ethical stance may not be the best position from which to decide the wisest course of action, when there's the risk of facing a possible misconduct charge, Pat…"

"Patricia."

"What…?"

She rose to her feet and held his eyes. "My name. It's Patricia, Peter. And to be honest, I am heartily fed up with being called Pat…"

His eyebrows rose like startled birds. He took a step back, as if half expecting she might lunge at him. "Really…? Well, if it's that important…"

"It is." She bent to retrieve her brief case. "You've made it clear Chloe is my problem, which is fine by me. I'll sort it my way and let you know what I've done. Was there anything else…?"

"Er…no, I don't think so…"

"Good." She flashed him a smile, but her eyes and the set of her jaw sent a different message.

Ψ

The Icelander came bounding into her consulting room wearing a broad smile. He looked her up and down and gave a approving nod.

"You are wearing red today…"

"Er…yes…"

"Do you know what that means…?"

She glanced down at her blouse. "That I liked it…"

"It is the colour of courage and fire and will power…" He raised a clenched fist. "They chose it for the Roman legions to wear when they marched out to conquer the world. Did you know that?"

"Really...?"

"Also a symbol for the force of fire itself. It cleanses...burns away that which is not pure. Think of the alchemist. Red for energy and determination..." He nodded again. "A good colour for you, no?"

Responding to Caitlin's only half playful accusation that Patricia wore clothes which were dull and dowdy, Patricia had purchased that particular crimson silk blouse in a Brighton boutique months before, but had never worn it. This morning, however, as she sorted through her wardrobe it seemed to slip from the hanger and into her hands before she knew it.

"Well, perhaps..." she conceded. "It's not a colour I wear often..."

"Then you should start..." He spread his hands. "Don't you want Patricia's flame to burn strong and bright...?"

"You might have a point." She recalled with satisfaction the look of surprise on Peter Wingfield's face as she strode out of his office.

She nodded at a pair of leather armchairs, flanked by emerald-leaved peace lilies, occupying a corner of the room; her visitor shook his head. He chose instead to examine a monochrome photograph on the wall beside her desk. It showed an elderly, balding man with intense eyes and a walrus moustache, smoking a battered meerschaum against a backdrop of snow-topped mountains.

"A good strong face. Your father?"

"If only..." She smiled. "You've heard of Carl Jung..."

Olaf nodded. "Of course..."

"Taken in the grounds of his house. Which I actually glimpsed once from a trip-boat on lake Lucerne..."

Olaf's beard and moustache were no longer so neatly trimmed; two days' worth of stubble darkened his cheeks. Eyes rimmed with red gave him the look of a man with an overdraft on his sleep account.

"I'm sitting over there," she told him, picking up his file and leaving her desk. "You're welcome to do as you wish…"

With a lingering look at the photograph, Olaf glanced round and headed for the window. He seemed like a restless bird, reluctant to perch in one place for long.

"Your friend Peter's room gets a lot of sunshine," he remarked glancing left and right. "But you have only a view of walls and cars. You do not mind?"

"I'd prefer something more picturesque," she admitted, "but I don't have much time to admire the view. So," she went on, "tell me how you're feeling after your trip?"

"You knew about it?"

"I was kept in the picture. It's routine. After all, you're a patient of mine…"

Pausing to rub his face with both hands he leaned back against the window frame and smiled. "Great. Yes, I feel great…"

"But tired…"

"I did not sleep so much…"

"Life too interesting…?"

"You might say that…" He grinned.

"It does seem an awfully long way to go for such a short stay though…"

"You think so…?"

"Olaf, I saw you and Morgana together just after we last met. And she said she was planning to go off to the Glastonbury area." She paused. "So I assume you went to meet her…"

He chuckled. "I thought you were a psychiatrist. Not a detective…"

"In my job sometimes I need to be a bit of both…"

"I knew where she was going, but we had made no plan to meet. Then…" He raised a finger, "I received a sign…"

"Did you really…?"

"I was looking at some of my research on Scafell, and something just...jumped out at me. I do not know why I never noticed it before..."

"Okay..."

"I realised if you link Ben Macdui to Scafell, and extend that line due south..." He swept a hand through the air, "it goes straight through the chalice well..."

"Is that in Glastonbury?"

"You never heard of it?"

"I'm afraid not..."

"It is magical, famous – I spent all Sunday night there. You should go there, feel the energy, it is extraordinary. So light that when you walk it feels as if your feet do not touch the ground. You float like...like a cloud..."

The man's smile was infectious; she found herself returning it. "And are you still floating...?"

"I think so..." He grinned. "Just a little..."

"So finding this line did the trick – off you went?"

"We have our own Scafell in Iceland. Ours is named *Ská-la-fell*," he told her. "Almost the same, no? And it has many meanings. In Greek *skala* is a ladder or stairway. So...stairway to heaven, perhaps? Skull, of course, and chalice..." He raised cupped hands to his lips. "There are places where people still drink from skulls..."

Relinquishing his place at the window he started in her direction but another photograph – this time a framed one on her desk – caught his eye. He pointed at it. "Your son and daughter, your husband and you, yes?"

"That's right," she said studying his face.

"What are their names, please, your children?"

"Caitlin and Colm."

"So, your son is Colm and you are Patricia...that is interesting..."

Ever since the separation she had had it in mind to replace it with one of the children and herself, but had never got round to it. In spite of everything, to exclude Liam felt like an act of betrayal. Not towards him – God knows, betrayal was his prerogative – but the children. "Ex-husband..." she added without knowing why. "Olaf, I'd like to talk to you about..."

He slumped into the chair opposite her own, sighed and stretched improbably long legs straight in front of him. "About what happened when I was a child...?"

"Amongst other things..."

He scanned her face and smiled. "Morgana?"

"Maybe it wasn't planned, but you did meet up with her, right?"

"She said she gave readings. I asked around..."

"We're both detectives then...?" she enquired.

"She is extraordinary, a beautiful being..." He cocked his head. "But you know that. You met her, no...?"

"Well, we—"

"She said you talked..."

"I can't really tell you any more than that..."

"Don't worry." He waved a hand. "I am not asking. It is not important."

"I have to respect confidentiality..."

"She was not there when I arrived. She was in Wales, looking for dragons. Well, a special one..." He frowned. "Did she tell you about her friend Mitch?"

"We didn't go into her private life..."

"Okay..." He chuckled. "Guess where this old dragon was..."

"You mentioned Wales..."

"A place called Great Rhos." He nodded. "Can you believe that...?"

"Why wouldn't I?"

"I checked, and it is right on that line I just told you about. So it is Scafell's southern guardian. Mitch found dragon energies running wild, out of control. Four churches meant to contain them are just ruins now, piles of stone." His smile faded; he pointed a warning finger. "That is serious. Rhos is red, red for danger, no? Bad things could happen – very bad. I told her to be careful but sometimes she does not want to listen…"

Olaf's rambling was not a cause for concern. People hovering on the edge of manic states often found boundaries hard to maintain; their customary control mechanisms no longer functioned efficiently. Rapid, incoherent speech and sleep problems were textbook symptoms. The condition was also known to carry a significant chance of sudden, intense relationships, often with others in a similarly vulnerable state.

"Is she…all right?"

"Morgana? No…" Olaf jumped to his feet, chuckling, arms wide. "She is like the Rhos dragon – running wild."

"Wild in what way…?"

"She is mad at people. Everybody. Her father, her mother, your friend Peter, you…the world…" He laughed. "But not me. I understand her and she knows it, you see. I can help her and she can help me…"

"How would she do that, Olaf?"

"She is a shakti…!"

"Meaning…?"

"…Don't you see, she is blessed with great gifts? Morgana possesses powers she promises to use to…empower me, guide me. Like the valkyrie did. You know about them?" He gave her no time to reply. "They choose the warriors who must die in battle but they are also their guardians." He waved a hand. "Of course, dying is not an ending, it is a transformation. One thing dies…another is born…"

He fell silent for a few moments, rubbing his chin and staring at the window through half-closed eyes.

"You look as if you could do with a rest," Patricia told him gently. "Won't you sit down?"

He gazed at her blankly, then did as she suggested. "Maybe

you are right..." He stifled a yawn. "I am sorry..."

"It isn't a problem," she told him. "So Morgana's angry, but not with you..."

"Me...?" He grinned. "No, no, not with Olaf."

"How about..." She paused. "How about with the *Order of Cosmic Consciousness*? They didn't treat her at all well, did they..."

"She told me about it on the drive back." He shrugged. "You know what I told her...?"

"What...?"

"People like that are monkeys..." He broke off, laughing. "Little demons, low consciousness beings. So greedy they are always trying to manipulate others, desperate to get as much money as possible. Sure, some of their teachings are good but they do not work in integrity. I gave her some advice..."

"Oh? Which was...?"

"To be careful of them..." He leaned forward eyes locked on hers. "Very careful. If not, she might put herself in danger, and get hurt. Monkeys are tricky and clever but they are also thieves – they want whatever you have. They want to steal her money but they are also jealous of her powers, you see – they want those, too. That would be much more serious, more dangerous..."

Patricia smiled.

"You do not believe me?" he demanded.

"Oh, I do, in fact I completely agree. I gave her much the same message, only in different words. What makes me smile is that coming from you it's great insight, coming from me it just makes her angry..."

"Because she trusts me."

"Doesn't it take time to build that kind of trust..."

"The first time we talked we both felt we already knew each other. Not like we'd met before – knew at a deep level. Did that ever happen to you...?"

"I've heard people talk about it..."

"Morgana thinks when they feel that, people must be from the same soul group. They often incarnate together, life after life. Sharing a soul group..." he murmured. "That is...a lovely thought, isn't it?"

"And do you believe the same thing?"

"While we were in Glastonbury, she gave me a reading..."

"Really. What did she tell you?"

"That I am blessed, favoured by the gods of this land and especially the spirit of Arthur. In fact, the energy of the grail castle drew me there. And I was chosen for my quest because I have the gifts the land needs right now. I am to help strengthen the mystical union between earth and sky, helping to heal the Fisher King's wound so life can return to the wasteland. And I must instruct others who are ready how to heal the land..."

"That is quite something, isn't it...?" Patricia observed. "How did you feel after that?"

Ignoring her question, he held up a finger. "But she gave me a warning. I should watch out for certain people – maybe one particular woman – who could have a part to play in my whole life journey. That is positive, but at the same time I must be on my guard against the forces of darkness, who fear the light and the power of universal healing, and do their best to block it. They will seek ways to stop me doing what I was sent to do..."

"Affirmation and encouragement but...watch points too. Quite a lot to think about..."

"Yes...but I felt okay about it..."

"It sounds as if you feel you can trust it..."

"She is like one of those bright coloured butterflies. Always fluttering from one subject to another, one mood to another. Now she is angry, now sad, now frightened, now...caring and gentle." His face softened. "Morgana is a moon-child. She needs someone like me – someone to hold her, keep her feet on the earth. You understand?"

"Well, I think so, yes. So you came back together last night..."

"She lives not far from here…"

"Do you mind me asking where you stayed?"

"I explained I must go to the abbey. She was not happy, but…"

"But…?" Patricia smiled.

"We agreed I was to stay there didn't we? I was worried if I did not, maybe you would send the police to find me." He cocked his head. "Would you…?"

"Things might have got a bit tricky…"

"Oh…?"

"You were detained under an order which expired after seventy-two hours," she explained. "But I would still have felt a clinical responsibility. Anyway, you're here so it's not a problem."

"So…" Olaf spread his hands, "what happens now?"

Not so different from his description of Morgana, he appeared restless, unable to settle. Wearing her professional hat, she was watching for hyperactivity and heightened mood, but his behaviour did not fall into either of those categories. Taking a common sense view, what could you expect of a young man smitten with an attractive young woman? Olaf's delusional traits remained in evidence, but did not appear to prevent him taking a sensible, balanced view of the burgeoning relationship. Most persuasive of all, the previous night, when he must have been sorely tempted to ignore them, he had honoured the boundaries they had negotiated.

"There's a lot going on for you. How do you feel you're handling it?"

"Pretty well, I think." He stared down at his hands for a few moments. "Don't you?"

"I wouldn't argue with that. You asked permission before leaving the abbey, and came back for today, so you respected our agreement…"

"You were surprised?"

"To be honest…no."

He gave a nod of acknowledgement. "Good…"

"You asked what happens now. You're wondering about a discharge, presumably?"

"Of course. Are you going to let me go?"

"I discussed your case with Dr Wingfield just now..."

Olaf looked thoughtful. "What did my friend Peter say?"

"We agreed there's no reason why you shouldn't be discharged immediately."

A smile spread slowly across the Icelander's face. "I didn't think you would say that."

"Oh, why...?"

"It has all been very strange...I could feel something was going on but...people were not telling me about it. Am I right, Dr Carragh?"

His eyes searched her own.

She bit her lower lip. "I'm being as honest with you as I can, Olaf..."

A faint smile tugged at the corners of his mouth. "So I am right."

"I always had your best interests at heart, and did the best I could for you..."

He took a deep breath and nodded. "I believe it," he told her. "So, I can just...go?"

"You can, but I'd like a few more minutes of your time. Is that okay?"

"Sure..." He shrugged. "I am not in a hurry."

"Last time you started telling me your life story. You described your childhood, losing your father and how the family then...is disintegrated too strong a word?"

"No, I do not think so." He shook his head.

"Okay. We got as far as you going up to university and..." She paused, "when we got to Bjorn's birth, you suddenly remembered you were meeting someone. That was Morgana, wasn't it?"

"Yes..."

"So I never heard the rest of your story. Of course, you don't have to tell me anything more if you don't want to, but it feels...incomplete. Do you mind finishing it for me?"

"If you like, but..." He shifted uncomfortably in his chair. "I do not understand why you people always want to go back into the past. The past is gone, finished. What is there except the present moment?"

"True, but in my experience what happened to us in the past can have a really powerful influence on the way we react to events in the present."

He sighed, then shrugged. "Okay..."

"You said you didn't plan a baby, but you were happy she was pregnant – both of you..."

He got to his feet, and momentarily she wondered if he had changed his mind but instead of heading for the door, he returned to the window and placed his fingertips against the glass, as if testing it. He had his back to her and she had to lean forward to catch his words.

"He looked like his mother, which I guess was lucky for him. But his body was like mine. Long, you know? And he had such good balance. He started walking very early. Like he was in a hurry to be up and moving by himself. Independent, that is the word. He knew just what he wanted from when he was small, yes..." his voice faded. "That might have had something to do with what happened. Who knows...?"

Patricia said nothing; her work involved a great deal of patient listening. Waiting, observing gestures, movements of eyes, head and body. Words can be designed to give a certain picture or impression but physical responses are unconscious, spontaneous; the insights they provided, she knew, were invariably reliable. Olaf was standing so still he might have been hewn from granite.

"It was so long ago..." the words somewhere between a statement and a plea.

"I really understand, it must be so painful to revisit..."

"Maybe he got bored, just wandered off by himself. That's

what we think..." He swung to face her. "I was working an hour's drive away. *Brynja* had been sick, and had to stay inside. She thinks it was some kind of flu. He was upset, desperate to get out, so she took him for a walk. To a hill which was a favourite place of his. We went there many times. And..." He shook his head, "after the climb she was exhausted. It was warm, and she lay down and closed her eyes. Just for a few minutes, she thinks, but he must have gone off exploring, I guess..."

"And...was never found?"

He frowned. "You knew that...?"

"All I know is what the papers said."

"About me...?" He glared.

"That he had never been..."

"You know what else those bastards said?" he demanded. "That I had something to do with it..."

"But you weren't even there..."

"That day I was working on my own. I could not prove where I was..."

"And people actually accused you...?"

"The newspaper people wanted someone to blame. They always do. They do not care about the truth – they want a story. If they do not find it, they make one up..."

"As if it wasn't already a nightmare..."

"They do not care."

"I'm sorry to say that's probably true."

"Not our own papers so much, but reporters came from everywhere: England, Germany, even America..." He waved a hand. "Pushing microphones in your face, asking stupid questions, taking pictures..."

"When all you wanted to do was find him..."

"It went on for days," he told her. "Weeks. So many people looking, always looking. Helicopters with special equipment for finding bodies. I do not know how that works. Maybe from the heat but..." He sighed, "what use is that if someone is dead...?"

"How long before you had to accept that was what had happened – Bjorn was probably dead?"

"How long...?" He took a deep breath and shrugged. "*Brynja* could not accept it. Not for a long time. She had dreams she was with him. She was sure it must be a sign he was alive, somehow...somewhere."

"And you?"

"I don't know. I mean, when you have searched everywhere and you do not find anything, in the end, any sane person has to admit..."

"You are a sane person." She smiled.

"A week, maybe. But until you find them," he added, "there is always hope..."

"Does any part of you still hope?"

"That he is being raised by wolves like the Roman twins...?" he offered, with a wan smile. "No, I do not hope..."

"So..." Patricia asked, softly, "when all hope is gone, Olaf, how does it feel...?"

"Numb..."

"How about right now, reliving it...telling me about it?"

"I am very tired..."

"You must have been trying to cope with so many things at once. The pain of the loss itself, obviously, which is hard to even imagine for anyone who hasn't been through it. But on top of that the cruel way the media treated you, so presumably feelings of frustration, helplessness..."

"All of them..." He waved a hand as if to dispel the memories. "But we had friends who were wonderful. Not just coming out searching with us, at all times of the day and night, but doing what they could to protect us from reporters and television people..."

"Which sounds great, but there is only so much other people can do. How did you manage to get through it...?"

"You do what you must do," he said, firmly. "You carry on,

survive, find a way. You...cope."

"Did you ever think maybe you couldn't...?"

"There were times I was not sure. I remember for weeks I could not sleep. Night after night. A doctor gave me pills. He said they were strong, they would help." He shook his head. "They just made me feel sick. They were useless..."

"Did you go to the doctor about how you were feeling?"

"Only the sleeping."

"And apart from friends, did you get any support? Medical...psychological?"

He stared at the ceiling for a few moments, brow furrowed. "I never asked. I had to stay strong for *Brynja*, you know? But it got more and more difficult between us. She felt everyone blamed her – even me. Sometimes we argued. In the end she wanted to go back to her family..."

"Leaving you by yourself?"

"I had been okay, held myself together. But when she went..." He puffed out his cheeks. "It got so bad I started thinking...dark, dark thoughts."

"People say things like that when they really mean they were suicidal. Were you...?"

"Once or twice, maybe..." he confessed. "But I knew inside that was not the answer. The answer was to get away. I had no idea how or where, just that I had to go..." He took a deep breath. "Then one day, a friend visited who had been there and started talking about what a great time he had in India. And something inside just...I knew that was it. Like a sign..."

"It was quite a way to go..."

"I did not care how far it was..." Crossing the room he eased himself down into his chair once more.

"And stayed...?"

"About a year.

"You went by yourself?"

"My friend offered to come but I wanted to do it alone."

"If you stayed that long, presumably it helped..."

The light was flooding back to Olaf's eyes, like the dawn breaking; he smiled a slow smile. "It was...like visiting another planet."

Patricia nodded; what better refuge for the victim of serial loss than another planet? All the more so when he already had an affinity with beings who inhabited other dimensions. His response to emotional overload, it seemed, was withdrawal into a state of numbness; absence of feeling. At what price, she wondered. What time-bomb of repressed emotions might be ticking away beneath the surface?

Olaf tilted his head, like an inquisitive bird. "So – is that what you really wanted to know? That I did not harm my son...?"

"It was important to hear the whole story in your own words. Even if going over it yet again wasn't easy..."

"I told you, I trust you. If you thought it was important enough to ask me..."

"Tell me one more thing, then. Did you have any sense that by walking away, leaving the tragedy behind, maybe you never really managed to complete with it?"

"What do you mean...?"

"Do you remember what I told you about unexpressed feelings...?"

He nodded, slowly. "You think I am like one of your dams...?

"I'm convinced the real process is more subtle. Expressing and releasing feelings may be beneficial in the short term, but I believe it's more about letting yourself go deeply into them. Stay with them, feel them, experience them at a deep level. If you can do that, it may take time but in the end you will probably integrate them..."

"You must drink deeply from the cup..."

"Exactly that. Transforming rather than just acting them out. Does it make sense?"

"It makes sense. You are talking about the path to inner

healing…"

"I don't know about the death of your father or your brother, but in Bjorn's case, do you feel you drank deeply enough, in your words, to complete that process…? With all those complex emotions whirling round inside you? The almost unbearable sadness and pain of loss, some guilt, maybe, anger with *Brynja* when you thought it might have been her fault, sheer blind rage with people who said you were responsible…"

Olaf lifted a hand. "Dr Carragh, I know you are trying to help. And I thank you for that. You speak of feelings and processes because that is how you were trained to understand the world. But it is not how I see it…" He paused. "I did not tell you before, but I have been blessed. I have met and communed with angelic beings who watch over and care for *Björn's* spirit. They taught me much, and helped me see why things had to unfold the way they did. That it was all part of his journey, his destiny. And because it was his, it was mine. When it was his time to leave, he left. And people who persecuted me…I forgive them. There is no point in being angry – they just did what they thought they had to do. Perhaps the most wonderful and powerful lesson I learned at the feet of the Indian masters, you see, was acceptance."

Patricia nodded slowly.

"Absolutely no sadness, then? No pain or regrets…not a shred of anger left with anyone…?"

"You do not believe me…" He smiled.

"It's just that a few moments ago you seemed sad. Very sad indeed…"

"Yes, but…"

"And the first time," she went on, "when you were on the point of telling me about Bjorn's death, you left in a hurry and I got the feeling you thought I might reopen a wound that had not healed. That is not so…?"

"I studied with wonderful masters." He smiled, "but that does not make you one. I am not skilled enough to stay in a state of acceptance. That may take a few more lifetimes…"

"And a lot of practice, I guess…"

Olaf leaned forward, elbows on his knees, chin resting on clasped hands. "Morgana told me to ask you why you did not let me go before. She said you must think I might hurt someone…" He shrugged. "I understand why you were so keen to know about *Björn*."

Patricia nodded. "That was part of it…"

"Do you believe I told you the truth?"

"I have absolutely no reason to doubt you. So," she went on, "what are your plans – are you going straight to Scafell?"

"I have to think about it. I am not sure…"

"Not sure about what…?"

He wore a sheepish smile. "Morgana has invited me to go with her to Stonehenge…"

"You're serious – for midsummer night?"

"Yes…"

"But Olaf, what about your mission… healing the mountain and…" She waved a hand, "everything?"

"I have not made up my mind yet. But," he went on quickly, "there is something else, which was why I had to know whether you were going to let me go."

"What's that?"

"Morgana is going to Canterbury tomorrow. A friend of hers is taking a party of tourists round the cathedral in the evening, but he is ill, so she is helping him out. She really wants me to go with her…"

"Sounds interesting. Well, you can tell her you're available. Oh," she added, "just one other thing. Are you likely to head off or do you plan to stay round here?"

"I think…" he told her with a smile, "I will be staying. For a few days, at least…"

"Good. I still need to do my research," she reminded him.

"I had forgotten about that…"

"I'm attending a meeting of the group tomorrow. In Canterbury, as it happens."

Olaf got to his feet. "Morgana's tour is in the evening. Maybe you would like to come. You would find it interesting…"

"I have a feeling Morgana might not be too thrilled if I turned up."

"I will tell her I asked you, because you have been kind to me…"

"Olaf, I've just done my job…"

He waved her words aside. "And I would like you to come. Please?"

"If you were still my patient there'd be boundary issues, but seeing that I've just discharged you…"

"There is no problem. I will find out the details and let you have them."

"Well…"

"It was meant to be," he insisted, "I can feel it…"

"Oh, really?"

He closed his eyes for a few moments before replying.

"Really, Dr Carragh. So you can celebrate the rose moon and receive its gift," he went on. "You may not believe it is true but you did not believe me when I told you your visit to Ireland would be healing for your son, did you?"

Patricia stared at him. "Er, no, I didn't…"

"But it was, wasn't it?"

"Yes," she told him. "As a matter of fact, it was…"

Chapter 12

Rose Moon

24

Wednesday 15th of June 2011

Trains to London from East Grinstead ambled along like elderly ladies taking a stroll for the first dozen miles or so until, seemingly remembering they were bound for the metropolis, they put on speed. Having completed her patient reports, Patricia closed her laptop just in time to catch a glimpse of the debris-strewn banks of the Thames at low tide, as they clattered over a wide bridge before easing into Victoria station. Ninety minutes later, watching Kentish hop-fields roll by, her thoughts returned to Olaf.

Appealing they might be, but she could not bring herself to do other than consign his tales of cosmic connections, guiding spirits and dream invasion to the realm of sci-fi movies and children's fiction. On his maps, she admitted, the jury was out; it was within the bounds of possibility he might have stumbled across some mystico-mathematical relationship between places possessing degrees of religious significance. Certain of the American founding fathers, Washington among them, were known to have arranged streets, monuments, and even cities in patterns enshrining Masonic beliefs; she could see no reason why they should have been the first or the only ones to do so.

His reference to contrasting atmospheres in England and his homeland resonated strongly with her and made sense of the sinking feeling she invariably experienced boarding a Gatwick bound flight from Dublin. It was like the last day of school holidays; that reluctant farewell to freedom before resuming the academic treadmill. While the feeling was triggered primarily by the prospect of resuming clinical duties and responsibilities, punishing schedules and endless meetings, he had reminded her of another dimension; a heaviness not in her heart alone, but somewhere even deeper within.

On the most recent flight she was able to watch with equanimity as the Sussex countryside rose smoothly to meet them, and needed to look no further than the adjacent seat for an explanation. The effects of his adventures might or might not prove enduring but thus far the signs were encouraging. Hardly had she accelerated away from the gates of the faux castle with its fresh decorated tree, before Colm was busy calling Frances to give her a comprehensive if dramatised account of events. Confessing he had been unable to secure her precious cord in exactly the prescribed manner he was visibly relieved to be assured it mattered not. Positive intention while carrying out the ritual was, Frances assured him, of greater importance than the act itself. Eavesdropping on one side of their exchange, Patricia particularly enjoyed his triumphant glance at her as he recounted there had been, as predicted, an eagle presence.

From a professional perspective, she had reservations about how much Colm's improved mood owed to spending a few damp minutes in a storm tossed corner of Sligo. Attaching a length of dyed and woven cotton to a particular genus of tree, even in a specific location, was unlikely to facilitate modification of her son's mental or emotional state. He had, however, been convinced that carrying out his great-grandmother's instructions would be beneficial, hence the ritual could be categorised as a placebo, the efficacy of which was established scientific fact. Wearing a mother's hat, of course, rational explanation was irrelevant. Colm was back to his old self, and nothing, even touching down on English soil, could lessen her delight in that.

Ψ

Special Interest Group meetings ranged from the dry, academic and theoretical to the stimulating, inspiring and thought provoking. Despite this one being at the latter end of the scale, Patricia speculated on more than one occasion how much livelier proceedings might have been had she agreed to the Icelander's suggestion she bring him along. It was, however, gratifying to be able to respond with confidence to enquiries regarding progress on her paper; she made a mental note to pin Olaf down to definite dates lest he and his butterfly flutter off together.

At the conclusion of official business, she needed minimal encouragement to accompany half a dozen fellow delegates to a wine bar occupying a cool cellar among the city's narrow, winding streets. Nursing a glass of crisp white wine she picked at a platter of assorted continental cheeses and enjoyed inconsequential chat, banter and gossip. It put her in mind of the simple pleasures of her Dublin student days and made her wonder why she so rarely allowed herself such indulgences. It was not until one of her companions announced they had a train to catch that she remembered her own appointment. Olaf had stressed the importance of punctuality; Mitch's party was among only a handful granted access to the cathedral grounds that evening and if she was not there in time to enter with them, she risked not getting in at all. Wishing she had worn sensible shoes instead of heels, she hurried down Long Market and into Burgate where she was relieved to spot Olaf among a throng in front of the entrance.

"You are now officially with *Dragon Tours...*" He smiled, handing her a pass.

"Thank you."

"I was starting to wonder if maybe you changed your mind..."

"Just forgot the time..."

"Have you been here before?"

"Never." She shook her head. "But I'm honouring a promise I

made to myself ages ago..."

"First time for us both..."

Morgana was calling his name from somewhere ahead of them.

"I am sorry, I must go..."

"No problem. Did you mention I was coming...?"

"Yes, yes..." He grinned. "I did..."

She watched him set off through the crowd, then headed for the clattering turnstiles. Presenting her pass and squeezing through, she positioned herself on the fringe of the group assembling round Olaf and Morgana, across whose slender shoulders a velvet cape of rich purple shimmered in the evening light. Patricia guessed the party numbered around twenty, the majority looking and sounding like Americans, with a smattering of Japanese. As they moved off towards the cathedral entrance, Morgana turned to address her charges.

"Hi everyone...Mitch is so sorry he couldn't come. You probably already know but he hasn't been feeling great since he and I went to Wales a few days ago..."

A sympathetic murmur greeted the announcement. Raising herself on tiptoe, resting a hand on Olaf's shoulder, Morgana did her best to make herself heard above the noise of the crowd. She had a high, child-like voice and an accent which hinted at an expensive private education. Patricia caught a flash of scarlet nails and glittering rings as she ran a hand through her ringlets.

"...But we're determined to make it a really great evening for you, and as Mitch couldn't make it, I invited a special guest. His name is Olaf Bardarson and he's come all the way from Iceland..."

She smiled like a magician producing a rabbit from a hat; the news earned a smattering of polite applause.

"Hello..." Olaf gave a self-conscious wave.

"Before we go in," Morgana continued, "Olaf's produced some handouts he'll explain to you. Later, he's going to tell us some really fascinating stuff about tonight's full moon..."

"Well, he sure looks a fine young man..."

A silver-haired matron at Patricia's side studied Olaf through large round spectacles and smiled at her.

"Are you another of little Morgana's experts, honey?"

"I'm afraid not..." Patricia shook her head. "I'm just here to...have a look at the cathedral."

Olaf brandished a sheaf of papers in the air.

"I have two maps for you. On one I drew a line joining Mont Blanc in France with Scafell, which is the highest mountain in England..." He handed the papers to Morgana. "And you will see the line runs right through where you are standing now..."

Morgana was circulating among the group, distributing Olaf's handiwork. She glanced at Patricia with a fixed smile.

"Oh...hi..."

"How are you...?"

"Busy, actually..." she said, gliding away.

"I invite you to join a little experiment," Olaf told them. "Keep Canterbury and these mountains in your awareness while you are inside. And see if you have any thoughts or feelings about them..."

The silence which greeted this suggestion, thought Patricia, might have signalled respect or bemusement. Most of those studying their maps, she noticed, wore puzzled expressions.

"...And if you like to tell me about your experience, please do."

"And the other one?" called a woman. "Looks like a plain old plan of the cathedral to me..."

"It is," Olaf told her. "I will explain that one later, nearer the hour of full moon..."

"Did you understand that, honey?" enquired the silver-haired lady in a lilting southern drawl. "Did you figure out just what it is we're supposed to be doing exactly...?"

"Not really..." Patricia admitted. She nodded at people

clustering round the tall Icelander. "He's probably explaining it. You could ask…"

"Chances are it wouldn't help…I think we'll just head right on in and have ourselves a look-see." She extended a lace-gloved hand. "I'm Ramona Duluth, and this is my hubby, Lincoln. Everyone calls him Linc."

She tugged at her companion's arm. A burly, crew cut man in pale yellow safari suit and tasselled brogues, he was puffing on a cigar and appeared absorbed in a glossy cathedral guide.

"Linc don't hear so good any more, honey," she confided. "Folks think he's ignoring them, but in truth he just ain't heard…"

"Where have you been to so far…?"

"Oh, a bunch of real wonderful places…just wonderful. There was Saint Michael's Mount – so cute, all little winding streets and alleys and such-like. And we've been to Stonehenge and Glastonbury…" she lowered her voice. "I'm sure young Olaf is just wonderful, honey, but Mitchell…such a pity he ain't here. That man is a walking encyclopaedia, I swear. He knows every last thing about every last place we've been…"

Patricia nodded. "Sounds as if you're enjoying yourselves."

"We have just loved every second, haven't we, Linc?"

The man in yellow picked a piece of tobacco from his tongue, flicked it away, and turned a page of the guidebook. Patricia wondered if his deafness might be strategic.

"Mitchell is steeped in the history of this wonderful country of yours." Ramona's outsized glasses gave her the appearance of an amiable owl. "Real steeped in it, believe me. All those wonderful Arthurian legends, and his knights with their Round Table…Mitchell knows every single one of them by heart. Oh, that Guinevere and Sir Lancelot, honey! How romantic is that…?" Fanning herself with her maps, she chuckled. "…And he tells us all about nature spirits and elves and fairies, and devas and…heaven knows what else." Her voice sank lower. "Mind you, to my mind, what he has to say on subjects of that kind comes right out of left field, if you follow me..."

"Does it...?" Patricia nodded. "Tell me, that young lady in charge..."

"Morgana...?"

"Yes. Is she...wonderful, too?"

"To tell you the honest truth, honey, we havn't see a whole lot of her until the last couple of days. She kind of flits in and out, like a fairy, you might say. Now, Linc, he sure likes that little lady," she added with a wink. "And she sees things. You know what I mean – *sees* things? Like disembodied creatures and all..."

"Does she really...?"

"Well, she says she does. Now, being as it's only her doing the seeing, you could say it's kind of hard to be certain..."

Mitch's clients were not alone in enjoying the privilege of an evening tour; Patricia saw other groups, shepherded by guides in dark uniforms. Heels clattering on flagstones worn smooth with age, she joined a stream filtering through the massive arched doorway leading into the nave. She hung back, allowing Mrs Duluth and her mute husband to join those following in Morgana and Olaf's wake like a troupe of nervous ducklings. To her surprise, Patricia realised witnessing an association between her two former clients made her faintly uncomfortable. Liam would have dubbed the girl a man-magnet, so perfectly did she fit the profile of those diminutive, doe-eyed, gamine creatures he seemed to find irresistible. On that basis alone, that the girl should trigger both Patricia's lack of trust and resentment, she decided, was probably inevitable.

A glance at her watch confirmed there was no need to hurry; Olaf had said the highlight of the evening would not take place until around ten, which gave her plenty of time. Sauntering the length of the nave she found her gaze constantly drawn upwards, ascending the full height of columns appearing too slender, too delicate to support the vast expanse of vaulted ceiling above. Had she only invested in a guidebook, she would have known if the columns were Norman or perpendicular. Gazing upwards made her feel slightly dizzy, and she sat down in the nearest pew to examine Olaf's maps.

The instructions, as far as she remembered, were to concentrate on the mountains and cathedral and see what happened. She closed her eyes. Trying to conjure up an image of Mont Blanc, she could recall only a skiing holiday when Liam had pointed it out to her from the plane. Or had that been the Matterhorn? She had no more success with Scafell; it was there on the map, but she had no idea what it looked like. As for the cathedral, how were you supposed to visualise a place you were in? With a sigh of exasperation she opened her eyes. Olaf had a habit of making things sound simple which in practice proved less so. Folding the maps and stowing them in her shoulder bag, she decided she would visit Becket's tomb.

Murder in the Cathedral was among the prescribed texts for her school leaving certificate and she had found herself enthralled and captivated by its hero. She had promised herself that when the opportunity arose, she would make her own pilgrimage to honour the saint's memory. It might have taken a full quarter of a century to do so, but the moment had arrived.

She got briskly to her feet only to find she had to clutch the back of the pew to steady herself. The combined effects of an early start, a tiring day and a large glass of white wine – or had it been two – were exerting an unwelcome influence. She sank back onto the polished wooden seat and took a deep breath. Glancing round to see if she was observed, she allowed her eyes to close.

A sudden flash of light startled her into wide-eyed consciousness.

"Sorry, ma'am. Did I disturb you...?"

Tall, rugged and deeply tanned, the speaker had a mass of shoulder-length white hair and a Zapata moustache which nestled beneath a patrician nose. Clutching a bulky camera, he wore an expression of concern.

"No, I was just…" She waved a vague hand. "Really, I'm fine…"

"I was so busy trying for a good angle on that entrance to the choir I didn't see you…" he went on. "Which was just plain careless. Sure you're okay?"

"Certain, thank you…"

The man hovered, unconvinced. Patricia nodded at his camera.

"I didn't know people used those any more. I thought the world had gone digital."

"Well now, you have a point. It very nearly has…" He patted his battered Leica. "Call me old fashioned, but I enjoy the whole process and procedure, as I call it. Checkin' the light level, settin' aperture and exposure, composin' the picture, clear through to processin' and printin'. If you ain't ready to go the whole nine yards, I don't see as how you can call yourself a photographer."

"And do you…?"

"You could say I try my best on that score, ma'am…" He shrugged.

Patricia smiled. She recalled a client who, on a visit to America, had embarked on a whirlwind romance with a man half her age. The affair ended abruptly when police arrested her lover, charging him with a number of murders. From the outset, she said, she had been enchanted by the young man's impeccable manners. He had always addressed her as ma'am – even in bed.

"The name's Westerberg…" he leaned down to extend a large hand. "Karl Westerberg. Mind if I join you?"

"Not at all. Are you with *Dragon Tours*?"

"Indeed I am…" Dark eyes studied her from beneath eyebrows like a pair of white caterpillars. "But I don't recall seein' you before…"

"You wouldn't. I'm a friend…well, acquaintance of Olaf's."

The rangy American placed his camera gently on the seat of a pew worn smooth by generations of worshippers; he had to turn sideways to accommodate long legs. He wore pale blue trousers, a white cotton shirt and stitched moccasins.

"So you've come a long way for this."

"True enough, but that is one long story. I'd better not get started or you'll wish I hadn't..."

Becket's tomb suddenly seemed less important than a stranger's story. Patricia smiled.

"Can't be that long..."

"Don't have to be, I guess..."

"So...?"

"Well..." He ran a finger along the underside of his moustache, "truth is I ain't never had no interest in the metaphysical, as you might call it. I'm a farmer from Oklahoma and you could say, as a breed, we're down to earth folk. Literally and every other which way..."

There was an engaging quality about this big, raw-boned man. In his late fifties or early sixties, he spoke and moved with unhurried ease, and judging by tell-tale lines etched at the corners of his mouth, he smiled easily and often. Farmer he might be but to Patricia's eye he needed only Stetson and horse to look at home in any western.

"Yes, I imagine so..."

"But six years ago come July, I lost my wife to cancer. Mary, her name was. Married twenty-nine years and she gave me two beautiful daughters. No finer woman..."

"I'm sorry..."

"Thank you, ma'am..." Reaching into his collar he drew out a plain gold wedding ring on a matching chain.

"This here was hers..." Glancing down, he cleared his throat. "And it was on the first anniversary of the day we buried her it all started..."

He tucked the ring back. People drifting along the nave were chatting in low, respectful tones. She might have recognised

Olaf's voice, but her gaze did not leave the stranger's face.

"All started...?" she echoed.

"The messages. Well..." He waved a hand, "can't say I thought of them that way at first. They were just...peculiar happenin's, you might say. Like her picture by my bed fallin' to the floor. Not just once, mind...three nights, one after another. Don't have no pets, weren't no wind, neither..."

With a sigh, he stretched out his legs and crossed them at the ankles.

"Then there was the perfume. Mary's favourite, it was. No one else noticed it – but I did." He tapped his chest with a bony forefinger. "Yes, ma'am. And there was dreams too...but in the day-time, you understand?"

"Not really..."

"Like one evening, I was out on the porch watchin' hawks lookin' for jackrabbits. Next thing, she was standin' next to me. True as I sit here and she set off talkin' like I am to you right now, ma'am. After that she kept on comin' by. Never for long, mind..."

He shot her a hurried glance, as if fearing he had said too much.

"...But I couldn't tell no one, else them fellas in white coats would've come callin'. Psychiatrist fellas, you know...?"

"Indeed I do," she assured him.

"Why, they'd have locked me up with a chocolate key and tossed it to a five year old. And I wasn't havin' that, no ma'am. Anyways, Mary kept on tellin' me I had to go across to England, where her folks came from a hundred years or more back. Go, she said, and follow St Michael's line." He shrugged. "Tell you the truth, I never heard of the darned thing but I dreamed up some excuse, got one of my daughters to go on her computer and find out all about it." Leaning back, he folded his arms and smiled. "She found Mitch's website, where it talks about that very line. So there's your answer – that's how I come to be in Canterbury Cathedral tonight." He leaned forward. "I reckon you must think you've wound up talkin' to a fella that's just plain crazy..."

"Are you really so different from the rest of us?" She smiled. "Anyway, you did what Mary said, and has it been worth it? Have you found out why she was so keen for you to come?"

"To tell you God's honest truth, ma'am, not yet. Don't get me wrong, I've enjoyed myself so far and, like they say, it ain't never over 'til the fat lady sings..."

"True enough..."

"Mitch, he's told me plenty about this Michael line, but still..." He shook his head. "You know him?"

"Of him. We've never met."

"I like him, he's a regular guy. Mind you, he has a few wild and wacky ideas. And Morgana – now, there's a gal..." He lowered his voice. "Back in the day, they'd have burned that one at the stake, if you get my drift..."

"I do..." Patricia could not suppress a wry smile.

"Maybe Mitch, too. Did they have men witches...?"

"I have a feeling they did. They were called warlocks, I think..."

"His big thing is what he calls earth energies. Says they're kind of underground rivers and you can find 'em with a couple of bent metal rods. Dowsing, he called it. I read somewhere Native Americans look for water the self same way, usin' plain old twigs. According to him, they put churches over them currents, so folk going to pray would vibrate with the energy and have visions and such-like..." He pursed his lips. "Sounds like them holy rollers to me. Mitch sure believes it all, but to my mind there's only so far a man can go down that track..."

"True, but then there are people who'd find it hard to go along with the idea a sane, intelligent man like yourself would come all the way to England because his late wife appeared and said it would be a good idea..."

"Ma'am, you are so right!" He slapped his thigh. "Definitely, indubitably right…"

"Karl, I've really enjoyed talking to you," she told him, "but there's something I promised myself I'd see while I'm here. Then I shall go and find the others. I don't want to miss whatever Olaf's got planned…"

Rising to his feet, the big farmer retrieved his camera and slung it over his shoulder.

"And I have more pictures to take. Ma'am, it has been a real pleasure, yes, indeed. Who knows, we may meet again…"

Patricia had no difficulty finding the martyr's tomb. She lingered longer than she intended, transfixed by the stark beauty of the altar of the Sword's Point, with its cruciform metal frame and cruel, jagged swords. Becket's dignity, integrity and courage had shone through Eliot's dense text, touching something deep within her. Even in a setting so magnificent was there anything more inspiring, she wondered, than this memorial to such an extraordinary man of God? With a final genuflection she made her way through the deserted choir to Trinity Chapel, to find Olaf already in full flow.

"…You have all heard of a honeymoon, yes…?" He glanced at those round him. "Well, the full moon tonight is truly a honey moon, or what some call a rose moon. It is the third moon period after the equinox, which started on June the first and ends on the last day of the month. In ancient spiritual traditions, people believed the phases of the moon were important and celebrated them. Then Christianity came along and did what all new religions do – adopted existing festivals. They literally re-christened them, gave them Christian names. Easter is a good example. Does anyone know how the date of Easter Day is decided…?"

Glances were exchanged and heads shook but no one offered an answer.

"Astrology. It is based on the timing of the equinox and full moons. So…" He spread his hands, "Christian or pagan…? And what about the wise men in the nativity story? Who were they? Probably Persian astrologer kings – looking for the rising star..."

His words were endowed with an eerie, echoing quality by the vastness of the spaces surrounding him. They brought a subdued murmur from his audience.

"...At full moon, spirit reaches its highest level of potency and intensity. So this evening, every one of us may experience awareness and consciousness we have never known before..."

His eyes glistened. There was no need to talk about energy, thought Patricia; he was practically crackling with it. She caught a glimpse of Morgana gazing at him and wondered whether the moon-child was prepared to be eclipsed for much longer.

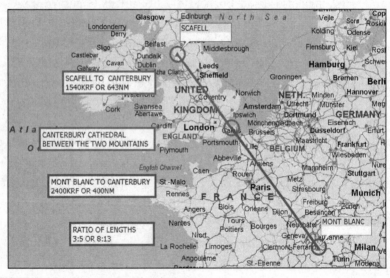

Image 06 Scafell and Mont Blanc

"...Understand, please, this is not just because the Moon is full. Remember you are standing in what has been a sacred space for centuries, which means there could hardly be a better place to be, tonight of all nights. Because the spiritual currents here are like the Moon – at the very peak of their powers. Now I want to show you what makes this moment so magical. Look at your second

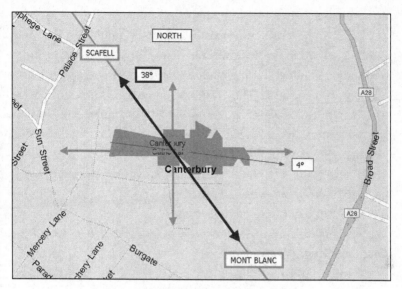

Image 07 The Canterbury Cathedral

map, please..."

He paused until the rustle of paper subsided. "This ancient place of worship is not aligned only with Mont Blanc and Scafell. Tonight it is aligned with the Sun and Moon..."

"Is that why they put the cathedral right here?" a man's voice enquired. "They knew about this line way back then, is that what you're saying, Olaf?"

"I believe they did." He shrugged, "unless you believe such things happen by chance. So at this moment we are experiencing another alignment. The Sun is behind Scafell, the Moon is above Mont Blanc. As you see from my map we are on a point between them. So, another little experiment. For this, try closing your eyes for a few moments and see if you can sense the interaction of Sun and Moon...sense it in your body..."

Patricia closed her eyes and waited. If spiritual energies were indeed wandering the cathedral, they were not flowing in her direction. She was less aware of cosmic alignments than a nagging ache in the centre of her brow. She resolved to exercise more restraint when visiting wine bars.

"…Sun and Moon can represent opposites, polarities. Day and night, masculine and feminine. The same is true of our mountains. Think about them. One is to the north of us, while the other lies to the south. They might remind us of our own polarities, the opposites which we represent. For example, some of you may be responding to what I am saying from your heart, your feelings…"

He paused to scan their faces; Patricia had the uneasy feeling his gaze lingered on her as he went on.

"…For others it may be their minds…"

Morgana touched his arm; they exchanged a few words in voices too low for Patricia to catch.

"If you would like to, we can explore that idea a little more later on," Olaf announced, "but there are other things I am sure will interest you. I spoke of the presence of spirit in different forms here tonight. Let Morgana tell you how she experiences it…"

Silver bracelets clinked and glittered in the light of chandeliers as she brushed the ringlets from her brow.

"This man is amazing, isn't he? Now you understand why I was so pleased when he said he'd come along, even at really short notice…" She gave him a heavy-lidded glance. "…Now, you may not realise the mountains on his map have their own guardian spirits. As a matter of fact, they're right here around us and have been ever since we came in…" Spreading her arms she gazed upwards. "Maybe some of you can see them, too…"

"Not as good as you, I reckon, ma'am."

Patricia smiled at Karl's stage whisper. Waiting for a ripple of laughter to fade, Morgana half closed her eyes.

"…Inhabitants of the angelic realms are present sharing every moment with us…including Scafell's own guardian. She is the most exquisite being…"

She sighed before continuing in a dreamy tone. "…And

surrounded by light...shining, shimmering golden light...oh, and I see purple, too...the very highest note on the colour scale..." Staring at one spot, she nodded to herself. "Her aura is lighting up the spaces round and above us...everything and everybody...including every one of us, of course...in fact, she's looking down with an expression of such tenderness, such love..."

A handful of passers-by paused, curious about the woman wrapped in velvet and intoning in a hypnotic voice. A man in dark tunic and clerical collar caught Patricia's attention. Tall and balding, his face was so pale she wondered if he only came out at night. Arms folded, he was peering intently at Morgana, brow furrowed.

"...Do you remember Olaf talking about polarities? That's so interesting, because the guardian of Mont Blanc is definitely masculine. His aura is stunning, too, but the colours are completely different...I see sapphire, the colour of the Aquarian age...and dazzling white, like...like a snowy mountain in the sun..."

Her voice faded and she shifted her attention to another area of the ceiling. The man in the clerical collar edged forward, as if determined not to allow a word to escape him.

"...They are both magnificent and..." She spread her arms wide; the cloak across her shoulders shimmered. "...Huge...I mean, they practically fill the whole space with fantastic beauty and power. We're really blessed to have beings like them looking after us, protecting us..."

She took a deep breath and lowered her arms, pressing her hands to her chest. "The cathedral has its own...resident guardian angel," she went on, "with a buttercup yellow aura...which is a healing colour, of course. And surrounding the yellow I can see a ring of emerald green. As you may know, green is a mixture of yellow and blue, which signifies spiritual wisdom...and at the edges I can just make out another ring of pale, pale violet..."

"Do you see such things, Mr Olaf?"

The question, from a plump Japanese woman with gold hoop earrings and a pink silk blouse, seemed to take him by surprise. He glanced at Morgana.

"Me...? I have a strong sense of their presence, yes. Once you acknowledge spirit you attract it, you see. Your attention and awareness activate its energy..."

"Remember Tinkerbell?" enquired Morgana. "She's a fairy in the *Peter Pan* story and she says if people stop believing in fairies, the fairies will die. It's the same with spirit, too..."

"Do you want to say more?" Olaf asked her, but she shook her head.

"I don't think so. It feels like a good moment for your visualisation."

"Sure. Now, Morgana has told us about her experience, so let us all go within and explore our own. Tune in and...see what happens..."

"Folk talk about tuning in, but I'm not sure what that means, Olaf," said a hesitant voice. "How are you supposed to do that...?"

"A good question. " He nodded. "Well, it is simple. Just close your eyes, and be aware of your breathing. Feel the air enter your lungs... and leave again as you breathe out. Let go of any thoughts which pop into your head. Instead, focus on any feelings or sensations in your body..."

"Do you think you could maybe lead us? Kind of...talk us through it?" asked the woman.

"Is that what people would like...?"

Several hands rose into the air and there was a murmur of assent.

"Okay. Well, I suggest we spread out and join hands, form a circle. If you wish, of course..." He smiled. "I do not ask anyone to do anything they are not comfortable with..."

A handful of people retired a few paces, watching their companions form a ring with Morgana and Olaf at its centre. The pale young man took his place among the observers, shifting feet as if he would have preferred more distance between himself and whatever was to take place.

"...Turn your right hand palm upwards, ready to receive...and your left hand palm down. Now let your hands slip into those of the people next to you..." He toured the circle, gently repositioning hands here and there. "...The left hand delivers...the right receives. It helps the energy to flow..."

Aware of a figure looming at her shoulder, Patricia glanced up to see Karl's leathery face.

"Well now, ma'am," he said, in a low voice, "I sure hope you ain't aimin' to abandon ship. Not just when your friend is going to lead us into the mysteries, as you might say..."

"Well, I thought I'd just..."

"And miss out on the main event? Well, shame on you..." He wore an expression of mock reproach. "I thought this was the very thing you came along for..."

For all she knew the man from Oklahoma might be right. Perhaps there was a greater purpose to the evening than homage to St Thomas, and mixing with rainbow-hued angels. She might even learn more about what it was that kindled such a bright flame in the Icelander's wounded heart. Karl was bowing, offering his hand as if inviting a southern belle to dance. She hesitated. Observe, with a mixture of envy and admiration, those courageous enough to accept the challenge, or choose a road less travelled? A flock of teenage butterflies swarming in her stomach, she allowed him to take her hand.

"Thank you, kind sir..."

The circle opened to embrace the newcomers; Olaf flashed her a smile. She had a moment of panic; which hand received...which delivered? Standing between Karl and the Japanese woman in pink, she felt her hands slip into theirs.

"...Let us first create a welcoming space for all beings present. Whatever their nature, wherever they have come from. Let us ask them to help us open ourselves to the healing energies around us..."

Eyes closed, listening to the rhythms of his voice, Patricia felt uneasy. Linking hands with strangers troubled her little, but she was engaging in a ritual alien to the traditions in which she had been raised. She felt a flash of anger towards well-meaning, gracious Karl, without whose intervention she would have maintained a safer distance.

"Hail to you, blessed father Sun
Hail to you, blessed mother Moon
Hail to you, lady of Scafell, the chalice mountain
Hail to you, father of Mont Blanc, the white mountain
Hail to all the stars of our solar system
And all beings inhabiting this world and all others, near and
    far
Hail to all Holy Beings who watch over this place of worship
We ask that you guide all those who come here seeking
Spiritual knowledge, wisdom and healing
We ask you to be with all of us, now and at all times
And help us open our hearts and minds to the presence of the
    divine."

He spoke softly, but each syllable rang clearly through the stillness.

"Now, imagine a pillar of light at the centre of our circle. And imagine that pillar is stretching down from the highest heavens...going down deeper and deeper until it reaches the heart of Planet Earth...And as you breathe in, imagine drawing its light into your body, through the centre of your chest...then flowing out from your heart, along your left arm...into the hand of the person next to you...while light enters your body through the other hand...Then, relax...do nothing...enjoy the sensation as loving energy flows round the circle, gently passing from hand to hand...and you become one with infinite heart energy..."

Patricia's palms felt unusually warm. No mystery there; Olaf had said it would be so and her mind obediently created the illusion. It was simple auto suggestion – the hypnotist's stock in trade. No doubt Karl and the Japanese woman also experienced this strange, unfamiliar heat. She would ask them when it was all over. Now to summon an image of a pillar of light, draw it into her and pass it round the circle. That, she discovered, was easier than she had expected. It was accompanied by the sensation of warmth flowing through her entire body. She felt herself relaxing, breathing more easily; her brow no longer ached...

"...Now let us introduce a little extra magic...Mont Blanc and Scafell are no longer where you thought they were. In some way you do not need to understand, they have been transported right here – to Canterbury...In fact, they are now standing on each side of the cathedral like huge sentinels. Imagine them towering above it, making us all look tiny, minuscule...like ants. They are vast and magnificent, yet..." his voice dropped to a whisper, "infinitely gentle and protective towards us. Now imagine the Moon emerging from behind Mont Blanc...a perfect, shining silver sphere, with a halo of red and white light...and from behind Scafell, imagine the Sun rising...a flaming ball of gold, dragging behind it a trail of fiery orange..."

She could actually see it. Everything, just as he was describing it; the cathedral flanked by soaring mountains, Sun and Moon emerging simultaneously, brilliant against a star-strewn sky...

"...And as you behold those images, sense the power of Sun and Moon pouring in and filling our circle and each of us with the loving energy of the infinite...the eternal...the divine. Let go, surrender to the light...aware of whatever enters your consciousness...'

She watches, awestruck, as the cathedral walls dissolve, melting away like wax in a furnace, revealing the mountains. Dwarfing everything round them: regal, magnificent, they tower into a night sky in which both Sun and Moon radiate light. The Earth is suffused with dazzling, blinding brilliance of silver and gold.

The warmth in her hands has become a current, now pulsing through her entire being. The image flashes before her of a perfect ring of dancing flame, flickering round all those who had linked hands, passing through them in an unbroken circle of fire. But they are no longer separate beings holding hands. They are one, single, unified body of humanity. In an ecstatic, blissful moment, Patricia is one with Karl, with Morgana, with Olaf...with all of them...with all humanity. There is no separation...ever...

She opened her eyes; her cheeks were wet with tears. Karl, face buried in sinewy hands, wept silently at her side. She hugged him, resting her head on his broad shoulder. The trembling subsided and he stepped back, dabbing awkwardly at his eyes.

"Are you okay...?" she asked.

He nodded. "I told you I didn't know why I'd come all this way..." he said, with a wan smile. "Well, now I think maybe I do..."

She took the proffered handkerchief and nodded.

"I'm glad," she told him. "And I don't understand what just happened, but...maybe I know, too."

Chapter 13

Mitch

Thursday 16th June 2011

A cacophony of alien sounds dragged the reluctant Patricia from deep sleep to the edge of consciousness. Opening her eyes resulted only in disorientation; nothing she saw was familiar. The noise filling the room became louder and more insistent; wailing guitars and someone angry pounding drums. Not her kind of music, least of all at half-past eight in the morning. Managing to locate the source, she seized her mobile from the bedside table and jabbed at it until silence reigned once more. Every time Colm laid hands on the thing, half the settings changed; it began announcing callers' names, or greeted incoming emails with a sound like a demented cockerel. On this occasion it was the alarm. She had chosen Vivaldi to ease her gently from her slumbers; he had substituted something hideous and tuneless. It called for a polite but extremely firm request that he restore her own settings, which were never to be tampered with again. She was settling back for a ten-minute snooze when the house phone rang.

"Good morning, Dr Carragh. It's Emma from reception. I have a message for you…"

"Oh…?"

"From Mr Ward."

"Ward…?"

She put a hand to her forehead, trawling her memory for anyone she knew of that name. No one came to mind, and, in any case, how could they possibly have known where she was?

"For me – are you sure…?"

Emma from reception rustled some papers. In the background a radio announcer intoned the news.

"It definitely says Dr Patricia Carragh but I didn't take the message myself and the writing's a bit hard to read. It looks like Ward. Oh, there's another name. Mr Bandston or maybe...Bandison?"

"Couldn't be Bardarson could it...?"

"Oh, yes, I think it is...sorry."

"No problem. What's the message...?"

"You're invited to have breakfast with them in our coffee shop at nine. There's a mobile number for you to let them know..."

What Mitch's clients told her about him intrigued her. Nine o'clock still gave her time for an indulgence she reserved almost exclusively for her infrequent hotel visits; a leisurely soak in a foaming, scented bath.

"Would you be a pet and call them back for me?"

"Yes, of course..."

"Tell Mr Ward thanks, I'll see them there..."

Ψ

Lingering over her bath longer than planned, it was quarter past nine before Patricia entered the coffee shop. A glance at the table told her the others had arrived some time before. Morgana, sporting dark glasses, sat with legs folded under her, guru-style, studying a gossip magazine. She glanced up, acknowledging the newcomer's arrival with a brief, tight-lipped smile. Olaf joined his palms and inclined his head; Mitch waved her to a chair.

"Morning, Dr Carragh. I'm Mitchell Ward," he told her. "My friends call me Mitch."

"Mine call me Patricia..."

Stocky, barrel-chested and broad shouldered the owner and managing director of *Dragon Tours* possessed a poker player's shrewd eyes, a nose which looked as if it had been broken and

290

badly set and a head of thick, greying hair, drawn back tightly across his scalp into a ponytail. A goatee sprouted from his square jaw.

"Sorry I'm late…"

"No problem. Glad you could make it. Olaf tells me it was you that certified him sane."

"Indeed?" She raised an eyebrow. "That might be an over statement…"

"I hope he is. He's busy reorganising my business…"

"Just a few ideas I have…" Olaf began, but Mitch held up a hand.

"Some of which I like. Others, well…" He shook his head as he handed Patricia a menu. "Now then, I haven't felt too good the last couple of days but my appetite's back, thank God. I can tell you the smoked salmon and scrambled eggs are done to order – none of your reheated rubbish. Coffee's pretty good and according to Morgana the almond croissants are to die for. That right…?"

"They're okay…" she said from behind her magazine.

"You're a guest of the company by the way," he told Patricia.

"That's very kind…"

He waved her thanks aside.

"It's nothing of the kind. Entertaining's an allowable expense. Any gratitude is due to Her Majesty's Revenue and Customs, God bless their generous hearts…"

"Amen…" Patricia scanned the menu. "I fancy a latte please, and if they're that good, I shall spoil myself with a croissant…"

A waitress materialised at Mitch's side and Patricia studied him as he placed the order. In his late forties or early fifties, he might have the face and physique of a nightclub bouncer but he offered few rough edges to the world. He wore a plain, white, open-necked shirt and stone washed jeans; an aviator style jacket of soft black leather was draped across the back of his chair. Planting his elbows on the table he clasped his hands and gave her a crooked smile.

"So, what did you think of last night?" he enquired. "Are you signing up for the rest of the tour?"

"Pity you couldn't make it, but I thought these guys did a grand job. Mind you," she added, "I have to admit I'm a novice when it comes to that kind of thing."

"What kind of thing...?"

"What would you call it...the supernatural?"

"A novice? You're kidding me." His smile broadened, revealing uneven teeth. "With Finn McCool and Brian Boru and all those banshees and wee folk? You must've been fed that stuff with your mother's milk..."

"It's a bit of a jump from the odd leprechaun to moveable mountains and invoking spirits..."

Mitch put down his coffee to frown at Morgana.

"You didn't say anything about..."

"Mitch, it was okay, really..." Patricia was quick to assure him. "I just meant some things were...let's say, unfamiliar to me."

Mitch, eyes narrowed, shook his head. "I still want to know..."

"Like she says, it was fine." Morgana sighed. "Absolutely fine..."

"We've done the tour a few times. I just wanted the same kind of thing we normally..."

"Which I did..."

"So what's the doc talking about, then...?"

"If you'd just let me finish, I was going to explain – Olaf came up with some new material, that's all. Which everyone loved – absolutely lapped it up. Ask her..."

Mitch smiled at Patricia. "What did you really make of it, be honest now?"

"It was extremely interesting, Mitch. I thought so, anyway. Especially the bit right at the end..."

"Okay. Nothing too...weird, then?" He glanced at Morgana.

"She can get a bit…"

"For God's sake, chill out," Morgana groaned. "You heard what she said."

"I'd be surprised if most of the others didn't feel the same…" Patricia told him, looking round. "Where are they, by the way?"

"Late night – we give them the morning off for souvenir-hunting, sightseeing and so on. We'll round 'em up and get them back on the coach again later." He glanced at Olaf. "Did you talk to many people afterwards?"

"Quite a few. It was hard to get away…"

"And…?"

"A Chinese lady did say she was feeling a little nervous towards the end, but by the time we spoke she was fine. People seemed to enjoy it…" Olaf reached for a piece of toast. "One man said he was blown out…"

"Away…" Morgana turned a cool smile in his direction. "The phrase is blown away…"

"Yes, thank you…"

"Did the lady say what made her nervous?"

"A little exercise based on one of those maps I showed you…"

Mitch took a deep breath and met Patricia's eyes. "But all in all you'd reckon it went down all right?"

"I don't think there's anything to worry about, Mitch…"

"I hope not," he told her. "They let you know fast enough if they've got any gripes."

Morgana lowered her magazine. "No need to get your knickers in a twist then, is there…"

Olaf's gaze flickered from Mitch to Morgana before catching Patricia's eye.

"So you liked the last part…?" he enquired.

"Definitely. In fact…"

She was tempted to describe that intense, climactic final experience, holding hands in the circle of fire, but it was not the moment; not here, surrounded by strangers.

"It's still, well…settling in my mind. But the people I spoke to," she told Mitch, "were pretty complementary about it…"

"Good. It's tough pleasing all the customers all the time…" He sipped his coffee. "You can only do your best."

As the waitress delivered their order, Patricia glanced round the room; practically every table was occupied and the place was buzzing with morning chatter. The croissant was warm to her touch; she broke off a piece and slipped it into her mouth.

"Did you see that young chap spying on you in the chapel?" she asked Olaf. "He did not look very happy. I'd say he might have been a priest…"

"The pale guy? More like a bloody ghost if you ask me…" Morgana offered in a bored voice. "He wasn't though…"

"Spying – really?" Olaf frowned, "I did not notice him…"

"But then you wouldn't, would you, sweetie…?"

Olaf glanced at her but she turned the page and avoided his eyes.

"I don't think he knew what to make of your angels…" Patricia told her.

"You'd hardly expect him to – not that they're mine…"

"No, I meant—"

"You talked about angels, did you…?" enquired Mitch, unimpressed.

"I did, actually…" replied Morgana, glaring at him. "Any objection?"

"And ruffled a few ecclesiastical feathers in the process?" He grinned. "Wouldn't be the first time, won't be the last."

Patricia cocked her head. "You don't think *Dragon Tours* might get banned…"

"I doubt it, somehow." He rubbed thumb and forefinger together. "They don't hand out late tour permits free, gratis, you know. Sounds like it might have been risky, letting this one loose on my little flock…" He jerked a thumb at Olaf, "but she reckoned he'd be okay."

Morgana had exchanged her romantic ensemble of the previous evening for a loose, flowing, peacock-print shirtdress, over skinny black leggings. The change in mood was equally marked. Gone was the softness; anger glittered in her gaze like distant lightning.

"I told you he'd be absolutely fine, which he was..." She nodded at her empty cup. "Would you ask them to get their finger out, Mitch. I ordered hot water ages ago."

Whatever domestic drama was playing out, Patricia had no intention of becoming drawn into it, nor letting it spoil breakfast. When she had finished her breakfast she would plead train schedules and make her exit.

"Do you do many tours on the scale of this one?"

"As many as I can fill..." Mitch shrugged. "Hasn't been so easy the last couple of years, though. We're feeling the pinch, same as most, I suppose."

"I can imagine..."

"They're pretty good business, though – nice money-spinners. Smaller ones are my bread and butter – day trips, mostly. They pay the mortgage – or would if I had one," he corrected himself with a grin. "Carting punters off to see stone circles, earthworks, megaliths, and crop circles, of course. Very popular they are, if you can track them down."

"Can't you just slip out and mow a few...?"

Mitch's smile faded. "You're joking, are you?"

"I was actually. All I know about them is what I've read..."

"Most likely churned out by idiots who don't know what the hell they're talking about..." he said, with feeling. "I never take my people anywhere unless I've checked it out and it's authentic..."

"I don't doubt it," she told him. "You'll be pleased to know one southern belle described your knowledge on such things as encyclopaedic..."

"That would be Ramona...?"

"It would."

He shook his head. "That one's a character. Haven't heard her old man say a word yet..."

"He's probably given up trying..."

"Mitch and me have a lot of interests in common," Olaf told her. "Before you arrived we had a good talk..."

"We...?" Mitch rolled his eyes. "He did most of the talking. Hard to get a word in edgeways with this one. Did you find that...?"

Patricia nursed her tall glass in both hands and gave the question a moment's thought. She could only guess how much Olaf had told Mitch about his stay at Maidenbloom or the circumstances surrounding it.

"I plead client confidentiality."

Morgana did not join in the laughter.

"Which I'll take as a yes," Mitch told her. "He's right, though. We're into similar stuff..."

"Oh? Like sacred sites...?"

"And ley lines. Hobby of mine, ley lines. And rocks, burial sites...standing stones..." A gold ring glinted as he waved his hand. "Old churches...and trees of course."

"All trees?" she enquired.

"Yews in particular..."

"Really?" Patricia tilted her head. "Why them?"

"The very old ones, anyway. Did you know their heart eventually rots away? Makes 'em bloody difficult to age. They reckon we've got some in this country upwards of three thousand years old..." He pursed his lips. "Three thousand years, think of that. God, think of the stories they could tell..."

Patricia licked flakes of croissant from her fingers.

"Is that why you like them – because they're old?"

"That's part of it. But if you want a genuine, real live energy field, there's not much beats a yew. There's a few I know – as you get nearer you can actually feel it..."

"Feel what…?"

"The energy. It's hard to describe. It's a bit like…a tiny electric charge they give out."

"You get a shock?"

"More of a tingle," he said, smiling.

"It is very subtle," offered Olaf. "A warm feeling…"

"Come and visit one, you'll see for yourself. We had a bloke on one of the tours," Mitch went on, "who'd got himself smashed up in some car crash years before. Said he was in pain twenty-four seven. I took him along to this big old yew in Worcestershire and he was absolutely gob-smacked. While he was within eight or ten feet he was right as rain. No pain at all. He couldn't believe it but it didn't surprise me. They're special all right…" Leaning forward, he dropped his voice. "Some people believe they can help you develop, well…gifts."

"Really? Tell me more…"

"Healing for one, and divination. They were supposed to be witches' trees, weren't they? But…" He held up a warning finger. "You want to mind your step. If you don't treat them respectful like, you can find yourself in trouble…"

A waitress bustled up to place a stainless steel jug of steaming water in front of Morgana, who did not acknowledge its arrival. A young woman at a neighbouring table who had been eavesdropping on their conversation caught Patricia's eye and looked away.

"Told you I'd been under the weather, didn't I? Sick as a dog." He grimaced. "Now that's what can happen. Morgana and me had been down to this little place called Great Rhos. There's a local legend says it's where the last dragon in Wales was buried. Tricky old stuff, dragon energy, so to pin it down and make sure it didn't get loose and cause trouble…"

"Olaf mentioned it," Patricia told him. "They used churches for that, didn't they?"

"Four of them." Mitch nodded. "All dedicated to St Michael.

You know who he was...?"

"An archangel...?" she ventured.

"He was a dragon-slayer before he got Christianised..."

Mitch suddenly thrust out a hand. Patricia recoiled as he impaled the remains of her croissant with a fork. Waving it aloft, he grinned.

"...That's how you always see old Michael in your stained glass windows and statues and suchlike, isn't it? Pinning dragons with lances or chopping them up with a sword."

Patricia frowned. "I'm getting confused. Wasn't that St George?"

"Kindred spirits – literally. Dragons and snakes, all the same thing, you see. They represent basic, earthy human instincts..."

"Primal ones..." added Olaf.

"So whether he's called George or Michael he's supposed to get us to stop and think. Have we got those wicked urges under proper control...?"

With a gleam in his eye, his pony-tail, goatee and lop-sided grin, central casting would have picked Mitchell Ward for the role of Pan.

"Are you having sex strictly for the purposes of procreation – which the church says is okay – or for pleasure, which is not? Are you a slave to your urges – do you control them or do they control you? That's what dragon-slayer stories are all about, you see..."

"Which puts a new slant on England's patron saint..." Patricia smiled.

"And what about St Patrick?" Olaf grinned.

"Good point..." she agreed.

"Not really new," Mitch pointed out. "It's just that people have forgotten what it really means, that's all."

Flagging down a waitress, Mitch ignored Patricia's protestations and ordered a replacement croissant.

"They were supposed to make people reflect – send them on

an inner journey," offered Olaf. "You find characters like Michael as far back as Egyptian myths. You know about Horus killing Set as a crocodile...?"

Mitch held up a hand. "Hang on my friend...I haven't finished telling the doc about Wales. The story goes that, if those four churches went to rack and ruin, the dragon would break loose and run amok..."

"Which is not good..." Olaf drew down the corners of his mouth.

"You ain't kidding. Anyway, in I went to dowse the last of the four. It's a ruin – only a few bits of wall here and there still standing. I should've asked permission first, but I was running late so I skipped it. Mistake..." He puffed out his cheeks. "Wasn't feeling too great by the time I'd finished, so I got Morgana to drive back but I didn't really think anything of it. Then, over the weekend, it hit me. I'll spare you the gory details." He patted his belly ruefully. "But it taught me a lesson. You've got to be careful with rogue energies like that. I won't be making that mistake again..."

"What should you have done?" Patricia wanted to know.

"Make sure I didn't upset the guardians," Mitch told her with a shrug. "Start off by asking if what I wanted to do was okay with them – simple as that."

"It is important to do that." Olaf nodded. "Ask permission to enter and seek their help."

Patricia took a sip of coffee.

"There's a yew in a churchyard not far from me which I've heard is one of the oldest in the country..." Patricia told him. "Might it be one of the special ones?"

"In a churchyard...?"

"I haven't seen it myself, but I think so, yes."

"Sure, could well be..."

"So if I went along, how do I pacify the spirits – what's the etiquette?"

"You should definitely go," Mitch insisted. "And it's dead simple. Treat it the same as you would a person. It's a living creature, isn't it?"

"Is it, really?"

"You may not realise it," Mitch told her, leaning forward, "but every tree you walk past knows you're there. It registers your presence..."

"I see..."

"So say hello to it. Explain who you are and why you've come. And, like Olaf said, maybe a quick prayer to the guardians..."

Patricia nodded. "I think I could manage that..."

She was back in Sligo, listening to Colm, straining to catch Frances's invocation above the rain beating on the car roof. Watching him race off through the rain, heading for the storm-pummelled yew while the gale threatened to tear the boy's shirt from his back. She was wondering what the others would make of her story, when a metallic chime signalled an incoming text message.

"Excuse me..." She reached for her bag. "Better check. Might be work..."

She glanced at the screen.

hi mum hope u r ok. Gr8 party thanx 4 letin me go now work promise love you lots xxxxx.

"It wasn't," she told them. "My sixteen year old. I let him go partying last night. He had a great time. Funny, I was just thinking about him..."

"So..." Olaf smiled. "Maybe he sent you a different kind of message, an even faster one, just by having you in his consciousness..."

She glanced at Mitch and shrugged.

"He doesn't believe in coincidence."

Mitch folded his arms and raised an eyebrow.

"Ooops. Outnumbered, am I? Change of subject, then. It occurs to me you have pulled off a trick most people only dream about. Making a pretty good living out of something you love."

"It didn't fall into my lap – took some work, but what you say is basically true, I guess. Came to it late, mind. I trained as a surveyor. Boring as hell but the kind of steady job parents like mine want for their kids."

"Quite a jump," she observed. "Surveyor to tour guide."

"Entrepreneur," he corrected her.

Olaf grinned. "The land called him…"

"You could say that…"

Morgana sighed. "Except it's complete and utter bollocks…"

"Really…?"

"Really. His wife left him."

Mitch shot her a sharp glance. "What's wrong with you today, lady…?"

"Saying it like it is doesn't mean there's anything wrong."

"What would you know about it anyway?" Mitch demanded.

"What you told me, which was – the reason you got out of London was…"

"You…" He jabbed a finger at her, "have been bloody moody ever since Great Rhos…"

"She seemed fine…" began Olaf, but only Patricia seemed to hear him.

"Moi?" She gave a humourless laugh. "There's a word for that. Which I think is…projection. Ask Patricia, she'll tell you."

Retiring behind her magazine, she left Mitch to glance at Patricia and roll his eyes.

"As a matter of interest," Patricia enquired, "which version is true?"

"Bit of both, probably…"

"Explain how the land called you…"

"Well, while I was a surveyor, I went on a site visit down Marlborough way and ran into an old boy who told me to be careful because the ground was unstable. Said it was on an aquifer. When I asked how he knew, he waved a couple of pieces of coat hanger and just walked off. I decided to get a digger in and it turned out he was spot on so I got interested and tracked him down. He said he was a druid – which meant sod-all to me – and started rattling on about dowsing. Claimed water was an earth energy, and there were other kinds, too. Still hadn't a clue what he was on about, so I gave him a few quid to show me how to dowse – and got hooked. That's the land connection, I guess..."

"Makes sense..." She nodded.

"It was just a hobby to start with but when my marriage went tits up – if you'll pardon the expression – I moved down to Somerset. I was fed up to the back teeth with what I'd been doing but I needed an income and hit on the idea of running tours." He shrugged. "And here I am..."

"The emperor of *Dragon Tours...*"

"I've been called worse." He grinned.

"I was wondering about the accent. You're not really west country, then?"

"Fools most people." He chuckled. "Three parts Bermondsey and a dash of Somerset."

"Do you teach people on your tours how to dowse?" Olaf asked.

"I sometimes mention it..." Mitch paused. "Never actually showed anyone how..."

"You should. It would be good for them..." the Icelander told him.

"Good how...?"

"Tuning to external fields can activate inner ones..."

Mitch caught Patricia's eye and shook his head.

"He still doesn't get I run sight-seeing tours. He wants to turn them into workshops or therapy courses or...God knows what."

"No, no. I do not suggest you change anything..." protested Olaf. "But maybe you could add something...a new dimension."

Mitch looked doubtful.

"New, maybe, but would it be commercial? That's what it

comes down to..."

"Bookings aren't great, you said so yourself," Morgana pointed out. "What do you have to lose? Could be exactly what DT needs to create some excitement – get new people coming along..."

"How do you know it won't frightened off the old ones? Not everyone goes for that...spiritual stuff."

"Loads of younger people are seriously interested in it. The kind who come to see me..." she insisted. "Just because it scares the hell out of you, don't think..."

"Hang on, who said it scared me? I'm listening to your friend here, aren't I? All I'm saying is—"

"Sometimes you talk such bollocks..." she snapped.

Grim-faced, Mitch leaned forward and tapped his temple. "Sounds like your cosmic mates got right in your head..."

"Bastard..."

Morgana grimaced and launched her magazine at him. Mitch thrust out a hand to send it fluttering to the floor like a wounded pheasant. As a dark stain from his upturned coffee cup spread across the cloth, faces at neighbouring tables turned their way.

"You can be such a sod...!" she hissed.

Olaf bent to retrieve Morgana's magazine. Passing it to her, his gaze flickered uncomfortably between the young woman and Mitch. Olaf appealed to Patricia for support. "What do you think, Dr Carragh?"

"About...?"

"Mitch trying, you know...new things."

"Hard to say. Some people would probably go for it. It rather depends what they're looking for, doesn't it...?"

"I'm not rushing into anything," Mitch announced turning his cup over and placing it back on the saucer. "What I'm doing now works pretty well."

Olaf folded his arms and smiled at Patricia. "Perhaps dowsing lessons would be good for your patients..."

"As well as chanting..."

"Yes, yes. Be holistic. Treat them all – spirit, body and mind..."

"Olaf, I wouldn't argue with that. But you keep forgetting, I'm a psychiatrist, not some kind of faith healer..."

"See what I mean?" Mitch nodded. "Me, too. I just run tours..."

Olaf gave Morgana a sideways glance. Lips pursed, she folded her arms and leaned back but said nothing.

"I know." Olaf nodded. "But you could do more than take people to standing stones or corn circles or cathedrals. You could offer them journeys which are exciting, profound..."

"Yeah, but not everyone..."

"Inner ones..."

"Sounds great, but you don't know my punters like I do. I'll give you long odds hardly any of them would be up for personal growth or whatever..."

"That's the whole point, don't you see? He's not talking about people like this boring lot." Morgana waved a hand. "You'd attract new customers, younger people..."

"Boring they may be, but they've got money..."

"And some of the old ones," Olaf countered. "Plenty of them enjoyed last night..."

Mitch scratched his chin. "Maybe, but all that soul searching? Deep, meaningful experiences?" He sighed. "You've got to be careful with that stuff, my friend. Before you know it you're deep in woo-woo territory..."

"Woo-woo...?" Olaf echoed shaking his head.

"Weird and wonderful," Mitch told him dryly. "Look, I already have enough hassle from health and safety, for God's sake. The last thing I need is men in white coats coming calling..."

"Or women...?" enquired Morgana bestowing a thin smile on Patricia. "You should actually listen to him, Mitch. All you tour people do the same dull stuff. Visit the same old places, regurgitate the same historical facts, tell them the odd ghost story and...that's about it. Why not think outside the box for once – be original..."

Mitch took a deep breath. "He's got a couple of ideas I could probably develop that might – might, mind – give us an edge over the competition..." He smiled at Patricia. "Like he said, me and him are into the same kind of things. We may come at them from different angles, but basically..."

"Not different...I would say matching," Olaf offered, joining his palms together, fingers interlinked. "We would amplify each other's understandings. Making them deeper, richer..."

"How would you see it working?" Patricia wanted to know. "In practical terms..."

"Well, he showed me the maps he did for last night. They went down all right, apparently and he says he's got plenty more..."

Olaf nodded at Patricia. "She has seen them..."

"He has, yes," confirmed Patricia. "There's no shortage of maps..."

"It'd make sense if I stick to what I know best. Historical background, local legends...oh, and the ecological stuff, of course. Healing the planet. Always goes down big with the Chinese, God know why – they're major league polluters..."

"Which would be the perfect place to introduce dowsing..." Olaf added. "Show people how to receive messages from nature..."

"Might be a runner..." Mitch nodded, tugging at his goatee.

"What about Olaf?" asked Patricia.

"He's got it all sorted..." he said with a wry glance at the Icelander. "Go ahead, tell the lady..."

"Mitch is good at leading groups on what I call the outer journey. They concentrate mainly on the physical, the material, but he does give people a taste of the..." he reached for the word, "esoteric..."

"Dunno about that..." Mitch frowned.

"It sounds like that to me," Olaf insisted. "So let me guide them along a parallel path. Different in nature, sure, but parallel. With Mitch they explore the surface, I invite them to dig a little deeper..."

"You make it all sound ordinary, but to a lot of people it's anything but, my friend..." Mitch pursed his lips.

"As long as we do it in the right way..."

"What do you think would be the right way, then?" Patricia asked.

"Gently. With sensitivity. First maybe introduce them to the idea of symbolic meanings. Then the kind of thing you did last night: simple rituals...visualisations. How did you find that? "

"Fine..." Patricia assented. "Better than fine, actually..."

"So..." Olaf looked at Mitch and spread his hands.

"As long as we avoid anything too far out, too weird," insisted Mitch. "I'm not having people scared off..."

Olaf glanced at Patricia, eyebrows raised. "Have you done visualisations before?"

"Not really..."

"But it was okay..."

"It was certainly powerful. I'm not sure enjoy is the word I'd use..."

"Would you like to do more?"

Patricia took a deep breath. Morgana sipped hot water and studied her.

"Yes, under the right conditions. But my opinion probably isn't worth much. I mean, a middle-aged Irish woman with a medical training? Hardly the *Dragon Tours* demographic..."

"Fair point," Mitch agreed.

"And my maps come from different understandings, but they go really well with Mitch's ley lines..." He spread his hands. "I would not frighten anyone, just encourage them to look at what their experiences really mean. Go a little bit deeper..."

"Not so bloody deep my punters start running round babbling in tongues or leaving their bodies, thank you very much..." He winked at Patricia. "If he's coming on board maybe we should have you too, Doc. Fancy being our resident shrink...?"

Morgana shot Olaf a withering glance. "If you're thinking of working for him," she said in ominously soft tones, "a piece of advice for you, sweetheart. Get a good lawyer and a proper contract."

"You will have noticed..." Mitch said, with a weary sigh, "that employee relations are my top priority..."

"Crap. Your top priority is Mitch. And whatever he says, don't think he'll actually let you do anything remotely spiritual," Morgana told Olaf. "If he'd been around, last night would never have happened..."

Mitch drew a gold cigarette lighter from his pocket. He flicked it and stared at the flame for a few moments before shutting it. "Me and her have never seen eye to eye on that subject. But," he added placing the lighter on the table, "after what Patricia's said, I might give it some thought..."

Morgana opened her mouth to speak and changed her mind.

Patricia drained her cup and looked at Olaf. "So you might join Mitch. Rather different from what you had in mind when we first talked..."

He smiled and gave a wry nod. "Isn't it wonderful what unexpected gifts the universe sends...?"

"This really appeals to you, then..."

"I would enjoy working with Mitch...He is grounded and practical. I am..."

"Not...?" Morgana's tone was edged with acid.

Olaf met her eyes and forced a smile. "I was going to say, Mitch is earth and I am air. Together, we give people the best of both worlds..."

Mitch chuckled. "What he means is he's into all the invisible, floaty, airy-fairy stuff. I keep my feet firmly on the ground. Rooted in nature, the planet and earth energies…"

"And money," Morgana donned a saccharin smile. "Be honest. When it comes down to it, you're really about money aren't you?"

"I'm running a business, for Christ's sake…" The big man planted his hands flat on the table as if to prevent it flying away. "Listen, if you've got something to say, feel free. Just go ahead and say it…"

"I just did," she retorted. "You probably weren't listening, as per usual. You make it sound like all you want is to get people hugging your precious trees. Which is crap. You don't give a shit about saving the planet, do you?"

Mitch ran his hand across his eyes. "Oh, Jesus…" he groaned.

"Seriously, you're in it for as much as you can get…"

"What the hell's wrong with doing both…?"

Morgana's fresh onslaught drew an unhappy glance from Olaf. Mitch appeared to be her principle target, with the Icelander no more than collateral damage; an innocent bystander caught in the crossfire of what bore the hallmarks of a festering feud.

"How come," Morgana demanded, "you always ignore my suggestions, but when your new best friend comes up with exactly the same things, suddenly they're bloody brilliant…?"

"Hang about. They're not the same things. They're not even remotely…"

"Of course they are, don't you see…?"

Mitch shook his head wearily. "No, Morgana, they are not…"

"How can you say that…?"

"Because it's true. What you want is my lot to have those bloody readings of yours, don't you? Talk about woo-woo…"

His protestations were swept aside like bamboo huts in the path of a tsunami.

"God! That just proves you never listened to me…" She leaned towards him, stabbing an angry finger at the coffee-stained tablecloth. "Always made a big joke of anything I came up with. Said it was all about bloody fairy music and angels..."

"If it wasn't, what was it, then?"

Her eyes on Mitch's face she gestured at Olaf. "What he's been telling you! Don't just go on feeding people old churches and folk stories for God's sake. Give them something serious to think about. Something important. Like who are they, how are they living their lives, why are they...?"

"If that's what they wanted, they wouldn't be on a tour at all. They'd have buggered off to church..."

"You weren't even there last night, how can you say that?" she shouted, nodding at Patricia. "Didn't you hear what she said...?"

He held up a hand. "For Christ's sake, keep your voice down..."

"Shut up, you mean. Just love that, wouldn't you? Don't make a fuss, let good old Mitch run the show..." Under the cotton shirt, her chest heaved. "Everybody always has to do what you want. You are such a bloody control freak...!"

He shook his head. "I don't have a clue what you're on about..."

"Which proves you're still not listening...!"

He raised his palms towards her. "I am..."

"To her, maybe..." Morgana dragged clawed fingers through her hair, sending her sunglasses clattering across the floor. "Not that she gets the spiritual stuff any more than you do. We know that for a fact, don't we, Dr Carragh...?"

"Do we...?"

Half closed, Morgana's dark, deep-set eyes searched Patricia's with disconcerting intensity. She tilted her head and spoke in a soothing, softer voice. "Odd, isn't it? You used to be really open to it back in the day, didn't you? Way back, when you were a kid, I mean. Isn't that right, Doctor...?"

"You obviously think so..."

"Don't pretend you've forgotten. Listening to the old lady...you know who I mean, of course you do. After all, she was such a special person in your life. And she told you wonderful stories, didn't she? Scared you sometimes, but you loved those stories all the same..." She paused. "You even wanted to grow up to be like her, see what she saw...do things she could do."

Mitch grimaced. "Hey, Morgana, give it a rest..."

She gave no sign of hearing; her eyes remained locked on Patricia's.

"It was all too much for you, though. Easier to tell people she was away with the fairies wasn't it? She's not, though, far from it..." She shook her ringlets. "After last weekend you must know that..."

"I've no idea what the hell you're on about," Mitch told her, "and she probably doesn't, either..."

Morgana shivered and sat bolt upright, blinking. "Why don't we ask her...?"

Patricia folded her arms. "I don't think this is..."

But Morgana had swung back to glare at Mitch.

"Now it's all about you and Olaf. I'll do the earthy stuff, he'll do the spiritual bit..." Her lip curled. "Oh won't we work beautifully together? Isn't everyone going to love us? Won't we make such a fucking brilliant pair...?"

"If it's what you wanted, what are you bitching about...?"

"Why him? I've worked for you for ages..."

"You never really worked for me. Sure, you've helped out..."

"Helped out...?" Her jaw was clenched so tightly the words could barely escape from between small, even teeth. "That's what I was doing in your bed was it, you bastard..."

Patricia was studying Olaf's expression. It told her that, however uncomfortable Morgana's words might be, they came as no surprise.

"Look at you, old enough to be my father..." she taunted Mitch.

"What is it about you and young flesh, ehh? Does it help you forget how old you are...?"

"That's enough..." he snapped.

Olaf flattened his palms on the table. "Morgana. Please...?"

"If I were you I'd be very, very careful," she told him with a grim smile. "Because Mitchell Ward will use you and kick you out like a piece of shit...Your problem," she went on, "is you live in la-la land. You can only see the best in everyone and every-thing, which is just great except...it's not how the world actually works. Sorry, sweetheart, but there's bad stuff, too. Dark stuff..."

Olaf nodded. "You think I don't know that...?"

Morgana laid her hand on Olaf's. "You know it, but you dance round it, don't you? The *Order* has a great phrase for that. Patricia won't like me quoting them, but I don't give a toss if she does or not..." She paused. "They call it a spiritual by-pass..."

Olaf shrugged. "Perhaps you are right..."

"God, you're always so bloody nice..." Glancing at the others she shook her head. "Why don't you lot get real? Say it like it is, be honest – at least with yourselves..."

Jumping to her feet, she seized her bag and slung it across her shoulder.

"You'd never admit it, Mitch, but it's taken two people to make your precious tours a success, and neither of them's him..."

Turning on her heel she strode off, blouse billowing like a galleon's sail. A grey haired man at a nearby table had retrieved her glasses. He half rose and proffered them as she strode by, but she brushed past without a glance. Wrenching the door open she disappeared into the street.

Mitch puffed out his cheeks and leaned back. "She's like those volcanoes of yours..." he told Olaf. "You never know when the bloody things are going to blow, until they do. Mind you, I've seen worse..."

"Did you say you both went to Great Rhos...?" murmured Patricia.

"Yeah…"

"Perhaps that's it, then."

"That's what…?" Mitch frowned.

"The dragon bit you both…"

A smile spread slowly across his craggy features.

"Do you know, Doc, you're getting the hang of this stuff, aren't you…?" He nodded at Olaf. "I reckon that's a pretty good call, don't you…?"

Chapter 14

Into the Unknown

54

Thursday 16th June 2011

"Honestly, it was so cool. They had this fantastic DJ. Some of his mixes were like, awesome. There's clips of him on YouTube…"

"I need to finish this, pet. Maybe later…"

"Check him out. He's called Hazchem…"

Colm, in T-shirt and tattered jeans roughly scissored into shorts, lay on a moth-ravaged tartan blanket, head propped on one hand. Amid a clutter of books and papers, mobile and iPod within arm's length, he recounted the events of the previous night. Patricia sat in a candy-striped deckchair, trying to divide her attention between her son and a research paper on the benefits of EMDR in the treatment of post-traumatic stress disorder. She reached for her apple juice.

"Where's he from? Sounds Turkish…"

"Croydon. That's his DJ name. He got it off a lorry…"

Patricia's brow furrowed. "Off what…?"

"You must have seen them…"

She shook her head. "You've lost me, pet…"

"Those signs. It means hazardous chemicals…"

"Oh, those…okay."

"He's reading psychology at uni. Exeter or somewhere, I think. But he doesn't do much like, work…"

"A toast to Hazchem…" she murmured raising her glass. "Role model for any young person…"

"Only because he doesn't have time…" Colm rolled his eyes. "You'd be proud if I was a big name DJ, wouldn't you?"

"Enormously. And I shall definitely come and watch you

when you are," she warned. "Just by walking in I shall double the average age…"

"He's played at quite a few big events already. He said there were over a thousand people when he did the Safe Sex Ball in Exeter…"

"Really…?" She paused. "That's certainly a lot of people."

"But his like, dream is playing a gig in Ibiza."

"It's still going is it…?" she enquired mildly. "I thought Ibiza got closed down for bad behaviour…"

"Still going…?" From his pained tone, any vestige of street cred she might have enjoyed had evaporated. "Mum, it's mega. It's like *the* place…"

Arriving home half an hour earlier, she had received an unexpected reward for slipping the leash to enable him to party beneath the rose moon. Trying to make the point she needed his help both inside the house and out, she had been nagging him to attend to the lawn. Not only was their ancient motor mower temperamental, awkward to start and heavy to manoeuvre, but her priorities lay elsewhere. Her efforts seemed to have been in vain until, climbing out of the Volvo, the unmistakeable, summery scent of freshly cut grass told her a small miracle had occurred.

"Did Sophie enjoy it…?" she asked, keeping her enquiry casual.

"They've got such a nice house…" Turning onto his back, he shaded his eyes with an arm. "With a pool. They said we could go and swim any time."

"Her mum sounded nice…"

It earned her a suspicious glance. "You talked to her?"

"Don't panic, I'm not the fun police. I wanted to thank her, that's all."

"Oh, yeah…" He brushed lazily at a fly. "Okay."

Patricia ran her gaze over the lawn with its neat, variegated stripes. A plump pigeon, carrying out a closer inspection, paused now and then to peck at the earth.

"She said you were a charming guest..."

"Yeah?"

"What did you do – mow their lawn?"

His brow furrowed. "Did I what...?"

"Just wondering how you charmed her."

Ice cubes tinkled like unseasonal sleigh bells as she sipped her drink.

"It does look great, by the way. Did I thank you?"

He sighed. "Twice, Mum."

"To make sure you get how much I appreciate your support. Speaking of which, I've got someone coming later – a kind of work thing. Only for an hour or so but I'll need the sitting room."

"A patient?"

"You know I never bring patients home. I was seeing this fellow, but he's been discharged. He's helping me with a project..."

"No probs. Thought I might have an early night, anyway."

She watched him stifle a yawn. It appeared Sophie's mother's idea of a curfew might have been optimistic. She returned to the article.

"And, Mum...?"

"Yes, pet...?"

"Dad rang."

Months down the line, yet her limbic system remained on hair-trigger setting; even casual mention of Liam could still make her catch her breath. She took time to drain her glass before replying.

"Oh, and...how was Dad?"

"Sounded okay. Said he wanted to talk to you."

"Did he say what about...?"

"Not really..." Now on his hands and knees, he was busy assembling his possessions. "What's for dinner?"

"Lasagne..."

"Cool..."

"Don't forget the blanket..."

"My hands are full..." He flashed one of those brilliant smiles she found it impossible to resist. "Can you...?"

"Lazy wretch." She pointed at the house. "Be gone..."

"Thanks..."

Inherited from his father, of course: the damned smile that convinced you his needs outweighed your own. That could make you say yes when the only sane answer was no. God, how flattered she had been at first to find those smiles beamed her way. Miss Patricia O'Leary, fresh from the bogs, taking the eye of a lecturer. Not some young buck, either, for wasn't the man twelve years her senior? She knew she was not the sole object of his attentions; she might be young but she was not born yesterday. Just as she was well aware of the man's reputation, but was that not all part of the appeal, the buzz, the excitement? Even being one of a crowd was intoxicating; all the more so for a young woman none of whose admirers in far-off Mayo had succeeded in raising her ardour.

How could she have been so naïve, so blind, so...bloody stupid? Not to mention vain. How was it possible to have convinced herself in the face of overwhelming evidence to the contrary that she could put manners on the wild man; she could tame the beast when others had failed? Ignoring the counsel of female friends more experienced in the ways of the world – and specifically the ways of attractive, manipulative and unprincipled men – she had clung blindly to the belief she could pull off the ultimate trick. She could transform the philandering Dr Liam Carragh into an honest, trustworthy and, above all, faithful partner.

Clambering out of the deckchair, she shook her head. Might this not be the time to revert to her maiden name; turn back the clock, resurrect Patricia O'Leary and give her a second chance?

"Mum..." A plaintive cry from the house. "Can we eat soon?

I'm starving..."

His grades in domestic science had been outstanding. Once exams were over she would give him cooking lessons. No son of hers was going to grow up into one of those men who seemed rendered helpless by simply walking into a kitchen.

"Mum...?"

"Coming, pet..."

Ψ

His tap on the kitchen door startled her. The Icelander must have moved as quietly as a cat; few people traversed the little courtyard without her hearing. He had retreated a few steps to give himself a better view of the house; she found him surveying the buttery stonework, pitted oak framing leaded windows and undulating roof like a potential purchaser.

He nodded approval. "Beautiful...it must be very old..."

"About five hundred years..."

She walked out and stood beside him, following his gaze.

"I fell in love with the place the moment I saw it. It had been on the market for ages, but for some reason it didn't sell..."

"Maybe it was waiting for you..."

She glanced at him. "Not very likely."

"Why not? I love the roof, look how it goes up and down." He traced the contours of the mossy tiles in the air. "And the brickwork of your chimney, so...elaborate. Is that the word?"

"Yes. Elaborate...ornate..."

"We have nothing like this..."

"Builders seem to like it," she told him. "Probably because it always needs some kind of work done. Anyway, come on in..."

"Morgana said she would collect me in one hour, but if we have time I would like to see your garden, please."

Accompanied by a squadron of tiny insects, they strolled the length of the narrow lawn occupying the upper terrace. As they approached the low stone balustrade marking the top of a flight of irregular stone steps giving access to the lower level, Olaf paused. He nodded at a spreading tree from the lower branches of which dangled a faded, fraying hammock.

"You and Mitch were talking about yew trees. You did not say you have your own…"

"It's so familiar I'd forgotten. Anyway, it's only a baby compared with the kind he likes. I'm told it was probably planted about the time that was built…" She pointed at a small grey stone building whose low, arched, wooden doorway was almost hidden by a blanket of ivy. "It's a privy…"

"Privy…?"

"Old word for loo. It was believed yews cleansed the soil – absorbed impurities…"

Olaf nodded, glancing round. "You live in the middle of a town, but it is so peaceful…"

"Apart from aircraft. We're close to the flight path into Gatwick…"

Hands clasped behind him, Olaf studied the steps leading down to a ramshackle wooden shed, the kitchen garden, a compost heap, and a pond which had been home to Colm's goldfish until a heron came calling. Gazing at an expanse of higher ground in the distance, he pointed out a steeple just visible on the horizon.

"There is a ley line running through your garden to that church," he told her. "Did you know…?"

"I didn't…"

"Is there a church close to here?"

"St Swithuns. Just the other side of the high street."

"That may explain why it was built in that particular place," he observed, turning away.

Patricia cocked her head. "How do you know about the ley line?"

Olaf pursed his lips. "I see it. Look – maybe you can."

"What am I looking for…?"

"What I see is pale and silvery – like the tracks of a snail…"

Narrowing her eyes she scanned the landscape, searching for anything fitting the description but seeing only a mosaic composed of different shades of green. She shook her head and glanced back to find him smiling.

"No? Maybe you are looking too hard. Some things are easier to see if you just…let them be there."

"Okay…"

"I can feel it, too. A stream of clear energy…" he told her. "I wonder if that is what drew you here. The ley line and the yew…"

"Yews have started popping up rather a lot recently…"

He cocked his head. "How is that…?"

"Colm hasn't been in the best form lately, what with exam pressure and, well…" She shrugged, "the stuff kids his age go through. While we were in Ireland we visited my grandmother and when Colm told her how he'd been, she sent him off to carry out a ritual. It involved tying coloured cord to a tree and she was very insistent – it had to be a yew."

"And what happened?"

"It was only a couple of days ago but, fingers crossed…so far so good."

Olaf stepped forward and stood for a few moments, head bowed. Placing a palm against the rough bark he smiled at her over his shoulder.

"Wise old grandmother knew exactly what to do, then…"

"It looks that way. Touch wood…"

He turned back to face her. "Morgana sensed a presence round you this morning, do you remember?"

"So she said…"

"Do you think it was the same lady…?"

Spectral manifestations might be commonplace in Olaf's life but his casual acceptance of them still came as a surprise. Even so, she could not deny she knew exactly who Morgana had meant.

"Quite possibly. Look, if we've only got an hour," she went on briskly, "we'd better go in and get down to work..."

They retraced their steps through evening air heavy with the earthy aroma of mown grass, mingling with the scent of sweet peas, like swarming butterflies on a wall-mounted wooden trellis.

"I'm glad you came...she told him. "After the fun and games this morning, I had my doubts."

"Me too," he admitted with a rueful grin. "But Mitch told me she would calm down and she did. We drove back as we planned."

"She can be a fiery lady..."

He shrugged. "She is a Cancerian."

"I'm afraid I don't know what that means..."

"That she is likely to be, well...unpredictable. And full moon would be a particularly difficult time for her – it probably makes her feel out of balance."

"I'm not much the wiser, but I'll take your word for it..."

Collecting a tray set with glasses, a cut glass jug of elderflower and a plate of biscuits, she led her visitor into the cool of the sitting room and nodded at a black leather sofa.

"That's fairly comfortable..."

"Thank you, but I prefer the carpet..." he told her.

He dropped down, folding his long limbs into the familiar cross-legged pose. The sofa had been a bone of contention between Liam and herself. He saw it as stylish and elegant; to her eye it was too big, too expensive, and depressingly dark. They faithfully adhered to the choreography of such conflicts; Liam refused to negotiate while Patricia fumed, resisted, and finally, resentfully, acquiesced. One day, she promised herself, the monster would be consigned to a charity shop or, failing that, the community rubbish dump. She swivelled a Scandinavian bentwood chair to face Olaf.

"When I asked you to help me, I'm not sure I explained exactly why…"

"You spoke of wishing to introduce a spiritual element into your work."

"That might be an overstatement. As a group we've committed to exploring whether there's a place for what you could call a greater metaphysical dimension in modern psychiatry." She paused. "If we agree that is the case, we'll have to tackle a much tougher issue. How on earth do we achieve that?"

"So," he asked, leaning back, "how do you think I can help you?"

"My paper focuses on one specific aspect of spiritual experience, and that's communication. You believe you are in touch with…let's call them non-physical beings, and messages pass between you. I want to find out as much as I can about what actually happens – how that kind of interaction takes place."

"Oh…" Olaf shrugged. "That is all?"

"We'll probably touch on other things, but that's the most important one, yes. I'd better explain I'm more interested in process than content, by the way. And if I'm to really understand your experiences it's going to help if you first give me an idea of where they fit into your life story…"

Opening a Maidenbower Hospital note pad and smoothing it across her lap, she uncapped a biro.

"Oh, and it's all confidential. I may quote you, but I will not identify you…"

"As you wish – it is not important," he told her. "So where do you want to start?"

"Right at the beginning would be good. When and how your paranormal experiences started. Assuming you remember…"

"Would I forget such a thing?" He took a deep breath. "I told you my mother married again after my father died, and how bad it was..."

"You did."

"I hated being anywhere near him because he frightened me. I stayed out of the house as much as possible. I went to the sea, into the hills, the mountains..."

"By yourself? You must have been awfully young."

"Seven or eight. Sometimes I went with my brother but mostly by myself. And that was when it started. Meeting...beings." He paused. "It did not seem strange because I already knew about spirits, you see. My grandparents told me stories about them..."

"Children's stories?"

"No. The sagas. They are about warriors and giants and the spirits who live in the land. They can take on different shapes and become people, birds, animals...anything. And they do all kinds of magic. Sagas are very simply written – literal, not poetic. The earliest ones were written on skins, but skins were very valuable, so they did not waste words." He smiled. "May I have a drink, please?"

She poured him some elderflower. He took a sip and sat for a moment or two staring at the glass, nursing it in both hands.

"My favourites were called Bárðar saga Snæfellsáss, the Ármanns saga, and...one called Hrana saga hrings..."

"Why those in particular?"

"I loved the ones about great heroes and battles between the forces of good and evil. Stories on a big scale, you know? I quite enjoyed the folk stories, too, but they were...different..."

"How so?"

"Everything is smaller. They are mostly about ghosts and demons, gnomes and trolls..." He shrugged. "So from very early I knew about all kinds of beings – they were already familiar, like old friends. The first time I came face to face with one, it did not seem strange..."

Patricia glanced up from her notes. "Tell me about that..."

"Well, I remember climbing a hill one day and the weather

was getting worse and worse. The wind was so strong it nearly blew me off my feet, then it started raining really hard. I got a bit frightened and started looking for shelter, and managed to find a gap in some rocks. Only a small one but I was not very big then, and I could just squeeze through. I found myself in a cave, with just room to sit down, and that surprised me because I expected it to be dark..." He rubbed the back of a hand across his chin. "It was as if the rock was luminous...it glowed. And pretty soon I realised I was not alone; there was someone else in there. And there he was..."

"A being...?"

"The very first..."

His voice tailed off until the loudest sound in the room was the rhythmic ticking of a grandfather clock in its polished mahogany case.

"That sounds...scary."

"I could not believe how big he was. I mean, huge – as tall as your yew, maybe taller. I suppose it could have been scary, but he was gentle. He told me he lived in a mountain I knew really well, right above *Snæfellsjökull* – which means 'snow-mountain glacier'."

"You're telling me you weren't the least bit frightened...?"

"Not really..." He shrugged.

"That's pretty extraordinary, Olaf..."

"Yes, he was big, but kind and gentle. I knew it – I could feel it the moment I looked into his eyes. And the first thing he said was – I was safe. He gave me his blessing and said he was my friend. He promised to always protect me, so nobody and nothing could hurt me."

"Quite something, especially for a child who was only out there because he was scared of exactly that..."

"Just so..." he assented, softly. "Can you imagine how I felt?"

"Only guess at it," she told him. "And when you say he 'said' things, what exactly does that mean? He spoke, like we are?"

"No..." Olaf shook his head. "It is hard to describe..."

"I appreciate that, but it's what I really want to understand," she reminded him.

"Okay. Try to imagine energy flowing between us, carrying our thoughts. So whatever you think, I know instantly. You and me sitting in silence, but knowing one another's thoughts – like two radios tuned to the same frequency..." He paused. "Have you ever known what someone is going to say before they say it?"

"Occasionally..."

"That is how it was. I could hear his thoughts..."

"And vice versa..."

"Yes..."

"How did you know that was what was happening?"

"I felt it, sensed it. If a thought came into my mind, he would know."

"Sounds simple enough..." she told him, busy scribbling.

"Beautifully simple." He smiled. "You see why I asked if that was all you wanted to know...?"

"Does it sound right if I describe it as a 'sophisticated, instinctive telepathic process'?"

"If that is the language you understand..." He shrugged.

"What would yours be...?"

"Mine..." He considered the question for a few moments, eyes half closed. "I would say we both resonated with the field of the mountain we were in. Entering the same field means there was no separation between us; any thought was automatically a shared one..." He shrugged. "So the idea of something passing from one to the other becomes meaningless..."

"I get what you're saying...sort of," she told him, tapping the pen against her teeth, "but I'd better stick to concepts my group are going to understand..."

"Then I would like to add one more thing..."

"Go ahead."

"Tuning in and sensing messages in this way works best if you are in a calm, happy state of mind. If I am tired or upset, my mind is not so clear. Like interference on your radio...you know?"

"Okay. So the ideal conditions are when you're emotionally calm and your mind is not cluttered..."

"When you can enter what the Buddhists call 'space of clear mind'," he agreed.

Patricia spent a few moments amending her notes before glancing up and nodding.

"It may be simple to you but this is great, Olaf. Really helpful..."

He touched his palms together and smiled. "I am happy..."

"I think I'm pretty clear so far," she went on. "That was how it began. Getting in touch with...what would you call it?"

"Reality," he offered without hesitation.

"Which makes this...?" She gestured at the room. "I think of this as reality but to you it's something else?"

"Maya..." He smiled. "Illusion."

"I'm tempted to try, but exploring that might take more time than we've got," she told him. "Before we go on, is there anything else you think it might be helpful for me to know about that first encounter...?"

"I do not think so..."

"And did you ever meet that particular giant again?"

"Often. I still do. He has always been my special guardian. In fact, it was he who appeared in my dream last mid-winter, when I was asked to get ready for this journey..."

"The gentle giant..."

"*Bárður*. And he really is gentle. People often think giants are ugly – that's how they are drawn in children's books..."

"And they're not...?"

"That is a reflection of people's fear of the unknown. I have met many of them – they are no more or less ugly than the rest of us," he told her. "Like anything else, how you see it depends on you, not them."

"Sounds like Iceland is full of giants...?"

"More than you could count. It was as if Bárður pulled back a curtain and suddenly I could see all kinds of beings who must have always been there but they'd been invisible..."

"When you say 'all kinds'?"

"Well...there were the spirits of people who have left the planet, nature spirits who live in trees and flowers, and mountain guardians like Bárður." He paused. "His mountain abode is called Snæfell. It is also called Þríhyrningur, that you may be interested to know means triangle. "

"It explains a lot." Patricia smiled.

"So, as I was saying, there are spirits everywhere."

"Really?" Patricia tapped her teeth. "As a matter of interest, can you see any right here, right now...?"

"In this room...?"

"For example..."

Eyes narrowed he glanced round and nodded towards the window. "You see that crystal...?"

Caitlin had placed it on the ledge inside the leaded window, long ago. Like a rough-hewn cylinder of opaque glass, it was an inch or so thick and no longer than Patricia's ring finger.

"It's my daughter's. I've no idea where she got it..."

"Did you know there were beings living in it?"

Patricia peered at it, but it looked exactly as it always had done.

"I had no idea. Presumably they're very small...?"

"I see tiny specks of light going in and out, like bees round a hive. Beings like them inhabit crystals, stones, pebbles, rocks..."

"Not only living things, then?"

"A rock is not alive...?" he asked in mock surprise.

"You'd say it was...?"

"Wherever there is matter, there is consciousness. Just as

wherever there is power there is consciousness. So, rocks and stones are conscious, and so are rivers, waterfalls, hot springs...seas and oceans." He raised a finger. "And if wherever consciousness is found, so is spirit, then that which has spirit must have life..."

"Interesting idea. And...could you communicate with the beings in that crystal?"

"I could ask them if they wanted to. It depends on whether they say yes or no..."

"If they said yes, would you be talking to the crystal, or..."

"Its essence... spirit if you like." He nodded. "Just as I am not having a conversation with your body but with the spirit which inhabits your body..."

She spent a few moments leafing through her notes. At a very early age he had already been through a succession of harrowing and destabilising events: bereavement, separation, disintegration of the family unit, insecurity and anxiety. His instinct would have been to find a way to survive and cope with their combined effects on his psychological and emotional state. She had enough experience of work with disturbed youngsters to know how adept they could become at creating imaginary worlds offering a panacea for emotional scars. The man in front of her had been blessed with a ready made fantasy realm in the form of Iceland's myths, legends and sagas. That realm was richly peopled by giants and gods, magical beings and mystical creatures so real to him that perhaps they eventually took the place of a family that had been denied to him.

"You talked about the giant coming to you in a dream," Patricia reminded him. "Is it not possible you fell asleep in the cave, and that first meeting with him was actually a dream...?"

"I was awake. It was very cold. If I had gone to sleep I do not think I would have woken up. I wonder," he added, after a pause, "if that is a reason he came at that moment...to make sure I stayed awake..."

"These encounters when you're awake." Patricia glanced up from her pad. "What word would you use to describe them...?"

Olaf shrugged. "I am not sure...visions, maybe?"

"Thinking about dreams," she told him, "in mine people seem to speak to one other. But when the giant told you about coming here, was that telepathic communication, or..."

"It's like that in my dreams, too, but in visions and meditation we do not use words."

Watching her as she recorded his reply, Olaf stretched. "You are going to put all this in your paper...?"

"A lot of it, I expect. Why...?"

"You will send your friends to sleep..."

"You think so...?"

"What is so interesting about sending thoughts? Surely we do it all the time, even if it is not conscious...?"

"I'm passing on that, Olaf," she told him, brushing the hair from her brow. "And the group will be fascinated. You forget that very few of them – maybe none – will have direct personal experience of the kind of thing you're describing. And even if they had," she added, "I'm not sure they'd admit it. We're beginners you see, still at the stage of exploring simple, basic principles..."

"Have you thought of letting me talk to them?"

"You...?" She paused. "Well, it's an idea and I could certainly propose we invite people like you along..." Closing her notepad she leaned back and cradled her head in her hands. "Let's suppose I suggest it and they all jump at the idea. Imagine this is it. The floor is yours, Mr Bardarson. What would you like to tell us...?"

"Something about me and my history, I suppose. Not too much because that is not important. Then, maybe...a little of my experiences with beings like *Bárður*..."

"Only a little?" Patricia smiled.

"Their own experiences are much more interesting than

hearing about mine..." He rubbed his hands. "So they would have practical exercises..."

"Like...?"

"Putting them into pairs, so they can to tune into one another and experiment with sending their own thought messages..."

"That could be interesting." She nodded. "I'm not sure if we could do it, but..."

"Some – probably the women – would find it comes naturally. The important thing is to help them develop awareness of their own gifts. How can they introduce something into their work if they have only heard about it from me...?"

Patricia held up a hand. "Good point, but say a bit more about what you'd tell them about you and your life..."

He shrugged and waved a hand. "That as a child, of course, I understood nothing of spirit. All I knew was that sometimes my life was difficult and other times...magical..." He paused. "For example, I can remember lying in bed staring out at the stars. We have almost zero pollution so our night skies are wonderfully clear. And one night, I don't know exactly how old I was, I discovered I could fly..."

"Fly, or imagine you could...?"

"It was not imagination," he insisted. "Just by thinking about it, I could slip out of my body and...up into the sky. My body stayed in bed, but I was free to go wherever I wanted."

"Not imagination, not a dream...?"

He gave an impatient shake of the head. "I used to go to the airport and play with planes taking off and landing. I could fly beside them the way people...swim with dolphins. I loved it. Without my body I felt completely free and safe..." He peered at her. "You never did that as a little girl?"

"I can remember gazing into the sky and thinking how amazing the Moon and stars were and wishing I could do something like that. But actually leave my body...?" Patricia shook her head. "Never..."

"In India, you can learn how to do it."

"Why would anyone want to...?"

"At the moment of death, spirit and body separate. That could be frightening. But if you have already experienced it, you don't worry..."

"But you found that kind of thing out much later. As a little boy presumably you just did it for fun..."

"Imagine giving a child permission to fly off wherever they want, any time they like..." He smiled and spread his hands. "Another favourite game was slipping into people's dreams..."

"You could do that?"

"Yes, and the next day I described every detail of those dreams. People could not understand how I did it..." His grin faded. "The trouble was, a lot of them thought I was a pretty strange kid..."

"Wasn't that tough for you?"

He stopped, and took a sip of elderflower. "Feeling I was different? Yes, sometimes. I worried maybe there was something wrong with me. I remembered what happened to my mother, you see. That did frighten me. And I felt...lonely. To tell you the truth..." He shrugged, "That can still happen, even now..."

"Not at this moment, though...?"

"No," he agreed with a firm shake of the head. "No, not right now..."

"That's good. While we're on dreams, Olaf, do you remember we once talked, very briefly, about a dream of mine? That morning I ran you to the abbey..."

His brow furrowed, then he nodded. "Yes, I think so..."

"And you hinted – well, you were pretty clear about it – you knew about it because you had entered, or shared it, or dreamed the same dream or..." She shrugged, "or whatever..."

"Yes, that is true..."

"Which for some reason I found – and still do find – a bit disturbing. It's not on our agenda, but I'd like to ask about that. Is that okay?"

"Of course…"

"How could that happen, Olaf? I can't get my head round it. I mean…"

She placed her hands over her eyes and shook her head.

"I guess my question is this. That night, did you just decide to…come into my head, into my dream? Which, I have to tell you now, I would find pretty hard to believe. Or," she went on, "was it random – did you just find yourself there? Or is it like the way you communicate with spirits – did you pick it up from me later by some kind of telepathic process?"

"No to all of them," he told her with a grin. "Sometimes, without meaning to, I just find I am in someone else's dream world. And it happened that night…"

"I hear the words, but I still have a problem. On one hand I happen to believe no one can do that – because it's impossible. But on the other, you told me something you could've known only if you had done…" She sighed. "Do you see my problem…?"

"First, then, it will help if you understand there was no conscious action or intention on my part…"

"But you just said – it's a game you played…"

"Played…" he broke in, "not play. As a little boy I had no idea what I was doing, but now I do. And I know gifts like that must be used with respect, with…integrity."

"So what happened that night…?"

Olaf grinned. "I did not get into bed and think hey, why don't I go and see what that nice doctor is dreaming about…"

"That's a relief." She grimaced. "At least, I think it is. Go on."

"It is not something I wanted, but I believe it happens for a reason. That may be because I am needed to play some part in the dream – to take a role. Or it could be so I can help the dreamer or perhaps let them help me. I believe I have been guided by spirit to that place, at that time…"

"Do you have any sense what was going on with my dream?"

He paused, tracing the line of throat and jaw with a fingertip.

"It was as if your dream acted like a magnet and attracted me, drew me to it by its energy, its psychic vibration if you like. But you must understand, I do not see it as your dream or mine..."

"It felt like mine to me..."

"We were on a mountain, I think..."

Patricia reminded herself this was comfortable, routine territory for him. For her, exploring his inner world was like agreeing to an out-of-body experience; abandoning the familiar and safe to push the boundaries of what her mind could accept.

"That's right..." she said, slowly.

"So the dream actually took place in the field of consciousness of the mountain. You might say it was dreamed by the mountain." He leaned forward, "and for some reason we both entered that same field..."

She reached for the biscuits and offered them. He shook his head; she took one and broke it in half.

"To tell you the truth, I'm way out of my depth with the last bit," she admitted. "But if you're saying at some deep, unconscious level, we chose the same dream, I haven't the foggiest idea why."

"Nor do I, but does 'why' matter?" Olaf waved a hand. "Maybe we know one another from a previous life – or more than one. Maybe you have a connection with my soul journey, or I have something to do with yours – or your son's. Who knows? And if we knew the answer it would change nothing, would it? If we are meant to know, the answer will be revealed..."

"And if we aren't...?"

"Then it will not..."

"Having a philosophical mind rather than an enquiring one has its advantages," she observed with a wry smile.

She folded her arms; she was no nearer to grasping what had happened but then neither was Olaf himself it seemed. Tempted to pursue the question, she realised she was faintly uncomfortable with anything involving past lives and soul journeys.

"Can we go back to that time Bardur sent you off on your Scafell mission?"

"He just said England. I learned it was Scafell later. After that dream I began discovering messages in the land..."

"Tell me about them," she asked, gathering up pen and paper again.

"I was working in a part of the country I did not know very well, called *Fáskrúðsfjörður*. And I started buying all the maps of the area I could lay hands on. Then spent hours and hours looking at them, learning the names of all the villages, farms, mountains, rivers, even small streams, off by heart." He chuckled. "People thought I had gone completely crazy..."

"Understandably..."

"But I realised something strange was happening. I began to sense, to literally feel the energy linking different places together. The clue might be the names of the places, or the sound of those names, or what they meant. And when I drew lines on the maps linking them together, I found I was looking at amazing patterns..." He paused. "You will like the first one I ever found..."

Patricia looked up from her notes and met his eyes. "Why...?"

"Near *Hoffell* I discovered goats. You remember our goats, I hope?" Without waiting for a reply, he hurried on. "*Hafur* means goat and there were three of them on a perfect straight line – *Hafranes*, *Hafrenesfell* and *Hafrafell*. Next I looked at places with *Græn* – which means green – in their name. Three more – *Grænanípa* and two called *Grænafell*. And they formed a triangle with mount *Hoffell* at the centre point of its base. Soon patterns were jumping out at me the moment I opened a map. Later, I realised my discoveries were inspired by the goddess of *Hoffell*..."

"You say inspired. I would call it, well...activation of an

intuitive process."

"For you, activation, for me inspiration."

"Tell me more about activation, then."

"When I started spotting all these patterns on the earth, the mountain guardians became aware I was tuned to their wavelength – I had entered their realm, their consciousness. So they invited me to meet the great goddess *Védis* the wise, wife of *Vémundur*. She guides and instructs those who are ready to read and understand what is inscribed on the land. She helps people uncover the Earth's secrets..."

"It sounds as if *Bardur* was very specific when he said you were to come to England. Do you often get such clear instructions to do things?"

"Not often." He shook his head. "Usually, when I meet those in spirit, they give me blessings and maybe we pray together. Sometimes there may be healing work to do...things of that kind."

"But this time it was a direct request. Did you feel you had choice? Could you have refused?"

"Said no to him...?" He frowned.

"If you'd had other plans or it hadn't suited you...if you didn't fancy a trip to England just then."

Olaf drew down the corners of his mouth. "That is hard to imagine..."

"So it never has?"

"No."

"Really? You've never felt like saying, no thank you, I don't want to do that...?"

Olaf pursed his lips. "I think you do not yet understand..."

"That's what we're here for. Maybe you can help me..."

"Well, imagine I ask you to do something. You might think it would benefit me, but not you. Or there might be something else you want to do which is more important, or would give you more pleasure. There are a hundred reasons why you might say yes or no."

"Agreed…"

"But those from the spirit realms are perfectly attuned to us, who inhabit the physical plane. If they make a request or suggest a course of action, it is because it is in our best interests…"

"Always…?"

"Always."

"It sounds as if you have enormous trust in them. Surely there must be tricky, bad, malign…evil spirits?"

"None of the ones who guide me are…"

"You're certain?"

"I am not denying some may try to deceive or control us, or maybe tempt us away from our true path. That is possible. But even then," he went on, "I do not believe that means they are bad or evil."

"Oh, really? Olaf, explain to me how something that tries to deceive or control you could be anything but evil…"

Getting to his feet; he thrust his hands into his pockets, crossed to the window and gazed out across the garden. On the lawn, Patricia glimpsed her neighbour's cat, black as polished ebony, sharpening its claws against a leg of her old, teak, garden table. It glanced skywards, tail flicking as a blackbird swooped low and vanished among the branches of the yew.

"You said your son is taking exams, yes…?"

"In the middle of them…"

"Would you call them bad?"

"No, but…"

"They will challenge him. That is the intention. Just as life challenges are the only way human beings learn and mature." He swung to face her. "So, why call spirits who set us challenges bad? I do not believe it is so…"

"Olaf," Patricia offered with a wry smile, "I'm beginning to wonder if there's anything in your world that's actually bad…"

"Bad? I do not think so…" He shrugged. "There are uncomfortable things or those which are difficult or inconvenient. Some I wish were different…"

"But ultimately you see them all as blessings…"

"Surely everything is how we choose to see it…"

His perceptions, forged in the fire of early life experience, made perfect sense to him. Not that he was alone in that, she reminded herself; perhaps you needed only to believe fervently enough that tying a length of crimson cord round a certain type of tree will banish demons, and banish them it will.

"Which raises a pretty fundamental question," she went on. "How do you know any of your experiences are real? Meeting giants, seeing spirits in crystals, slipping into other peoples' dreams, astral travelling…why shouldn't they simply be products of a highly developed and, dare I say, over active imagination…?"

"Another question to which I have no answer," he told her, eyes twinkling. "Maybe it is exactly as you say; all a dream, a fantasy…"

"But in that case…"

"And exactly the same might be true for you, Dr Carragh. But even if it is, even if there is no external reality and we all live in our own subjective dream world…" He spread his arms, "what difference does it make…?"

"So tell me, what difference does it make?" she enquired. "For you."

"What are you asking…?" He furrowed his brow.

"All your understandings and insights, your interactions with the…unseen. Do you believe they help you cope any better with life and its challenges than the rest of us?"

"Because I am me and not other people, I have no way of answering." He smiled.

"A slightly different question, then. Are you absolutely certain that your wonderful world is nothing more than an escape, a refuge? A place you created in your mind to avoid having to face the anguish and the challenges of real life...?"

The Icelander's smile faded. His eyes searched her face for a few moments before he replied in a soft voice. "In my wonderful world, Dr Carragh, I allow all possibilities..."

Birdsong drifted gently in through the open windows. The only other sounds were the steady ticking of the grandfather clock, and muted rumble of traffic passing along the high street. "In that case, I'm puzzled."

"You are...?"

"We've established you trust the beings who guide you. And you say their guidance, in whatever form it happens to come, is always in your best interests..."

"That is my experience..."

"And right from the start you were convinced they'd sent you on a very specific mission. You weren't certain what the exact outcome would be, but you knew you were to climb Scafell on midsummer night..."

"That is what they said..."

"Yet last time we spoke, you told me your plans might change," she reminded him. "It seems there is a genuine possibility you'll be going off to Stonehenge with Morgana instead..."

Silhouetted against the window it was difficult to see his features, but he shifted feet uncomfortably. "I have not made up my mind yet. I am thinking about it..."

"Even though it would mean ignoring those you trust...?"

"Not ignore. But things change, you know?" He moistened his lips. "Life unfolds. The universe offers new options, different opportunities. If we are too attached to old ones we are not open to—" He turned, his gaze flickering to the grandfather clock. "Is that the time...?"

"Within a couple of minutes..." She nodded.

"Morgana will be here in a minute. I told her one hour..."

"Not going to Scafell would be a very big decision, wouldn't it, Olaf?"

"If I don't..." he reminded her, edging towards the door.

She got to her feet and stood with the notebook clasped to her chest.

"Tell me," she asked, "I don't quite know how these things work. If you wanted to, could you...summon Bardur and ask his advice?"

"You mean...rub the lamp?"

Beneath the playful tone she sensed discomfort; his eyes strayed to the clock again.

"Or whatever you do..."

"If I asked, I am sure he would come..."

"Do you think you might...?"

A car horn blared, twice, from near her garage.

"I am sorry, I must go..." He shook her hand. "I hope it was useful..."

"Very," she told him. "I'm really grateful for your time..."

He glanced at her, eyebrows raised as if expecting her to speak. Expecting or inviting? She had a sense of unfinished business, something yet to be resolved.

"Olaf...?"

"Yes...?"

The horn again, abrupt and insistent.

"I'd really like to have another chat some time soon. Would that be okay?"

"Yes, of course..."

To her surprise, his answer was delivered without hesitation.

"I'm in the book. Call me. We'll sort out a time..."

"I will, yes..."

She stood in the arched stone doorway, watching him. Graceful as a cat he crossed the patio, pushed through the curtain of ivy surrounding the gate, and was gone from sight.

Chapter 15

The Visitor

Friday 17th June 2011

She had no clear idea where she was which made her feel uneasy and vulnerable. She had a sense she might be at home in Ireland, but it was not anywhere she recognised. Not that she could see much of it through a patchy mist, which dimmed the light of approaching dawn. Now and then she could just make out the silhouette of a low hill to the west – and she knew she had to reach it before the Sun climbed above the horizon. But she could not see how she was going to manage it; however tantalisingly close the high ground might be, she first had to find a way to cross a wide, fast-flowing river, and there did not seem to be one. Fear rose from her gut and gripped her throat like a choking hand. She hurried on as fast as she dared but underfoot the terrain was rocky and treacherous.

Following the sound of rushing water she succeeded in getting to the riverbank. She stopped to catch her breath and peered down at the menacing torrent, foaming and eddying between boulders black as a witch's robe. Perhaps she could clamber down and wade across. But the very idea was madness; she would be swept away in an instant and disappear among the rocks. Hurrying on, she stumbled to her knees with a muffled cry of pain and frustration. In a few minutes it would be too late; her chance would be gone. As she dragged herself to her feet the mist lifted for a few moments and she glimpsed a bridge.

Tears of relief streaked her cheeks as she ran towards it; she was all but there before she caught sight of the wolf. With a coat grey as the morning mist, and eyes like glowing coals, it blocked her path, challenged her to try to pass. She stood rooted to the spot, breath frozen in her lungs, a trapped bird beating its wings frantically in her chest. The huge beast padded silently forward, head low, tongue lolling between cruel fangs. Every instinct told her to turn and run, but she heard another voice; a clear, calm, inner one, commanding her to stand her ground. She obeyed; the wolf was now so close she could see its breath clouding the chill air.

Woman and wolf stood still and silent, as if hewn from rock, their eyes locked. The sky grew lighter as precious moments ticked away. She thought it must be she who was shaking, then realised it was the ground beneath her feet. She wanted to look down but if she flinched or dropped her gaze the wolf would hurl itself on her. The shaking grew ever more intense, spreading through her legs and hips, rising to her chest, until her whole body was vibrating. A sudden convulsion almost threw her off her feet as a surge of energy, like an electric shock, raced up her spine and seemed to burst through the crown of her head. She gasped, sucking in air before giving vent to a full-throated roar of defiance which echoed back from the hills.

The wolf, ears flattened, backed away and slunk out of her path. She ran as fast as she could; nothing could stop her now. Feeling the smooth, damp stones of the bridge under her feet, she threw her arms wide and let out another great cry, of triumph. That cry, too, echoed back as the Sun edged above the horizon, its rays, like golden arrows, shooting high into the sky.

Ψ

Pen and paper in hand, Patricia tugged open the fridge-freezer. Tapping her teeth with the pen, she ran an eye over the shelves in preparation for her weekly supermarket foray; a Friday evening ritual designed to avoid the weekend crush. She added steak to her list: preparing a dish making greater demands on her considerable culinary skills would have been more satisfying, but it was Colm's current favourite, and he had earned a treat. According to the Swiss railway style, wall clock, with its button-ended second hand, he had already begun what was, thank God, the last of the current exams. She doubted he had any inkling that her relief would be scarcely less than his own. Caitlin had responded to exams quite differently; apparently impervious to pressure, she appeared to sail serenely through them. Despite Patricia's wealth of maternal experience, the contrasting styles in which the siblings dealt with life's challenges remained a source of wonder.

The front doorbell chimed, drawing another quick glance at the clock, and a grimace. It was far too early for the postman or, she hoped, a visitation from the Jehovah's Witnesses. Tossing shopping list and pen onto the pine table, she padded down the short corridor to the door and unlatched it.

"Hiya. How are you...?

She caught her breath and gazed blankly at her visitor. Hands thrust into his pockets, shoulders hunched, Liam's feet were set wide, like a sailor balancing on a rolling deck.

"Oh...hello."

His smile slowly faded.

"You weren't expecting me..."

"I was not. Should I have been...?"

"Colm didn't tell you?"

"Tell me what...?"

With the exception of a few more pounds on what used to be a spare frame, a sprinkling of wrinkles round his eyes, and a frosting of grey at the temples, Liam's appearance had changed remarkably little over the years. Approaching sixty, yet there remained an enduringly youthful quality to the deep-set eyes and the way his dark hair flopped across a broad, high brow. The first time she laid eyes on him, she remembered thinking he looked more like an undergraduate than a senior faculty member.

"He didn't say I was coming by, then...?"

"He did not."

She folded her arms.

"It was only the other day..."

"He did mention you'd called. Probably forgot the important bits..."

"Christ!" He rolled his eyes. "Where's that boy's head at...?"

"Exams, where it should be. In the last one even as we speak..."

"Oh..." He looked past her. "You weren't off to work yet were you...?"

Her intention had been to reach her office sufficiently early to spend at least a couple of hours bringing some semblance of order to the clutter of files and papers which had accumulated on her desk. After that she would be working her way through a full appointments diary.

"Well, to tell you the truth..."

"Look, I'm here aren't I? Don't tell me you can't spare a few minutes..."

Since the divorce became absolute, contact had been limited to rare occasions when one of them – usually Patricia – felt something was sufficiently important to demand it.

"I'm sure I could manage that..."

The next moment he was past her, heading for the kitchen. She closed the door and followed. He had always possessed that knack, the ability to side-step obstacles and evade barriers in order to access what he wanted. She recognised it the first time he turned up in her pokey little flat in Rathmines, like a magician materialising through a cloud of smoke. Once focused on a goal, his determination became a force field which she had never quite learned to resist. Yet, when she did finally summon the resolve to break the magician's spell, it felt so easy she could never understand why it had taken her so long.

"Colm will be sorry he missed you..."

Watching him glance round the room gave her the uncomfortable feeling he was registering changes she might have made
to it.

"It's a bit since you've seen him, isn't it?" she went on.

"Not really..." He shook his head, dismissing the charge. "We
speak and text now and then. When the mood takes us, you
know. He never tells you...?"

"Tells me?" She flashed him a rueful smile. "Listen, he never
tells me anything. I'm just his mother, remember?"

"Like that, is it?"

"I'm pretty sure he's planning to go to a mate's house when
he's finished. Why not surprise him – pick him up? They should
be out in about an hour..."

Liam consulted his watch and pulled a face. "Not sure about
that. I'll see..."

He leaned against the heavy table, glancing down at her
shopping list. She felt momentary indignation, as if she had
caught him reading her diary. He was wearing an open-necked,
flax-blue shirt, sleeves rolled to the elbow; his wrinkled, dark
trousers hinted at a thickening waist.

"Do you want a drink," she enquired. "Tea, coffee...?"

"Coffee would be grand, thanks. I usually take the train up to
town, but I'm driving today so I thought I'd drop in. You know,
say hello...see how you're doing..."

Their communications, usually by phone or email, were
invariably brief and to the point. It was not Liam's habit to drop
by to enquire about her health, and she found it mildly irritating
that he should expect her to believe it was so on this occasion. It
never failed to amaze her that men – even those as intelligent as
Liam – seemed unaware how effortlessly women decode unconscious signals, like tone of voice and body language, in order to
distinguish truth from falsehood.

"Me? Can't complain, I guess," she told him, filling the kettle.
"Well, I say that, but work is actually a bit of a grind. My

esteemed medial director insists on upping my caseload. I might be able to handle that, but departmental budgets keep getting slashed, and my team's shrinking faster than a polar ice cap. But I'm still hanging on in there…"

She was making noises with the mouth; buying time. If only Colm, bless his heart, had remembered the message, she could have prepared herself. It was extraordinary how you could spend twenty years with someone, and within months they could become a stranger. She opened a cupboard and chose a mug decorated with hearts; symbolic of how she should feel, even if she struggled to do so. Taking it from its hook and she placed it beside the kettle, on the marble worktop.

"And yourself…?" she enquired.

"Same as you, it sounds like." He shrugged. "Money's tight with my lot, too. Same everywhere, I guess…"

"I thought there were supposed to be hordes of foreign students flocking in and filling the uni coffers…"

"Bloody media…" He shook his head. "Never get their facts right, do they?"

"Really…" She was surprised by his vehemence.

"If it's that bad…" He cocked his head, "did you ever think of quitting…?"

"Quitting…?"

"Yeah. I mean, it sounds as if…"

"Why would I…?"

"Because of what you just said. Your case load's up…"

"Yes, but leaving would be crazy." She shook her head. "To go where, and do what? It's not an option…"

"Just wondered, that's all…"

"Well, now you know…"

He was no more relaxed than she. Tossing his keys onto the table, he pulled out a chair and eased himself down.

"I've been…looking round, actually," he offered, his tone overly casual.

"You always said you enjoyed it where you are…"

"Yeah, I did. It suited me pretty well for quite a long time…"

"But…?"

"Well…pastures new and all that shite…"

"Are you looking?"

"Kind of…"

"Whereabouts?"

"Wherever…" He shrugged. "Early days, you know…"

She spooned coffee from a cylindrical, stainless steel container into a cafetiere. Colm teased her that it was easier to count scoops but she declined to change her habit of judging by eye. Wondering where the conversation was leading she glanced at him.

"You haven't quit, have you…?"

"Me? No," he insisted. "No, it's not like that…"

"What is it like…?"

"Ah, Jesus…" He grimaced. "Call it politics…"

She folded her arms and waited.

"Always comes down to politics in the end, doesn't it?" he went on. "Must be the same for you at the funny farm. Doesn't matter how good you are at what you do or how long you've been doing it. When the chips are down, what matters is whether you're licking the right arses. Am I right?"

"What you're saying is you haven't been."

"I was never your archetypal political animal now, was I?"

"That's true enough…"

Patricia was not going to contest that. Neither did she have any intention of reminding him that political acuity was founded on awareness of and atunement to the needs and aspirations of others; not a narcissist's strongest suit.

"Black, no sugar…?"

"Don't tell me you've forgotten…" He gave a wry smile.

"Habits change…"

"Not that one…"

She added boiling water to the grounds and stirred.

"So, like I said, I'm having a look round to see what's out there."

"Any luck so far?"

"Nothing you'd call definite yet but I've a couple of irons in the fire..." He traced a knot in the wood with the tip of his ignition key..."But there's no rush, I've got plenty of time..."

Putting the key down, he rubbed his eyes with his fists. His manner might be casual but it did not conceal the fact he looked drawn and weary. Patricia pushed the plunger and rested her hand on it.

"So what you're saying is you haven't actually quit, but you might leave anyway. Is that it?"

"Pretty much, yes."

"Well, you surprise me, but I assume you know what you're doing..."

"Sure I do..."

She walked across to place mug and cafetiere in front of him. It earned a quick nod of acknowledgement before he poured the coffee and glanced at her.

"Not joining me...?"

"I've had my ration. Too much makes me jumpy."

"I know what you mean..."

She resisted the impulse to join him at the table. Sitting together would have felt too intimate, too cosy, as if this were a meeting of old friends. She leaned back against the worktop and folded her arms. Inviting him in might have been ill judged; she was finding his presence as disconcerting as it was inconvenient.

"So, what are these irons of yours...?"

"Do you remember that nibble from Duke, a while back?"

Her jaw tightened. It had been three years ago, when his star was in the ascendant. A newly published treatise on globalisation was earning him plaudits from his peers, television interviews and invitations to speak at heavyweight business seminars. And the call from North Carolina: prestigious Duke University, sounding him out for a resident senior lecturer's post on the faculty of their business school. Liam was cock-a-hoop; Patricia's elation stemmed more from the unrealistic notion that new horizons might herald a fresh start. Within days, a friend's unguarded remark alerted her to his latest infidelity. Plummeting from hope to despair, she fled to Ireland with the children and agonised for a dark and desperate weekend. Determined that betrayal would be the last, she flew back to tell him the marriage was over. It was evident he no longer remembered a sequence of events etched indelibly on her memory.

"Yes. I do, actually..."

"Okay, well..."

"So you might be off there after all..."

She wished him anywhere but in her kitchen. Unwilling to risk him reading her expression she stooped to pull open the dishwasher and set about transferring the contents to the draining board.

"Depends what kind of deal they come up with..."

"Last time it wasn't what you thought you were worth, was it?"

"I don't really remember the details..."

"I do. They pissed you off royally. You said Americans call themselves a classless society because they have no class..." she offered over her shoulder, "and something about if they paid peanuts, they'd get monkeys..."

"I don't think I'd have said..."

"Well, you did. Anyway..." She pushed the dishwasher shut with her foot and met his eyes. "What can I say? Good luck...?"

"Thanks. Here's to...the future..."

He raised his mug and she just managed to return his smile. Picking up a tea towel she began wiping the cutlery.

"So, is that what you came to tell me – you could be leaving the country?"

"That's part of it…"

"And the rest…?"

"Don't rush me, I'm getting there." He peered at her over the rim of his mug. "Or are you that keen to get rid of me?"

Patricia let the question hang in the air, unanswered.

"Are you…?"

"Liam, I've got a lot to do today, and I wasn't expecting you…"

"That's not my fault…"

"I didn't say it was. But the fact remains I wasn't…"

"Look, if there's something you particularly want to discuss why don't we fix a day that suits us both and…"

"This won't take long. Come on now, at least sit down for God's sake…" He reached for a chair and turned it towards her. "You standing there is kind of…"

"Makes you uncomfortable…?"

He rolled his eyes. "Spare me the bloody therapist's questions…"

"If you want to talk now," she told him, "go ahead. But will you please explain what we're supposed to be talking about, because so far…"

"The house…"

"What about it…?"

"I'm answering your question. I came to talk about the house…"

She draped the dishcloth over her shoulder and frowned at him.

"This house…?"

"Do we have any others…?"

"I don't get it. What is there to…?"

"If you'd stop interrupting, sit down and listen for a minute, you might get it…"

"I'd get it…" She waved away the chair, "if you'd stop beating around the bush…"

"Okay, okay…" He placed his coffee carefully on the table. "The situation is very simple. My contract runs until the end of the year – a bit over six months. But there's a problem. Contracts used to be renewed pretty well as a matter of course – certainly for senior staff. But the game's changed pretty radically. These days they're recruiting a lot of new people who are generally, surprise surprise, younger and thus cheaper…"

"You said it was about politics…"

"I'm trying to explain, and you're not bloody listening…"

She clenched her fists. "This is my kitchen, Liam. If you can't be civil, I'd like you to…"

"That's the whole point…it's not," he told her, wiping his mouth with the back of his hand.

"Liam, I haven't the faintest idea…"

"You just said this is yours…" He spread his hands and glanced round. "Not so. Or maybe you'd forgotten…?"

"I live here…"

"Which doesn't alter the fact it's half mine…"

"I know that…" She waved his words aside. "Now could we get back to the point because I'm no clearer what it is…"

"I want to put the place on the market…"

She stared at him, slack-jawed. He delivered his bombshell in the tone he might have used to enquire if she still had the Volvo, or whether Colm suffered dental problems. Maybe she had misheard, maybe what he had said was quite different, quite innocent.

"Sorry…I still don't know what you mean."

"What part of putting it on the market is so difficult to understand…?" He sipped his coffee. "I want to sell this place."

"I thought that's what you said…" She frowned. "But now you're forgetting something, aren't you?"

"I don't think so."

"How about the agreement we made, giving me the right to live here…?"

"Until Colm graduates from university, or reaches the age of twenty two, whichever is the sooner..." he recited. "I'm well aware of that."

"So what are you doing – asking me to waive it...?"

"Effectively, yes..."

She paused to pull the dishcloth from her shoulder, fold it neatly and place it beside the kettle. Her heart was racing, and she was aware her tone was shrill; this was no time to lose her composure.

"Then you need to get I won't do it. I love this place. I always have. If you thought for one moment I'd dream of letting it go before our agreement expires, forget it..."

"This isn't just some whim, you know..."

"I don't care what it is. The courts are not going to change the terms because it happens to suit you..."

"I've taken legal advice..."

"Good for you..."

"According to which if, in six months time, there's a realistic possibility, no..." he corrected himself, "a strong probability I shall no longer have a job and hence no income..."

"What was all that guff about Duke then...?" she demanded.

"It's not guff. I've been in touch with them..."

She paused to allow disconnected pieces of information he had supplied to rearrange themselves, like scattered pieces of a jigsaw coming together, and create a recognisable picture.

"Hang on, I'm getting it..." She nodded, slowly. "I was wondering why you weren't giving me straight answers..."

"I have given you..."

She planted her hands on her hips. "Duke didn't come looking for you at all, did they...?"

"You assumed that. I never said..."

"Just made it sound that way. That is so bloody typical. I'll bet you just emailed on the off chance they might still be interested..." She shook her head. "I'm right, aren't I?"

"Which I am perfectly entitled to do..."

"But it turned out they're not, which should come as no surprise the way you played so hard to get last time. And you're far too vain to admit you missed your chance, and now they don't want you..."

"They have not given me a definite..."

"Come on, Liam, get real. And it's the same kind of story with the LSE, isn't it...?" She raised her eyebrows. "You didn't say so, of course, but you already know that come December they're not offering you..."

Jumping to his feet, he sent his chair tumbling. He leaned forward, palms flat on the table, glowering. "Will you stop babbling, shut up for one minute and let me..."

Someone once told her Liam was a typical Scorpio. Enquiring what that meant she learned their anger was reputedly akin to a scorpion attack; fast, without warning and potentially dangerous.

"No. I bloody won't. You seriously think I'm going to agree to you tearing up a legal agreement..."

"Made at a time when I was in secure employment." He reminded her angrily. "With a decent income..."

"Which you still are..."

"But almost certainly won't be come, the new Year. My solicitor's advice is, if I go back to the court and present credible evidence of a material change in my financial situation, the judge is practically certain to agree to amend the original terms..."

"Oh, really...?"

"Yes, really. That's the way it works, whether you like it or you don't. All they'll want to know is whether your financial situation has changed, and it hasn't, has it? So selling this place now," he went on, "simply alters the time frame..."

"Pretty radically. And you think I wouldn't fight it...?"

"What you do is up to..."

"It's not just my home, it's the kids' home, too which you

conveniently overlook. I loved this place the moment I clapped eyes on it, and I still do…"

"Maybe so, but if you think the courts care…"

"I have no idea what you thought I was going to say, but…"

He held his palms towards her. "Listen, we agreed a fifty-fifty split and I'm not suggesting any change to that. I mean, I'm trying to be reasonable here…"

"That's a relief…"

"You never could do sarcasm," he told her. "But surely you can see there's no earthly point going back to court. Think of all the hassle, and all the bloody solicitors' fees, not to mention the time those meetings take up. Why can't you and me sit down together like reasonable people and sort this out ourselves…"

She watched as he retrieved his chair and sat down again. Constructing arguments designed to make ideas which were neither fair nor reasonable sound both was another of Liam's skills; she was not alone in thinking he missed his vocation as a lawyer.

"Fine. So, what are you offering, exactly?" she enquired, evenly.

"What do you mean, offering…?"

"Just that. You want your share of this place now. I've no intention of selling, so I'll contest it," she reminded him. "I can't believe you and this brilliant solicitor of yours didn't anticipate that was what would happen."

"Well, until we'd talked I didn't know…"

"Come on, be honest. Are you trying to tell me you and he didn't dream up a contingency plan, some little sweetener, some…" She rubbed finger and thumb together, "*je ne sais quoi* to persuade me to go along with it?"

"Fight it if you like, but it's going to cost you serious money…"

"Me and you both, and I know how much you hate putting your hand in your pocket. Let's see now, Colm is sixteen." She pursed her lips. "So he's not going to be through uni for, what…five or six years? Getting me to give up my right to stay here that long must be worth something. Come on now, what are you putting on the table…?"

"You're being emotional, you're not thinking clearly…"

"Oh, really…?"

"Look at the bigger picture. For a start, do you really need a place this size? I mean…for four of us it made perfect sense, but Caitlin is pretty sure to want to take off once she's graduated…"

"She's not said a word to me about taking off. Has she to you…?"

"That's what they all do at her age for Christ's sake. That, or she'll shack up with some guy…"

Patricia gave him a tight-lipped smile. "Oh, really? You're saying your daughter's the type who'll shack up with some guy…?"

"How the hell would I know? It's possible, isn't it…?"

"On the theory the apple never falls far from…"

"Christ…" He passed a hand over his eyes. "All right, then, if she finds some nice chap and settles down…"

"Go on…"

"Well, if she does," he continued, doggedly, "there'll be just you and Colm in a three bed roomed house. A listed building in good repair, great position, easy commuting distance…"

"You've had it valued, I take it…?"

Flyers from estate agents, claiming potential buyers were clamouring for homes in her postcode, seemed to land on her doormat daily, only to be consigned to the recycling bin.

"I remember what we paid, which gives me an idea. So…" He avoided her eyes and her question, "this actually works for us both. Sell and share the proceeds, but a bit sooner than planned. Obviously you'd need a new place. Smaller, maybe, making it more economical to run. You could probably find somewhere closer to work too, which would be a damned sight more convenient, wouldn't it...?"

"Closer to work would be further from school..."

"Yeah, well..."

"That must sound a lot more convincing to you than it does to me," she told him. "But then it would if you need the money that badly..."

"It's hardly going to make me rich, but I don't fancy being on the bread line, either. I've never lived that way and I'm too old to start now..."

"We're not talking the bread line, Liam. And you're not exactly an old man. You look reasonably fit..."

"What do you expect me to do? Stack shelves in bloody Tesco...?"

"Do you know how much shelf-stackers get...?"

"Don't be ridiculous..."

"I didn't say anything about Tesco. The point is, there are plenty of things you could do..."

"No, the point is, this place is way bigger than you need. If we pitch the price right, chances are it would sell really quickly..."

She shook her head. "It isn't just about selling a place where I'm happy. It also happens to be a lousy time to sell..."

"Swings and roundabouts. You'll be a cash buyer, downsizing in a buyer's market. Loads of people are losing their jobs or finding they're in negative equity, either way they're desperate to sell and mortgages are dirt cheap..."

"In six years who says there won't be in an economic recovery and another housing boom..."

"You're a psychiatrist not an economist," he reminded her, draining his coffee. "This is my field, and believe me that is not going to happen..."

She crossed to the table, picked up the mug and cafetiere and returned with them to the sink. "So, you're full of good reasons why I should give up my home," she told him as she rinsed the mug under the tap. "The principle one, as far as I can tell, being that it suits you…"

"What is your problem…?"

"My problem is that so far, I've not heard anything…not one single thing, that persuades me it would be the slightest benefit to me, or the kids." She glanced at him over her shoulder. "Or have I missed something…?"

He sighed and shook his head. "I had a feeling you might see it that way – to begin with, anyway…"

She returned the mug to its hook, folded the tea towel and nodded. "You got that one right…"

"Okay, then…" He sighed and folded his arms on the table. "Why don't we look at how we'd divide the proceeds of sale…"

"Yes, let's do that." She turned to face him. "I'm really interested. Did you and your legal eagle come up with an offer I couldn't refuse…?"

"Before you and I had even talked about it? There was no point…"

"Are you serious? You're not even going to make me an offer…?" She shook her head.

"Look, I haven't really…"

"No problem. I'll save you the trouble, anyway. You see, I really don't give a damn what you offer, because I'd turn it down."

"That's absolutely ridiculous. I'm giving you an opportunity to…"

"Liam, you're not giving me a thing. All you want is to take as much as you can get, which is all you ever wanted…" She paused. "And I used to let you. But I don't do that any more. I simply will not be used…"

"You're being stubborn, and stupid and you'll regret it…" he warned. "The kids aren't going to thank you for turning it down, either…"

"Oh, you are so wrong…"

"If you want to be completely unreasonable and refuse to

even discuss it, that's up to you, but it's not going to help your case if I put that in my statement to the court. Which I intend to because I am going to push the sale through…"

"Push it through how…?"

"What do you mean, how?" He frowned. "I told you, I've got a bloody strong case…"

"No you don't. In fact, you haven't got a hope in hell of the court even reviewing, let alone revising, have you…?"

"That's shite," he snarled.

"Because if you had, you wouldn't even be here…" she told him. "Liam, I've known you a long time, and you don't change. All you can see is what's in it for you. If you were sure you'd got such a marvellous, cast-iron case, you'd have told your lawyer to get on with it. But you're not, so you came here, hoping I'd…"

"Absolute, utter shite…"

"Why would I believe you had, anyway? In fact, why would I believe anything you say…? You've lied to me so often, that's what I've come to expect. Don't you get that…?"

Teeth clenched, he swept his keys from the table with one hand and caught them in the other.

"By the way, why have LSE kicked you out?"

"Who said they'd…?"

"Not another affair with a student was it…?"

"You bitch…" he snarled, rising to his feet. "You fucking bitch…"

The trembling began as a tremor in her calves and thighs, growing more intense as it rose through her body. She gripped the worktop behind her to steady herself.

"I'd rather be a fucking bitch than a doormat," she retorted, cheeks burning. "That's all I was. A sad, pathetic doormat, who let you do anything you liked to any woman who'd let you do it…"

"That's not true, and it's not fair…"

"Fair? Don't lecture me about fair. Was it fair you were

screwing every doe-eyed little slut who'd drop her knickers…?"

"I'm not staying to listen to any more of your…"

"Struck a nerve, did I…?"

"I don't have to put up with your shite…"

"Like I put up with yours…?"

"If it makes you feel better to hate me…" He shrugged, "go ahead…"

"Liam, I don't care enough about you to hate you…"

The trembling was so strong she wondered if he could see it. "…But I'm still angry. Bloody angry…"

"Well, I'll leave you to enjoy it…" He took a step towards the door.

"Not bothering to see Colm?"

The words brought him swinging round to glare at her.

"Since you mention him, what the hell were you two doing last weekend…?"

"Meaning…?"

"You know what I mean. He told me about some bloody nonsense with Frances…"

"Nonsense it was not. We had a grand time…"

"That's what you'd call grand, is it? He spouted all kinds of rubbish. Picking up angels, looking for trees and nearly getting struck by lightning…" He gave a reproachful shake of the head. "I mean, what were you thinking even going over there, when the kid's in the middle of exams…?"

"He came back in damned sight better shape than when he left. He adores Frances, you know that…"

"God knows why. That old crone's not the full shilling," he added, tapping the side of his head. "You of all people should know that…"

"Don't be ridiculous…"

"Me…?" He took a step forward. "It was you let her put a rake of crazy shite in his head about spirits and magic bloody trees. Come on, you're not seriously pretending that's good for him…"

"How would you know what's good for him? You never see him…"

"You love throwing that at me, don't you…?"

"Isn't it true…?" she demanded, fists clenched. "Isn't it…?"

"I see the boy as much as I…"

"And I live with him twenty-four seven. You have no idea what he's been like the last few months. Stressed, moody, withdrawn…night terrors. At one point I was really worried he might be…"

"He told me…"

"Good, so you know what I've been through…"

"He told me you're making him see some chum of yours, some…psycho-terrorist…"

"Making him…?" she bristled.

"Without even consulting me…"

"Why the hell would I?"

"I am his father for God's sake…"

"And you'd have been against it…"

"Teenage angst." He waved a dismissive hand. "Adolescence, hormones…all kids go through it…"

"You're an expert on the subject…?

"…Without a bloody therapist holding their hand…"

She bit back the words which sprang her lips and glared at him. Like angry children in the playground, she realised, they were trading taunts and insinuations, insults and accusations. Each dredging up old hurts and wounds, neither listening to the other. It was familiar, pointless and futile.

"You said you were leaving," she reminded him, running a hand through her hair. "I think that would be a good idea…"

If he heard her, Liam would not be deflected.

"That boy needs more exercise. He needs to be out kicking a ball or…something physical, not bloody…therapy." He pointed at her. "I'll tell you what's wrong with Colm…"

Patricia closed her eyes. Her mind might be calmer, but her body refused to follow suit. The trembling brought her morning dream flooding back.

"You're too soft, always have been..." he snarled. "You mummy him..."

"You don't think he could do with a bit more daddying, then...?" she enquired.

"It would stop him spending all night at parties during exams..."

She turned her back on him, looking out at the peace and beauty of the garden. Her heart was pounding; if he said one more word, just one, anything might happen. She ran her gaze slowly the length of the neatly striped lawn. Near the balustrade, a thrush was prospecting for worms in the shade of the tree which, if Mitch Ward and Olaf were to be believed, was a sacred being.

"I'd like you to leave, please..." she said softly, without looking round.

"When I am good and ready..."

The faintest stirring in the flowerbed propelled the thrush into flight. A fox emerged from amongst the foxgloves, brushing aside their delicate, bell-shaped clusters of flaming red. It padded light-footed across the lawn, early morning sunlight painting flanks and bushy tail a coppery gold.

"As you wish," she told him, "but don't say I didn't warn you..."

The fox paused in mid-stride, one paw raised. It remained motionless for a few moments, facing the window as if sensing her.

"About what...?"

"I will not let you punish me..."

"You're out of your mind..."

"Everything I did was to support him and you know it," she insisted, her voice shaking.

Liquid as its own shadow the fox continued on its graceful, unhurried way. Patricia turned.

"I won't do what you want, so you're trying to punish me..."

"Absolute drivel..."

His face had become a mask; lips curled, eyes ice cold. Glancing about her, Patricia reached out and plucked a blue enamel milk pan from the hob. Liam's gaze flickered uncertainly between her face and the pan.

"You wouldn't do that..." he said, without conviction.

"You don't think so...?"

Anger fading into anxiety, he retreated towards the door. "You're acting like a child..."

"Not any more..." she hissed.

"Don't...!" Hands clasped round his head, he took to his heels, ducking into the corridor at the same moment she hurled her missile with every ounce of strength she could summon. His footsteps echoed down the corridor as the pan spun through the air, cannoned off the doorframe and shattered into shimmering blue pieces.

"Get out...!" she screamed. "GET OUT...!"

Chapter 16

On the Forest

Friday 17th June 2011

Her plan had been to drive down, collect Olaf from Morgana's cottage and bring him back to the house. Within thirty seconds of stepping out into a balmy early evening she revised it and went in search of walking shoes. After day-long incarceration in the hospital she was in need of gentle exercise in natural surroundings, sunshine on her skin, breathing unconditioned air.

She was nursing the Volvo through a series of tight bends on the descent to Forest Row when an orange convertible roared by in the opposite direction. She caught no more than a glimpse of the driver's billowing mane of blonde hair but it triggered a pang of jealousy. Where was that kind of glamour and excitement in her life? The very thought brought a wry smile to her lips; what would people make of seeing practical, sensible Dr Patricia Carragh at the wheel of something like that?

Passing a parade of shops in the centre of the village, she swung off the main road and soon found herself entering a maze of narrow, winding, rutted lanes, bordered by old brick cottages, packed together like too many teeth in a small mouth. Bracing herself against humps and bumps she eased through a series of potholes, scanning walls doors and gateposts for house names and numbers. A tattered yellow sign pinned to a telegraph post showed a figure in a tall hat astride a broomstick with the caption 'neighbourhood witch'. She grimaced as the Volvo's undercarriage made grating contact with the ground. Liam had complained that the only suitable mode of transport for these lanes was a Centurion tank.

It took her two walking-pace passes along Inkpen Lane before she spotted *Moonraker*. The cottage's walls and small sash windows had practically vanished under a blanket of Virginia creeper, which all but hid the small oval nameplate by the front door. She was looking for somewhere to park when Olaf appeared at the gate.

"No problem getting away, I trust...?"

"No." He shrugged. "Not really..."

"I can't bear the idea of being indoors," she told him as he fastened his seat belt. "How do you fancy a walk in the forest?"

"Grand." He grinned. "That is what you say, yes...?"

"It is indeed." She glanced down at his trainers. "It can get a bit rough and boggy, but we'll avoid the worst parts. Are they up to it?"

"It is not a problem," he assured her. "They dry fast in this weather."

They joined a stream of traffic heading south on a road ascending through heavily wooded, undulating countryside, dappled by sunlight flickering between the leaves. Reaching the top of the incline they halted at traffic lights.

"See the Wych Cross sign? They use to burn witches round here, poor creatures."

"Burn...?" Olaf grimaced. "How long ago did you do that?"

"Not us," she corrected him, turning left as the lights changed. "We were more civilised. It must've been around the time my house was built."

A narrow road took them through open country for a minute or two before she pulled onto a patch of rough ground shaded on three sides by tall, slender birch trees. Switching off the engine she waved a hand at the expanse of rolling heath land spread out before them.

"Welcome to Ashdown Forest..."

"Beautiful..."

"A lot of it's common land, so anyone has the right to come and wander about on it. It's on my doorstep so I should know its history, but I'm afraid I don't. In Henry VIII's time I believe they kept deer here for hunting. Nowadays there doesn't seem to be any of that and there are so many they've become quite a problem. They stray onto that main road and a lot get hit by cars. That's horrible for everyone..."

While she laced her walking shoes Olaf produced a square of faded green cotton, folded it into a bandana and knotted it round his head. They set off through scrubby grass and bushes, following a rutted track etched deep into cracked, chalky earth.

"You are blessed to have a place like this so close to where you live."

"I don't get down here much these days. I used to when the kids were small. Their favourite game was stalking me, hiding behind bushes so I wouldn't spot them. I had to pretend I hadn't – even if I had – and be suitably amazed when they jumped out at me..."

"When you said you wanted to talk again, I was surprised," he told her. "I did not expect it."

"And you said okay, which I wasn't expecting. But here we are..."

"For more research...?"

"Partly, yes..."

"There is something else..." Hands clasped behind him, he glanced at her.

She took a deep breath. "Yes. To be honest, partly to satisfy my curiosity..."

"I had a feeling it might be."

"And came anyway..."

"Do you remember the first time we met, I said maybe you were sent to guide me?"

"You did. I'd forgotten." She paused. "Do you still think so?"

"Do you think Dr Wingfield would have discharged me?"

Patricia pursed her lips. "Probably...it might have taken a bit longer though."

"Perhaps a lot longer..."

"Olaf, I really don't know," she admitted. "I don't know whether it's wise to assume I'm some kind of guide, either. I was just doing my job..."

"Maybe," he assented. "But I thought if we talked again I might find out..."

"We're both looking for answers, then..." She smiled. "So, why don't we start by you clearing up a few things for me?"

"No notebook?"

"In here if I need it." She patted her shoulder bag. "So, you described a number of situations when you've had contact with non-physical beings. Dreams, visions, meditations and so on. And I got the impression they were all instigated by the beings rather than by you. So I'd like to know whether that kind of communication is always...one way. Like having a mobile that receives calls, but you can't dial out..."

Olaf smiled. "I don't think you understand..."

"Help me..."

"Yes..." He tugged at his beard. "Well, for that kind of contact or connection to take place, first I need to enter a space of receptive consciousness..."

"Meaning what, exactly?"

"First quieting all the mind-chatter. Stop thinking. Then open myself for...whatever comes..."

"How do you do that...?"

"It helps to be very clear about intention," he explained. "And part of that is being completely open to receive whatever comes. As you get used to doing so, you will find you naturally enter a clear, luminous space in which all is peaceful, all is..." he dropped his voice to a whisper, "...thundering silence. Then you know you are ready. In the Indian tradition you have entered a state called *turiya*. It means moving beyond personality, beyond ego..."

"That's fine if you're awake. But quite often it sounds as if these happen when you're not."

"True, but when we dream we are no longer under the control of our conscious, are we? The conscious always tries to keep us in the physical realm. Asleep, we attune to the non-physical."

"What about meditation...?"

"With practice you can consciously create a dream-like state. I think a psychiatrist might say the ego is no longer in charge. He smiled. "Then you can be truly receptive..."

"Does that mean any non-physical being who wants to can then connect with you? And by the same token, presumably you can communicate with them whenever you feel like it...?"

"It is easier if you forget what you are accustomed to in the physical world...including your self. And do nothing. Simply exist...be. After all, we call ourselves human beings, not human doings, don't we?"

"Fair point..."

"We are speaking of a realm in which you naturally connect with the beings who resonate with you. Those who enter your field of consciousness. Does that make sense?"

Patricia ran fingers through her hair. "Beginning to, I think..." She paused. "I can see they would be able to enter your consciousness. That's what the giant did that first day in the cave, didn't he...?"

"That is how I described it," Olaf agreed. "But remember, we are talking about a state of being in which there is no separation as we understand and experience it on this planet. In that state, at that level of consciousness, all is one. It is total unity..."

"But I'm still not really clear. Suppose you wanted to communicate with one particular being – the giant, for example – could you make that connection at will? Do you see what I'm getting at...?"

"Once you enter a receptive state, it is really about the level of attunement. Needing and wanting may be part of our earthly reality, but they are no longer an issue. Think of the guiding power as the universe itself, rather than one individual who is part of it..." the Icelander advised. "Attune and see what happens. Sometimes it is exactly what you expect, sometimes it is quite different. Letting go of all expectations helps the process..."

"Do you have a sense of why that would be?"

"I can hold the intention of meeting a certain being, but for that to come about we must both be ready..."

"Has that ever happened? That you've held an intention and invited a spirit to come to you, but...they didn't?"

For a few moments they walked on in silence. Patricia glanced across at him and knew the answer.

"Did you experience that with *Bjorn*...?"

"Yes..."

"Of course..." She nodded. "I'm sorry..."

"It's all right." He forced a smile.

They altered course to pass behind a pair of middle-aged ladies recording the scene in oils. One was perched on a shooting stick, her companion preferring to stand. They had set their easels in the lee of a thicket of silvery birch trees; an overweight black Labrador snored at their feet as they dabbed at their canvases. Beyond them the ground fell away sharply. Patricia pointed out a group of oak and ash trees at the bottom of the incline.

"Down there's a favourite spot of mine," she told him, "near a little stream. As long as you don't mind a bit of a climb back..."

"It will not be a problem," he assured her. "In Iceland running up mountains is a popular sport, remember..."

"Feel free, but don't expect me to," she told him, dryly.

They began their descent. Patricia placed her feet with care, arms half raised to keep her balance, while her companion progressed with the easy grace of a man accustomed to traversing rough terrain. The slopes to both left and right were thick with ferns and bracken and dotted here and there with waist-high gorse bushes, flowers glowing gold in the evening light.

"I feel I've got a much clearer picture of the whole process now," she told him, "but things you said last time did raise a couple of questions. Maybe you'd clear them up."

"I will try..."

"I'd like to look at what you've described from a different perspective – one I'm more familiar with. The psychological one..."

"That is not my world..." he warned.

"It's easier than it sounds."

"I hope so..."

"Experiences when you access what sounds like another world, seem to play a big part in your life..."

"Very big, yes..."

"And now I've got a grasp of what you might call the mechanics, I'd like to get an idea of how they make you feel..."

Olaf shot her a suspicious glance. "Make me feel...?"

"I told you it wasn't complicated." She laughed. "What was your emotional response to that first meeting with Bardur, for example?"

"I have never thought about it..." He drew down the corners of his mouth. "I guess what you would call Olaf, the personal me, disappears for a while. It is less like me experiencing the moment than the moment simply being...experienced."

"Okay. But are there no feelings?"

"Well, it is certainly...intense."

"Surely you must feel something...?" She insisted, gently. "Like happy or excited...?"

"It is difficult..." He gazed into the distance, brow furrowed. "Afterwards, I do feel, yes. Calm, peaceful and...healed. Yes, healed and connected. Is that what you mean...?"

"It's a start," she told him. "When you say calm and peaceful,

I've had experiences I'd describe using those words. But surely they are more concepts than emotions?"

"Are they...?"

"There's invariably a body response accompanying feelings. If we're happy we smile, frightened we may shake, when we feel sad we often cry..."

"Well, I would say I feel joy at the time – of a very intense kind. And a sense of awe...and deep connection. Maybe the right word is...bliss. But," he added, "that is after the experience is over. It comes back to the personal. Feelings relate to an individual, don't they? But in that state of consciousness, Olaf as a person ceases to exist..."

"Okay. So, there's calm and connection afterwards but at the time you're not really in a feeling state. In fact..." she went on, "it sounds a bit like trance, when someone...moves beyond emotion. Does that sound right?"

"Yes, maybe..." He nodded assent.

"How about the beings then? Take the giant, for example..."

"Bárður."

"When you attune to him, have you any sense how Bardur feels...or whether he feels anything at all?"

Olaf closed his eyes for a few moments. "Loving, I think. No, I am sure. In fact, they all feel that way. And," he added, "I guess I feel the same way towards them..."

"Fine. Love is an emotion..."

"But it is not quite the same as what we call love..." He broke off. "Some of this is hard to explain...

"You're doing great..."

"With them, I get a sense of connectedness at a profound level..."

Patricia considered his answer. "Maybe the problem is finding the right words. I don't know about Icelandic but we only have one in English to cover all the myriad kinds of love. I've heard that Eskimos," she went on, "have dozens of words to describe different kinds of snow. There's one for newly fallen snow, another for crisp and icy snow, another for melting snow, et cetera. So while they can be absolutely precise about snow, whether I'm talking about loving marmalade or loving my children, I've only got the one word..."

"When they speak of love, people are often thinking of a flow moving from one person to another person. You understand...?"

"Yes, I do..."

"But in the realm of spirit, it is not like that. We come back again to everything being connected. You may be aware of it or not, but love is surrounding you, suffusing you. It is like..." He spread his arms, "like you are always in an eternal, infinite field of love. Just as we, at this moment, are in a field of light, or warmth, or..."

"It's as if you move out of feeling states altogether. Transcend them..." She took the pad from her bag. "Yes, that would make sense..."

They reached the bottom of the slope, and Olaf followed in her footsteps as she picked her way gingerly through a tangle of briars, nettles and brambles, heading for a fallen elm. Its roots, torn from the ground and exposed as it fell, had become a natural bridge spanning a narrow, winding gully cut by a stream. Brushing bark and moss from the trunk Patricia shrugged off her shoulder bag and sat down. In the course of the hot, dry spell, the stream had dwindled to little more than a sluggish trickle, stained rusty gold by iron leeching from the soil. Here and there sunlight slipped between the leaves and branches of elms and the broader oaks to dance on the ground beneath.

"When I have time – which isn't often these days – I love just sitting here and listening to the birds and the water. Occasionally I can get Colm to come with me but he can't sit still," she added with a wry smile. "He has to be doing something – usually playing with the stream. He likes clearing out leaves and sticks, or moving rocks to do a bit of dredging...he seems to have a thing about making it flow faster..."

"Excellent." Olaf gazed down at the water, nodding approval. "He seeks to release the natural energies, help them move freely..."

"He calls it hydraulic engineering," she told him, opening her notebook. "I call it interfering with nature..." She busied herself scribbling notes.

Olaf picked up a twig and snapped it in half. He dropped the pieces into the water and watched them drift downstream. "Are you writing about my feelings?"

Patricia shook her head. "About the absence of them, actually."

"Is that important?"

"Perhaps. Professionally, I find it interesting."

"Why?"

"Well...it supports a theory of mine."

"Now I am interested."

"It may not be one you would subscribe to."

"Now I am even more interested." He smiled.

"Okay..." Crossing her legs, she cupped a knee in her hands. "Well, it's fair to say that your first entry into the spirit world, with Bardur, came at a pretty traumatic time in your life. Is that fair...?"

"I suppose so..." He shrugged. "And...?"

"And from what you just told me, you seemed to find yourself in a realm in which you cease to experience what most people would think of as normal, everyday emotions..."

Olaf folded his arms and nodded. "You are saying there is a connection...?"

"I am saying I wouldn't dismiss the possibility..." she told him. "Because it might have made a very painful, unpleasant experience just a little easier to bear..."

"You mean I made it all up...?" His jaw jutted at a belligerent angle, and she caught a hard, defiant edge to his voice which she had not heard before.

"I don't know if that's what you heard, but I didn't say anything of the sort…"

"What are you saying, then?"

"That if an anxious, frightened child has an experience, as a result of which they no longer feel anxious and frightened, for a time, at least, then it would be absolutely natural for them to want to repeat it. Does that sound like an accusation?"

"Is that what you will put in your paper?"

"Hang on," Patricia spread her hands. "I haven't got as far as…"

"No…?" Taking a couple of steps towards her, he planted his hands on his hips. "Maybe you will remind your group that frightened children dream up imaginary friends and invent places to escape to. But it's all in their heads, it isn't real…"

"That is exactly what some do, but I never said I thought you were one of them…" She paused. "You're not, are you…?"

His eyes searched her face; it was several moments before his expression softened and he shook his head. "No…" he told her. "No, of course not."

"You seem pretty…sensitive about it."

"When *Brynja* got angry, she accused me of that. It hurt me a lot, but…it does not matter now." He took a deep breath. "I would like you to show me more of your forest…"

"Let's do that…" Patricia got to her feet, slinging her bag across her shoulder.

"Do you have more questions for me?"

"I do, actually. You said you came along today partly to find out if I really am some kind of guide. Have you decided yet?"

"Not yet."

"How will you know?"

"I will…"

"Come on. Tell me how…"

"I will sense it…feel it in my body."

"Really – a physical sensation…?"

"Probably..."

"Will you tell me if it happens?"

"If you wish..."

"Okay. We're going to swing round in a loop which will bring us back to the car..."

Leaving the cool of the shade beneath the trees, they set off once more. A length of frayed rope dangled from the branch of a sturdy oak: an area of scuffed, bare earth beneath it marked the place someone had chosen to create a rustic swing.

"You mentioned you once hoped to connect with Bjorn in spirit – but it didn't quite work out."

"Not yet." He shook his head. "Later I found out why..."

"Found out, how?"

"It is a long story..."

Patricia smiled and spread her hands. "We're in no hurry are we...?"

"Well, after he disappeared it was terrible. You have children, you can imagine. There was a big search, of course. People swarmed all over the place, looking everywhere. There were helicopters, rescue teams, a volunteer group called the *Hjálparsveit Skáta*..." He paused to take a deep breath. "It went on for...I do not remember how many days, but a long time. When everyone else gave up, *Brynja* and me could not. We never found anything. No one did. No clothes, no...not one clue what might have happened. His picture was in our papers, papers from other countries, on posters, on television...everywhere. People called from other countries saying maybe they saw him, but it never was. Some had crazy ideas, like he was taken by aliens, or fairies or...We kept hoping, searching...sometimes together, sometimes alone. Long, long past when we knew it was hopeless, I guess. But...you cannot just sit and do nothing."

"But you stayed together...?"

"For a time, yes, but in the end it got too difficult. What happened was not her fault, no one could say that, but sometimes she thought I blamed her. Then she went crazy at me. Why did I leave her alone when she was ill? That made me mad, because I had asked if she wanted me to stay. She said no, it was okay if I went…It is a terrible thing to say, but it would have been easier if we had known for sure he was…" He sighed and moistened his lips. "Just known what happened. Nothing was for sure, nothing was certain. When you do not know, you start imagining…"

He loosened his bandana and slipped it off. Wiping his face and hands he knotted it round his brow once more.

"You said I could imagine…" she reminded him, "but quite honestly I don't think I could begin to."

"No, maybe not. Anyway, in the end we were making it worse for each other, not better and…I do not remember where I went. I moved from place to place, staying with friends, family…different people. Everyone was kind; they fed me, looked after me. One was a priest I had known all my life, we grew up together, and she talked to me about what she believed in. We understood God in different ways, but it got me thinking. I even went to her church and tried praying. It did not help, but it made me wonder what would. And the answer was so obvious I could not understand why it took me so long to see it. Go talk to *Bárður* and the others who rescued me when I was a kid…"

"So you'd stopped all that…"

"As I got older it was like I needed it less and less. Life was easier after I left home, and of course I got interested in other things…" He smiled. "Like any boy does…"

"When testosterone kicks in…" She nodded. "So you reconnected?"

"Exactly."

"How did you manage that?"

"Doing what I said. Clearing my mind, meditating…"

"As easy as that…"

"It took time. At first, I could not stop thinking about *Björn* –

so many thoughts it made me dizzy. But slowly I learned to calm down. And there they were, just like the first time. *Bárður*, then others..."

"That must have felt good."

"Sure..." He nodded, "and I was pretty relieved. I had worried that because I had kind of neglected them, they would be angry..."

"But they weren't..."

"They are loving. Beings of love do not punish..."

"Presumably you asked them for help."

"I had a thousand questions. Where was he now, what happened, why to him...why to us, was it our fault, something we did wrong...?" He shrugged. "And they always gave me the same answer. Be patient. In time you will understand."

"Kind of frustrating when you must have wanted proper answers?"

"At first, yes. But when the message never changed, and they always answered in a gentle, loving way, I started to accept." He nodded to himself. "And that was when I was taken on a journey. Which made things clearer. A little, anyway."

Their track ran roughly parallel to the stream, which had become little more than a succession of glistening puddles on ground so soft and damp, the pair left a trail of footprints in their wake. Patricia glanced at her companion. Hands clasped behind his back, he had a far-away look in his eyes.

"One day I climbed *Eilífsdalur*, which is not so far from where he disappeared. I sat on the ground with my back against a rock, and meditated. And my grandmother came to me. *Friðrika*, the one I lived with after my mother had her breakdown. You remember...?"

"Sure. Was she still alive...?"

"No, no. She died a few years before *Björn* was born. Anyway, she said she wanted to take me somewhere special and the journey might be uncomfortable. I told her that was okay. And she told me to be aware of the place we started from..."

"Which was where *Bjorn*..."

"No, she meant we were between two mountains. *Eilífstindur*, which means the eternal mountain, and *Skálatindur*..."

"Skala," echoed Patricia. "As in chalice, is that right...?"

"I wondered if you would notice..." He gave an approving nod. "Well, pretty soon it did get uncomfortable. As she led me deeper and deeper into *Eilífstindur*, it felt like being suffocated. As if the whole weight of the mountain was pushing down on me. You have seen fossils in rocks?"

"Sure..."

"That was how I felt. Trapped, imprisoned, completely helpless..." He puffed out his cheeks. "Just thinking about it makes my lungs hurt. Even worse, I felt the presence of dark forces. The kind that could keep me prisoner down there if they wanted. I have to admit I was getting pretty scared but *Friðrika* told me if I faced the fear and showed them I was stronger than them, they could not hurt me. And I guess I must have managed to, because soon I felt us going up again and..." He clasped a hand to his chest. "You know when you are swimming, and you dive down deep, then as you are coming up you can't wait to take a big breath...?"

"Oh, yes..." she assured him.

"Once we started going up there was more light. Soon all I could see were bright, brilliant colours everywhere. I realised wherever *Friðrika* was taking me was literally built of light. And we came to a huge temple, where the whole place – walls, columns, arches, windows...they were all beams of light. All the colours I had ever seen and some I hadn't..." He paused, smiling at her. "It is kind of hard to explain..."

"Don't worry, you're doing fine," she assured him.

"*Friðrika* said I was to go in by myself, she would wait for me. So I did and found three goddesses in gold robes. They said they were expecting me, and were happy I had come..." He broke off and chuckled. "All you are interested in is how they told me, yes?"

"It's all fascinating, but since you ask…"

"No words. They were beings of love, you see. The moment I looked into their eyes, I knew I was in the presence of amazing kindness, warmth and compassion. That, in a way, told me everything they wanted to tell me, too."

"Which was…?"

"I immediately knew *Björn* was with them, in the light, as they called it. He was being looked after, and he was well and happy. It told me they knew my sadness, and how much I had suffered. And that I should understand everything in my life was unfolding exactly the way it needed to…"

"That must have been a pretty hard message to hear after what you'd been through…"

"At that moment, sitting in such an extraordinary place, surrounded by beauty I can't really describe, it did not seem hard, really…" He pursed his lips. "You see, I absolutely knew I could trust them. You know I said they were beings of love…?"

"Yes, but even so…"

He held up a hand. "Love…" he repeated. "Think about it for a moment. Love always, always tells the truth. Why would I doubt them?"

"Well, okay…"

"I realised it would help me to never forget there is divine purpose behind everything. Every event and experience, every situation or circumstance. Without exception, whether it is something I like or do not like. The problem is, we become so caught up in our feelings, we forget that. As far as *Bjorn* was concerned, I knew he incarnated with soul work to complete. It only took him a few years. Then he was ready to return to his true home. It reminded me another mistake we make is thinking this planet is home, which is just another illusion. This is somewhere we come to learn about ourselves – a kind of graduate school…"

"I have to admit I don't really understand the concept of soul work," she admitted. "Did they explain what Bjorn's had been – did you learn anything about why he came or what he was supposed to do...?"

"Only that it was healing work, and sometime in the future everything would be made clear to me..."

"But you don't know when or how?"

"That's right."

"And...was that it?"

"I want to explain about reconnecting with him. I wanted to, of course, right then, but I knew it was not the moment. Well," he corrected himself, "not yet. But I was also certain we will meet again."

"You mean...when you die?"

Olaf shrugged and spread his hands. "Maybe. It will definitely happen, I felt that so strongly, but only when we are ready. Both *Björn* and me..."

They crossed a narrow, uneven bridge, built of heavy wooden railway sleepers darkened by age and weathering. On the other side their path began a steep ascent through tangled broom, ferns, and gorse. She had read reports of an unusually high number of adders in the forest during the hot spell, and Patricia stepped with care as they entered longer grass.

"And tell me, after that journey, when you...came back to earth again, did you feel any different...did it help?"

"Well..." He tilted his head from side to side, like an Indian dancer. "I would say so, yes. But it did not help *Brynja*. Definitely not. She said she did not care about reasons or explanations. He was gone and none of that stuff could stop her heart being broken. I remember," he went on, scratching his head, "she got really angry with me for even telling her about it. I never understood why..."

"And the part about meeting him again when you're ready. Presumably if he's..." She waved a hand skyward, "up there, he would be ready, wouldn't he?"

"I expect so, yes."

"So the real the question is, are you..."

He shot her a sideways glance. "I suppose..."

"An interesting one, isn't it? Have you ever wondered what you might have to do to be...ready?"

Sinking his hands into his pockets, he let his gaze range over the countryside before him and shook his head.

"I thought about it, but I do not really know..."

"Did you...ask?"

"When I was with the goddesses?"

"Yes..."

"Maybe I should have. I asked my guides one time..." he told her, kicking impatiently at a clump of earth. "But they told me when the time is right, I will know everything..."

"They're letting you sweat it out, then...?"

His only answer was a wry smile. For all she knew, his beings might really be independent, autonomous entities who inhabited a spirit realm. Equally, it was possible they were figments of his imagination. Not so long ago, she reflected, ideas like those could have earned him a one way ticket to Wych Cross. One thing he had made abundantly clear was that spirits provided nothing to him but positive, supportive advice and guidance.

"Are you absolutely sure about that...?" she asked, as they skirted a stand of silver birch.

He glanced at her, brow furrowed. "About what...?"

"Well, I just wondered. Could they have answered your question, only you didn't quite get the message, so to speak...?"

"What do you...?" He began, but halted in mid-stride, a finger pressed to his lips. It was several moments before, following his gaze, she glimpsed, well camouflaged by the play of light and shadow among the birches, a deer. Keeping as still as she could, Patricia watched it raise its slender head to sniff the air. Then, calmly, it turned and with a flick of its tail vanished into the shadows. She took a deep breath.

"I'm not sure why, but there's something special about seeing deer. Did you know the old English word for them was 'hart'?"

"Interesting…" He pressed a hand to his chest. "Maybe that is where they touch us."

"Possible." Patricia nodded. "I like the idea anyway. Over the last few years I've seen too many hit by cars. It's sad, really…"

Olaf grimaced. "I am sure…"

"You can buy whistles to put on your car that are supposed to scare them away…"

Topping the crest of the ridge, they saw the artists had packed up palettes, easels and canvases, woken the Labrador and left for home. The lowering sun glinted on the windows of the handful of cars left among the firs. Olaf emerged from thought to glance at his companion.

"I am thinking about our deer," he told her.

"What about it…?"

"Have you heard of somewhere called *Dharma Chakra Pravartana*?"

"I don't think so. Why?"

"People also call it the Deer Park."

"Still no wiser, I'm afraid."

"It is where the Buddha gave his first teachings…"

"Okay…"

"According to the legend, his presence and message were so powerful that even the animals came to hear and receive his wisdom. His devotees still consider it a very significant event."

"Are you one of them?"

"I honour all the great masters. And I believe Buddha is one of them."

"So seeing that deer…reminded you of Buddha?"

He stopped, turning to face her. "You remarked on there being something special about that moment. True for us both, perhaps."

"It's always nice seeing them but, I mean...it's not that unusual..."

"I see it from a different perspective," he went on. "When something like that happens, I stop and ask myself a simple question. If there was a reason for that particular event happening at that particular moment, if it held some kind of message for me, what might it be?"

"I'm not sure where you're going with this..."

"You may have noticed." He smiled. "I can never resist looking for what may lie hidden behind, or beneath, that which is obvious..."

"Hence many maps..."

"Very many. I see things not as important in themselves, but as clues to what might be important, or significant. So," he went on, "I am asking myself, why did I meet a deer at that moment..."

"It led you to Buddha. Anywhere else?"

He held up a finger. "A few moments before I saw it, you asked me a question. I do not recall your exact words, but I think it was about what I might have to do before I am ready to meet my son again..." He paused. "And you wondered if maybe I had been told already, but not heard..."

"Yes, but I still don't see..."

He placed a hand lightly on her arm. "My conclusion is this. Just as you ask me a question, I see the deer. And..." He tapped his head, "the first connection which enters my mind is with teachings of the Buddha..."

"So you think it meant...what?"

"Perhaps what Patricia was saying is important. Listen to her wisdom..." He paused. "What do you think...?"

"I can see how you got there, but what do I think? Quite honestly I don't know," she admitted. "There's a kind of logic, to one part of my brain. But another part just says: hey, come on, Patricia, so you saw a deer. There's no shortage of them around here. Do you have to make such a big deal of it?"

"In other words, it might be pure chance...?"

"It might..."

"Or not?" Olaf mimed weighing the possibilities in the air.

"That covers all the options," she agreed. "So, assuming for a moment that you're right, and it really was something deep and meaningful, what then?"

"Then...maybe it answers my question. You were sent to give me guidance."

"You really think so?"

He put a hand to his brow. "I feel tingling here. It tells me, yes..."

"I'm flattered..."

"I must consider very carefully the question you were asking."

"I'd say the answer was pretty obvious..."

He smiled. "More wisdom? Tell me, please."

He might be playing a harmless game, teasing her. Scrutinising his face for clues, she saw nothing but polite curiosity. Faintly uncomfortable, she hesitated. He might be convinced she had a role to play, but she risked straying into territory which was surely his alone to enter. It might also be an invitation to assume a level of responsibility she was far from sure she wanted. She took a deep breath; he had asked in good faith and the best course of action was to respond in kind.

"Olaf, the way I see it, that's one of the reasons they sent you here in the first place," she told him. "I mean...it's all part of the process. By doing as they ask, you show you're...ready."

"Oh..." He frowned. "You think so...?"

"Look, I'm not saying that's definitely it. How could I? I'm telling you how it feels..."

"It's okay..." He held up a hand. "Maybe you are right..."

"Good..."

"Better than good..." With a sudden spring in his stride he led the way towards the cars. "It is wonderful. A sign I am on my path. Doing what I need to do..."

"That's not quite what I meant..."

He glanced at her as if she had spoken in a language unfamiliar to him. "No? Like you say, they asked me to come here, and I have done that..." He hesitated, "Now it is up to me where my path leads..."

"That sounds as if you think seeing the deer just meant whatever you decide to do is fine..."

"I think it was...important. So," he continued, briskly, "have you done all you wanted to do? Do you have everything you need for your research?"

As far as he was concerned, the subject was closed. For him perhaps, thought Patricia, but not for her.

"I don't get it, Olaf. You're talking about seeing where your path leads," she reminded him. "But surely that was never in doubt..."

"No, but..." He seemed reluctant to meet her eyes. "Anything can be a sign. Meeting a deer or...meeting Morgana. You understand?"

"I...yes, I guess so."

"She is a very sensitive person. In tune with spirit. In fact," he went on, "she is exactly the kind of person they would also send to guide me...perhaps in a new direction."

Patricia smiled. "That's interesting. I mean, I'm nothing like her, am I? The opposite, maybe. But you seem pretty sure I'm a guide, too."

"I was to go to a sacred place and..." he insisted, "Stonehenge is another ancient one. Very ancient, and also now misunderstood and so neglected. In great need of healing. If my mission is to align myself with earth energies to aid a healing process, one place is no better or worse than another."

"I'm sure you understand all that better than I do..."

"That may be true..."

"But the fact remains you weren't told to just go anywhere,

Olaf..."

Olaf spun to face her. "You do not like her, do you...?"

"Morgana...?"

"You just do not like her," he repeated, more loudly.

"It has nothing to do with liking..."

"And you are angry she will go back to the people who are complaining about you..."

"Olaf, let's just stick with you..."

"No...!" He jabbed an accusing finger at her, "you are talking about her. I know it. She said to be careful of you. I did not understand, but maybe she is right. Yes, you helped me, but I will not let you interfere in my life..."

Snatching the bandana from his head he strode off. Patricia watched him go. He was in no mood for rational discussion, but when the anger and indignation faded he might see it differently. Or not: either way it was beyond her control. The only sensible thing to do right now was return him to his lover. She found him with his hands on the car roof, fingers beating an impatient tattoo. She had carefully parked in a patch of shade, but the interior was stifling. She sat with the door open, hand on the ignition key.

"You may not feel like listening, but I'm going to tell you one more thing," she said, evenly. "One more thing about that bloody deer..."

The Icelander sat stiffly at her side, looking straight ahead, hands clasped in his lap. A car went by at walking pace, pausing briefly at the entrance before accelerating away towards Wych Cross.

"Maybe you've understood the real message, maybe not. I have no way of knowing..." She glanced at him but saw no response. "But my gut feeling is it's vital you get this right. Important for you..." She hesitated, "...and for Bjorn."

"Please take me back now." His voice was flat, expressionless.

"So," she continued, starting the engine, "I am inviting you to come with me tomorrow morning to visit that yew I told Mitch about. According to him they have healing powers. And maybe that's exactly what you need right now…"

They completed the return journey in stony silence, punctuated only by the drumming of tyres on tarmac ridged and rutted by the ravages of a harsh winter. She drew to the kerb outside the village church with its stubby tower, waiting while her passenger climbed out. He stooped to peer in at her.

"I understand."

The colour had drained from his face, giving it a pale and haunted look.

"I'll come by at nine tomorrow morning," she told him. "If you're here, we can go together. If you're not, I shall go alone…"

"I understand," he repeated, joining his palms. "Namaste…"

She sat for a few moments watching the tall figure cross the road. She wondered if he noticed the sign for Hartfield Road.

Chapter 17

At the Buxted Yew

Saturday 18th June 2011

"Working...?" Colm's expression registered somewhere between surprise and disbelief. "On a Saturday? How come...?"

"To which the answers are, in that order..." Patricia replied, "sort of...yes...and because it's really important..."

"Mum..."

"Something tells me you have other plans..."

"Yeah. I wanted to go to Crawley to upgrade my mobile. You said we could..." He sprinkled another spoonful of sugar over a bowl overflowing with cornflakes. "And that's important to me..."

They were taking breakfast al fresco at the edge of the lawn, warmed by a morning sun already high in the sky. The garden chairs were in urgent need of their annual rendezvous with rag and teak oil, and she added it to the mental list of things Colm would strive to avoid doing over the summer holidays. She paused, distracted by butterflies executing an exquisitely choreographed aerial ballet, among bushes heavy with hydrangeas the colour of old bruises.

"Mum...?"

"Yes, I'm sure it is, pet, and we shall. How about this afternoon...?"

"I'm doing something this afternoon..."

"Oh, what?"

"Going for a swim..."

"Good for you. Where?"

"Over at Soph's..."

"What I've got to do shouldn't take long. An hour or so, no more..."

"I got up early specially." He heaved the sigh of a love-lorn Romeo. "And you say an hour or so, but it never is. It's always hours and hours..."

"There are buses," she reminded him, "if it's that urgent..."

The information was received with scant enthusiasm; being chauffeured was infinitely preferable to using public transport for any journey, however short. She wrestled a jar of homemade marmalade and lost.

"Can you do this for me...?"

She tossed it to her son, who plucked it out of the air one handed.

"What's so important, anyway?" he enquired, reluctant to concede the battle.

"I'm going down to Forest Row to pick up an ex-patient. The guy who came to talk to me the other night, remember? He's helping me with some research, so we're meeting again," she explained. "At least, that's the plan..."

Colm opened the jar with a deft flick of the wrist and slid it back to her.

"So he might not pitch up...?"

"It's possible, in which case the mummy taxi company will be operating as usual," she said, with a saccharin smile. "If he does, we're going over to Buxted..."

"There's nothing in Buxted..." he protested.

"You are so wrong..."

"What is there, then...?"

"A two thousand year old tree..."

"Seriously...?"

"Scout's honour."

"Wow..."

Colm took a mouthful of cereal and digested her words.

"But why would you take this guy to, like, see some tree...?"

"Because I want to see it anyway, and I know he'd be really interested. He knows a lot about trees…"

"I still don't get it." Colm frowned, waving his spoon in the air. "Okay, it's old, but so what…?"

"It's a yew. Like ours," she added with a nod towards the end of the terrace, "only a lot bigger and much older…"

Colm remained unimpressed.

"So?"

"Have you forgotten last weekend…?"

"Course not…" He frowned. "What about it…?"

"And what Gran Fran sent us off to find…?"

"Oh, yeah…that's right. It was one of them, wasn't it?"

"Some people seem to think they're special…"

"She did. I'm still not sure why…"

"Nor am I. They're supposed to be sort of…magic, I gather. Anyway," she went on quickly, "your great-grandmother and the chap I'm meeting certainly think so."

"Oh, okay…"

She stretched, and stifled a yawn. She would have preferred devoting the morning to some gardening but fate had decreed otherwise.

"I don't really understand it," she admitted spreading marmalade on warm toast, "but with a bit of luck I might find out this very morning…"

"This chap…" Shading his eyes, Colm peered at her. "Is he, you know…like her?"

"Not really. He's about a foot taller with a beard…"

He groaned. "You know what I mean. If he was a patient he must be, like, a bit loony, yeah…?"

"Well, let's just say they seem to share certain unusual views…"

"Cool…" a grin crept across his face. "Can I come then…?"

"To Buxted?" She frowned. "Are you serious?"

"Totally…"

Pushing the empty bowl away he leaned back and closed his eyes, brow furrowed in thought. "If your guy is into the same kind of stuff she is...it might be, like, interesting, mightn't it...?"

She smiled. One minute gauche teenager, the next, young man. He wasted no time intuiting parallels between Olaf and his great-grandmother, nor had he shared his mother's ambivalence when it came to trusting the old lady's instincts.

"If you'd like to, it's fine by me," she told him, sipping coffee. "By the way, any snake ladies visit since we got back?"

"Nope." He opened one eye and grinned. "How cool is that...?"

"Positively arctic."

"You say that every time..." He sighed.

"I solemnly promise I will never say it again."

"And you say that every time," he pointed out, wearily.

"No," She held up a finger. "I've only promised. Never solemnly."

He shook his head. "Dad thinks Gran Fran is bonkers."

"Is that a fact?"

"I told him she's great, but I don't think he really gets her does he?"

"A lot of people wouldn't." She put down her cup and glanced at her watch. "You'd better get your skates on if you're coming, mister. I told him I'd be there at nine sharp."

Colm jumped to his feet. "Can we go even if your guy doesn't pitch up?"

"Could do. I want to go to Nutley, anyway."

"Why...?" He protested, picking up his bowl and mug. "There's nothing there, either..."

"Oh really? What about that place where they sell old sports cars?"

"Yeah, there's that..." he conceded as he padded towards the kitchen door. "So...?"

"I was thinking I might get one..."

He came spinning round, eyes wide. "Mum...you're kidding, right...?"

"Why would I be...?"

"Hey...what kind?"

"I haven't decided yet. But I think..." She pursed her lips. "I rather fancy a red one..."

Ψ

Olaf would be there or he would not; either way, she decided, en route to the village, would be fine. If he wasn't, she and Colm would simply make the trip on their own. She was not sure how much she recalled of Mitch's advice on etiquette for approaching sacred trees, or how comfortable she would be following it. Invoking spirits featured somewhere, but she doubted she would go as far as that. Not that it really mattered, for Olaf's spirits sounded a benign bunch; the kind who would make allowances, given the fact that such things were no part of a good Catholic girl's education. Mentally prepared to undertake the venture without him, she nevertheless felt a sense of relief, as well as pleasure, spotting the tall figure on the low, stone wall enclosing the churchyard.

"Is that him – the thin guy with the pack...?"

"It is indeed..."

"Looks pretty normal to me..."

"I think you'll find he is..."

Olaf deposited his backpack on the floor and climbed in, acknowledging Patricia's greeting with a faint smile. He reached for his seat belt and glanced over his shoulder.

"I'd like you to meet Colm. I told him what we're doing and he was keen to come along," Patricia explained. "I hope that's okay with you..."

"It is a pleasure. *Góðan daginn, Kolbjörn. Hvernig hefur þú það?*" he went on, extending a hand over his shoulder. "You understand...?"

"I can guess..." Colm shrugged. "I'm good, thanks."

Olaf did not speak again until they were approaching the crossroads at Wych Cross.

"Some things you said yesterday..." he told Patricia, keeping his eyes on the tree-lined road, "were not comfortable to hear."

"I'm sure."

"But..." He ran the tip of his tongue along his lower lip, "maybe...necessary. I thought a lot about them last night."

"I hoped they might help," Patricia told him. "That was my intention, anyway..."

"I hope so, too. If there is time today, maybe we should talk more..."

"Of course..."

He glanced over his shoulder. "Your town has quite a history. Do you know much about it?"

"Not really but my dad always said it's like, a magnet for loonies..."

"Really...?" A smile crept across the Icelander's face. "Is he right?"

"It certainly attracts an extraordinary number of cults, and what you might call fringe groups," Patricia agreed. "We've got Mormons, Anthroposophists, Pagans, Druids..."

"And Morgana's friends...?" Olaf offered.

Patricia glanced across and noted, with relief, he was smiling. "Yes," she assented. "Mustn't leave them out..."

"According to Dad they're all loonies..."

"Liam doesn't have much time for anything that smacks of religion..."

"I see them a little differently..." Olaf pursed his lips. "As spiritual seekers, maybe...?"

"They do some seriously weird stuff, though," Colm told him. "Like dancing round completely starkers at full moon..."

"Not all of them..." Patricia pointed out.

"The tree hugger guys do," Colm insisted. "Honestly, Dad said he'd seen them…"

"He probably meant the pagans," Patricia explained. "They're pretty active here…"

"But, Mum, you've got to admit that's pretty weird…"

"When we do not understand something, we often call it weird…" Olaf told him.

"So you've been busy researching?" Patricia enquired.

He nodded. "The name Grin-stead interested me. Did you know 'grin' and 'crom' have the same root…?"

"I did not," she said. "But then, I'm afraid I haven't a clue who or what they are."

"You do not know of Crom Dubh…?" Olaf wore a shocked look. "He is in Irish legends. He may even have given you the name of your capital…"

"Olaf, it must have been very obvious the first time we met, you know a great deal more about Irish mythology than me…"

"He was an ancient pagan god. The trouble was, when Christianity came along they did not like such gods – they were too popular. But the church was very clever. What they did was turn Crom and his friends from gods into either evil spirits, or Christian saints…"

"Neat…" grinned Colm.

"Very. I'm sure you know Saint Patrick's story…"

"Of course…"

"In the Christian version he fought with Crom Cruach – probably another name for our friend Crom Dubh. He was victorious of course, and threw him out…"

"Like with the snakes…"

"Exactly, but there are many different versions, you see. Some talk about Crom, others about Cruach. Sometimes it is dragons, and sometimes snakes…" Olaf shrugged. "But stories are just stories. The important thing is their true meaning."

"You'd get on really well with my great-gran. Wouldn't he,

Mum?"

Patricia glanced in her mirror to see Colm wearing a broad smile.

"I think he might..."

"She's got loads of books on saints. She gave me one on St Patrick, actually, but I haven't started it yet..."

"There wouldn't be many long, awkward silences once they got together," agreed Patricia.

"What are we actually going to do when we get to Buxted?" Colm wanted to know.

Patricia glanced at Olaf. "Over to you..."

"Well, this yew is very old, so it probably marks a sacred site. A place people have visited to worship for centuries."

"How could you tell..." Colm craned forward, "if it is, like...sacred?"

Hoisting his pack onto his lap, Olaf rummaged inside and produced two lengths of wire bent into an L-shape. "With these..." He passed them over his shoulder to Colm. "If you are interested I will show you how to use them. You can do it yourself..."

"They look like bits of cheap, crappy, coat hangers..." Colm frowned, running his finger along one.

"That is what they are," grinned Olaf.

"So what do you do with them...?"

"You know about magnets...?"

"We did them in physics..."

"If you know how to use those pieces of wire, you can detect even tiny changes in magnetic fields. So you can find the path of underground streams..."

"Yeah, but you talked about sacred," Colm reminded him, returning the rods. "That's, like, to do with God isn't it – not magnets."

"True, but..." Olaf shrugged, "I can try to explain, but it gets a little complicated, my friend."

"No prob…" Colm told him. "Go for it…"

"Not everyone would agree with what I am going to tell you. But it is my experience, so it is what I believe…"

Colm shrugged. "That's okay…"

"Well…" Olaf stared out of the window for few moments. "You know people from different cultures often hold different beliefs, and understand God in many different ways…"

"We do comparative religions…"

"And there are so many, aren't there? So you know some people like to think of God as a person. There is nothing wrong with that, but I understand God as pure energy. In fact, as the most powerful energy in the universe. From your physics, you know if you have the right equipment you can detect any kind of energy. Electricity, light, heat, magnetism…" He waved a hand. "Any of them. To me, our planet is a living being and the energy currents flowing through it and round it are expressions of one universal energy…" He glanced over his shoulder. "Okay so far…?"

"Kind of…" Colm frowned. "I hope. Go on, anyway…"

"Do not worry about it. The only thing you really need to know…" He flourished the pieces of wire, "is that you can use these to trace and map the paths of those earth current. As you will see for yourself."

"Cool…"

"So you call them crappy bits of coat hanger," Olaf added, "I call them low technology God-detectors…"

"Neat…" Colm grinned.

Patricia wondered if letting Colm come along had been wise. There was surely no harm in him hearing a few words designed to placate tree spirits – as he had done in Ireland, after all – but the conversation had progressed way beyond that. She suspected she might unwittingly have sent him out for a walk on the theological wild side – of the kind which would have sent Father Coyle into cardiac arrest on the spot. However sensible and level-headed he might be, she recognised Colm's susceptibility to Frances's tales of the supernatural; her concern was that Olaf's words might exert a less benign influence.

"We'll be there in a couple of minutes," she announced, with a glance at the Icelander. "Is there anything we should be doing...?"

"There are no rules. That may not be what you are used to..." he offered, with a smile. "I do not believe in telling people what to do or how to do it; what is allowed and what is not." He paused. "If you like, I will tell you what I am going to do. If you feel like doing something similar, please do that. If not, that is fine, too."

"When Gran Fran sent us to find her tree," Colm told him, "she wrote down this sort of...message thing I had to read out."

"Asking for help from the relevant spirits. Or something along those lines..." Patricia added.

"I can only remember bits." Colm paused. "Like...spirits in the sky, mountain spirits, yew spirits, creatures on land sea and air and...there were others as well..."

"You've got a good memory..." Patricia nodded approval.

"I hung onto the bit of paper, actually," Colm admitted. "I wasn't sure if I was meant to, but it felt wrong to, like, bin it. Actually, I still read it out loud occasionally. I had this idea it might help stop the nightmares coming back. And it seems to..." He glanced at Olaf. "Do you think that'd be okay? I mean, going on reading it...?"

"Better than okay," Olaf assured him. "A great idea. Each time you read it you honour the words, the intention, also the spirits..." He glanced at Patricia. "You named this young man well."

"Gran Fran told us loads about that, too." Colm nodded. "You know, the dove and stuff..."

"Did she mention the eagle...?"

"She told us to look out for them, didn't she?" Colm glanced

394

at his mother. "We didn't actually see one, but we found the tree at a place called Eagle Lodge..."

"So there was an eagle presence, but not in physical form." Olaf nodded. "Dove is a symbol of peace – as well as high consciousness. Eagle has many meanings – it has earth connections, but is also to do with flight, and seeing clearly from above. And of course it is a symbol of dragon taming, like Saint Patrick..."

"Gran Fran lives really near his mountain. She said it used to be called Eagle Mountain, didn't she?" Colm's eyes shone.

"Excellent...!" Olaf clapped his hands. "I like the sound of this old lady. She must be very wise..."

"I don't really get the bit about dragons, though." Colm frowned. "I thought it was snakes..."

"Over the centuries, different story tellers, different versions, using different creatures. Snakes and worms, lizards and dragons all stand for the invisible energies around us – the ones flowing through and under the earth, and all living things, including you..." he added, glancing over his shoulder. "So we will find them round the yew."

"What are we supposed to do when we get there, then?"

"What did you do last weekend?"

"Not much, really," Colm told him. "Just...tied a bit of cord round it..."

"After asking the spirits for help..."

"Yeah, right."

"So, first you attuned to that yew, connected with it..." Olaf reminded him. "You could do that today, if you like. Then ask it for help or guidance or...whatever you need right now..."

"Awesome," breathed Colm. "Do you understand all this stuff, Mum?"

"Still got L-plates on, I'm afraid..." She shook her head. "But aren't you glad you didn't go to Crawley...?"

Ignoring her question, he leaned forward. "Do we do one of

those message thing?"

"Because if so," Patricia added, "we're going to need it ASAP..."

She swung off the main road and into a queue of traffic. Moving at walking pace, they passed through a walled entrance leading into a broad avenue, lined on one side with evenly spaced poplars. At the far end stood a church with sandstone walls and squat square tower, topped by a low spire. It was dwarfed by a majestic yew which rose well above the tiled roof, almost as high as the spire itself.

"There's an awful lot of cars." Colm frowned. "Do you think all those people have come to see the tree?"

Patricia gestured at an expanse of open grass stretching away to their left. "I'd say it's got more to do with the midsummer fair..."

In the centre of the field, a team in hard hats was busy erecting a large marquee, while others worked on an array of tents and stalls. Pulling into an empty space amongst vans and cars, Patricia glanced at Olaf.

"I know what we do is up to us, but I'm interested what you'll do..."

"When I visit a special place like this, I take a little time to make sure I know why I have come," he told her. "Then I make a clear intention about outcome..."

"Which might be...?"

"Sometimes it is as simple as giving greetings, paying my respects. Sometimes I have a particular purpose." He explained. "Like seeking healing..."

"Or guidance?"

Olaf gave her a wry smile. "If that is what I feel I need..."

"Actually, I only sort of came because you guys were," Colm offered. "No other reason, really..."

Patricia glanced at him. "Why not just say hi to it, then. I'm sure that'd be fine."

"Absolutely," Olaf assented. "Another time, if you wanted something you can ask for it."

"Okay." Colm bit his lip. "If I think of something now, do I have to say it out loud?"

"No rules…" Olaf shook his head. "Do whatever feels right. Relax, enjoy, observe. Expect nothing, observe everything. If you do not wish to talk, try listening instead. It could have something to tell you…"

"Let's go…" Colm fumbled with the door.

"Sure, you go on…" Patricia told him. "I want to check something out with Olaf. We'll be along in a minute…"

"Well…" His eyes flickered from her face to Olaf's, "okay."

Patricia watched him move off towards the churchyard, shading his eyes as he stared at the bustle of activity in the field. Olaf unfastened his seat belt and cocked his head. "You have something to ask…?"

"First, I want to say I'm really glad you came along. I'd decided I'd bring Colm anyway, but…I'm glad. And what I want to say is less asking you anything than making a suggestion…"

"I see…"

"I have no right to, but I'm going to do it anyway." She smiled. "After all, you said there were no rules."

"I meant it." He nodded. "So this is not about your intention…"

"No. I've got one, but it's nothing to do with that. Actually," she added, "it's about yours…"

"Mine…?" He leaned back and folded his arms.

"Yesterday, we talked about whether I'd been sent…as a guide."

He gave a faint nod but made no reply. Drifting through the summer morning air she could hear cries, raised voices, laughter and rhythmic hammering.

"You didn't seem very keen to hear my views about your change of plan…"

"I did not say I had changed—" he began.

She cut him short. "Okay, but you're thinking seriously of changing it, aren't you?"

"It is possible..." he assented.

"So what I'm suggesting is you...before you finally make up your mind, you ask for guidance. From the yew," she added, "or its guides or...whoever."

"I see..." He took a long, slow breath, gazing at the scene before them. A cheer rang out as one of the massive marquee poles was hauled into place. Running the tips of his fingers across his moustache, Olaf chuckled. "She is a determined creature, isn't she?"

"Who is...?"

"The deer."

"Oh. How do you know it was a female...?"

"I felt it."

"Me too, as it happens. Determined she is," Patricia agreed. "Do you realise what she's done? Somehow persuaded a highly qualified, mental health professional to suggest someone goes and asks the advice of a tree. Now, you have to admit that takes something special, doesn't it?"

"Yes, but your energy today is more tigress than deer."

"Meaning...?"

"Strong, determined, courageous and..." He scanned her face, "it is unwise to argue with tigress."

"Really...?

"Really. But," he added, opening his door, "I think we should go now. We must not keep the white dove waiting."

Colm sprang lightly from his seat on the skimpy, metal fence surrounding the churchyard. He was wearing baggy, calf-length basketball shorts in a shiny blue material, and a long yellow T-shirt bearing a print of Michael Jordan leaping improbably high.

"So, Mr Colm, are you ready?"

"Absolutely..."

"Shall we ask for a little help...?"

"Go for it..."

Turning his palms skywards, tips of thumbs and forefingers touching, Olaf closed his eyes and intoned in a quiet, clear voice:

"Hail, O blessed angel of this church.

Hail, O blessed spirits of this churchyard.

And all living beings within its boundaries.

Plants and trees, insects, birds and animals.

Hail, O elemental beings of earth and air, fire and water.

Hail, O lady of this ancient yew tree.

Hail, lords of light and of darkness, of summer and winter

Of the inner and the outer, of day and night.

Hail, holy eagle of high space above.

Hail holy dragon of deep space below.

May we come to this sacred place with pure intention

With hearts, minds, spirits and bodies open

To receive your love and your compassion, your wisdom and
    your healing."

"Amen," breathed Colm softly.

"Now I shall touch the ground..." Olaf told him.

"Why do that?" enquired Patricia, recalling something similar had alarmed the security people at the airport.

"To honour the goddess who lives here," he told her, glancing at Colm. "The word in my language is *halló*. Like your word 'hallow'. So we are really saying: be holy..."

He unlatched the gate and led his companions into the churchyard, pausing to brush the grass with his fingertips before continuing past the church towards the place where the yew stood. Colm caught his mother's eye, grinned and slipped an arm through hers.

"I like him. He's kind of cool, isn't he?"

"Cool...?" Patricia paused, eyebrows raised, then nodded.

"Yes, I suppose he is in a funny way…"

"Doesn't seem loony to me."

"No more than most people, probably," she agreed, hoping it was true.

They followed the narrow gravel path which wound between rows of moss-encrusted, crumbling grey headstones, some upright, others which leaned at angles, or had fallen victim to gravity. Sparing the church itself only a brief glance, Olaf halted before the yew with hands clasped reverently in front of him. From the road it was impossible to appreciate its sheer size; at close quarters it overshadowed everything in its vicinity. Over the centuries it had separated into no less than five separate trunks which now radiated like a huge starburst from a space wide enough for an adult to pass through. A small, neatly lettered sign, dangling from a wire, attested to its antiquity, and sturdy metal braces had been fitted to steady and protect it from wind damage.

"It's humungous. Way bigger than ours in Ireland," Colm told him in awed tones.

"A truly regal being…" Olaf nodded. "I shall empty my mind – try not to think. Breathe deeply, and remain aware of anything I see or feel or smell. So I do not really do anything – only experience…"

"Do things ever happen – special things?" Colm wanted to know.

"Anything is possible, but I never worry about that. Whatever happens is okay."

"Oh…" Colm had clearly been hoping for more.

"Sometimes I feel sensations in my body…"

"Like…?"

"Tightness, tingling, heat…it could be anything."

"What should I do if I feel something?"

Olaf rested a hand lightly on Colm's shoulder.

"Just notice it. Be interested, be thankful and see what may come next. Become the observer..."

"Okay, I'll try..." Colm nodded.

"I shall begin with a greeting – a private, silent one. Then take a good, close look at our friend. Walk round it and see how it feels to be in its presence and whether the feeling changes when I move to different places..."

"Is it okay to touch it?"

"It's been here since before Jesus was born," Patricia reminded him. "You can bet you wouldn't be the first. I'm sure it wouldn't mind..."

"Whatever you do, treat it with respect..." Olaf counselled. "Sure, touch it, see how it feels. It might touch you first, who knows...?" He grinned. "And try turning your back and leaning gently against it..."

"Why do that?" enquired Patricia.

"We meet most things in life face-to-face. We are used to doing it that way, so it probably feels safer. Turning your back to make contact with something is a different experience. By doing something unfamiliar, you may find you are more receptive, more aware of how your body responds."

"I'm up for that," Colm told him.

"Anyway, take your time – we are not in a hurry, are we...?"

"No," Patricia agreed, "as long as I get this man to a mobile store before closing time..."

Olaf nodded at Colm. "When you have finished, would you like to try working with my coat-hangers..."

"Detecting God? You bet..."

Olaf's laughter echoed round the churchyard, sending a crow flapping hastily skywards from its perch on the fence. Watching it swoop low over the field, heading for the safety of the poplars, Olaf touched his palms together and bowed his head.

"I am sorry if I startled you, my friend..."

The gesture was naïve, childlike even, but Patricia was touched by the man's respect for nature. Offering a brief, silent greeting to the tree towering over her, she began to circle it.

It was easy to talk of stilling the mind's chatter, but Patricia's mind initially proved uncooperative; ideas, thoughts and questions clamoured for attention like a classroom of five year olds. What caustic, tree-hugger comment might Liam have made had he been here? Colm was clearly intrigued by Olaf, but was it possible this experience could harm him in some way? But this ritual was not dissimilar to their Mayo adventure, and she had not a single regret on that account. She stopped, and took a long, deep breath. Would it help if she tried transferring her awareness from mind to body, from mental process to experience? She closed her eyes and waited.

The circuit had taken her into the shade, but the air still felt warm on her face, shoulders and arms. Taking a couple more slow breaths she resumed her walk, letting her fingers trail lightly through the needles. Somewhere close at hand, a songbird trilled and she was aware of a deep-toned, musky aroma carried on the gentlest of breezes. Her progress was proving too leisurely for Colm who had been hovering at her elbow. As he slipped past her his arm brushed hers; his excitement was palpable.

She flattened a hand against the trunk's rough, ridged bark, and caught a glimpse of Colm occupying the heart of the starburst, standing with eyes tightly shut. Watching him, Olaf's suggestion drifted into her mind. She turned away from the tree, edging backwards until her shoulders nestled against it.

Her body moulded itself gently to the contours of the trunk, giving her a feeling of melting right into it. Closing her eyes she wriggled her shoulders until she found a comfortable position and let the tree take her full weight. The sensation was a pleasant one; reassuring and comforting. It was like relaxing into the arms of someone she knew she could completely trust. Someone on whom she could rely, who would never, ever let her down. She sighed; it had been such a long time since she had felt truly held, supported and cared for...

The sensation was one of peace, serenity and safety. Her body grew steadily softer and more relaxed; tightness and tension ebbing away with each breath. She smiled, tempted to let go completely, slide down until she was sitting on the bark-strewn earth at her feet. She might have done so had she not wanted to savour the feeling of being held in a gentle embrace. But that had changed in nature. Now she felt less held by the yew than, by some magical process, united with it. Inexplicably, she and the tree were merging into one...

The realisation she had lost all sense of time made her smile; sharing her existence with a living being two thousand years old, what did time matter? There was nothing to do but breathe, feel the air's warmth, enjoy the heady scent surrounding her, and wonder at the moment. But even in that euphoric state, she was aware of yet another change. She was holding something in her arms. It was a few moments before it dawned on Patricia it was a human being; a child. It was clinging tightly to her, its heart racing. She sensed fear of loss and abandonment in the small body. Hugging it closer, she imagined surrounding and comforting it with a wave of love, compassion and tenderness. As she did so, the child began to cry; anguished, racking sobs of long-held grief. Patricia rocked her gently, and waited. At last the tears subsided and the trembling died away until, finally, she surrendered herself into Patricia's arms, and slept.

Patricia continued to cradle her, stroking the child's hair until, finally, she stirred and woke. As they looked into one another's eyes, Patricia found she was gazing at Caitlin's tear-streaked face. And she found herself weeping tears she had denied far too long.

"Mum. Mum...are you okay?"

She opened her eyes. The arms holding her tight were Colm's. Drying her cheeks with the back of her hands she managed a pale smile. "I'm fine..." she assured him. "Honestly, I'm just grand..."

"Are you sure…?" He peered at her. "You don't look it…"

She felt for his hand and squeezed it. "Absolutely and completely sure. Trust me. How about you?"

"Yeah, I'm good, actually." He pursed his lips. "It was kind of weird, though."

"For me, too." She took a deep breath. "Weird, but good, I'd call it…"

"I was, like, thinking about Dad," he went on. "You know, I've been kind of pissed off with him…"

"I know. It's been tough, hasn't it?" Sliding an arm round his waist, she planted a kiss on his cheek. "Well, maybe today will help…"

"Yeah…"

"Do you want to talk about it?"

"Maybe later…" He glanced round, frowning. "Do you know where Olaf went…?"

"Isn't he here…?"

But of the Icelander there was no sign; mother and son were alone with the yew.

Chapter 18

The Fun of the Fair

Saturday 18th June 2011

An arched, stained glass window, decorated with colourful saints, apostles and mythical beasts, occupied the east wall of St Margaret The Queen's Church. Patricia, arms folded, stood beside a weathered gravestone, observing the two figures slowly and methodically criss-crossing a pebbled area beneath the window. Colm's eyes never strayed from the thin wires balanced in his fingers. The tall, spare Icelander hovered like a shadow at his side; hands behind him, he bent closer to murmur words of advice and guidance. Enjoying the calming effects of her experience beneath the yew tree, she was content to allow several minutes to pass before she called out to Colm.

"Hang on..." His gaze flickered her way. "I can do it. Come and see..."

"I will in a bit. You don't have to stop. I just want to talk to your dowsing master for a couple of minutes. Is that okay?"

"Yeah, sure..."

"Okay with you, Olaf...?"

"Of course..."

Passing pen and notepad to his student, Olaf spent a few moments speaking to him in a voice too low for her to catch.

"Can he really do it?" she asked as Olaf joined her.

"Definitely. Not everyone has the gift."

"He's really into it, isn't he...?"

"It comes very naturally to him..." He dropped to one knee to retie the lace of his trainer. "Do not be surprised if you find that young man has other gifts, too..."

"You think so…?"

"I do…" Hitching up his jeans, he nodded. "He could be a healer, like his mother…"

Patricia shook her head. "Where did you get that idea? I'm no healer…"

"Not everyone uses the gifts they are given…"

"I use all my talents in my work," she insisted. "I hope he'll do the same…"

"That young man is a sensitive being…"

"I wouldn't argue with that. I've been watching the pair of you. Everything you've told him and shown him – it's all gone in, that's for sure…"

"Do you mind…?

"About that…?" She shot him a sideways glance. "Why would I…?"

"I get the feeling you are not always…comfortable with my ideas."

"With my background that shouldn't surprise you. I was brought up with just the one God, Olaf. Not loads of gods and goddesses, and definitely no spirits…"

"What about the Holy Spirit?" he enquired, innocently.

"That fellow is of an altogether different order, I'd say…"

"Do you think so…?"

"Our parish priest, bless his heart, would have condemned practically everything you believe in as the work of the devil and the path to eternal damnation…" She gave a wry smile. "If I wanted help from God, I went to Mass and prayed. I did not wander off into the countryside looking for an old well, a stone circle, or, God help us, a holy tree…"

"So he did not believe there are many paths to God…?"

"Many…?" She recoiled in mock horror, "he certainly did not."

"And you…?"

"Ah, well…" She paused, lips pursed. "I like to think of myself as pretty broad-minded. Anyway," she went on quickly, "that's very interesting, but it's not what I wanted to talk to you about."

"I thought not..." He smiled.

"The first thing I want to tell you is, something happened just now. I'm not sure what, but I'm feeling great. A touch light-headed maybe, but...well, I think mellow would be the word. And something else..." She paused. "It's as if...a weight's been lifted from my shoulders."

The sound of hammering, good-natured shouts and bursts of laughter rang out from the field. Looking across she saw both end supports were now in place, and the main body of the marquee was being hoisted into position. All round it, tents were springing up like mushrooms. They sauntered back along the path leading to the tree.

"I'd made my intention," she went on, "which was to do with my daughter..."

"Caitlin...?"

"Right. Why is still a complete mystery to me, but when her dad and I separated she blamed me. The whole thing, apparently, was my fault and mine alone. I did try to talk to her a couple of times but we never got far. Since she's been at uni she hardly ever comes home and lately we rarely even email let alone speak." She sighed. "I do love the girl, but I'm angry with her and I've not the slightest doubt she feels much the same about me. So, impasse. I asked for help with sorting that out."

"It sounds as if you got it..."

"In the end. Emptying your mind isn't easy if you're not used to it..." She smiled. "The harder I tried, the faster mine cranked out questions, images and ideas...but that's minds for you, isn't it?"

"Mine, too..." he agreed. "But you did it..."

"Using something I learned in a yoga class years back: focus on your breathing and whatever's happening in the body. It must've worked because the next thing I knew I was leaning against old mother yew and…she started working her magic."

"Mother…?" Olaf cocked his head. "Interesting. I felt it too – a strong feminine energy."

"It was a bit like going to sleep and starting to dream right away. In fact, it was a kind of…waking dream, I guess. Or maybe I was so keen for something to happen I just imagined the whole thing. Who knows…?"

"Does it matter…?"

"Probably not…" She laughed. "To begin with, it felt like the tree was hugging me, which was nice, I really enjoyed it. Then after a bit I had the strangest sensation of holding a child. A sad and lonely little girl. I didn't do much, just cuddled and comforted her, and…let her know I loved her. And then it dawned on me it wasn't any little girl – it was Caitlin…" She bit her lip. "It may sound a bit silly, but I'm welling up just thinking about it…"

She took a deep breath and blinked away the tears.

"The most amazing part was that afterwards I knew exactly what's been going on for her. I don't know how, but I really got it. All that shitty stuff she's been throwing at me is a defence. Underneath, the poor kid is absolutely broken hearted…"

"A very clear message…"

"Well, it's obvious, really…"

"You must be very open…"

"I don't know about that…"

"You said so yourself…"

"Open minded. To ideas, not…the kind of thing you're talking about. Anyway," she went on, "the point is I also know exactly what I need to do…"

"Which is…?"

"Talk to her. Simple as that. And as long as I avoid turning into little Miss Angry, it'll be fine…" She paused. "So it really helped. And I wanted to thank you…"

"But I did not do anything. If there is anyone to thank, isn't it her...?" He nodded at the yew.

"You played your part, Olaf. On this occasion you were definitely the guide..."

He joined his palms. "I am honoured..."

"So...quite an experience." She cocked her head. "And for you...?"

"You are asking if I did what you suggested..."

"Don't tell me. Let me guess..."

"If you wish..."

She peered at him through half-closed eyes.

"You decided I was interfering, and it was none of my business. And that you were going to ignore every word I said..." She paused. "So once you'd set things up for Colm and me, off you went to dowse."

"I was not so disrespectful. I..."

"Olaf..."

"No, really..."

"Olaf..." Laughing, she laid a hand on his arm. "Listen, it's okay. I don't mind one bit. But you did go straight off to do some god-detecting, right?"

"You saw me...?"

"Absolutely not. I was far too busy doing my own thing," she told him. "But I had such a strong feeling that's what you'd do."

"And you would like to know why..."

"No." She waved the idea away with a sweep of the hand. "As a matter of fact, I wouldn't."

He frowned. "You are serious?"

Strolling a few steps closer, she gazed into the upper branches of the yew. However ancient, magnificent and majestic it might be, when you came right down to basics it was, after all, only a tree. Just as Canterbury Cathedral was only a cathedral, yet the experiences associated with them had been as potent as they were unexpected. She realised Olaf was speaking again.

"Sorry, you were saying...?"

"I have been thinking about yesterday and if maybe I am still under the spell of the hart."

"Come on, now..." She shook her head. "Let's keep things in perspective..."

"That is important, but just now you were very clear about what I should do..."

"I was," she assented, "but since then I think I've learned a couple of things..."

"Two thousand years of wisdom?"

"If only..." She laughed. "I think it has more to do with talking to you."

"You honour me again. Tell me your mysterious lessons."

"They're kind of hard to put my finger on," she admitted, "but one has to do with being more philosophical. I remember the first time we met, I was really struck by how laid back you were about everything that was going on. You seemed to take everything so calmly..."

"I was not always like that..."

"You weren't...?"

"Not at all. As a young man I was a rebel. Always looking for a cause, going on protest marches, sit-ins...anything I did not agree with, I wanted to fight..." He mimed throwing punches, dropped his hands and chuckled. "But in India I discovered a completely different approach to life. They did not fight; they accepted. When I adopted their way, I was amazed. It felt much easier, more natural..." Joining his palms, he closed his eyes. "No battles and no resistance meant no stress. Stress comes from fighting reality, which is madness. Accept what is, simply allow each situation and experience to be, and trust your inner wisdom to show you how to best deal with it..."

"I'm a great believer in acceptance. You wouldn't believe how much time and effort I put into encouraging my patients to be more accepting. But can I do it myself...?" She shook her head and gave a rueful smile. "I find it a real challenge..."

"And now you think you have changed…?"

"Sadly not. Not just like that. But I can feel something inside has shifted, even if it's only a start. I just wish I knew why it's happened now…"

"Perhaps there is no reason. It is simply the moment was right…"

"Could be. But what's frustrating is, I have no idea why this moment should be right when others haven't been…"

"Perhaps the universe is sending you a lesson in acceptance…"

"That may have to do for now," She assented. "And remember telling Colm there were no shoulds or shouldn'ts, and to do what felt right…? I've heard that message, or ones like it, God knows how many times…hundreds I expect. But again, for some reason, it suddenly made sense. I feel I'm actually beginning to get that one, too…"

"All these right moments all coming together. Wonderful…" He laughed.

"Seems that way. I got the sense something went on for Colm, too. Did he say anything to you…?"

"We talked only about dowsing…"

"He still might…" she told him. "It's possible he'd feel more comfortable telling you than me. Anyway, as far as I'm concerned, the most precious thing is realising what's going on between Caitlin and me…"

"So you do not regret coming here…" he asked.

"Absolutely not…"

"And what I did does not trouble you, either."

"Not one bit. What did trouble me…" She held up a finger, "was a voice in my head, insisting what you suggested we should do was pointless, stupid…sacrilegious, even. It was hard to ignore and just…trust the process."

"Even after what happened in Ireland…?"

"That doesn't happen to me very often. I'm not like you,

trotting round communing with trees every day..."

"Maybe that has changed, too."

"Don't hold your breath," she advised. "But there's more to it you see, which might explain why I'm not interrogating you about what you did or why." She took a deep breath. "I'm beginning to realise that before I can trust my own process, I have to learn to trust other people's – including yours, of course."

"Insight, acceptance...and now trust?" Olaf feigned amazement.

She searched his face, fearful of mockery. Talking about trust was all very well, but maybe she had been unwise to be quite so open, so trusting of him. Butterflies swarmed in her stomach; suddenly she felt vulnerable.

"That...may take a little time."

He nodded. "Which is natural...""

A burst of thumping brass band music from the direction of the marquee shattered the peace of the churchyard. It was followed by a chorus of good-natured complaints, and cries of protest. The music died abruptly, rang out at a slightly lower decibel level and stopped as abruptly as it had started. The ensuing peace was greeted by ironic applause.

"I have a question..." he told her.

"Ask away..."

"Why did you think it was so important for me to consult my guides...?"

"I'm not sure..." Patricia shrugged. "It was a feeling..."

"Why does it matter to you what I do...?"

"Several reasons, I guess..." She told him. "Maybe I got too caught up in what you told me. You know, dream messages from ancestors, the pilgrimage to a sacred site, healing the mountain..." She waved a hand. "The whole story..."

"Story...?" He shot her a suspicious glance. "You think it is just a story...?"

"There's always a risk in the kind of work I do of getting

hooked into a patient's narrative. We need to stay as objective and detached as possible, because our job is dealing with context not content. Maybe in your case I lost perspective..."

"I see." He nodded. "Is that all...?"

"And the part about being a guide," she reminded him. "I may have taken that too seriously, felt responsible for you..."

"Is that what happened...?"

"It's possible. But I honestly don't think it matters now. You'll do what you do, and I'm fine with that. Anyway," she continued, briskly, nodding towards the field, "there's a bunch of people over there setting things up for a fair, and I think I should take you to have a look round. Since you're here, you really ought to see how a typical English village celebrates midsummer. Let's see if Colm wants to come along..."

The trainee dowser was on his haunches, using a fallen tombstone as makeshift table. He had sketched an outline of the churchyard and was painstakingly charting the results of his labours. Patricia's invitation brought a firm shake of the head.

"No thanks, I haven't finished yet..." With a glance at Olaf, he added, "I'm pretty sure you're right. It looks like it runs straight down the middle of the church. I'm going to check it out..."

"I wouldn't do any dowsing inside, pet..." Patricia shook her head.

"Why not...?"

"Wait until you are alone," Olaf advised. "Always be respectful. Most people would not understand what you were doing. They probably have no idea their church is here because of the energies..."

"No, I guess not..."

"Or that with every service, every celebration, the spiritual current grew..." Olaf reminded him. "Over the centuries, from a stream to a mighty river..."

Leaving Colm to his work he and Patricia threaded their way through the cars, trucks and vans parked along the avenue of poplars, finally reaching the gate into the field. They found themselves in a stream of people ferrying bags, crates and boxes of equipment towards the tents and marquee. Through open flaps, they glimpsed men in overalls erecting a low stage and laying wooden flooring. Children were entertaining themselves, running in and out among the stalls and stands, while a man in a perspiration stained blue shirt, with a mobile clamped to his ear, scribbled notes on a clipboard.

Olaf paused to observe a middle-aged couple filling a large, circular table with neat rows of closely packed, narrow-mouthed, glass bowls.

"What are these for, please...?"

The man glanced up and took the cigarette from his lips.

"It's a pound for three ping-pong balls, mate. Toss them in and if you get lucky and one ends up inside a bowl, you win a prize." He grinned. "A goldfish. Perfect pets they are. No noise, no trouble. Come back when we're set up, see how easy it is..."

"I have been thinking," Olaf told Patricia as they walked on, "about what you said..."

But her attention was focused on a tall, slim man wearing an outsized red plastic nose, white-face makeup and clown costume. Casually juggling apples and oranges he had drawn a crowd of admiring children, some filming him on mobiles.

"Sorry, what was that...?" she asked, joining in the applause. "Good, isn't he?"

"You called what I told you...a story."

"I might have. Why, does it bother you...?"

"It depends what you mean. A story is some thing you make up – they are not the truth."

"Oh, I see..." She nodded. "You're worried I think you've kissed the Blarney stone...?"

"I don't understand," he told her. "But I wonder if you are too polite to say so, but you do not really believe me..."

"Olaf, I'm a psychiatrist. I've been trained to look at life from a psychological perspective. You're a..." She reached for the word, "...let's call you a visionary. So you see things from a totally different angle – a mystical, spiritual one if you like. We're not going to agree on everything, are we...?"

"Some of the things you believe seem pretty crazy to me, too," he reminded her, wryly. "But when you said you wanted to research your paper, I thought you took me seriously..."

"Don't get me wrong, Olaf. I take you very seriously, I really do. Our talks have given me all kinds of insights I'd never have got any other way. And they'll be extremely valuable. I am very grateful to you..."

Lips pursed, he walked on, staring at the ground before shooting her a sideways glance. "Are you going to use me as an example of people who make things up, and live in a fantasy world...?"

"Absolutely not. You've made it clear that's not what you do at all..."

"So I do not understand why you do not seem to believe me..."

"You have to remember it's not always easy to believe things we've never experienced. I mean, gate crashing other people's dreams, walking into mountains, flying with aeroplanes and chatting away happily to gods and giants...I haven't done anything remotely like that. But do I accept they're part of your reality?" She spread her hands. "Certainly. And I accept you've told me everything in good faith..."

A battered, rust-flecked generator van parked alongside the marquee wheezed asthmatically and roared into life, belching clouds of acrid blue smoke. They waited until they had put distance between themselves and its steady, low-pitched throbbing.

"That first day," Patricia told him, above the din, "when you showed me your map – remember?"

"The goats..." He smiled. "Oh, yes."

"I'm not pretending I accept all your ideas," she went on, "but I am open to the possibility you've discovered patterns which might represent some kind of cosmic consciousness. The same goes for your philosophy of life. Again, it's not about agreeing or disagreeing, but I can see wisdom in it…"

"So you do not quite believe what you call my stories, but you are open to the possibility there is truth in them…"

Patricia laughed, softly. "It often comes down to what you feel rather than what you know, doesn't it? And, by the way, you'll notice I am not quizzing you about your future plans. You've made your mind up and that's it…" She smiled. "End of story."

Olaf nodded, tugging at his beard. A horn at their backs sent them hastily out of the path of an old tractor. The driver lifted his hand in greeting as it chugged past, towing a flatbed trailer loaded with plastic chairs and rolls of thick coir matting. A gaggle of small boys dangled their legs over the rear.

"When I got back yesterday," he told her, "I told Morgana what you said…"

"Oh? What did she say?"

"You probably do not like her and think she is a bad influence on me…"

"Olaf, I hardly know her," Patricia told him, evenly. "We've only met twice. The first was a clinical assessment. In Canterbury, to be honest, I felt she acted more like a spoiled child than a grown up. But there must be reasons for that, and it doesn't mean she's a bad person. Anyway, I'm sure you've seen a very different side of her…"

"Yes, I have…"

"And her influence on you? I've no way of judging that, and it's not my business to even try," she pointed out. "Anyway, look at the bigger picture. After a rough start your trip seems to be working out pretty well, even if it's not what you expected. Think about it – a promising relationship and maybe working with Mitch, too…" She spread her hands. "That doesn't sound bad to me."

"Nor me..." he assented.

"You told me that when you embark on a spiritual journey, whatever you need just...materialises. Who am I to say your new lady doesn't come under that heading?"

Bells were tinkling somewhere close by; she glanced over her shoulder to see a group of men heading towards the marquee. Long wooden clubs in their hands, they wore identical uniforms: straw boaters festooned with coloured ribbons, baggy white trousers and loose, long sleeved white shirts with crimson sashes across the breast. Clusters of silver bells dangled from wrist and ankle straps.

"Morris dancers," Patricia told him. "Quintessentially English. The ones I've seen were dancing to fiddles and drums and it all seemed to involve a great deal of banging those clubs together. That's about all I know, I'm afraid..." She glanced at her watch. "Colm must have dowsed every inch of Saint Margaret's by now."

"He may need a little longer..." Olaf shook his head. "I did not realise that was the name of the church..."

"There's a notice near the gate. Apparently it's dedicated to Saint Margaret the Queen..."

"Another dragon-slayer..."

"Margaret...?"

"A female version of Michael and George." He gave a wry smile. "Or is that another of the crazy Icelander's ideas...?"

"Sounds plausible. Listen, after what happened in Ireland – and again just now – even talking to trees is starting to feel pretty ordinary."

"Quite a step for you..."

"Not really. It's like you say – it's my experience, so how could it not be real? If I'd spent my childhood astral travelling, I'm sure I'd think that was pretty ordinary, too."

"When I told you about meeting *Bárður*, or that time *Friðrika* took me to learn about *Björn*, do you call those fantasies or…what would you say, delusions?"

"This…" Patricia pursed her lips, "is where it gets slightly tricky."

"Why…?"

"Forget what I think," she instructed. "Were they real to you?"

"You know they were…"

"How about the dream when you were sent here?"

"The same…" he insisted.

"That," she said, "is why it's tricky."

"I still do not understand…"

"Okay. The way you described that dream has been consistent. And the same goes for the instructions you were given. They have never varied…"

"So what is your problem with it…?"

Planting her hands on her hips, she turned to face him. "Olaf, if that dream is real, what I cannot understand is why you've started acting as if it wasn't. As if maybe it was just…" She looked at him questioningly, "a nice story…"

"And I do not understand why you make such a big thing of it…" he retorted, as they passed a stall where two young men were taking it in turns to hurl wooden balls at a row of coconuts set on poles.

"Maybe you're right, maybe it isn't…" she agreed. "Maybe for some reason your compass is just sending you off in a new direction…"

"Guiding me south, instead of…" He threw out a hand to steady himself as he stumbled to his knees. "The laces are coming apart…" he complained, tugging at them. "I must get new ones…"

She raised her eyebrows. "Nothing to do with tripping up, or…the wrong trip…?"

"You are teasing me…"

"I'm not, actually. You've got me thinking about signs…"

"I see..." He straightened, brushing grass from his hands and knees.

"You could ask him..." she said, nodding at a nearby stall.

It consisted of little more than a sagging aluminium frame, draped with a collection of faded, fraying Indian wall hangings decorated with tiny mirrors which twinkled and sparkled in the sunlight. In the shady space beneath them, a stocky, balding man, a cigar clamped between his teeth, had spread a blue and white striped cloth over a folding wooden table and was now dusting a pair of olive-green canvas chairs. A glass ball in a wooden cradle occupied the centre of the table, from which dangled a hand-lettered sign reading: *Your Future Told Here.*

Olaf smiled and shook his head. "I do not think so, thank you..."

"When your reading with Morgana was so useful...?" she teased.

"She is a psychic," he reminded her. "Not a fortune-teller..."

The man took the cigar from his mouth and flicked the cloth in the air. Sunlight glinted on thick-lensed spectacles as he appraised his prospective customers. No taller than Patricia, he was barrel-chested, with the red cheeks and nose of a man who was no stranger to the public bar.

"Who'll be my first of the day then?" he called. "Only a fiver for your future? A bargain at twice the price. Now then, how about you, sir?"

"Thank you, my friend," Olaf joined his palms. "Not for me..."

"I knew you'd say that. See how good I am?" He grinned, switching his attention to Patricia. "What about the lovely lady, then?"

Overweight, cheeks dark with stubble, he wore grubby tennis shorts and his ample belly strained against a black T-shirt a size too small. He would, Patricia thought, have looked more at home behind a bar or hot dog stall. He cocked his head on one side.

"How about it, my dear...?"

She laughed. "If you're as good as you say, you know my answer, too..."

He shaded his eyes, squinting at her. "You hail from the Emerald Isle, do you not...?"

"Indeed, but you'll have to do better than that..."

"Oh, I will. Well now, an Irish rose," he added, with a crooked smile. "But what would she be named, I wonder...?"

Patricia glanced at Olaf, folded her arms and smiled. "Now there's a question..."

It was a few moments before he spoke in a slow, thoughtful voice. "Not Kate, I think...nor Siobhan, though it's a lovely name...Clare? No, I think not, and...no, you don't look like a Mary to me..." He snapped his fingers and grinned. "Ah, yes...I have it..."

"Good. Are you going to surprise me, then...?" she enquired.

"You were named in honour of Ireland's most famous saint..." He raised a pair of bushy eyebrows. "Am I not right...?"

If the man had got it wrong, he would simply have run through more of the most common names for Irish women her age; but he had not.

"I don't know if you could tell my future, but you're a good name guesser, I'll give you that..." she conceded.

"Guesser...?" he repeated. "You don't do me justice... Patricia."

"The answer's still no, thanks all the same..."

"The fair's not officially open yet," he called as she began to walk away. "So there'll be no charge, my lovely..."

"I would," she told him over her shoulder, "but my mother warned me not to take gifts from strangers..."

"And that there's an exception to every rule, didn't she...?" He waved a hand at his chairs. "Come along now, you don't have all day, do you...?"

Olaf had stopped to wait for her. She hesitated. The man

looked nothing like her idea of a fortune-teller, but there he stood, holding the chair ready and bowing like the head waiter of a five-star restaurant. Addressing Olaf, his tone had been playful, self-mocking, an invitation not to be taken seriously. His tone to her was different. It had an intensity, a compelling quality it was impossible to ignore.

"I'll be five minutes," she called to Olaf. "Why not check out those Morris dancers...?"

"Are you sure...?" He looked surprised.

"Of course she is." The man grinned through a cloud of cigar smoke. "She's a lady who knows her own mind, as you are aware, sir..."

Olaf shrugged, gave a half-smile and walked on. She found herself ducking into the makeshift tent and accepting the chair with a nod of thanks. The bulky figure eased himself down opposite her with exaggerated care, as if not convinced the chair would support his weight.

"So...your name is...Patricia."

"It is. And yours...?"

He puffed on the cigar, expelling a thin stream of smoke from the side of his mouth. She found it disconcerting that he should pause so long before replying.

"Merlin..." he said, at last.

"Like the wizard...?"

"Exactly like the wizard..." he said, as if she had answered a tricky question.

From somewhere close by the thin, reedy notes of an accordion rang out accompanied by the rhythmic thud of heavy boots on timber.

"Well now, what would you like to know, Patricia?" he enquired in a low, rumbling voice.

"Don't you just...tell me stuff? Isn't that how it works?"

"Have you never had a reading before...?"

"No. This is my first..."

"Well, well. And are you perhaps just a touch...sceptical?"

"Just a touch..." She glanced round and sniffed the air. "What's that smell...?"

"Incense. These old hangings reek of it..."

"Ah, right..."

"Are you quite sure there's nothing you want to ask?" He leaned forward. "Nothing...puzzling you?"

"Apart from why I'm sitting here, you mean...?"

She did her best to sound playful, but the canvas chair felt none too safe, and a cocktail of aromatic oils and cigar smoke was making her light-headed. Merlin, or whatever his real name was, seemed to be asking too many questions. She resolved to make her excuses, go and find Olaf, then see if Colm had completed his labours.

"I honestly can't think of anything, I'm afraid," she told him. "Look, perhaps this wasn't such a good..."

"Yes, yes, sure..." He brushed her words aside. "What about Stonehenge, then...?"

She stared at him.

"What...what about it...?"

"It's on your mind, isn't it...?

"Well..." Somehow she managed a smile. "Look, aren't you supposed to just tell me the...?"

"Patricia, I could tell you a thousand things, I really could..." He addressed her like a parent reassuring a nervous child. "But we don't have much time, do we?"

She ran her fingers through her hair. Maybe the best thing was to just let him talk.

"Okay then..." She nodded. "Stonehenge will do fine. Go on..."

"You needn't worry about it. Not at all. It's...cold."

"Cold...?" She frowned. "What are you talking about...?"

"You never played hide and seek as a kid? If you go the right way, people shout 'hot'?" He grinned, eyebrows raised. "Well,

Stonehenge is completely the wrong direction, you see. Forget about it."

He took another puff of his cigar.

"Okay..." She said, doubtfully, "I think I probably knew that..."

"You weren't certain though. Still a bit..." He waggled a hand, "concerned...?"

"Maybe..."

"It's not going to happen and that's that. Now then, what else...?"

"But Stonehenge isn't really my problem, is it...?"

"If it's on your mind it's your problem..." he insisted. "All right then, how about something that is yours? Something you don't know, but you'd like to. Anything..."

"Let me see..." She paused. "Okay...I'm planning to call someone I've...had a row with. But I'm not sure how they'll react, how it will go..."

Taking the cigar from his mouth, he pursed his lips and blew a perfect smoke ring. Like a writhing snake, it ascended slowly to hang above their heads. Merlin stared into the distance, eyes narrowed, stroking a stubbly cheek with his thumb.

"Have a look in there, dear," he instructed jerking his chin at the glass ball. "See the person you mean...?"

The ball was so chipped and scratched it was practically opaque.

"Quite honestly, I can't see a thing..." She leaned forward to peer at it. "It could use a good clean..."

Whipping out a rag, he wrapped it round the ball, rubbed it vigorously between his palms, and placed it back on the stand.

"There. Try again..."

She glanced at it and shrugged. "No improvement, I'm afraid..." she told him. "I think you need a new one..."

"Damn..." He sighed, stuffing the rag back in his pocket. "Don't know why it's there at all, to be honest. Pulls in the punters, I expect. Silly idea really. Anyway you're talking about a young woman, aren't you? Name begins with...C, doesn't it?"

She had said nothing to suggest it was a female, but he was off, playing his damned name game again. How did he do that? The odds were twenty-six to one; a bit less if you ignored the most unlikely letters and C was, after all, among the more likely. Not that Merlin was interested in her confirmation; he folded his arms and planted them on the table.

"It'll go fine," he said.

"What does fine mean?"

"Just the way you're hoping. One thing, though..."

"Which is...?"

"You won't call her..."

"Why won't I...?"

He made an impatient gesture with the cigar. "You have a son, don't you. Another C..."

"Are you good at names, or just lucky?"

He ignored the jibe.

"Going to be a traveller, that one. I see him in the good old US of A. Studying. Might do some teaching, as well. What do you think of that?"

"I'm not sure what to think..."

He flicked ash onto the floor and nodded. "Ever pick up hitch-hikers, Patricia? Nearly said Pat..." He grinned. "That would never do, would it...?"

She shook her head. "No, it wouldn't. I don't like..."

"That's what I meant." He paused. "So, where was I?"

"Asking about hitchhikers..."

"That's right. Do you? Pick them up...?"

"It depends. What they look like, what time it is, where I happen to be, you know. I mean, if it was late at night and I was alone, probably not..."

"You will..."

"Late at night...?"

424

"I didn't say that…"

"Oh. So what did…?"

"Don't worry. It'll be fine. You'll be glad you did…"

"That's all right, then. When will this happen…?"

"It'll be just fine…" He repeated. "That's all you need to know."

"It would be helpful if you told me…"

"There's going to be a meeting…" He ran a hand slowly over his eyes. "A committee…some kind of tribunal. Mean anything to you…?"

"Well, it's possible there might be a—"

"Bunch of old farts in suits. They think they're important. Someone's got it in for you, haven't they?" He frowned. "You know what I'm talking about…"

"Sort of…" she told him, faintly, "But I'm not sure it's actually happened yet…"

"Maybe it won't. But you've nothing to worry about even if it does…" He shrugged. "It'll all go away. The people who want to give you a hard time are bastards, aren't they…?"

"You could say that…" she agreed, remembering she had.

"Oh, by the way, you'll spend time in the States with your son. It'll be an important time for both of you." He discovered his cigar had gone out and grimaced. "He's going to make quite a name for himself that lad of yours. He'll make you proud of him…"

"I already am – of both of them."

"As they are of you. More than you know…" Merlin frowned. "Time's running out. You know that friend of yours…"

"Which one…?"

He pulled a face and jerked a thumb over his shoulder. "That one. The foreign chap…"

"Olaf, yes. What about him…?"

Merlin took off his glasses; he had eyes of duck-egg blue. Pulling out his rag once more, he gave the thick lenses a peremptory polish and put them on again.

"Let go of him, Patricia," said Merlin in a soft voice. "And let him go…"

"I wasn't going to try to…"

"He'll do what he does, and all will unfold as it's meant to. That goes for you, too. You fret too much, you know. Trust yourself, and others…" Rising to his feet, he pushed his chair back.

"Is that it…?"

"Follow your instincts, you'll be just fine. Okay…?"

"I'm doing my best…"

"I know you are." His voice softened. "But we had to be sure, you see…"

"We…?"

He tapped his watch. "You'd better go. Your son's right, you're always later than you say you'll be. No sense of time, you Irish…"

Patricia got to her feet and stared at him, suddenly reluctant to leave. Fresh from communing with a tree, she had spent five minutes talking to a complete stranger, who somehow possessed knowledge about her to which he had no right. He had treated her to a bewildering assortment of facts, assumptions, riddles and, for all she knew, rubbish. She wanted to discover which was which, but he shooed her away as if her presence now irritated him.

"Go," he ordered, "quickly, now. Go and find Olaf…"

"Thank you. But what about…?" she stammered, "I can pay…"

"Go with God." He dismissed the offer with a shake of his head. "But for God's sake, go. Oh, one more thing…"

"Yes…?"

"The car. Wonderful idea. But not a red one…"

She discovered Olaf outside the entrance to the marquee, mingling with a group of people watching the Morris dancers rehearse. Boots thundering, high stepping like soldiers on parade, they weaved in and out in a sequence of intricate patterns, punctuated by sounds like pistol shots as they struck at each other's sticks. She touched his shoulder.

"We should go…"

"So, now you know your future…?" he enquired, with a grin.

"I'm not sure. He was a really odd little guy, didn't you think so?"

"But you talked to him anyway."

"He did come up with some extraordinary stuff…" She shook her head. "I'd really love to know how those people do it. Maybe I should ask Morgana."

"She is not a fortune teller," he said firmly. "But you would find her interesting…"

"They're mostly women, aren't they…?"

"Maybe that lady is his assistant…"

Following Olaf's pointing finger, she saw they were passing the Indian hangings again. But there was no sign of the man with the cigar; his chair at the table was now occupied by a wraith-like middle-aged woman, with skin like parchment, and wispy grey hair.

"Would you like a reading…?" she enquired in a high-pitched voice. "All proceeds to charity…"

"No thank you…" Patricia shook her head. "I just had one with Merlin…"

"Oh? They promised I'd be the only one…" She frowned. "Where was that…?"

"Right here…" Patricia explained. "You must know him. Thirty-five or forty, short, heavily built, thick glasses…?"

"Merlin…?" The woman shook her head. "I don't know anyone called Merlin…"

Chapter 19

Dreams

Sunday 19th June 2011

The full moon painted the scene with a ghostly, surreal sheen. She and the man were crossing a swathe of misty, manicured lawn, dotted with trees and bushes; ahead of them she glimpsed a wooden hut. She could not see water but a lapping sound told her it must be close at hand. The scene was familiar, yet she could not quite place it. She glanced at the old man with his arm loosely linked through hers, but he was peering down at the pipe cradled in his hand and his face was hidden in shadow. While she was uncertain where she was, she had a reassuring sense she could trust him; she was safe in his care. As they got closer to the hut, she could see it was a wooden boathouse; a sailing dinghy swayed at its moorings just along the quay. Beyond it she could just make out an expanse of dark, mirror-smooth water, stretching away into the distance.

With a bow and gracious sweep of the arm, her companion wordlessly invited her to board the little vessel, and the gesture told her he was entrusting her with a precious possession. Slipping off her shoes, she steadied herself with a hand on the mast and stepped aboard. She glanced back, expecting him to join her, but to her surprise he bent, untied the mooring rope and pushed the dinghy away from shore. She was alone, but his cheery wave assured her all was well.

A breeze was soon ruffling the surface of the lake, propelling her further and further from land. A match flared as the old man lit his pipe and he gave her another wave as he and his garden began to vanish in the mist. Grasping the gunwales she gazed round. The mist hanging over the water like a pale shroud was stirred by the breeze and she glimpsed snow-capped mountains etched against a starry sky. She leaned over to trail her fingers through the water, surprised to find it warm against her skin. Two moons danced attendance on her; one sailing high above, the other a glittering disc escorting her vessel across the lake. "I am the Lady of Shalott..." she said aloud, and laughed. She drew her coat more tightly around her as the wind slapped the rigging against the mast and the little boat reared like a nervous pony.

Lightning flashed through the night sky like a rapier through velvet; thunder drum-rolled overhead. A storm was coming but she felt no danger; the old man's invisible presence still guided and protected her. A second bolt of lightning made her jump; it struck the water close by, making it foam and bubble like a witch's cauldron. As she stared at the spot, transfixed, she glimpsed a shape rising from the depths. She recoiled as it burst through the surface, showering her with spray. As she dried her face with her hands, she heard a woman's voice.

"Good evening, Patricia. I'm sorry if I startled you. Isn't this a beautiful night? I have come a long way, the length of the great Reuss river, to be here. I wanted us to meet under the Rose Moon..."

Patricia caught her breath; she was in the presence of a goddess. The dragon on whose back she stood hovered effortlessly above the dark waters, the scales on its flanks glistening like rubies at each breath. Languidly coiling and uncoiling its sinuous tail, it watched Patricia with ebony eyes.

"Don't be frightened," the goddess told her. "He looks menacing, doesn't he, but dragons are good as gold if you treat them well.

And I'm sure you know I would never let any harm come to you..."

"Thank you..."

The goddess stood erect and proud, her head held high.

Wrapped in a shimmering crimson robe, she cradled a willow branch between slender fingers. Gazing up at her, Patricia sensed warmth and love emanating from her.

"I have come to ask for your help."

"Me, help...? Yes, of course..." Patricia stammered.

"I am grateful. You see, someone else is soon going to ask for your help. Your first thought will be that their request is unreasonable, not to mention very inconvenient."

"Oh no, I won't mind..."

"Believe me, you will, my dear. You will be very tempted to turn them down, which is perfectly understandable," the goddess continued. "But you have a loving heart, the heart of a healer, Patricia, and I invite you to find the answer in your heart. Do you understand?"

Of course she did, she would do anything she was asked...but no words came. But it didn't matter; this being, whoever she was, read hearts and minds.

"Thank you..." She inclined her head and the moonlight sparkled on a headpiece exquisitely carved in the shape of a lotus blossom.

"To make your task more enjoyable..." The goddess smiled. "You will have help. I wouldn't ask you to do this by yourself..."

The wind must have changed; it brought the mist swirling back again. Almost as quickly as they had appeared, the goddess and her mount faded from sight, leaving Patricia alone once more. She leaned back against the mast, exhilarated but exhausted, enjoying the gentle rocking motion. With the goddess's parting message ringing in her ears, she felt herself slipping into a deep sleep...

Ψ

"Finished. It looks amazing..."

Colm came bounding up the narrow wooden stairway.

Looking up from her laptop, she found him leaning against the door, wearing a satisfied smile. Barefooted, clad in T-shirt and shorts, he had a damp chamois cloth in one hand. She tried to remember what she had asked him to clean.

"Oh. That's grand…"

The smile blossomed into a grin. "You don't have a clue what I'm talking about, do you?"

"Umm…kitchen windows?" she ventured.

"Mum…?" He dangled the creamy yellow cloth in front of her.

"Ah…"

It was all coming back. First, sauntering round the show room with its collection of venerable sports cars, then the glorious, wind-blown ride with Eddie in the green convertible. Charming, attentive, infinitely patient Eddie, who surprised her by casually suggesting she borrow the Jaguar to 'get the feel of it'. And Eddie's incredulity when she enquired if he had the same thing in red.

"You have never, ever washed a car before…"

"We never had a Jag before."

"We still don't," she reminded him. "It is on loan, for two days only, on condition it's returned in the same state it—"

"But it suits you, Mum." He spread his hands.

"Tempting, but although you may not have noticed, you can get the kitchen sink in the back of the Volvo, with room to spare," she pointed out. "You'd be hard pressed to find space for half a dozen kitchen taps in the boot of that thing…"

"Anyway, I've washed it," he repeated, unwilling to allow practical considerations to sway his judgement. "Why don't we go for a drive? I can take the top down. Eddie showed me, it's dead simple…"

"Okay, but I've got a couple of reports I must finish first."

He wrinkled his nose. "How long…?"

"If you'll go away and leave me in peace…half an hour?"

"Sweet." He turned to go.

"Okay, take the top down..." she called after him, "but for goodness sake be careful. That thing's so old it's practically an antique."

What year was it Eddie had said the Jaguar was built; the early nineties, was it? She shook her head; why would anyone in their right mind even consider buying a car that age? And how could she explain it to people – especially Liam, she thought, picturing his expression of pained disbelief. Turning back to her computer, she smiled; who cared what he thought, or anyone else for that matter?

Twenty minutes later, files stowed in an old leather doctor's bag, she took a deep breath and puffed out her cheeks. In the churchyard of Saint Margaret the Queen, clearing the air with her daughter seemed the easiest and most natural act in the world. The prospect of doing so, however, made her heart beat faster and her palms feel damp. She was reaching for the phone when it rang.

"Hello...?"

"Mum...?"

"Caitlin? My God...!"

"You sound...are you okay...?"

"You made me jump, that's all."

"What...?"

"I'd just about got my hand on the phone to call you..."

"Oh. Is anything wrong...?"

"No, nothing..."

"Really...?"

"Great minds thinking alike...?"

"What did Dad always say? Fools seldom differ..."

She had woken from her dream fully intending to make the call, only to find a succession of things needing her attention first. Merlin's words were fresh in her memory, but somehow they could not quite silence the voice in her head which insisted this would be just the latest in a series of stilted, awkward exchanges, ending as they always did; leaving her angry and frustrated.

"It's good to hear your voice. How have you been...?"

"Oh...not bad, you know. Once exams were over I started looking for a summer job. It's not easy though. Everyone's looking, but people just aren't hiring. We're all finding it really tough..."

"Don't worry, something will come up..."

"It had better..."

"Colm's just finished exams..."

"I know. He said—"

"He called you?"

"We text, chat on Facebook, you know..."

"Oh, good..."

"Yeah, and...Dad rang yesterday. Said he'd been up to see you..."

"Did he tell you what happened?"

"No. What did...?"

Patricia took a deep breath. She had not expected her resolution on clear, honest communication to be put to the test so early in proceedings.

"He didn't say...anything?"

"No. Just...he'd been up. Why...?"

"Actually...we had a blazing row."

"Did you...?"

"I finished up throwing something at him."

"Oh, my God..."

Patricia put a hand over her eyes and waited. How stupid was that? It was fine to tell her what went on, surely, but to blurt it out before they had even got talking... What if she just slammed the phone down? She cursed her stupidity, and it was several moments before she realised what she was hearing was muffled laughter.

"Are you serious...?"

"He must have said something about it…"

"No, honestly…all he said…" She broke off, no longer trying to hide her laughter. "All he said was…he didn't think you were in a very good mood…"

"He got that spot on…"

"Oh my God…and you threw something…?"

"A saucepan. One of my favourites, and I broke it…"

"Seriously…?"

"Seriously but inaccurately…"

"Thank God for that. You didn't actually hit him, then…?"

"Not even close. We started off all right, you know, being reasonably civilised. Then he started pressuring me to do something I absolutely do not want to do. I told him no, but he wouldn't drop it, just went on and on and…it all went downhill rather fast. By the time I completely lost my rag he was heading for the door. Hastily, if I remember correctly…"

"I don't blame him…"

"Neither do I…" She paused. "I was really angry but, well, it sounded like he's not having the greatest time, one way and another…"

"No, he's not. Anyway…" Caitlin hesitated. "You said you were going to call me. About anything…particular?"

"No. Well…yes. Mmm…covers all the possibilities, doesn't it…?" Patricia hesitated. "To tell you the truth, something happened yesterday and it got me thinking about you. Well, about us…"

"What was it…?"

"I was just talking to…someone. And I realised there were things I've wanted to say to you for a long time but never have. The first," she went on, "is I've been missing you. I mean, really seriously missing you. It's a big gap in my life…"

"Have you…really?"

"Of course I have. It's not just we haven't seen each other for ages. That was bound to happen once you went off to uni, wasn't it? What I mean is, even when we do talk, it's not like the old days, is it...?"

"You mean before..."

"Before Dad and I split, yes."

"Mum, nothing's like the old days. It's no use pretending it is..."

"But in the last few months it's started to feel like it's not just been your dad and me. We've separated...you and me." She paused. "Does that make sense?"

"Yes..."

Caitlin suddenly sounded young and uncertain; Patricia heard a child's voice.

"Obviously you and I see things differently – all the stuff between your dad and me, I mean. That's normal, natural – we're mother and daughter, but I don't expect you to always agree with me..." She paused. "But yesterday I suddenly got it. I realised what I've been doing. I wanted you to accept my version of what happened, side with me and say I'm right and your dad's wrong. Which was never going to happen, but because it didn't, I just got angry with you..."

"Like I did with you..."

"Okay, but the fact remains, you're an adult. You're entitled to see things any way you see them and feel however you feel – including being angry with me. I accept all that, I honestly do. But then to let it go on like that and turn you and me into strangers – that is not okay..."

Her words were greeted with silence. Dry throated, she switched the phone from one hand to the other. "Are you still there...?" she ventured.

"Yes, sure. I'm just, you know...taking it in."

"...And I was determined it shouldn't go on a minute longer. If you think I've made a total mess of things, maybe I just have to live with that. But you're my flesh and blood, you're very precious and...I love you. And that's it. That's what I was going to tell you." She sighed. "Speech over…"

Caitlin took a long, deep breath.

"Thanks, Mum…"

"All I've done was tell you how I feel…"

"We, actually…"

"We…?"

"How we both feel. Something told me I absolutely had to call you. That happened yesterday, too. Isn't that extraordinary…?"

"Maybe, maybe not…"

"What do you mean…?"

"I don't really know, but I've been talking recently to someone who absolutely refuses to accept there's any such thing as chance or fate or coincidence. He's got this bee in his bonnet there's a reason for everything, and it's all deep and meaningful…"

"God, and he's convinced you, has he…?"

"No, but it got me thinking. I mean, the fact the same idea came to us both at the same time…" She shrugged. "Anyway, go on…"

"The thing is, I sort of knew what I wanted to say but I didn't know how to start. I needn't have worried…you did it for me. So…thank you."

"I don't understand why it's taken me so damned long to see sense…" Patricia paused. "Or why we do things like that to the people we love most…"

"Not to mention ourselves…" Caitlin reminded her. "It was actually quite scary picking up the phone…"

"Tell me about it!"

"I wasn't sure you'd give me a chance to…well, if you'd listen…"

"When you think how much time I have to spend listening to people! Maybe I'm not as good at it as I thought…"

"I didn't say that…"

"I know, but the trouble is, when I feel I'm being blamed for something unfairly I get defensive…then I get angry."

"Right…"

"And then it's really hard to listen. Quite honestly, there were times talking to you, I was fit to be tied. You must have felt the same way. I mean, don't tell me you couldn't have strangled me…"

"Cheerfully…" Caitlin groaned. "God, that's a terrible thing to say to your mother, isn't it…?"

"What's so terrible? Surely you're allowed to love someone and still be bloody angry with things they do or say. It's all right, it's okay…"

"I guess so. And," she went on, "he could be a bastard sometimes. Dad, I mean. You two didn't say much about it, but I'm not stupid, I could see what was going on…"

"Yes, he could, and it got to the point I'd just had enough. This isn't the time to trawl through it all again but what hurt was that you seemed to be convinced I was the baddie. It was as if whatever he did was okay, and when I finally said 'enough, I won't put up with more' the fallout was all my doing. It was me who'd…torn the family apart…"

"No, no. It wasn't like that, honestly," Caitlin protested. "I mean, I was angry with you for loads of reasons…"

"Tell me…"

"Well for a start, how you let him treat you, Mum. And how you just went on doing it. It drove me absolutely crazy that you hardly ever stood up for yourself. Actually," she went on, "that's probably the single thing that pissed me off most…"

"God…I wish you'd told me."

"I tried to, but I got the feeling you didn't really want to hear it. I often thought if only she'd get tough, put her foot down, even threaten to walk out. Maybe, just maybe, he'd have got his act together…"

"I thought about leaving, but it was just too scary…" Patricia admitted. "Also, I clung to the completely insane idea that given enough time, I could change him. Call your mother delusional, but I can remember thinking that pretty much from the time I met him..."

"I don't think you realised how much he needed you, did you?"

"Did he, really...?" She took a deep breath, exhaling slowly. "It didn't feel like that..."

Patricia shook her head. What was the use of all that psychological training if she still couldn't see something so blindingly obvious? She would have spotted a pattern like that in a patient in five minutes flat, yet in her own life it could completely elude her. She sucked her teeth; self pity was the last thing she needed right now.

"It probably sounds stupid, but I never dreamed that's how you felt. It didn't enter my head. As far as I was concerned you'd taken sides, but why was a complete mystery..."

"What is it you tell me sometimes – you don't have to beat yourself up? You never claimed to be a mind reader, and if I never told you..."

"At least you have now. And I get it, pet – I do. It must have been really difficult for you. It's just frustrating I didn't see it before..."

"You're right in a way, I did kind of...stick with Dad, but that was because I just hated the thought of him being alone. Sure, he behaved pretty badly but I could see everything going pear shaped and him being left high and dry. I wanted him to know he had someone on his side, I suppose." She sighed. "I just couldn't bear the thought of him feeling, I don't know... abandoned."

"He made pretty sure he wasn't alone..." Patricia pointed out dryly.

"I know. It's not logical, Mum. But it's how I felt..."

She paused, transported to the churchyard. The towering yew was once more at her back, supporting her, immense, powerful and protective, a living force unimaginably old. Just the way a parent might feel to a child. Following Caitlin's birth, Patricia often felt overwhelmed by the task of balancing the conflicting demands of motherhood and her medical studies. Far from sure it would be forthcoming, she was reluctant to seek Liam's support. Fiona was willing enough, but never able to forge a close bond with her granddaughter. Could her own efforts have been so woefully inadequate they left a legacy of emotional wounding?

"Caitlin...?"

"Yes...?"

"Do you ever feel that way...?" She hesitated, fearful of what the answer might be. "Abandoned...lonely?"

"Don't most people, when they're feeling a bit down...?"

"You mean you do...?"

"Only what do you call them – fleeting thoughts? Never lasts long. I can bring myself out of it..." Her voice brightened. "I usually remind myself my mum's always, always been there for me. Which you have, haven't you...?"

"It hasn't felt that way the past few months but I've always tried, done my best..." Patricia nodded. "Listen, you'd better not say any more or I'll have to go hunting for tissues..."

"Likewise." Caitlin laughed. "God, aren't we a pair...?"

Patricia sighed; there was nothing wrong with tears, but they were for another time, when they were not separated by hundreds of miles.

"So..." she went on, briskly. "When are we actually going to see you, then...?"

"Well, I was thinking of..."

Her reply was drowned by thunder on the stairs, heralding her brother's reappearance. He had launched into an account of his efforts with the car roof before he noticed she was holding up the phone and pointing to it.

"Hang on, I'm talking to Caitlin..."

"Cool..." His eyes sparkled. "Did you tell her about the green machine...?"

"Not yet. We had other..."

"Here, let me..."

He lifted the receiver lightly from her hand and set about bringing Caitlin up to date with recent developments regarding the Carragh family's transport facilities. Leaning back, Patricia cupped her head in her hands, savouring the moment. Caitlin's call had turned out to be imbued with a magical, serendipitous quality. And it was Caitlin's call; events had proved bloody Merlin right again.

"Hey! I was in the middle of...!"

She was too late to prevent Colm ringing off. Seeing her redialling he groaned.

"You promised we could go. You guys can talk all you like when she gets back, can't you...?"

"She said she's coming...?"

"Wednesday evening. She'll text when she's on the train. Mum, come on, I've been waiting hours...please?"

Ψ

Colm studied the knobs, buttons, dials and switches arrayed on the polished walnut instrument panel, the leather bound owner's manual in his hands providing further proof of the Jaguar's pedigree. Glancing up at a stretch of empty road ahead he urged her to go faster.

"Not here..." She shook her head. "Too many deer..."

"Only at night," he protested. "Everyone knows that..."

"Except the deer, evidently..."

He rolled his eyes but did not deign to reply.

The cream leather upholstery had taken her eye in the showroom, but she had yet to adjust the driving seat to her full satisfaction. Equally, accustomed to the solid utilitarianism of her own car, the thin-rimmed, wooden steering wheel felt unnervingly fragile, as if applying pressure might be enough to break it. In Eddie's experienced hands the Jaguar had sped effortlessly along, leaving her free to admire the graceful curves of an improbably long bonnet, and simultaneously relish the wind tugging at her hair. Wrestling with unfamiliar steering, pedals set awkwardly close together, and unforgiving brakes, however, Patricia was finding the beast less appealing.

"How sweet is this…?" Colm grinned.

"Extremely…" she assured him, doing her best to sound convincing.

A dab on the accelerator was enough to send the diminutive speedometer's red needle creeping to the more adventurous side of fifty-five miles an hour.

"We are going to keep it, aren't we?" he asked. "I told Cat we were…"

"That did not escape me…" she had to raise her voice to compete with wind noise. "By the way, have you thought what you'd like to do this summer?"

"Some friends have offered Soph's mum and dad this villa in the Algarve. Sounds pretty cool, and they're going some time next month. Actually," he added, "they asked if I'd like to go with them. I said I'd talk to you…"

She wondered how he explained his family situation; she had never asked. Talking so openly to Caitlin had brought a sense of release and relief; she must make sure she did the same with Colm.

"Would you enjoy that, pet?"

"Yeah…! They showed me pictures. It's awesome. Got its own pool and jacuzzi and everything…"

"Do you know dates…?"

"Nope…"

"You'd better check, pronto. There'd be flights and stuff to organise. Are they nice? I mean, I've met them at parent evenings just to say hello and had a quick chat with the mum on the phone, but that's about all..."

"They're great. Soph's mum's a brilliant cook..." He shot her a guilty glance. "Not as good as you, but like, really good. Her dad's nice, too. Haven't seen much of him. He's something to do with insurance in London, gets home pretty late..."

"You like them enough to spend a holiday..."

"God, yeah..."

"Why don't I ring them, maybe invite them over to dinner? I'd better get to know my future in-laws, hadn't I?"

"Mum..." He grimaced.

"Sorry. Seriously slapped wrists..." She took a hand from the wheel just long enough to touch his arm. "Forgive me...?"

He pursed his lips, giving the question due consideration. "If you keep this..."

"The word for that is blackmail," she pointed out. "Listen, I've had an idea. I'd have to check with Dad, and I don't even know if he'd be up for it, but how do you fancy a holiday with the two of us? Might even get your sister to grace us with her presence..."

Family holidays had been collateral damage in the aftermath of the separation. They had crossed her mind but she never raised the subject; maintaining the necessary level of harmony had felt unrealistic. Caitlin travelled with friends from uni, while she created trips for Colm and herself; Switzerland the first year, Morocco the next. As far as Portugal was concerned, spending time with Sophie was an obvious attraction, but she wondered if the lure of family life was also a factor in its favour.

"Instead of the Algarve...?" He frowned.

"How about as well as? Mums need holidays too, you know."

She assumed his sigh was one of relief. "Where would we go...?"

"I have not the faintest idea," she admitted. "But that shouldn't surprise you, since I only thought of it about thirty seconds ago..."

"How about Venice Beach?" He turned shining eyes her way. "A guy at school went last summer and he says it's awesome. They've got these basketball hoops everywhere. Anyone can rock up and just like, join in. You know...?"

"I said I wanted a break, pet," she reminded him, "not to be broke."

"All of us? Yeah, that would be really cool." He leaned back, smiling into the distance. "Where is the Algarve, anyway...?"

"What do you do in geography lessons...?" She shook her head. "The Algarve is the southernmost bit of Portugal."

"Does it have mountains?"

"I'm not sure. I don't think so. Not big ones, anyway. Why...?"

"I had this dream last night, where I was up some mountain..." He leaned across and peered at the speedometer. "You're still miles inside the limit, you know..."

"Can't have that..."

The engine purred, the roar of the exhaust edged up the decibel scale, and a satisfying surge of gravitational force pressed her deeper into the cream leather.

"Good dream, bad dream...?"

"I haven't had a nightmare for ages." He shook his head. "Anyway, I was snowboarding like that time in...where was it?"

"Andermatt..."

"Yeah. That was it..."

"Interesting," she told him. "I had a dream last night. And I was in Switzerland, too."

"Hey, what if we'd met...?"

"I wasn't in mountains..."

"Does it ever happen, though? I mean, different people having, like, the same dream?"

"People say it does."

"You weren't skiing, then...?"

"Nope. In a small boat on what I'm pretty sure was Lake Lucerne..."

Rounding a long, sweeping right hand bend they emerged from beneath the canopy of trees which had lined their route for the last two or three miles, and found themselves on the crest of a hill offering a vista of the broad, undulating Sussex downs. Patricia slowed and pulled off the main road, onto a bumpy, rutted parking area.

"We're not going back, are we." Colm frowned. "Not yet...?"

"No. My seat doesn't feel quite right. Job for you," she told him. "Eddie's legs must be longer than mine."

Giving a wide berth to a garish pink van with a giant glass-fibre ice-cream on top, beside which a queue had formed, she circumnavigated the worst of the pot-holes and parked facing a grassy bank.

"I'd like it forward a bit, closer to the pedals, and not leaning back at that angle. Would you ever have a look and see if you can sort it? First, though," she added, "I'd love to hear about this dream. Do you remember it...?"

"I think so, most of it..." He nodded, opening the handbook.

"Do you mind telling me...?"

"It was just a dream, Mum..."

"How about doing it the way I get my patients to?"

"Do they have to tell you their dreams...?" He shot her a suspicious glance.

"They don't have to, but sometimes it's useful," she explained.

"And then we're going on, yes...?"

"Once you've fixed the seat..."

"Okay, then. What do I do...?"

"Don't look so worried, there's nothing to it. First, sit back and get comfortable. Once you are, close your eyes..."

"It won't take long, will it...?"

"It won't take long..."

Settling into his seat, he folded his arms. "Now what...?" he enquired, opening his eyes again.

"The idea is you keep them closed until you've finished," she explained, patiently. "Okay, now imagine you're seeing the dream again, only this time you're watching it on a screen. Imagine it's a video…"

"Cool…"

"Then tell me what you see and feel. Okay…?"

"No prob…"

Lured by the prospect of another baking summer's day, a steady stream of traffic was passing along the main road at their backs, en route for the coast. A posse of gleaming motorbikes roared by in noisy convoy, leather clad riders hunched low.

"I was on this mountain, boarding…" He opened one eye. "That first time I kept falling off, remember…?"

"Only too well…" She nodded.

"But this time I didn't, not once. It was so cool. There weren't any bumps or anything, the snow was perfect. It felt brilliant. I just…" He drew lazy curves in the air with a hand, "did it, you know? Oh, did I say it was at night." He paused, "and full moon…?"

"Was it really…?" she said, softly. "How interesting…"

"Yeah, it was amazing, like being under floodlights, you know? Anyway, I went down and down into this valley, didn't fall off once. Awesome…" A broad grin lit his face. "Then what happened? Yes, I know, I pitched up at some chair lifts. Three or four I think, but I didn't know which one to take. And there was no one around to ask…" He wiped his nose with the back of a hand. "And I'm kind of standing there when a really random bunch rocks up…"

"Random…?" she echoed.

"Yeah. Appeared out of nowhere, playing music. Like a band, only they were just making noises. No tune. It was totally mad. Guitars, drums, trumpets, and those…" He put a hand to his mouth and waggled his fingers, "you know…?"

"Flutes…?"

"Right, yeah…" He paused again. "All following this big guy. I mean, humungous, like, you know…a giant. And they've got these crazy outfits and masks on…like they've been to a fancy dress party. Anyway, they're laughing and singing and having a really good time. And then…" his voice faded. "I'm sure there was more…"

"Sounds like they were having fun," she prompted.

"Yeah, definitely…"

"Do you remember how you were feeling…?"

"Me? I felt great…"

She waited for a few moments. "And…was that it?"

"Don't think so…" He frowned. "Yeah, I asked this giant which lift to take, and he said it didn't matter. And I said that couldn't be right, it must matter. But he just started laughing and pointing at these mountains all round us and said it didn't matter but I must go up. And…" He opened his eyes and shrugged. "That was it…"

"When you woke up?"

"Must have…" He yawned. "Kind of spooky, though, isn't it, seriously? I mean, us both dreaming we're in the same place. Do you think it might mean something…?"

"If it does, I've no idea what…"

"I do…"

She glanced at him. "Oh, really? Tell me…"

"That's where we ought to go. Switzerland…"

"Now there's a thought. Well, I guess we'll find out." She opened her door and got out. "Now, get twiddling those knobs and levers, mister. We're not going anywhere until I get comfortable…"

Ψ

If the sleek green convertible had initially felt like an amphetamine-fuelled carthorse, ninety minutes was long enough for it to metamorphose into a well-schooled and compliant thoroughbred. The Jaguar was proving exhilarating and exciting, occasionally unpredictable but generally willing to submit to her control. She eased her way off East Grinstead's busy main street and through the narrow gap separating her house from the neighbouring one, aware that any encounter with brickwork could be disastrous.

"Would you ever hop out and open up for me, pet?"

"You always say garages are too good for cars…"

"That's ours. This is a different class of machine, it's not mine, and I think it needs putting under cover…"

Heedless of her exhortation to treat the upholstery with care, Colm planted a trainer on his seat and vaulted onto the cobbles. At the third attempt he succeeded in wrenching open a wooden door to which only traces of its original black paint now clung. He swung to face her and gave a rueful smile.

"No way you'll get it in there…"

He stepped aside, gesturing at a jumble of old bicycles, cardboard boxes overflowing with books and papers, metal-edged tea chests bearing stencilled numbers, bulging black plastic bags and assorted furniture in varying states of disrepair.

"I didn't realise it was that bad…"

"Doesn't matter. I mean, it's not going to rain…"

"I'm not risking it. Better put the top up. But," she added with a grim smile, "that tip needs sorting. Job for you, darling…"

He groaned. "That would take ages…"

"This summer, not this minute. During which you will have time on your hands, okay?"

"Mum…" His shoulders sagged.

Pushing through the heavy, arched, wooden door leading into the garden, she pondered how, in the unlikely event she exchanged a large sum of money and the Volvo for what Eddie insisted was 'a collector's item, Dr. Carragh, a modern classic,' she would transport the contents of the garage to the municipal dump. On the other hand, there was no denying their outing had left her feeling pleasantly elated. Running her fingers through a mass of tangled hair, she decided this was no moment to become bogged down in practicalities.

"Hello…" She spun round, clapping a hand to her chest. He was sitting on the ground, backpack propped against sun-warmed bricks, arms folded and long legs stretched out in front of him.

"Olaf…you made me jump…"

"Forgive me…" He joined his palms.

"Have you been here long…?"

"Not very…" He climbed to his feet, brushing earth from his jeans. "I need to talk to you…"

"Okay…"

"You do not sound sure. Do you have time…?"

"I…will it take long…?"

"I am not going to Stonehenge…"

"Oh, really…?"

He spoke in a casual, matter-of-fact tone, as if the matter had never been in doubt. He hoisted the pack onto his shoulder and studied her face.

"You are surprised…?"

Patricia shrugged. "Nothing about you surprises me any more." She shook her head, smiling. "So, it's back to plan A, is it…?"

"Plan A…?"

"Scafell."

"Oh. Yes, that is where I am going…"

"Well, well. To be honest, I am a bit surprised. When I didn't hear from you for a few days I just thought…" She shrugged. "Anyway, is that what you came to tell me?"

"It is a long journey…"

"It must be. Scafell is way up in the Lake District, isn't it…?"

"I checked. It is three hundred and fifty-nine miles. They

estimate it will take us six hours and twenty minutes and will cost sixty-eight pounds and eighty pence for petrol. That is a great deal of money." He frowned. "But I am not sure how accurate that is..."

Out of the corner of her eye, she saw Colm had followed her into the garden. He advanced a few paces, nodded to Olaf and stood, hands on hips, listening.

"You said 'us'..."

"Yes..."

"You and Morgana, you mean...?"

Olaf shook his head. "She has left for Stonehenge..." He paused. "So, I came to ask you to take me, please, Dr Carragh..."

"Oh..."

There was more than a touch of the surreal about this scenario. It was Sunday afternoon. Monday was often her busiest day of the week, with tomorrow no exception; her list of assessments, appointments and meetings began first thing, and ran through to early evening. And this man had the gall, the effrontery to appear out of the blue and calmly ask her to cancel, rearrange or reschedule everything in her diary. All so she could act as his chauffeuse for a round trip of over seven hundred miles and thirteen hours behind the wheel. In addition to which, she would presumably be expected to climb the bloody mountain. She took a step towards him, shaking her head.

"Olaf, do you have the remotest idea what you're asking...?

"Yes," he replied, without hesitation.

"No, I don't think you do. I mean, if at least you'd given me warning, maybe I..."

"I quite understand if you say no," he told her. "It is a most unreasonable request..."

Patricia stared at him, frowning. "Unreasonable...did you say?"

"And very inconvenient..."

"Oh, Jesus..." her voice was little more than a whisper.

"Mum, are you okay...?" Colm moved to her side, slipping an arm round her shoulders. "You look kind of..."

"I'm fine, really..." she told him.

"Did Olaf say he wants to hitch a lift somewhere?"

"Leaving first thing tomorrow morning. Not to any old where, pet. To a mountain in Cumbria and it's a three hundred mile drive..."

"Three hundred and fifty-nine..." Olaf murmured.

"Wow. Great..." Colm's eyes glistened. "Did you know we've got this new car..."

"Have you...?"

"No," Patricia said, wearily. "We've borrowed it..."

"Is this trip something special...?" Colm wanted to know.

"Yes, it is..." Olaf nodded. "Very special..."

"Hey, can I come? It'd be great, Mum. I mean, you don't have to do it all by yourself..."

"All right..." Patricia threw her head back and looked skywards. "Okay, I get it, I get it...!"

"Mum...what are you doing?"

"What I'm told..." She looked from one puzzled face to the other and began to laugh. "And the whole idea is madness..."

Olaf joined his palms. "If you can't, I will find another way..."

"I said it was madness, not I wouldn't do it..." She turned and set off for the door. "Come on in, the pair of you. I think we'd better talk about this thing..."

Chapter 20

To the Heights

Monday 20th June 2011

When Patricia set her alarm for 6 a.m. she was unaware her body clock was programmed to wake her a good deal earlier. Without opening her eyes she stretched, yawned and listened to the soundtrack of a midsummer dawn. Blackbirds were calling from their favourite vantage point on the redundant television aerial, their song punctuated by deep-throated pigeon chants and thrushes tirelessly repeating higher notes.

Memories of her wedding morning tiptoed into her consciousness, uncomfortable as they were unwelcome. Her finals were fast approaching but she was a diligent and dedicated student, expected to achieve good grades. The relationship with Liam Carragh, twelve years her senior, was three stormy years old. Even a woman far more worldly, self-confident and self-assured than she would surely have found it profoundly challenging. Thoughtful, attentive and charming one minute, the next he could become cold, distant and punishing. There were women who, perversely, seemed to find his very unpredictability an attraction, but she, was not among them. Having fallen under his spell, however, she felt powerless to escape from a dizzying, bewildering, emotional roller coaster ride of blissful highs, interspersed with depths of almost unendurable pain. When she fell pregnant, the last thing she imagined was that he would almost casually agree to marry her. Not for the last time she misjudged him.

She had spent much of that bleak, November night tossing and turning, trying to convince herself she had chosen the right option. Marriage would, unarguably, provide her unborn child not only with a father but a degree of security. In addition, she would avoid the fate of unmarried mothers in what could be a brutally unforgiving environment. However difficult her path might be it would also preserve her dream of achieving a psychiatric qualification. The most alluring, seductive fantasy, however, was that given enough time she might transform Liam into a loving, supportive and faithful mate.

That morning – God, was it really over twenty years ago – the nausea had little to do with her condition; her body was rebelling against the tyranny of her mind. The arguments in favour of going through with the marriage were compelling yet, to her consternation, she was unable to silence a relentless voice insisting she was committing an act of self-betrayal. Patricia rolled onto her back, cradled her head on her arm and wondered why such memories should come knocking like uninvited party guests on this of all mornings. Perhaps, she mused, to remind her that even with two additional decades of life experience, she found it no easier to resolve the conflicting dictates of heart and head.

Long after Colm and Olaf had gone to their beds she was still busy making phone calls and dispatching apologetic emails in a frantic attempt to reschedule her commitments. She was also troubled by the question of transport; while the Jaguar represented a tempting alternative to her own car, was it sensible to embark on such a long trip with three people jammed into a space designed for two? Even if it were, the agreement had been she would test drive the Jaguar for a day or two. Eddie's oleaginous charm was unlikely to survive the revelation she had covered the length of the country in that time. Perhaps the question which really nagged at her, however, was what on earth the trip could possibly achieve.

She took a deep breath, kicked back the duvet and padded to the bedroom window. The brightening sky was cloudless; logic might not be on her side but the weather was. Turning on the shower she smiled to herself, picturing Frances's delight when she learned her granddaughter had responded to the call of adventure rather than submit to the dull, dead hand of convention.

Olaf, to whom she had assigned Caitlin's room, had declined her offer of a wake-up call on the grounds that he was an habitually early riser. Entering the kitchen, it was therefore no surprise to find him standing at the window with a glass of water in his hand, gazing out across the garden. He turned to salute her.

"We are blessed with a beautiful morning…"

"I didn't realise you were up," she said, reaching for the kettle. "In these old places the staircases creak like mad, and I usually hear every step. You'd make a good cat-burglar…"

"A habit from my time in India. We were encouraged to step lightly…"

"Why was that…?"

"It is considered an act of respect for the planet to place our feet upon it with consciousness…"

"Would you mind mentioning that to my son? He thunders around like a herd of elephants…" she told him. "Olaf, I'm going to put some food together. Sandwiches, fruit, maybe hard-boiled eggs, just snack stuff and it'll rather depend on what I can find. What do you fancy – you'd better start with a decent breakfast inside you…"

"Thank you, but I carry seeds and nuts in case I get hungry. Also…" He drew a piece of paper from a pocket, "I would like to share this with you…"

"Our path up the mountain…?"

"I have printed that out for you, but this is a map I drew. In case you were wondering about the reason for our journey…"

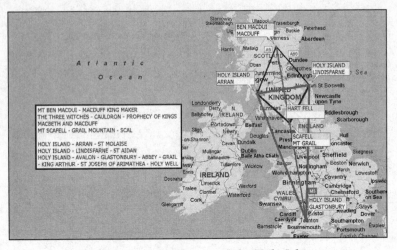

Image 08 Glastonbury and the Holy Isles

Pulling a box of eggs from the fridge, she glanced at him.

"It had crossed my mind..."

"This will explain..." he told her, smoothing it flat.

"Olaf...if it can really tell me why I spent half last night cancelling today's schedule, just so I could drive for God knows how long to get to God knows where," she gave a rueful smile, "it is one hell of a map."

"It is one hell of a map..." He grinned, waiting until she moved to his side. "Now, please observe this line running due north from Glastonbury, up and up...all the way to Ben Macdui. And notice it passes straight through..." He paused, eyebrows raised.

"Scafell, yes..." Patricia shrugged. "But that doesn't actually explain..."

"Wait, please..." He stabbed a finger at the map. "This line cuts the first at right angles, linking Lindisfarne with St Molaise in the firth of Clyde..."

"You're not planning on going that far, I hope."

He smiled and shook his head. "Iona lies west of Scafell, on the midsummer sunset line. This means it is a gateway for sacred beings to approach the mountain. Beings with powers to heal not just Scafell, but the whole land. The gateway is always there, but the holy intention of anyone entering it at midsummer sunset, as we will, is made far stronger, reinforced by a tremendous charge of spiritual energy..." He paused, eyes scanning her face. "Now do you see?"

"You think it's a good time to be going, I realise that..."

"More than good. The perfect moment..."

She crossed to the cooker.

"Which is probably all I need to know right now. To be honest, I still struggle with those maps. It's hard to see them as anything more than, well...random patterns."

She lifted a saucepan from the stainless steel rack above the cooker, filled it with boiling water and lit a gas ring on the hob. Using a spoon she carefully placed half a dozen eggs in the water and set the timer. Olaf waited patiently for her to complete her task.

"I understand, but can I tell you why this one has special meaning...?"

"I'll be working away, but I'll listen. Go ahead..."

"It shows you the spiritual significance of our physical journey. People chose to commune with their gods on Scafell. It makes sense – up there they felt closer to heaven. Over time the holy intentions of a constant stream of worshippers charged it with its own aura of holiness..."

"Meaning...?"

"It became imbued with spiritual energy..."

"Okay..."

"Round the solstice, the rising point of the sun stays in practically the same place on the horizon for about five days. That makes tonight even more special. You could say time stops and gives us just the tiniest glimpse of eternity..."

"I bet there aren't many other people who'd see it that way..."

"You are probably right..." he conceded. "But human life is

more closely attuned to natural cycles and rhythms than people realise. The most powerful being astrological ones – the dance of the planets…"

She spooned coffee into a polished steel espresso maker, added water and placed it on the burner next to the saucepan. Olaf at least had his patterns to justify the journey; she wished she had something as substantial. The most compelling reason for the journey to which she was now committed was, she had to admit, a dream meeting with a crimson-robed female deity whose favoured mode of transport was a dragon. Patricia would ensure he completed his mission, but she had had all the cosmic consciousness she could handle for the moment.

"Olaf, I'm sorry but we need to focus on practicalities right now." Looking up from buttering slices of dark, seeded loaf, she gestured at the wall clock. "Which means checking if Colm's vertical yet…"

"Yes, of course…"

"One thing, before you do," she told him as he turned for the door.

"Yes…?"

"I'm wondering why you changed your mind about Stonehenge…"

"Ah, yes. Well, when I got back from our trip yesterday, I needed time on my own, time to think. Morgana told me how to get to the forest, and I found a quiet spot near a pool where I meditated…"

"Asking for guidance…?"

"Asking for nothing, but…"

"Open to everything…?"

"Just so." He smiled. "And my ancestors came to speak with me. The same ones who sent me…"

"To ask why you weren't following instructions…?"

"To remind me I had free will, and could choose to do anything I wished. But they gave me a warning. If I do not take this opportunity, I might have to wait a long time for another..."

"Opportunity for what...?'

"They did not say..." He shrugged.

"So you're nearly there, and you still don't really know what it's all about?"

"With your help I will soon find out..."

"How was Morgana with that...?"

"Very accepting. To tell you the truth I was a little surprised..."

"You and me both..."

"She said she had sensed what I would do, and I went with her blessing..."

"Supportive..." Patricia pursed her lips. "But not enough to take you there herself..."

"She said she was not meant to do that..."

"Oh, really...?"

"She told me to ask you."

"It was all her idea...?" Patricia could not hide her irritation.

"She had a strong sense about it..."

"I'll bet. Next time you see that lady, tell her she owes me a favour," Patricia instructed. "Time to rouse sleeping beauty. First floor, turn right, second door on the right and don't take no for an answer..."

She paused for a few moments, head cocked, listening. For all the noise he made the man might have been weightless.

Twenty minutes later, while Olaf gently persuaded Colm it was not yet warm enough to dispense with the roof, she struggled to find room in the boot for nothing more than a plastic cooler bag of refreshments and an armful of jackets and hiking shoes. Yawning, Colm was preparing to enter the confines of the rear bench seat when Olaf touched his shoulder.

"Here we are on midsummer morning, setting off on a very special journey. I think we should seek help, guidance and protection, don't you?"

"Sure..." Colm gave a weary nod.

"Treat the world with awareness and respect and it responds by opening to you. Invocations are my way of doing that, you see..."

"Makes sense..." Colm agreed. "Mum...?"

"It won't take long, will it...?"

"Not at all..."

Palms turned towards a pale early morning sun, Olaf closed his eyes.

"Hail Father Sun and Mother Moon, on this sacred day of
    midsummer.
Hail to all life and consciousness on this planet,
Hail to the spirit guardians of Scafell and of all this land.
May we come safely to your holy mountain.
Trusting in the thunder of your transforming power.
May we enter this sacred space with love
May we enter this sacred space with trust
May we enter this sacred space with humility
May we enter this sacred space with clear intention
And may we receive your blessings of healing and wisdom."

Ψ

Glancing at the neat analogue clock on the dashboard, Patricia felt a sense of satisfaction. It was barely half past nine, and not only had she satisfactorily negotiated rush hour traffic in the vicinity of two international airports but was increasingly comfortable with the Jaguar's idiosyncrasies. A decision which only a few hours earlier she was tempted to dismiss as madness, now felt little worse than mild eccentricity. Muffled grunts suggested that Colm, who had somehow folded his lanky frame into a position sufficiently comfortable to resume his slumbers, was surfacing. She glanced at Olaf.

"How are you feeling...?"

The Icelander took a deep breath.

"I am happy, excited and grateful. The journey we have shared," he added after a pause, "has not been long, but it has been eventful, don't you think...?

"True..."

"With many twists and turns and..." He inclined his head, "you have been a good teacher."

"You think so...?" She frowned. "I felt more like the student..."

"Both could be true..." He gazed at a quartet of concrete cooling towers, looming on the horizon like massive mushrooms, set against the bleak, charmless skyline of England's second city. "You reminded me how easy it is to be distracted and stray from your path..." He smiled. "But hart and tigress were persistent, determined I must walk my talk..."

"That tigress went AWOL too long." Patricia nodded grimly. "It feels good to have her back..."

"Tigress...?" Colm stifled a yawn. "What are you two on about...?"

"I am she, so you'd better watch your step from now on, mister..."

"Definitely..." Olaf agreed. "Do not pull the tail of the tiger..."

"If you say so..." Colm scratched his head with both hands. "How much further...?"

"Quite a way, but we're making good time..." she told him. "I just saw a sign for services in four miles. Let's grab a drink, stretch our legs and you guys can change places for a bit..."

Leaning against wooden railings enclosing a children's play area containing slides, swings, roundabouts and climbing frames in primary colours, Patricia watched Colm execute bends and stretches she recognised as part of his basketball warm-up routine.

"Are you okay? It looks pretty cramped back there..."

"It's not that bad. As long as we swap occasionally..."

Joining fellow travellers seeking rest and refreshment, they were entering the sliding doors of the angular plate glass structure when they met Olaf heading the opposite way.

"Too many people and too much loud music..." he told them. "I will wait for you in the open air."

"Won't be long..."

A few minutes later she was sitting on a bench in the sunshine, sipping indifferent coffee as Olaf knelt on the grass explaining the new map to Colm. Not for the first time, she marvelled at his openness to what he was hearing when her own response was usually so sceptical.

"Mum. You work with loonies, don't you...?"

"Not a term I'd use..."

"You know what I mean..."

"Why...?"

"Olaf says full moons can drive people crazy..."

"I've met paediatric nurses who swear they can tell when it's full by the effect on children – especially really small ones." Patricia nodded.

"I often have vivid dreams," Olaf added. "Maybe we are closer to the non-physical world – the world of spirit..."

Colm tugged at a piece of grass and slid it between his lips. "You mean, like...ghosts and stuff?"

"Ghosts...?" Olaf waggled his head. "It is possible. To me, spirit includes all that which has not taken physical form. Those things our senses can not detect..."

"But people see ghosts, don't they...?"

"True. I should have said most people can not detect..."

"But if you can't see or touch something how do you know it's, like, even there...?"

"By experiencing it. Dowsing, could you see the energy...?"

"I guess not..."

"But rods helped you experience it..."

"I suppose..."

"You know what an amplifier does...?"

"Makes sounds louder...?"

"Think of Mother Moon as an amplifier for spirit energies..."

"What about the Sun, then – is it as important?"

"Without it there would be no life on our planet, my friend. No light, no heat, no weather systems to create rain." Olaf grinned. "Is it important? If you asked that question a few thousand years ago people would have called you a mad man. Then, they believed all life depended on the phases of Sun and Moon. Every festival and celebration was linked to something in the lunar or solar calendar. Eclipses, new moons, full moons, sunrise and sunset..."

"And midsummer, yes?" asked Colm.

"Definitely. Solstices were very important." Olaf agreed. "Imagine the journey of the sunrise point from midwinter to midsummer as travelling north, from dark to light. Then there is the daily journey west, from sunset to sunrise." He paused. "On the longest and shortest days, sunrise and sunset take on even greater significance..."

"And that..." Colm took the grass from his lips, "is why you absolutely had to be there tonight. Right?"

"Call it a cosmic imperative..." The Icelander smiled. "An opportunity to approach the divine..."

"Belief or experience...?" Patricia wanted to know.

"A story for you," Olaf replied with a smile. "One midsummer a few years ago, I climbed one of our mountains called *Hoffell*. It was dull and cloudy but I timed it so that, at the moment of sunset I could be deep in meditation. I sat there, opened my heart chakra, and radiated loving energy and joy. I sent blessings to every living thing in and on our planet. And what happened...?" He waved a hand skywards. "The clouds melt away and disappear, the sun comes out, and birds fly up from the valley to circle round me. Why? Because when you send out the energy of lovingness, all life responds. Even the mountain lords came to dance with me..."

"Hey..." Colm gazed at him wide-eyed. "Do you reckon that might happen to us?"

"Why not?" Olaf spread his hands. "Be open to it. If you allow anything to be possible, then it is..."

"I get this is important to you..." Colm chewed his lip, "but what about Mum and me? Might it be the same for us or are we like, just along for the ride?"

"Good question..." Olaf told him.

"Isn't it?" agreed Patricia. "I'm hoping you have an equally good answer...?"

Olaf narrowed his eyes and took a breath. "When we stand together on top of the mountain at the magic hour, my young friend, I promise you will have your answer..."

Getting to her feet Patricia brushed at her jeans, crumpled her coffee cup and jammed it into an overflowing litter bin.

"I hope you've done your homework," she told Olaf. "I'm relying on you for the navigation – finding the best place to start from, and a nice easy path to the top. One even I shall be able to manage..."

"There is a place to park your beautiful motor car just before Wasdale Head. And we will have plenty of guides to see us safely up..."

"We have guides...?"

"Of course. I am sure the Lingmell dragon and St Michael, lord of the dragons will attend us. And the Lady of Wasdale Lake, of course. Did you realise," he added, getting to his feet, "our journey takes us from the depths to the heights? From Wast Water – the deepest lake in England – straight to the top of its highest mountain."

One of the cars flanking their own had departed. In its place stood a venerable VW camper, its original sky blue paintwork all but hidden beneath suns and moons, rainbows, shooting stars, swirling planets and signs of the zodiac. Two older women in dresses as colourful as their transport relaxed in the sliding doorway. A slender teenage girl lounging nearby poked at the ground with the toe of her shoe and scowled at the new arrivals.

"Cool." Colm, nodded his appreciation. "A hippie van..."

The elder of the women took a long-stemmed pipe from between stained teeth, and winked at him. "And doesn't this yoke have more years on it than you and your ma together..."

Sunlight glittered and sparkled on an array of necklaces and bracelets, hooped earrings and the sequinned scarf draped across the old woman's shoulders.

"It's grand. And you did all that fine artwork with your own hand, did you...?" Patricia smiled.

"Me? Not at all..." The crone cackled, gesturing at the girl. "My granddaughter, Colleen. Now that one's an artist, and no mistake..."

She exhaled a thin stream of smoke, studying them with knowing eyes set deep in a face as creased as an old shoe. Her companion in the doorway sipped from a leather covered hip-flask.

"You've a rare talent, Colleen..." Patricia told the girl, but her smile was not returned.

The women passed the flask between them, watching Colm lower the Jaguar's roof. Hands clasped behind her, the girl walked lightly forward, peering up into Olaf's face. Barefoot, she wore a flowing white blouse and flared, knee length skirt.

"Would you look at the eyes on your man, now..." She cocked her head and ran her fingers slowly through a mane of waist length copper-red hair. "One like a thrush's egg and the other green as a leaf..." her own eyes narrowed. "Your path has not been easy, has it, handsome...?" Stretching out a long-fingered hand, she went on. "If you're generous as you are good looking, you shall learn what life has in store..."

"Try her. She has the gift..." the woman with the flask encouraged him. "Make it folding money. You won't regret it..."

"Ah, come on now, handsome..." the girl wheedled, tossing her head. "You can spare five pounds, easy. If not..." Her lip curled, "twelve months ill-fortune could be your fate. What do you say?"

Olaf smiled. "I have a better idea. If you solve a riddle I will pay."

The girl turned to her companions and shrugged. Struggling to her feet, the pipe-smoker waddled towards Olaf, stiff hipped and ungainly as an old goose.

"Riddles, is it...?" she grinned, waving her pipe. "How about this, then? Answer one I'll give you, first time, or pay up..."

"Both of us," he suggested. "Each must solve the other's..."

"If we get yours, we win...?"

"Only if I can not answer yours," he told her. "Fair is fair."

"Agreed..." She nodded. "Are you ready...?"

"I am listening..."

"I washed my face in water that was never rained, nor run, and dried it with a towel that was never wove, nor spun..." With a satisfied grin, she jammed the pipe back between her teeth. "What was it I did, eh? Tell me that if you can..."

"That is not easy." He frowned, tugging at his chin. "I need a little time..."

"You'll never get it..." the girl insisted. "Pay up..."

"Pay...pay...pay..." chanted the older women in unison, laughing.

"One minute, ladies. You have to answer mine..." Olaf reminded them.

"Try us, then..."

"Fuglinn flaug fjaðralaus, settist á vegginn beinlaus" Olaf intoned. "Fuglinn flaug fjaðralaus, settist á veginn beinlaus"

"Hey, not fair..." the girl broke in. "Stop, stop..."

She took a step back, glaring. Her grandmother chuckled and

shook an admonitory finger.

"Don't you think you can cheat us speaking an alien tongue, now…"

Suppressing a smile, Olaf held up his hand like a teacher bringing an unruly kindergarten class to order.

"In your own language, then," he told them. "What flies in the sky as silent as a bird, but has no wings, and comes gently to earth, though it has no feet? Your rules," he reminded them, "you must get it right first time…" The trio huddled together, exchanging whispers, heads bobbing and shaking. Patricia turned the ignition key and the Jaguar's engine purred smoothly into life. Waiting for Olaf to take his place on the rear seat, Colm slipped in beside his mother.

"Over to you…" Patricia told Olaf in a low voice. "I've not the foggiest idea…"

"What was yours?" Colm asked.

"A snowflake…" Olaf told him.

Leaving her companions, the girl ran to press her hands against the Jaguar's gleaming green flank.

"We're beat, but it's not fair, you talked some foreign shite…" she complained. "What about ours, then…?"

"Come on, now, fair's fair," called her grandmother. "Don't you go running off…"

"Yours is foreign to me…" Olaf pointed out, gently.

"You have to pay…" the girl insisted.

"Maybe…" Olaf replied. "Is it…you washed your face in morning dew and…dried it in the sunshine?"

Planting her hands on her hips, the girl pulled a face.

"This one's a cute whore, and no mistake…" she complained.

She was wheeling away when Olaf reached out and touched her arm. Her scowl turned to a smile as she glimpsed the bank note he held. Snatching it, she skipped away in triumph, flourishing her prize.

"Do I go with your blessing, not your curse…?" Olaf called.

As Patricia sent the big car gliding slowly away she glanced in the mirror to see the girl running after them, hand cupped to her mouth.

"You do, handsome..." she shouted. "Bless the three of yous..."

Ψ

The Jaguar devoured the motorway miles with effortless grace, the speedometer needle rarely dipping below the legal limit. When Olaf guided her off the highway, however, Patricia found herself on narrow, winding country roads which made rapid progress impossible. Negotiating blind bends, an occasional tree encroaching on the tarmac, crowded village thoroughfares and lumbering lorries all demanded new levels of concentration, vigilance and care. On long stretches bordered by dry-stone walls, she was acutely aware that even a minor misjudgement could spell disaster.

On the rare occasions she had an opportunity to admire the landscape, it did provided some compensation for the reduction in speed; lush meadows dotted with sheep, and rolling hillsides, their slopes painted myriad greens and browns. Gaps in walls and hedges offered fleeting glimpses of sparkling streams, and lakes which lay like great mirrors reflecting clouds and sky.

"We should be there in fifteen minutes..." Olaf told her, studying his map.

"Thank heaven for that..."

"Unless we go to Ravenglass," he added. "Where St Patrick was born. We are close..."

"Absolutely not." Patricia gave a firm shake of the head. "We're going to get where we're going..."

"It lies on the midwinter sunset line from Scafell," said Olaf, undeterred. "So it is the first gate to open up at that time, when the slumbering dragon energy begins to reawaken..."

"Even so…"

"But this is midsummer…" Colm pointed out.

"True, but both are parts of the planetary pattern. The energy that begins to reawaken at midwinter prepares the way for what will happen as the sun sets tonight. If we went on further, to Wasdale Head we would reach your midsummer line…"

"Do I have one…?"

"St Columba does…"

"Okay…"

They were encountering fewer and fewer vehicles, which enabled them to gather speed over the last few miles to Scafell. They sped along an uneven road winding through a broad, open valley flanked on both sides by higher ground. With their destination almost in sight, they followed the contours of Wast Water, a long, narrow lake nestling between gorse-covered hillsides, and rocky scree which plunged almost vertically into its depths. The sky had become dull and overcast; cloud cover was dense and wisps of mist hovered like ghosts round the peaks of some lower hills. As they reached the sign for Wasdale Head, Olaf groaned.

"I am so sorry," he said. "I missed the sign for the parking

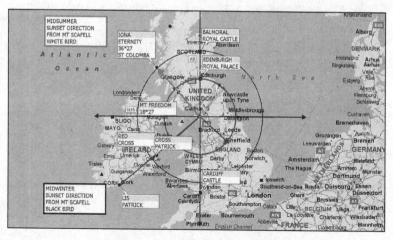

Image 09 Scafell and Isle of Iona

place..."

"I'll turn round..." Patricia told him. "Is it far?"

"Only a minute or two, but can we stop here just for a moment, please?"

"But we're practically there..."

"We are, but..." He turned to Colm, "you remember that midsummer line?"

"Sure..."

"It runs through this village and on past Mount Freedom, all the way to the eternal summer island of Iona. At sunset," he went on, eyes sparkling, "the energies of dragon and eagle will be fully awakened and at their most potent. It will become a path for a host of sacred beings to come and put their healing powers to work on Scafell..."

"Can you see stuff like that...?" asked the awed Colm.

"Anyone who enters their space can see them," Olaf explained. "There will be a strong link between the depths of the earth and the highest heights of the heavens. It means our experience will be even deeper. We have already entered the sacred field of the feminine," he added, glancing at Patricia. "We are in it at this very moment..."

"Are we, now..." She smiled. "Do you think we were meant to miss that turning...?"

Olaf glanced at her and smiled, but did not reply.

"On the way back," he told Colm, "the high ground to the right is called Yewbarrow..."

"Hey, cool..." He grinned. "Another one..."

Locating the right turning, they were soon bouncing along a bumpy farm track. A scattering of vehicles on the stretch of rough grass serving as a car park, told them they were among only a handful of people who had come to celebrate the solstice. Climbing out from behind the wheel, Patricia reached up to rub her neck and shoulders.

"I honestly didn't expect I'd feel this good. You must have

done something magic to my seat," she told Colm. "I wouldn't have wanted it to be too much further, though..."

She unpacked the boot, handing Colm trainers and a jacket. They would be going a good deal higher and there was already a cool edge to the air. Kneeling to lace her hiking boots, she nodded at tiny figures on the lower slopes.

"Are we going that route...?"

"I chose one of the easier paths..." Olaf told her, handing them both maps. "It is clearly marked..."

"How far to the top do you reckon?" Colm peered up at the higher ground.

"About three and a half miles..."

"Seven there and back, then." Patricia puffed out her cheeks. "That's quite a way..."

"We do not need to hurry and it will be light until very late..." Olaf reminded her. "The climb is less than a thousand metres, but some parts look a little steep so we must take care. You will not be able to see Scafell at first, because it is hidden behind Lingmell..."

Throwing her arms wide, Patricia took a deep breath and smiled at him. "You made it!"

"We have made it..."

"I didn't think I would be, but I'm quite excited myself, now I'm actually here," she told him. "Your ancestors must be pleased with you. How are you feeling...?"

He stood with eyes closed for a few moments before replying. "I told you at home we run up mountains, didn't I? Well, Scafell's energy is like an electric current running up my spine. I almost feel it would be easier to fly than run. And," he continued, "my forehead is just blown open by golden light, like when I look straight at the sun..." He smiled at her.

"My back's tingling a bit," she told him, flexing her shoulders, "probably from sitting for so long..."

"And I feel I am exactly where I am meant be," he went on,

saluting his companions. "I thank you both for making it possible..."

"I guess it's where we're meant to be, too..." added Colm.

"Of course..." Olaf gestured towards the mountain. "Scafell summoned us. We all heard, and answered its call..."

He broke off to gaze at Wast Water, dark and mysterious, stretching away into the distance to the south. "Do you see the lady of the lake...?" he enquired, softly.

"Afraid not..." Patricia told him. "Just sunlight glinting on the water..."

"But there isn't any sun..." Colm pointed out.

"Trick of the light, then. Anyway," she went on, taking a deep breath. "It's certainly quite a view, isn't it...?"

The hills surrounding them were not only beautiful but possessed a reassuringly solid and immutable feel. Olaf's assertion they had come to a place charged with spiritual potency somehow no longer seemed quite so fanciful.

"Ready to roll, mister...?" she put an arm round Colm's shoulders.

"Absolutely. Let's go..." He glanced at Olaf.

"One last thing..." Handing Colm a piece of paper, he lay down on the ground, on his back with arms outstretched, legs together. "Look at that map again, please..."

"Okay." Colm smoothed it across the Jaguar's warm bonnet.

"If you imagine Ben Macdui at the top of my head," he instructed. "What is at my feet...?"

"Hang on..." Colm chewed his lip. "Looks like...Glastonbury?"

"Exactly so. And on my shoulders...?"

"Lindisfarne on the left, and..." He traced the line with a fingertip, "this St Molaise place on the right..."

"Excellent. What about here...?" Olaf tapped his upper chest.

"I'd say that was...Hartfell."

"With Scafell a little lower down?"

"That's right…"

"Both expressions of heart energy, you see. One masculine, the other feminine." Rolling over, he jumped lightly to his feet. "On the climb I shall hold those places in my consciousness, which is like imprinting the map on my body. It invites the energies of all those sacred places to give me added strength…"

"Cool. Can I…?" asked Colm.

"Of course. See how it feels," Olaf advised. "So, shall we hail the mountain guardians and their friends, seek their blessing…?"

"What if we didn't…?" Colm wanted to know. "I bet most people don't. Do you reckon the spirits would, like, mind…?"

"If someone visits your house do you like them to ask permission to enter…?"

"Definitely…"

"You are seeking entry to a sacred place. The first step is to enter an outer space. The inner reality is still closed to you, still in the distance. Respectfully asking permission to enter brings it that much closer. And," he went on, "you would want a visitor to treat your house with respect."

"Who wouldn't…?"

"You have your answer…" Olaf spread his hands. "Acknowledge the mountain as a conscious being. Offer it respect and request it blesses us with its gifts…"

"Sounds good…" Colm nodded.

"I just want to make sure I am facing the right way…"

Consulting a compass slung on a lanyard round his neck, he shifted feet before lifting and spreading his arms.

"Hail O Guardians of the Eternal Mysteries of Spirit

Hail O Guardians of the Mysteries of the Mountains, Fields, Forests and Seas.

Hail O Guardians of the snowy mountains of Iceland, England and Ireland

Hail O Rose, Lady of Scafell

Hail to the black Ravens of winter, and the white Doves of summer

Hail to the Cistercian Saints of the Grey Abbey of Rosemount and the Nunnery of Rosedale

Hail to the Saints of the Holy Islands, Lindisfarne, St Cuthber and St Molaise

Hail O Chrom Dubh, hail O Lady in Mount Aigli

Hail O St Patrick in Ravenglass, the point of midwinter and upon Mount Aigli

Hail O Diarmund, Grainnem, Finn McCool and St Finnian in Ben Bulben

Hail O Fianna warriors in Ben Bulben in the west,

Guardians of the High Light and of the High King of Ireland

Hail O St Columba – the eternal luminous spirit in Ben Bulben

Hail O spirit of Mount Freedom that releases us from the chains of the mind

Hail O Isle of Iona as you lie on the Sunset line of Mount Scafell this very evening

Hail O Lady of the Lake in Wass Water

Hail O Dragon in Lingmel, in Great Rhos and in all the Land…

Hail St Patrick's Head,

Hail O Kings of Spirit, McDuff and MacBeth in Ben Macdui

Hail Bran the Blessed the ancient one,

Bearer of the chalice and fountain of youth and immortality

Hail to all sacred beings in and around this Land

May we enter the sacred space of Scafell

With love, trust and humility,

And receive your blessings and your healing."

Dropping his voice, he laid a hand on Colm's shoulder. "Do you think I forgot anyone…?"

"Didn't sound like it…" Colm shrugged.

"Our great adventure can begin!" Olaf announced.

They set off through a scattering of low, slate roofed, farm buildings, keeping to a well-trodden path bordered by waist-high walls built of flinty stones slotted together as neatly as a jigsaw puzzle. A pair of identical stone footbridges took them across shallow, fast flowing streams and out into open countryside. Patricia could hear a low, humming sound; it was a few moments before she realised it was Olaf, chanting softly:

Iona...Iona...Iona
Aion...Aion...Aion
Aionas...Aionas...Aionas
Aionias...Aionias...Aionias

He fell silent and glanced at her, smiling. "My homage to the sacred isle of the West. And this," he added gesturing at the wider of the streams, "is Lingmell Gill, one of two dragon rivers which spiral round Mount Lingmell to the north of Scafell. The other is Lingmell Beck..."

"Why dragon rivers?" Patricia asked.

"I sense something special here; a mystical coming together of the sacred tree and dragon energies. Tree representing our spine. The dragon rises along it cleansing all the darkness held at our core, healing and transforming us..." He paused. "Remember your caduceus..."

It was not long before they began an increasingly steep ascent through rugged, rock-strewn ground, weaving their way among boulders, scrub and golden-flowered gorse bushes. Patricia sensed Colm was reining himself in, matching his pace to her slower one and she was aware of the growing gap between the eager Olaf and his companions. Even on stretches where the footing grew treacherous or the ground slippery, the Icelander effortlessly maintained rapid progress, negotiating the terrain with instinctive balance, and the sure-footedness of a mountain goat.

"Look, no way am I going to keep up with you guys," Patricia told Colm. "But it's okay, I've got my map and I'm perfectly happy to take it easy and soak up the scenery. You go on with Olaf, pet..."

"Are you sure...?"

"Certain. All I ask is if you think the path may not be obvious from the map, someone waits and points me in the right direction..."

"Don't worry, we will. See you up there..."

Planting a hasty kiss on her cheek he was off like a greyhound from the traps. Covering the ground with long, loping strides, he soon caught up with the Icelander, and the two tall figures were matching each other step for step. Grateful for sturdy walking boots and a cool breeze, Patricia reached level ground at the top of the next incline, where she paused, hands on hips, to recover her breath.

Earlier that summer, encouraged by her son, she had signed up at a local health and fitness centre, largely frequented by trim-figured young men and women with no obvious need for one. She began well, but after a few weeks her enthusiasm waned. Nibbling a banana and admiring a waterfall cascading from a high, craggy outcrop, she solemnly promised any mountain spirits within earshot that if they granted her the stamina to drag her aching limbs to the summit, she would exercise on a regular basis.

Unfolding her route map she scanned the surrounding landscape. Assuming she had accurately identified landmarks so far, it dawned on her that the majestic peak looming ahead must be Scafell. Featuring so often on his maps and spoken of by Olaf in such reverential tones, here she was at last, face to face with the mountain in all its majesty. She caught her breath, shivering as a chill of excitement ran through her, and to her surprise tears sprang to her eyes. Brushing them away she searched the slopes ahead for the others, noticing as she did so that mist or low cloud had descended, blanketing some of the higher ground. She bit her lip, wondering how wise she had been to volunteer making the final ascent alone.

Ψ

In spite of the surge of excitement on finding her goal was within sight, her resolve to complete the climb had begun to fade. Not only was her fatigue growing with every passing minute but each slope seemed steeper than the preceding one. Even if that were a trick of the imagination, there was no question that the ground underfoot was increasingly treacherous and unstable. In places the shale offered scarcely more grip than she would have expected on a skating rink. More than once, the only way she could keep advancing was to do so on hands and knees, her heart racing, focused grimly on keeping her balance and avoiding slithering helplessly back down the slope.

Pausing to suck in air she reflected that while Olaf might find the experience inspiring and uplifting, she was more aware of the emotional and physical toll it was taking on her. If this really was, as he had casually dubbed it, one of the easier climbs, she was glad he had not chosen anything more taxing. She stopped to peer round, anxious lest she might have somehow strayed from the path. It was hard to see how she could possibly have done so, but she could not be absolutely certain. Suddenly she felt very alone. Her calves and thighs aching and her brow beaded with sweat, her unease increased when she saw the way ahead was shrouded in mist.

She was trembling, whether from fear or exhaustion she could only guess, although she suspected it was a combination of the two. Enveloped in an eerie bubble of luminous grey light, she could see only a few yards to either side of the path. Stones dislodged with each step bounced and clattered away in her wake. She halted once again, breathing heavily, and wearily swept a lock of damp hair from her forehead. It was decision time. She might be able to find the stamina to struggle on, but perhaps the wiser option was to retrace her steps and wait for the others on level ground where she could rest and recover her strength. Even as the thought came to her, she dismissed it; having glimpsed the summit before the mist closed in, something in her rebelled at the idea of abandoning her efforts now. If she could just summon the determination, surely she must soon emerge from the gloom and join the others on the summit of the mountain. Charged with renewed hope and energy she had just set off again when she heard a familiar voice.

"Mum...? Hey, Mum...are you okay...?"

"Down here..." She cupped her hands to her mouth. "I'm fine. Be careful though..."

Wraith-like, he materialised out of the gloom amid a minor avalanche of rocks and pebbles. Arms outstretched, he slid the last few yards to her side snowboard-style, sank to the ground and grinned at her. "You okay, really...?"

"Got tired, had to stop for a bit. Give me a minute, I'll be grand..."

"Great..."

"What about you guys – where's Olaf...?"

"We're good, no probs," he assured her, puffing out his cheeks. "In a couple of minutes you'll be above the mist. Just wanted to make sure you were okay..."

"It's good you did..." she told him. "I seriously thought about turning back..."

"No, you can't do that..." he protested, aghast. "You're nearly there, honestly..."

"Best news I've had all day..."

"Seriously, another hundred yards, maybe less, it's clear. And the view's amazing..." he added, getting to his feet. "Hey, you know those two who just came down..."

"What two? I haven't seen a soul..."

"You must have…"

"But I haven't…"

"This is the only path…" He frowned.

"I'm certain…"

"A lady and a little boy…"

"A lady and…?" She stared at him. "What about them…?"

"You haven't seen them? That is so…I don't know…" He scratched his head.

"Tell me what happened…"

"Well, Olaf and me just ran into them. Five minutes ago, max. We'd got to where the mist gets pretty thin and they were, like, on their way down. This lady and her kid…well, seven or eight, maybe. I was pretty gob-smacked he made it all the way to the top. I mean, it's tough in places, isn't it?"

Patricia's spine was tingling. Her first thought was of fatigue, but the sensation was warm and not unpleasant. It spiralled up from the soles of her aching feet, travelling along her legs and spine. She steadied herself with a hand on Colm's shoulder.

"Mum…?"

"What, pet…?

"I said it's steep, isn't it…"

"Steep, yes…" she repeated, her voice little more than a whisper.

Colm peered at her. "You look funny. Are you absolutely sure you're okay…?"

"I'm just a bit tired, that's all…"

The trembling would not stop; it was making her dizzy and light-headed. She tightened her grip on his shoulder, doing her best to keep her tone casual.

"So, you were saying…you saw these two. And was that it…?"

"No. That's the whole thing. It got kind of weird…"

"How so…?"

"Well, when they got quite close to us this lady – she must

have been his mum – bent down, sort of...whispered to him and pointed at Olaf. And the kid just, like, ran to him..." Colm shrugged, "into old Olaf's arms. And Olaf grabbed him and swung him right off his feet and just stood there hugging him. I mean, really hugging...like he wasn't ever going to let go, you know...?"

"I think I do, actually..." Patricia murmured.

There was a knot in the pit of her stomach. Tears threatened to fill her eyes; she brushed at them with the backs of her hands.

"What's wrong, Mum...?"

"Nothing, honestly. Then what?"

"Well, the kid had this bottle of water. He offered it to Olaf, and he drank the whole lot. That was kind of odd, too, because a few minutes before I'd had a drink and asked if he wanted any and he said he wasn't thirsty..." Colm shrugged. "Anyway, the mum just stood there watching. She looked okay with it, you know, she was smiling the whole time. But she didn't say anything – not a word. Don't you think that's kind of weird?"

"It must have looked that way..." she agreed, running her fingers through his hair.

"He must have known them," Colm insisted, "because he hugged the kid for ages and he was...sort of, crying. Crying...but laughing at the same time. Like he was sad...but happy. And the kid stroked his face, and he was laughing, too. You could see they were both really, really happy..." He scratched his head. "Anyway, after a bit Olaf put the kid down and he ran back to his mum. And the two of them walked on past us, coming this way. Then Olaf called out, and did that thing where he bows with his hands together, and they did it back. Then they kind of...disappeared into the mist. And that was it. But I still don't get how you didn't see them..." He broke off, shaking his head. "Hey, Mum, why are you crying...?"

Her answer was to wrap her arms round him, draw him close and hug him with all her strength. She buried her head in his shoulder and gloried in the strength of the long arms encircling her.

"I promise at this moment there is absolutely nothing, not one single thing wrong..." she breathed through her tears.

"Then why are you sad...?"

"I'm not sad. I'm so, so happy because you're my son and I haven't lost you. And I love you more than you'll ever know. I can't help it if that makes me cry..."

Epilogue

By Moonlight

July 13th 2011

The sun was floating down into an uneven smudge of dark cloud which lay like an artist's careless brushstroke just above the horizon. Turning deeper shades of burnished copper as it descended, soon only the rim gleamed above the glittering surface of the sea. Cicadas woke from the heat to begin their evening chorus. A freshening sea breeze rustled the palm fronds, cooling the bronzed bodies of the two young people stretched on loungers, beside the pool of a villa overlooking the beach.

"Wind's from the south. What did your dad say it was called...?" Colm enquired, opening one eye.

"Sirocco. They're pretty strong..." Sophie stifled a yawn. "I don't think it's that..."

"He said everything gets covered in pink dust they pick up from the Sahara. I'd like to see that..."

"Papa knows loads of seriously useless stuff like that..." She raised herself on one elbow. "Hey, you know what tonight is?"

Her companion opened his other eye, the better to enjoy his view of the girl smiling at him, eyebrows raised. Slender, nearly as tall as he, Sophie van Moppes had a mass of tight blonde curls and wide set eyes the colour of cornflowers. Colm returned her smile and wished life had a pause button.

"Thursday..."

"Obviously. I didn't mean that..."

"Oh. What are you on about then?"

"And you told me you were a romantic..." She shook her head.

"I am…" he protested.

"Look, then. There's your clue…"

She was pointing at a range of low hills bordering the ocean. As the sun descended, a ghostly disc had replaced it in the darkening sky.

"The moon, you mean…?"

He caught his breath as her arm dropped to rest lightly across his own.

"Not just any old moon, though, is it…?"

"Well…looks like it's full. Is that what you mean?"

"So the party was exactly four weeks ago…" She shot him an impish grin. "Or have you forgotten?"

"Oh, yeah…I mean, no…"

They both laughed; he wanted her to go on talking. Perhaps it was her Dutch accent, and that throaty quality she imparted to certain words; he had never heard anyone make his name sound the way she did. He reached for her hand; her long fingers gently entwined with his own.

"You know the trip you went on, with your mum and that guy from Iceland…?"

"Yeah…"

"You told me the bit about meeting people, and then they disappeared in the mist…but not what happened afterwards."

"Didn't I…?"

"You went a bit sort of…vague. Said you'd tell me, but you never have…"

"Oh…right."

He scanned her face, wondering how she would react if he told her the whole story. He had risked confiding in her about the Irish adventure, and she took that in her stride, but Scafell was a different ball game. He was happy with the way it was going between them; the last thing he wanted was to make her wonder if he was a bit of a nut case.

"It sounded kind of interesting, that's all." She shrugged,

squeezing his hand. "Why are you looking so worried, *schatje*...?"

"I'm not..." he protested, too quickly. "It's just, it might sound...I mean, it all got kind of weird..."

"Now you have to tell me everything!" She laughed. "You got to the bit where you met this woman and her little boy, and you thought they must know your guy, what was his name...?"

"Olaf. They did, definitely. It was obvious from the way he hugged the kid. Anyway," he went on, "after they'd gone, I thought I'd better check Mum out – the mist was pretty thick down where she was. I found her okay, but she was a bit wiped out. When I asked her if she'd seen them, she said no. That was pretty odd, because there was only one path down and she was on it. And another thing was, when I told her about running into them it was like, you know, she wasn't that surprised..."

"You didn't ask her about that?"

"Didn't really think about it until much later. All I wanted right then was to find Olaf. Anyway, she got her breath back and reckoned she was okay, so we went on up. Took about ten minutes, and by the time we got to the top we were above the mist or cloud or whatever it was, and there was Olaf..."

"Did your Mum ask him who they were, or anything?"

"She didn't get a chance. I mean, it was like the guy was on something, you know? As soon as he saw us he came running up to Mum and hugged her, then he hugged me and started on about all this stuff he could see..." He puffed out his cheeks. "I kid you not, it was like some trippy movie..."

"More a horror one..."

"Why?"

"Strange people appearing out of the mist and then just...vanishing?" she protested. "That sounds like a ghost story..."

"There's probably some explanation..."

"When you find out, I would like to hear it. Anyway," she

went on, "what was this stuff Olaf said he saw...?"

Colm paused. He was on the fringe of risky territory. If she was already thinking in terms of horror movies, what would she make of the next part? He took a deep breath and plunged on, trying his best to sound matter of fact.

"Loads of people, apparently. But not, you know...people. He sees things the rest of us don't. Comes off like he's some kind of psychic..."

"Does he? Cool..." She nodded. "Go on..."

Reassured by her wrapt attention, he did as she asked. "I don't remember all the details, but according to him we were surrounded by gods and goddesses and all these other, well...spirits. And they were dancing and singing and thanking us, saying it was great we'd come. Mum and me must have given him really funny looks, because he burst out laughing and said if we didn't believe him to close our eyes, tune in and maybe we'd see them too..."

"Did you...?"

"Well...I'm not sure, actually."

"What do you mean, not sure...?" She shook her head.

"I told you, Olaf was pretty much out of it. I mean he kept on about being in a state of bliss and feeling one with the land, and stuff like that. And," he went on, "I was feeling pretty amazing too – it reminded me of the time I put the ribbon round that yew tree..."

"The one in Ireland...?"

"That's right and I told him my Gran Fran talked about this magic line connecting the mountain we went to with Scafell. And he got even more excited, and said she must have special powers..."

"Hey. You still haven't said what you saw..."

"Soph, I'm not certain what actually happened and what...I imagined."

"It doesn't matter, does it?' she pointed out, gently. "Tell me whatever you remember."

"Okay. I didn't really see anything, but it was like..." He hesitated. "I think I heard singing...you know. Not an actual song – more like in church..."

"A choir...?"

"Yeah...something like that." He nodded. "And a lot of laughing, but that was probably him, not spirits..."

"Maybe, maybe not." She grinned. "What else did he say about them...?"

"Before we started the climb he did this invocation thing, asking a whole load of them for help. According to him all of them rocked up, plus a few he hadn't mentioned. He says they usually do, if you ask them..."

"Wow..." she murmured, wide-eyed. "Pity you couldn't see them. I'd love to know what gods and goddesses look like..."

"He got very excited about a couple of them. Let me think..." He furrowed his brow. "Oh yes, there was some goddess called Vedis who hangs out in a mountain in Iceland. She's been one of his guides for ages. And another called Bran..."

"Sounds more like a breakfast cereal." Sophie drew down the corners of her mouth. "I never heard of either of them..."

Colm waved a hand and grinned. "Nor me. Maybe he made them all up..."

He had wanted to sound cool, but succeeded only in feeling as if he had betrayed a friend. He did not know Olaf that well, but he was certain whatever else he might be, the odd Icelander was no liar.

"Only kidding..." he corrected himself. "If he said he saw them, then he did. The way he went on about Bran he must be pretty important. Like, you know, the main man..."

"Do you think there are alpha gods...?" she enquired.

"You'd better ask him..."

"There's loads I'd like to ask him," she said. "I'm kind of used to stuff like that. My Mum does yoga and meditation, and she's

into angel cards, you know. Some of her friends are a little..."
Smiling, she tapped her head. "Papa calls them the *heks*, the
witches, but most of them are okay, they're nice..."

He took a deep breath; he need not have worried. His mum
said Forest Row attracted more than its fair share of people with
odd ideas, and from the sound of it Sophie's mother fitted into
that category.

"Yeah, Olaf's okay, too. I really like him..."

"What else did he say...?"

"He was pretty hyper for a time, waving his arms around and
gabbling away..." Colm yawned and rubbed his eyes. "To be
honest I didn't understand most of it. It wasn't just gods. He was
rattling on about kings and dragons and healer spirits. He said
Saint Patrick was up there, too, and my guy..."

"You have your own saint...?"

"Sure, Saint Columba...oh, and Macbeth and Macduff..."

"Like in Shakespeare...?"

"I asked him about that on the way home. According to him
they were real people, and in Norway the MP's still take an oath
to Duff. Olaf called him the lord of the mountain," he added.
"Mid-summer is a really big deal for spirits. It's when they go
visiting their special places all over the world..."

"And is Scafell one of them?"

"Big time. He calls them portals. They're places spirits use to
get around..." He glanced at her. "Sounded a bit like the Tube to
me..."

"Seriously, you have to introduce me to this Olaf guy. Will
you, when we get home, *schatje*?"

"Sure, if you want..."

"Definitely..."

Colm liked Sophie calling him *schatje*, even though he was not
entirely sure what it meant. He liked the sound of it, and she
smiled whenever she said it so it had to mean something good.
She let go of his fingers, rolled onto her back and cupped her

head in her hands. He studied the curve of her lips; it would have been the perfect moment to kiss her, if she hadn't been so absorbed in his story.

"What did your Mum make of it all...?" she wanted to know. "You said she didn't really seem that surprised when the ghosts turned up..."

"They weren't ghosts," he protested. "Olaf picked the kid up and hugged him. You can't like, hug a ghost..."

"Okay. So what did she say?"

Colm shrugged, and shook his head. "Not much, actually..."

"What do you mean, not much...?" Sophie demanded, indignantly. "An experience like that, she must have..."

"You'd think so, but she just didn't seem to want to. It sounds kind of odd, but the more excited Olaf got, the quieter she went. On the way back he did calm down a bit. He talked to me about the mountain being healed, and us three being healed as well. According to him, that's the way it works..."

"What did he mean about the mountain?"

"He said it's the king of the land – which is to do with being the highest mountain. And because of that, whatever happens to Scafell affects the whole country. So when these spirits turned up to heal it, the same thing happened to the rest of England..."

"What about Holland...?" she demanded.

Colm glanced at her.

"Only kidding. But where does he get all this stuff from?" Sophie breathed, shaking her head.

"He talked about Scafell like it was alive...almost like it was a person, you know? It got sick the same way we do, because of all this negative energy it's soaked up. But when we turned up and brought all these spirits, they kind of...cured it. And he reckoned," Colm went on, "we got healed too, me and Mum and him. That's because he reckons what he calls personal healing and healing the land go together..."

"Cool..." she murmured. "Wouldn't it be amazing if that

happened to the whole planet...?"

"Including Holland...?"

"If we need it." She grinned.

"Olaf's keen to go round teaching people whatever they need to know so that can actually happen."

"I so want to meet this guy," Sophie told him.

"No prob, he's hanging out with some girl in Inkpen Lane..."

"Great..."

"He said we should watch out for changes in our lives. Mum's apparently going to be an even better shrink. He kept on about her needing to be more of a tigress, too, whatever that means..."

Sophie chuckled. "You can't guess...?"

"Well..." His brow furrowed.

Baring a set of even white teeth, she gave a throaty growl. "He means she must be a powerful woman, not a mouse..."

"How do you know that...?"

"Easy..." she told him, her smile more Cheshire cat than tigress. "You're looking at one. And...?"

"And she could get these amazing healing gifts. Like knowing what's wrong with someone just by looking at them. No idea how that works, but she'll just...know."

"Good for her. And..." She leaned closer and placed a finger lightly on the tip of his nose, "what about you...?"

"Me? Well, he said I was really cool, and so good-looking I'll probably be a film star and..."

"Be careful, *schatje*..." She raised a playful hand.

"He reckons I'm going to get into the same kind of stuff he is. Didn't say how or where, or anything like that, but..." He took a deep breath, "he said if I work at it, I can heal the land, too..."

"How do you work at something like that...?"

"He said it'd come naturally – I'd just know. Like I knew to keep reading that message my gran gave me when I went to Ben Bulben. But he said if I ever wanted to talk to him about it. I could..."

Sophie grasped his arm. "That is so amazing..."

"Why...?"

"Why...?" She shook her head in disbelief. "How could it not be? To be like him, and do the stuff he does? I mean, would you rather be like my dad, doing boring old insurance, or like yours and be a lecturer? Wouldn't you rather go round healing the land...?"

"Sounds good to me..." He laughed. "But I have a feeling my mum would prefer I was in insurance..."

"No way..." Sophie insisted. "She drove the guy all the way to Scafell. She wouldn't have done that if she didn't believe in him. I tell you, she'd absolutely love you to be like him..."

"I thought so too, at first. I mean, for a few days we talked quite a lot about how amazing the whole thing had been. She said she saw life in a new way, and I said I'd get her a T-shirt with a tiger on it, and she said it was a brilliant idea..."

"What about her work?"

"For a time that was great – like Olaf said it would be. Sometimes a new patient walked in and she knew absolutely everything about them before they'd even said a word. It really, like, blew her away..."

"I'm not surprised." Sophie smiled. "That must have been pretty amazing..."

"At first..." he reminded her. "Then something must've changed in her head, because that stopped happening..."

"What do you mean?"

Colm did not answer; her grip on his hand tightened.

"Schatje...?"

"Well, I asked when we were going to see Olaf again, and she gave me this funny look and said we probably weren't. When I asked why, she'd decided he was crazy after all – he just imagines things or makes them up..." He shrugged. "I couldn't believe it. One minute she's convinced he's a really special person, the next he's just...out of his mind."

"What do you think happened...?"

"No idea, it was really weird..."

"But that's just what your mum thinks. What about you...?" she asked softly. "I mean, you saw those two up there – so that couldn't have been him making stuff up, could it?"

"Soph, I saw them as clear as I see you..."

"There you are, then. It was real. He didn't imagine anything, and neither did you, right?"

The sky was suffused with pale, silvery light; the breeze had grown stronger and the evening air cooler. He felt Sophie shiver; it was time to go inside. In the bushes, cicadas were busy saluting the full moon.

"Imagine...?" He shook his head. "No way. Absolutely no way. God knows why Mum changed her mind about him, but I haven't."

"I've got this really strong feeling you're right, *schatje*..."

The sun had long ago sunk beneath the horizon, and darkness was deepening round them, but Sophie was bathed in her customary golden glow. It was something he wanted to ask Olaf about. Ever since midsummer night, everyone he saw seemed to radiate coloured light.

About the Authors

Dr Haraldur Erlendsson MD DCN MSc MRCPsych, 58, is an eminent psychiatrist and director of HNLFI, Iceland's premier private medical rehabilitation clinic. For more than two decades his hobby has been researching the symbolic interpretation of myths from around the world and also religious texts and artwork. Since his teenage years he has also engaged in meditation and a variety of ancient shamanic practices. His inner journey has involved exploration of the sacred history of the land as a result of which he has succeeded in decoding messages based on the names of places as well as naturally occurring geographical features. His discoveries form the groundwork on which this book is based. Harald works tirelessly to find ways of integrating the most advanced modern psychological treatments with spiritual healing practices including ritual and quests.

Born in 1944 Keith Hagenbach attended Rugby School and Trinity College Dublin, graduating with degrees in Business Studies and English. After three years with Unilever as a management trainee he managed and later bought his father's boat building business. At 34 he made a radical change to his life-style and Ibiza became his home for the next 10 years. In 1980 he wrote his first novel and its success earned him a contract for two more and also a BBC commission for three radio plays. He did some writing in France and travelled widely including to the USA, India and Australia. Returning to the UK in 1988 he married Kitty with whom he had sons Max and Sandy. Completing a psychotherapy training in 2000 he worked in the NHS until 2011 and now has a flourishing private practice.

By Keith Hagenbach

The Fox Potential, W H Allen, 1980
The Rat Quotient, W H Allen, 1980
The Fat Cat Affair, W H Allen, 1982

The Mind Body Spirit Workbook, C J Daniel, 1999
co-authored with Dr Christine Page

COSMIC
EGG
BOOKS

If you prefer to spend your nights with Vampires and
Werewolves rather than the mundane then we publish the books
for you. If your preference is for Dragons and Faeries or Angels
and Demons – we should be your first stop. Perhaps your
perfect partner has artificial skin or comes from another planet –
step right this way. Our curiosity shop contains treasures you
will enjoy unearthing. If your passion is Fantasy (including
magical realism and spiritual fantasy), Horror or Science Fiction
(including Steampunk), Cosmic Egg books will
feed your hunger.